# THE SELLING PARTY

*By Michael Granat*

 **FriesenPress**

Suite 300 - 990 Fort St
Victoria, BC, Canada, V8V 3K2
www.friesenpress.com

Copyright © 2014 by Michael Granat
First Edition — 2014

**ISBN**
978-1-4602-4637-5 (Hardcover)
978-1-4602-4638-2 (Paperback)
978-1-4602-4639-9 (eBook)

*1. Fiction*

Distributed to the trade by The Ingram Book Company

# Table of Contents

# THE SELLING PARTY

*A Novel by Michael Granat*

*In memory of my loving* parents

# 1

## THROUGH THE MAGNIFYING GLASS

Michael was preparing breakfast in his one bedroom sixth floor condo apartment in downtown Hamilton. He carefully washed and broke kale and spinach into pieces and placed them into a bowl. Sardines and sunflower seeds were added next. Then virgin olive oil was poured liberally all over the work in progress. With a firm squeeze, a wedge of lemon was coaxed to squirt out its succulent tanginess. A pinch of Celtic sea salt was all that was needed to complete the masterpiece, and it came next. The salad looked delectable—all the ingredients were organic. Michael was pleased: not only had he put together such a fine concoction, he would now devour it!

The late morning light lollygagged in every nook and cranny of Michael's combination living room and kitchen, reposing on the oversize worn out couch and chair he inherited from his parents, making clear but refusing to clean the large dining room table covered in pragmatic disorder with papers, files and a laptop computer. Unseen, the sunlight had slipped in without a peep at the speed of invisible stillness. Now it basked in egotistic brilliance, content to fill all space, slyly deflecting attention away from itself to the objects of its reflection.

However, on this particular morning Michael did notice. A switch had been turned on. His pacific state had shattered into shards of fancy—expressions of escape often called *day dreams*—whether or not they occur in the day or during the night.

"How nice it would be," Michael mused, "to slide open these glass balcony doors and step out to a green blue sea to eat my breakfast ocean view and feel a warm fragrant breeze blowing all over me while I chomp on olives, cheese and sundried tomatoes. How rich would that be?"

But was it in reach? There he was bent over, his right hand dipping in swirls of receding waves, deliberately moving slowly, testing and teasing the water's temperance as his feet sank in the sand, a broad smile beaming across his bronzed face.

Oh how he pined for a real land full of decadently docile broad-leaved deciduous trees, beaches that beckoned bared feet, streams winding through lush green fields surrounded by majestic mountains roaring grandly as far as the eye could see. This was his *Shambhala*, his private Idaho: a land of beauty and peace. The villa, the scooter, and the old brown corduroy sports jacket he wore, all these he visualized clearly, together with the sound of the beating and lapping waves licking his ears like an excited, panting dog. "Oh, if only it were so!" he lamented.

Michael turned on his computer and made coffee in a French Press. That was his custom, to kill time by performing other tasks to give his middle-aged laptop ample latitude to be fully functional. In a few minutes his homepage displayed a news headline proclaiming: *"Justin Trudeau admits to smoking pot while sitting as a member of parliament."*

"What a riot!" Michael ruminated. "What was once banned and hidden is no longer latent or occult. Smoking pot has become so common and prevalent that it is now done in the open with complacency, unlike a woman baring her breasts, which though legal is seldom seen. But what is really hidden beneath the sweet smooth words that politicians speak? Their words are no doubt meant only to seduce. They are deceptively laden with lack of meaning."

Michael figured that *"Justin's smile"* would be a good code for smoking pot if one were ever needed. But since some states in the United States of America had recently legalized recreational use, such word games might no longer be necessary. "My, how relative truth and morality are," he thought.

Michael's mind meandered to the elder Trudeau, a former Liberal Prime Minister of Canada, and the famous father of Justin. Michael recalled how popular he, Pierre Elliott Trudeau that is, was when Michael began articling at a large downtown Toronto law firm for his first kick at the legal can of *"professional indentured servitude,"* otherwise known as articling.

Michael recalled an incident which occurred at the start of his articles. He was walking down a corridor feeling good and laughing aloud when stopped and asked by a senior partner what it was that he found so funny. Michael interpreted by the tone and wording of the question that his laughing while alone was a breach of protocol and decorum. "It's not like I'm dressed in taboo attire, wearing only a grass skirt exposing a body covered in tattoos," Michael seethed to himself. "Who would have guessed such behavior is *verboten*? No sign is posted. Nobody gave me notice."

To be sure it was not a hanging matter subject to capital punishment. Even though Michael tried to minimize the incident, he could not let it go. Was what he did wrong, should he be faulted for having an overgrown and overblown sense of humor? He was just launched on his career trajectory—an innocent so to speak. Had he made a mistake in choosing law? Was he to be cannon fodder?

Michael was sent with his first file to the Masters' Motions Hearing Room in the old Supreme Court building on Queen St. in downtown Toronto near University Avenue, which building has since been torn down. A Master is a strange judicial creature resembling a judge but who deals only with technical and procedural matters otherwise not fitting the elevated estate of a Judge of the High Court.

Michael, like a *hero* (in terms of "*here*" and "*oh*" exclaimed) wore a red rose in his lapel as did the Prime Minister father of Justin at the time. Michael felt cool and suave as he swaggered up to the man in a suit sitting at the head of a large conference table, who he assumed to be the Master, flanked by ten men in suits to the right, and ten men in suits to the left. Michael's instructions were clear: have the Order signed and bring it back to the firm.

This was the first time ever that Michael had stepped into a court room of any kind in a legal capacity in his entire life! Unbeknownst to him, Motion's Court had already commenced and was in session, and the Master was in the midst of deliberations. The Master, who in this case was a frustrated mini judge transfused with hunger for the flesh taste of fresh meat and thirsty for virgin legal blood, stared intently at the captive prey before him. Then he pounced inquiring: "What is the action number?"

Michael was bewildered! He was caught off his arrogant guard—knocked off his rosy stride. Though thoroughly familiar with every detail of the material, no matter how hard or long or frantically he searched, all he could find on the documents was a "file number." He had learned that if the law was anything, it was precisely precise. He just stood there and said nothing so as not to mislead the court. No words emanated from his lips: they were two sealed portals made of stone. There he remained, frozen with a bewildered look in his eyes, like a dazed deer caught in the headlights of a Mack truck barreling down the highway heading directly towards him. Michael had yet to learn that "file number" and "action number" were one and the same, *and not more or less*!

Then the Master, who no doubt thought it unjust that he had not been appointed a judge, justice being denied him, went on a five minute tirade lambasting lawyers for sending unprepared students to his courtroom. Michael took the dressing down as if he was the butt of its bitterness. It was like being in a nightmare appearing in court almost completely naked, dressed only in his skimpy white briefs, totally unprepared to argue the case let alone move. He was totally terrified—scared stiff! Three years of law school and a three year B.A. in Philosophy had not prepared him for such an abusive and embarrassing nightmare.

Michael left the courtroom downtrodden. Although dejected and despondent he would return another day. He had learned a very important lesson in the school of real hard knocks. *Never* interrupt a master in deliberations. The rose did not seem to help. It attracted too much attention. Its flowery beauty juxtaposed the savage belittlement he received: the derision of the dressing down he suffered. Quickly he hid it in his pocket. The blood red rose, like a symbol of life itself, must forever remain hidden in the dark halls where the *paper chase* is practiced.

During the short period that Michael articled for such downtown firm, perhaps it was only a few weeks, he felt his manic, living exuberance trampled on, as if stepped on by faceless robotic clerks lining up endlessly to file court papers and register documents. Long anxious waits to speak to minor matters in large formal courtrooms were the norm. Images of big, hard covered books falling on him, bruising him, chasing him, trying to swallow him up, could summarize the way he felt, and he often faced them in his nightmares unable to scream or run.

Why had he not been able to answer the Master's very simple question? Over and over the scene replayed in his mind; over and over again he obsessed over the same question: Why had he been a *Master baiter*? But what choice did he have? Was it his *ipso facto* failure to probe and penetrate below the surface of the court's superficial machinations to find its esoteric recesses that led to his perceived misplacement, or was the reverse in fact the case? He was lost, aimlessly adrift without an effective exculpatory clause or credible excuse, a handle to grab hold of, a rudder to steer him through the ocean of precedents, *stare decisis*, statutes and regulations.

"What does the dusty old law know of my life anyways?" he quixotically queried. "I the rose wearer humiliated shall depart from these hallowed halls that have been like gallows to my ego and self esteem, and shall take the $99 specially priced Greyhound bus all the way out west to Vancouver to find my destiny." For "never again" and "nevermore," he vowed, "shall I be so humiliated."

But beaten, failing to find his fortune and destiny, Michael returned the following year to recommence and be re-shackled to articling-at-law. It was a necessary condition precedent to his becoming a fully fledged and pledged lawyer in the Province of Ontario, and so providence would have it. This time however, he chose a two man law firm in Malton, Ontario, which by then had already become part of Mississauga and Punjab. Here, Michael could laugh as loudly as he liked; the hall was not so highly hallowed, and there was only one.

Although Michael lived in Hamilton, he was raised in Toronto, and his current business, a health food store, was located in Toronto. The name of the store, "Wild Rice," was based on a pun of Michael's last name, which he conceived and contrived three quarter score years ago. Michael was actually born in a foreign country but his parents immigrated to Canada when he was young enough not to remember much if anything of the "old" country; not even to have a hint of a foreign accent when he got old enough to smoke and have sex legally.

As many people know, Toronto is the largest city in Canada and sits on top of Lake Ontario, being situated north of such great lake. Hamilton however, Michael's current home via a circuitous route through marriage, divorce and an only child, is considered a gritty shadow of Toronto's mega incandescent glow. Hamilton lies, not sits, south of and *under* the aforesaid Great Lake. This accounts for Hamilton's inferiority: that it lies *below* that great body of water instead of *above* as Toronto does. Such location not only makes Toronto superior, but all directions in Hamilton confusing. It is easy to get lost in Hamilton as anyone from Toronto like Michael knows, for he was always getting lost—at least in his own thoughts!

Toronto at one time was known as "Toronto the Good," but alas, no longer! It would stretch the rubber band to the breaking point to call Toronto "good" now. Perhaps some of Hamilton's sketchy shadiness rubbed off. Soot, coal and coke hauled from "Steel Town" via her majesty's highway, Queen Elizabeth's Way, to "Hog Town," smoked and cured the once benevolent town of York to pork. Yes, Toronto is a veritable land of wine and money—but it is not glutton free. They from the tower of power love to pick the taxpayer's cherry; the feeding trough is lined by snorting politicos!

In his condo apartment in Hamilton, the radio was turned on to Michael's favorite station, WARP 98, Eclectic Radio, *"resonating at the speed of mind."* It was 11:30 AM. News had surfaced about a video showing Toronto's mayor with a pipe in his hand, smoking what appeared to be crack. "What a refreshing change!" Michael chuckled, "most politicians get caught with their pants down, or with their hands in the cookie jar."

The mayor had campaigned on cleaning up corruption, as well as other things. Getting caught with a smoking pipe in his hand was pretty good evidence indicating on which side of the highwayman mayor Ford parked his Cadillac SUV. Michael had often been told by his mother not to be holier than the pope, so perhaps he was a bit critical, but doesn't everyone think that the views they hold are right? Michael, like his mother, definitely thought he had the right to think that he was right in what he thought to be right.

Michael now drank his coffee and it was good; some shady hill-grown, fair trade organic variety received as a free sample from a Wild Rice supplier. Michael had recently started on a self improvement kick trying to exercise a bit and refrain from smoking weed. Perhaps that is why he was so uptight, wound up with negativity. It is funny how when one tries to do something they believe will make them feel better it often makes them feel worse instead. Hell, if it doesn't kill you, it should at least make you stronger!

Michael wandered into the washroom to pee, and then studied his face in the mirror while washing his hands. White spikes of hair, like minute missiles waiting to be launched, speckled his chin. Thinning unruly brown hair stood stuck-up on his head. His round ruddy cheeks articulated an impish smile.

"Not bad for almost 60," he said to himself, "but I would look better without the stubble," so he shaved with that little common plastic blue disposable razor called "Good News." Thank god it is not called "bad news" with the sharp blade coming so close to the throat. God knows there is enough of that—bad news that is! Michael smiled at his now clean shaven face with just a reddish brown uneven triangle of hair remaining above his thin upper lip. Some skin under the chin sagged, but his eyes were still shiny, although his right eye, more closed than the other, stared slightly askew.

Michael had been cross-eyed as a child. Seeing two base lines or two balls flying at him at once was interesting but too challenging so he took up chess and gave up baseball at an early age. That his eyes stared in slightly different directions was unnoticeable to the untrained eye, but may have changed the cosmetics of his brain accounting for some of his far out ideas and theories, like the possibility of someone having two brains.

Michael's brother told him that whales were recently discovered to have two brains. The riddle as to why a whale never slept was thus solved (it being believed that all mammals must sleep). The answer was that one brain slept while the other was awake. Michael stretched this theory to the point of believing that some people might have two brains—the one split brain possibly evolving into two separate ones due to something as simple as being cross-eyed! Could he have two brains, and could this account for his changeable moods?

Then suddenly out of nowhere, as if two massive metallic hands in Michael's mind clapped, his thoughts began to ring and race: "It's time to sell the business and retire and travel and lead the easy life." He knew however, that the real reason he sought to get out of the health food store business was not because of the pull of that which was wanted, but rather it was due to the repelling force of that which was no longer desired: the situation he now loathed, his sentiments being stained by the dye of dread as if left in the tanner's tub for more than a fortnight.

Why was it that each project, each improvement he planned for the store become more difficult to do, year after year? How often had he told people that he was going to build bulk bins; that he would prepare and send out direct mailings, organize and print out new inventory sheets? But he would not complete any of such plans—not even get started. He was only able to maintain; pay the bills and eventually do the government filings at the twelfth hour. And then there were the thefts and the break-ins: not too frequent, so he would forget in time. After each he went to bed anxious, always expecting the worst, the dreaded phone call at 4 AM.

These worries, among others, weighed heavily on him. There was never enough money to go around, so he had to put his own money into the business: money that he had inherited; money that he had earned in the buying and selling of a house or two; money that he had borrowed and kept borrowing from credit cards and lines of credit and mortgages—the more he borrowed the more he was lent. And finally, he had put in money from the sale of his principal residence which he recently sold when his son moved out to go to law school. The house that was never cleaned or repaired where the foliage grew wild and the parties were well liked even if not well remembered.

And he profited well from his hesitation for the area had grown above his level of gentrification at the time he was forced to sell. So it had turned out well: he downsized to a condo near the Go Station in Hamilton where he now resided. But now, once again, the money was starting to run out.

Michael could not handle the money slowly dwindling, trickling away: a death by a thousand cuts, the steady seepage of red ink. He could be travelling, living on a tropical island, walking, talking, sitting, eating, waking up, yawning whenever he liked, drinking espresso—perhaps even smoking a cigarette now and then, but never inhaling—he had given that up when his son, Samuel, was born.

If not for the oppressive financial burden Michael carried, he would be living the good life. Why was he now unable to do anything, not take any action? He knew that the load, his burden, was of his own making. He created the gravity of his own grave situation. Had he not only four years ago, eagerly and manically, moved his heath food business into much larger premises? Now, he cried the blues, *"Whoa ho oh!,"* for no longer could he bear the cross that he bore, the cross that bore him, born from his aspirations and ambition.

So then, which is now, Michael felt that he had to decide. He made his determination in a manner not unlike so many other decisions—it was simply a matter of compulsion! The reflecting thought that could lead to indecision was nipped in the butt. Like a pin-pricked balloon it quickly deflated, flying aimlessly and futile, propelled by the air escaping in accordance with a driving and overriding universal law of nature. With a rude rushing sound it drowned out any doubt or hesitancy. This then is the plan Michael hatched:

First, and for the purpose of clarity, it should be noted that the level of stress and distress that Michael experienced was clearly expressed in a dream he dreamt a few nights prior when he woke up in the middle of the night wired, Justin's smile long gone and withdrawn from his face after days of attempted exercise and self improvement. He could not sleep! The electricity normally used to motor his limbs should have been in neutral and at ease but instead sparked all around him in invisible sub-ionic mocking. Was he drinking too much coffee?

In banal profundity and clarity Michael saw the arc of his life, his fifteen or so years studying law and practicing as a lawyer, and his fifteen years or so in the health food business, from one store to three stores and then to his current one, as representing his almost achieving success, but *not* quite. When he was almost there, success being within his grasp, he could not close the deal, he was unable to grip and grab what was rightfully his! All his efforts had added up to naught—he had failed! Or so he thought.

What then was the dream that so filled him with such dread? It was just the image of two large waves breaking, one after the other, and their outline appeared clear, so simple. The waves, though they had come and gone, might have otherwise been meaningless blips, mere lines on a monitor, but not so in his mind. They delineated his life. The dream, he knew, mockingly alluded to the murky waters of his submerged subconscious. It resonated so trite and true that it freaked him out! He was at a loss to understand the intense feelings that he could not understand, could not put into words (his life seemed so smooth on the surface, so successful to someone on the outside looking in). "I've got to get away. I never finish anything. I need to undertake something new not to finish either," and so his worries wove and wore on.

# 2

---

# THE PLAN

In the clear light of day in his sixth floor condo apartment at noon Michael saw his plan hatch like a dynamic chicken with rippling muscles exploding out of its shell while the shell remained intact. As the mighty chicken flew up triumphantly, all phases of its life were still visible—the chicken, the chick and the egg! The plan also appeared like a snake with the tail placed in its menacing mouth forming a perfect circle: the inside and the outside were one, joined and united.

"I will take active steps to sell the store and list it with a real estate agent who deals with the sale of businesses. I will then have a thank you party for the customers, which will also be a party for my 60th birthday. I will invite my friends and relatives, many of whom live in Toronto. Perhaps there will be a buyer for the store to invite in time. I will thus be the *"selling party"* in any contract to sell the store; and the party that I will hold and host to celebrate the event of my selling could no doubt be rightfully called a *"selling party."* Oh, how glorious it will be!"

Michael thought of the invitation to the party. A fine, formal invitation was in order. Thick off-white paper stock with raised black printing in fancy script would be just right. Mass mailings in the immediate geographical vicinity could be sent through Canada Post to penetrate the masses of high rise condos and office buildings surrounding the store.

Although he had thought of sending out mass mailings many times before, he never followed through. He always found some reason, made up some excuse like: "I don't feel like it. I'm not ready yet. I'll do it after my holiday." Oh! What can fly when procrastination rules the roost?

But now was different. It was the last straw. He could take no more! The ecstasy of freedom, the climax of his working life, lay in his hands. He needed to have the strength to complete, to take the last strokes necessary to reach orgasmic delight, to go out on a pun of a party where everything was rolled into one! Oh, how sweet it would be! Justin would surely smile.

But that is not all. When one has the courage to take the first step, the vista changes and transforms completely; things look different because one has moved into a different space. The past is left behind—*welcome to a brave new world*!

Ideas imploded in Michael's mind as if the barriers between all dimensions had crumbled. He was definitely on a roll! His previous big ideas now seemed trivial, dwarfed by the lightning storm of his grand new idea.

In the past Michael had had parties. They were always well liked, well attended affairs with ample alcohol, food and delectable consumables. Conversations flowed freely as did the beer and wine. Goodwill engulfed the guests like thick smoke from a Lebanese hookah. People danced and felt a kinship with one another! The invitations to these parties had been in the form of parodies so the partiers were up for a good time even prior to their arrival.

One party, when he was still a young lawyer, was held in the 3rd floor apartment of a semi-detached house converted into apartments in the Annex area of Toronto that he bought totally with borrowed money. The invitation for this party was in the form of a *Writ of Summons*, a legal document commanding the invitees to attend. Or perhaps the invitation to this party was done as a *Notice of Party*, a play on the *Notice of Motion* form used in law suits in accordance with the Rules of Civil Procedure in Ontario.

The *Writ of Summons* invitation, he now recalled, was for the party held on the non-working farm he bought with the profits from the sale of the aforesaid Annex property. The farm was located in Grey County. A small dilapidated farmhouse sat at the front near the unpaved concession road. At the rear, past acres of hardwood stands lay a small secluded spring-fed lake: one of the "Negro Lakes." Michael pretended that he was the "Earl of Grey," and called his estate "Negro Manor." How the guests were ready to be well lubricated! This *was* Southern Ontario for that matter—*no more and no less* was expected!

In his adolescent years Michael wanted to be a writer. Several times his father had mentioned being related to a famous writer, but Michael did not give much weight to a lot of what his father said. For example, his father had claimed to be descended from the house of David and that a record of such lineage had actually existed! Michael knew David had so many wives, probably more than prudent to record. After Michael's father died almost a dozen years ago, where and when interestingly enough the hospital clock stopped at the very moment Michael believed his father had shed his earthly robes, Michael tried to discover if such author ever existed.

Michael performed a search on the internet of the name he recalled his father mentioning, something like *"Appetoshen."* Nothing turned up. But a few years ago when Michael googled the name again, lo and behold, Opatoshu, Joseph Opatoshu, was serendipitously found, and he was famous indeed!

Michael was eager to read such author's works but there was a major hurdle over which Michael could not leap: none of the works were written in a language Michael could understand. They might as well have been in hieroglyphics! All of Opatoshu's novels and short stories were written in Yiddish, a language Michael had spoken at home with his parents, but could not read a word of. Fortunately, there were some English translations available through Amazon.

Both Michael's father and Opatoshu were born in that infamous Jewish town in Poland called Mlawa. People from Mlawa were reputed to be simple-minded—*yokels* in English—so much so that Michael believed they were blessed with a special name, a pet name of sorts, and referred to as "guppies" in honor of the fish known for doing nothing. Michael's mother was always calling her husband a *"Mlawa gapa,"* particularly in respect of his inability or lack of desire to effect household repairs. Michael thus understood *gapa*, whether it was a Yiddish or Polish word he was uncertain, to mean guppy.

Having discovered that he was related to a famous writer rekindled Michael's desire to write. He had written quite a lot of poetry in his youth, starting when his sexual urges were awakened, followed up by poems of reflection which were somewhat existential, and finally graduating to reflections on reflecting which might have been *meta*, if he were *hip* at the time.

Michael continued to write while taking a B.A. in philosophy at the University of Waterloo, along with adequate intake of alcohol and whatever else was prevalent and available, even to rise to an executive position as the social convener of the Philosophy Undergraduate Association. But writing seemed a dead end. The plots for his stories, and a play preformed at a party thrown for that purpose where an acted punch was actually thrown, centered on deception and betrayal. The novel he was writing at the time dealt with crimes, madness and endless repetition. He only got to the tenth page. Maybe the Nietzsche and the Dostoyevsky were getting to him!

After three years of university with his B.A. in hand, Michael thought it would be a good time to take a year off school and get a job. He quickly learned however, that the only thing he could do with the paper his degree was written on was to sell life insurance. He loathed the fact that three years of hard partying and doing well in university only qualified him for such position. Even though he had a degree in philosophy, he still didn't understand what life was or is—how could he sell life insurance? He was so naïve at the time, that when asked out for lunch by a life insurance agent he thought it was for purely social reasons, rather than to be sold life insurance!

So Michael, who was good at writing tests and very fond of words, ended up going to law school instead, attending the University of Western Ontario situated in London, Ontario. It was rumored that lawyers were paid by the word, *once upon a time*, so law seemed a perfect career choice!

The dean of the law school at Western then was David Johnston, now the Governor General of Canada. Dean Johnston was famous for being the character on which the captain of the Harvard Law School hockey team was based in the movie and book, *Love Story*—but Dean Johnson was a real person, not just a character in a movie or a story!

Michael engraved the names and years of the courses he took while at law school on a little wooden table that served as his desk. It had stayed with him since the days he and his brother shared a bedroom in the flat where his family as recent immigrants to Toronto lived. Even though his parents' bedroom doubled as the living room, Michael was glad his family lived in such ample and roomy conditions compared to some of the other immigrants in the neighborhood. The table now sits at the centre of the Wild Rice store displaying health food products.

Michael filled up and lit a little pipe full that set Justin's smile aglow again. Then *eureka*—it stuck him—another lightning bolt of an idea! He would make the invitation to the selling party a short story. Such story would not only serve as a façade for an invitation but would explain how he felt and why he was doing what he was doing so that all could understand! The invitation/story would be jam-packed with all the persuasiveness his lawyerly learning had taught him to cram in. The brilliance of the idea seemed simply luminous! Had he not had a party for many years—not since his wife left him some twenty years ago? Surely, now was the time to have a party; and what great subversive marketing, definitively light ages above and beyond gorilla!

When Michael first met his ex, he thought he had retired from working for good. It was not the first time, nor would it be the last time, he was mistaken. He had just sold his law practice in downtown Toronto, and as well had made a tidy and handsome profit from the sale of his house in the Annex. He thought himself set for life, and blessed by the benedictions of youth, humor and disputable good looks (often being considered cute except for the beard, check shirts and large rimmed glasses which were fashionable at the time). He had money, owned a large recreational farm property with its own lake, and was debt free. At last he was totally free! He could travel around the world and do as he pleased—or so he thought.

Perhaps in hindsight, the separation and divorce had caused him more pain and cast a deeper and longer shadow than envisioned. He *thought* he knew the difference between pleasure and pain having experienced them both, and he came to the conclusion that pleasure was preferable.

The writing of his invitation in the guise of a story, a story clothed as an invitation, would be his *coup de grace,* his phoenix rising from the flames, his resurrection from the grave, his *fait accompli ueber alles.* It would tie and join everything together, transcend levels real and imagined, lead to the understanding of the secret forgotten language, knowledge of Shangri-la, Utopia, and perfect contentment! Like the *ouroboros,* it would include and exclude nothing, be without beginning or end! It was at hand, at the tip of his tongue, he needed only to find the right words. His invitation in the form of a story to explain everything would be called *The Selling Party*!

Was Michael rash or foolish? Perhaps the answer to this question will be clear in due course as the story of Michael, his plans, and his party unfolds. For those who have the ears to hear, let them hear this. All men, women and children are mortal unless they live forever, which is a proposition that would take a very long time to prove. Therefore, one should not be hasty to judge, nor should anyone forget *caveat emptor*!

Michael was proud of his idea. He did not mind being proud because he was not a Christian. He didn't even mind Jesus— they were both brought up Jewish—weren't they? In Michael's mind whatever Jesus might have uttered had definitely been misrepresented and manipulated by the greatest empire in which after-effects the human race now finds itself mired; the greatest and most awe inspiring (to the point of awful) empire ever. The speakers of Latin were the ones who crucified the words of Jesus killing their true meaning in plain public view, as sure as blood drips and dries!

Michael was proud of his family. Had they not survived the war which still haunts modernity in a world where the cult of pseudo-science cares not for the sanctity of life, but only the winner of races under the rubric of survival of the fittest? Did not the perpetrators of the last great war try to rival Rome, but were able to last only one one-hundredth of the time? They came so quickly, U-boats filled with semen, the raging *blitz-krieg*, ready to sterilize the world. How many horrors does a lost and wandering race still have to face in a lost and wandering place that is mind space?

Michael's father, Mendel, worked as a sewing machine operator, like Mendel in *Fiddler on the Roof.* Michael's mother worked as a "finisher," sewing items by hand on clothes such as buttons and bows, and thus the apt appellation, finisher. The movie version of *Fiddler on the Roof* came out in 1971, the same year as the movie version of *Romance of a Horse Thief* did, based on a book by Joseph Opatoshu, which had as its heroes the simple-minded townsfolk of Mlawa. The movie, *Romance of a Horse Thief,* flopped! Some speculate that this was because *Fiddler on the Roof* was such a good movie, and there was no appetite for two "Jewish movies" in one year. It is more likely however that the movie version of the *Romance* did not steal people's hearts, for horse theft is not something to scoff at in the wild western world. But everyone loved the *Fiddler: "oy oy bibby bibby boomm."* Is there anything more that needs to be said or sung?

Michael's parents were honest and hard-working folk who survived to set up a new life in the new world. They worked, saved, didn't like to spend too much, and left Michael with a good inheritance.

But now, Michael was at his ripe age sick and tired of being constantly immersed in commercialism like a brisket that never cooks no matter how long it boils. He no longer wanted to look at life through the glasses of greed and desire; but how could he see otherwise?

Many able writers, thinkers and analysts of psyche such as Erich Fromm have harped and piped in symphonic eloquence on the loss of meaning in the post-war world and the alienation of values and disorientation resulting from commoditization. Michael was familiar with some of Fromm's books having read them in university when they were in vogue, and having reread some recently. He was still interested in *The Art of Loving*— even at his age!

Even though Michael considered himself an able person, at least in his up times, there were two aspects of his life which he believed suffered from the impotence of inability that brought him down. One was his failure to make lots of money from the practice of law; the other was that he was not reaping a good profit from his current business, the Wild Rice store.

In the past, Michael had in fact practiced law not once but twice, the second time coming after he retired and moved to the farm and got married and had a child, starting all over again with excitement, only to finish unexcitedly without a hard-on for life. Could Michael's inability to complete, *sign, seal and deliver* in the last four or so years, be construed as able? Would and could the *Selling Party* really be the answer?

Michael recalled a story that his mother told him about what he did when he was a baby. She said he would take his *"caca"* or *"poo"* and exclaim: "Want to see what I can do?" and then fling a brown handful at the ceiling. Whether it stuck or not, she never said, but the way she told the story evinced the pride and love she felt for Michael. If one loves someone, they don't mind cleaning their shit. Some parents might have seen the incident in a different light and reacted otherwise. Love makes everything smell like roses when one looks through its sensuous fogged-up (perhaps "fucked up") lenses.

Michael's mother did not come from Mlawa. She was not a guppy, a *"gapa,"* or a daydreamer like her husband, but instead came from a place of hard work and bridled expectations. Shunning all gifts and giving freely of her opinion, she baked, cooked, cleaned and worked.

Then after working a lifetime, she was replaced by a machine. She could finish by hand no more. Her blood dried up and she turned white, frail and thin, though once a stout hardy woman. In the face of infirmity she refused to transfuse her blood, possibly from pride or independence. Michael understood this sentiment for deep inside he felt that one's blood was sacred too. She finally gave in to having regular blood transfusions which prolonged her life somewhat, and abated her bloodless anger, but only on the threat of her failing to follow her doctor's advice being exposed to the relatives. What would her nephew, the doctor, a specialist and son of her brother, the titular head of the family, think?

Michael was with her at the end. He recalled her white and withered body lying on the shiny hardwood floor of his parents' North York bungalow. She lay helpless in a pool of blood, whining and crying. The ambulance attendees suspected foul play until they saw Michael's father enter the room, a shrunken and stooped 88 year old man smiling cryptically. He could hurt no one.

Michael remembered the ambulance stopping and starting, bumping along as he sat beside his mother as if they were in a dark crypt. Finally at the hospital, each doctor asked Michael about his mother's condition, testing his patience. Michael insisted that they should know his mother's condition better than he. They had treated her for years. Why would they ask him—he was not a medical man!

Then, the passing: Michael saw his mother's lifeless body draped only in a hospital smock, lying more lifeless than any inanimate object or stone, contrasted with the small heap of polyester, acrylic and rayon lying in the corner of the room, the pile of his mother's last worn clothes. The rags of her exterior cladding exhibited more traces of her energy and vital force than the lifeless vessel which lay abandoned, dormant and discarded in the centre of the room.

Condolences rang hollow. It was not a time of mourning or lamentation, but a time of destiny and blessedness, of opposites untied.

Michael's father died a few weeks later although in relatively good health at the time of his mother's death. "She must have dragged him from this world" Michael mused. "She was always jealous that he would outlive her even though he was more than thirteen years older." Michael wondered whether someone could drag another person into another world, dimension or paradigm, or from this world, dimension or paradigm; or if these matters were even worth thinking about.

Michael's life had been filled with so many seemingly coincidental but meaningful events which may have been idiotic to group together as meaningful. They may just have been a result of coincidence. A case in point is that when in grade 1 Michael lived on Montrose Avenue but went to Grace Street Public School. Later when he moved to Grace Street, he went to Montrose Avenue Public School. Such idiosynchronicities are the threads sown by hand in the garment of one's lives. Michael was the thread of the finisher and sewing machine operator.

Another case in point is the word *"beshert."*

# 3

---

## ON FINDING LOVE

Michael had heard the word "*beshert*" used by his parents and thought it meant dear or cherished when referring to a loved one amorously. Little did he know that this word was by no means an ordinary word; that it was worth far more than its weight in ornamental embellishment even for a word minted of foreign coinage. From the people of the word, who through oppression, deprivation and meandering were never short on words, where even the one word "*oy vey!*" was worth a thousand complaints, "*beshert*" was a whole doctrine with specific times, dates and happenings where the number 40 comes into play.

Michael was caught in the vortex of love whereby the divine divines and humans get to begetting. "*Beshert*" refers to the fated mate, the preordained loved one, or for chess playing intellectuals: the mated fate. Michael however, was not cognizant of such details at the time.

When he first met Samuel's mother all he knew was that he was madly in love: the world bubbled with bliss! Even when the bliss burst, as it always will, joy like a flapjack flipped becomes but negative joy, not really as ugly as pus or puke; the visible manifestations are more in the moping and groaning. But then and there love was everywhere. His to be mate was the first to say "'yes" to his entreaties of matrimony when he was broiling in the heat of lust!

People say that love is blind. Hogwash! Love is like its own Broadway or Vegas—enjoy the lights! Perhaps Michael should have remembered what he had yet to learn: that there is no perfection except in the path we paint before we step into it. No one says "love stinks," or else everyone would be more wary. Why would a daughter of a salesman, battle hardened through engagement in silent war with her lovely moody mother, not paint herself as the oyster of Michael's eye? Michael's ex was the silver tongue orator, not lacking in humor. When she spoke "pearls *would* drip from her mouth" Michael's mother would say in her broken English. Michael just drooled over his oyster.

But she, the one that said "yes" to Michael's "will you?" was his "chosen" or "*beshert*," so what choice did he have? His emotions were scattered like pieces on the chessboard of the game of life. The fingers of fate played against his white or black. He was helpless not to take advantage of fate's gambit.

Many years later and several years prior to now, Michael would well learn the meaning of "*beshert*" when he was looking for a loophole to bring his then Cuban girlfriend to Canada without having to pay for it, sort of like having his cake and eating it too, that he stumbled on the doctrine of *beshert*. He was looking for a *Charter of Rights and Freedoms'* argument that might recognize a religious marriage for immigration purposes without his then being subject to the property obligations and encumbrances that a civil marriage under one of Canada's provinces' law would entail. He uncovered that in

Judaic jurisprudence on wedlock it is written that it was written that each one of the chosen ones has a chosen one that they are destined, or predestined to meet; thus the fate of fate of mate.

Not only that, but one would know of their *beshert* because the conception of the offspring begotten by their carnal union was to occur 40 days on the button nose after the preordained scene of first encounter. Tingles went up and down Michael's spine when he read this. His body broke out in chicken skin. He could feel the *Twilight Zone* music vibrating within. Had he not met his future bride, his former betrothed, exactly 40 days prior to the conception of their son? But it is so hard to think clearly and count in order when the head is filled with grandiose doctrines! Was it an idiosynchronicity? *Welcome to the Twilight Zone!*

How does one know the date of conception of the issue of their loins, when love is fresh as the spring, and satyr's flute is buzzing like a bee? Michael knew, and he knew it at the time it happened, and he knew it at the time that he was peering into Jewish law and lore. It was on the Labour Day weekend, and not as in labor which signifies the load carried before the delivery, but that statutory holiday that occurs on the first Monday of September in the province of Ontario and probably in most provinces in Canada.

Michael had met his ex in July while he was living at Negro Manor after selling his house and law practice in Toronto. A few days after the initial encounter he was engaged. He was as rash as rash could be rushed. If that is not love then what is, considering this all happened in mid-western Ontario and not Vegas?

The engagement party took place on the Labour Day weekend at Negro Manor. Michael made sure that the invitations were appropriate for such an important occasion. He invited all of his friends, and his future bride invited all of her acquaintances. Before the wedding Michael was still allowed to associate with his friends!

The engagement party was a great and fated party, but it was crazy, or at least that is how Michael saw or didn't see it, and thought he recalled it. Fists of unwound emotional pounded on heaven's door in an attempt to seek shelter from the breach of the boundary between fact and fancy significantly exaggerated by the full moon's light causing the gate of womankind to swing wide open. The internal throbbing was thus externalized and the seed was sewn. Michael knew at the time of planting that something happened because he was spent, though he was yet to understand what his future and past father-in-law meant when he said "hide the plastic" in the in law's speech at the wedding to be held at the Pride of Sinai Synagogue in North York on the first day of winter later that year.

Michael did not yet ascertain that the stage was set for the scene where he would get his fly caught and stuck in Charlotte's web. Charlotte was the name Michael and his bride to be were going to call the dog they got after buying the red 4 wheel drive Toyota pickup truck while they resided at Negro Manor, but instead they called that noble beast, the creature that soothed Michael's soul after separation, "Jenny," short for "Jennifer."

Michael's labor began when the ex's child bearing labor began and she dropped any notion of work unless shopping can be laborious, and he set up a re-practice of law in Owen Sound buying a stately old house on a visible and prestigious intersection in that fair city.

It is funny, but not so humorous, how feelings can be exacerbated by a motivated angler. Once the catch is hauled in it's time to filet the fish and fry, and she cried: "I'm pregnant, I can't live on a farm!" so they moved to the Beverly Hills of Owen Sound: 4th Ave. West, know as Millionaire's Drive, although in Owen Sound you could be a millionaire for a couple hundred grand. The house they moved into was built by a delirious dentist and backed onto the Sydenham River.

Checked shirt, beard, wide rimmed glasses, a pregnant wife, a red 4 wheel drive pickup truck, and a dog named Jenny pulled into the driveway between the lawyers McClung and the orthopedic surgeon with the unruly children. The next door lawyer's wife was poor of hearing and sight, and thought Michael's name was Manfred Wright; but she was wrong, although it was a pretty awesome sounding WASP name Michael thought.

The practice went well. There was a real estate boom banging up business at the time and Michael had experience in the "ins and outs" of all types of cases, motions and actions save and except criminal law. The two partners in pre-matrimony cohabited in premarital bliss watching TV and eating together, he being able to come home for lunch. They drank sufficiently, and both smoked—only cigarettes for her. But as all good things must have a heads and a tails, a beginning and an end, even *beshert* has it's *"shert,"* which means *sheared,* or *cut* in the past tense.

The wedding of Michael and Mrs. Michael Rice was held at the Pride of Sinai Synagogue in the City of North York, now being the City of Toronto. It was a beautiful wedding where the beer and alcohol flowed like the 6 piece music, *"Always,"* over the flowers and fabulous food. Witty speeches and well dressed men, women and children, and even the elderly danced and jumped and lived and sang! Michael was happy and content in his black tuxedo, with full head of hair, reddish brown beard, white orchid and gold embroidered white skullcap, to be joined in holy matrimony under the law of Moses (how legally binding uncertain) to such a beautiful and expensive dress!

The wedding took place on December 21, being the first day of winter and the shortest day of the year. The significance of this seemingly insignificant detail will be revealed and exposed in due course. The video of the wedding attested to the fact that Michael's friends got progressively drunker, and one even wished him well, singing a line from that famous and happy song at the time: *"don't worry, be happy."*

Michael tobogganed down the slippery slope of bliss blithely, and the to be father practiced hard and even took his Dictaphone (registered trademark) to the hospital as there was a real estate boom clanging away at the time, for the crying time of his wife and the camel through the eye of the needle: the separation of the one into two, the opening of the floodgates, the birth of their son, Samuel, who Michael saw first and held and noticed he was perfect (at least in number of digits and appendages). Michael recalled the tranquil face of the family doctor as he hummed and rhythmically sewed the floodgates of motherhood together while whistling a melodic tune. That was *something* you could not expect in Toronto!

When one is of the Jewish fold it is obligatory to circumcise a male child on the eighth day of life, if health permits. "Why?" one may ask. *"Go ask Isaac when he was just small. But don't go chasing rabbits because you know you're going to fall."*

Michael invited everyone he could think of, or that he ran into, to the circumcision party. One might think that Michael being a lawyer wanted witnesses in case anything went wrong, but the kernel in the shell of the matter is that he was in joy— one might say high on life—in an elevated state, long term mania, in begetting progeny, a biological imperative.

In truth the reality might have been more vicious and ironic. He was but the *"dredel"* (i.e. a Jewish top spun by children to gamble on the feast of Hanukah for chocolate coins or future considerations) in the twisted digits of fate untwisting, twirling and unwinding; manifesting what was scribed in the unwritten book of his life as evidenced by the following idiosynchronicities:

1)    Michael was married on the shortest day of the year being the first day of winter, and the circumcision party or *bris* fell on the first day of summer, the longest day of the year.

2)    Michael was born in Wroclaw, Poland, which used to be Breslau, Germany, where one certainly famous German air ace, the much heralded and sung about *Red Baron*, Baron von Richthofen, was also born. Samuel, son of Michael, was born in Owen Sound, Ontario, the birthplace of one almost as famous air ace, Billy Bishop, about whom there is a play. Said Billy Boy Bishop reportedly and purportedly shot down the more infamous and higher ranking *Red Baron*. Samuel was thus able to spitfire to victory in any argument, essentially a battle of hot air, to shoot his father down, even though the father should by the rights and rules of heredity, chivalry and seniority be entitled to claim victory in any father/son verbal dog fight. But "what is" always trumps "what should be," and *that's life and no one can deny it*!

The major issue with having a circumcision party in Owen Sound was that there were no *"moyles"* or professional circumcisers who had the required skill and expertise to snip while performing the proscribed song and dance to be found. Many *moyles* were available in Toronto, but all were too busy to go up to Owen Sound. Only a former coroner, *Dr. Name Forgotten*, could or would do it. He was the last choice, but as there was no choice he was the chosen one to perform the deed, and Michael and his wife agreed. The good news was that the circumcision was to take place on the first day of summer, the longest day of the year, which permitted more time for the drive up from Toronto while there was still daylight.

"How hard could it be to perform the task?" Michael wondered. "Surely there must be a fool proof surgical instrument designed specifically for the purpose, even if the wee wee is wee at that wee age, eh." But at all *brises* he had been to, he was never able to get a close look. The skin was so quickly snipped, in a snap, like a magic trick or sleight of hand. Once there was foreskin, and then no more skin!

The ex-coroner looked a bit slow and shaky. Michael pondered whether he should have deputized *Dr. Name Forgotten* to be his surrogate to perform the ancient ritual. Only for *one second* did Michael contemplate being an Abraham to his Isaac. Even though Michael was a bit drunk, and an adventurous sort, often acting very rash and foolishly, he was not such a complete imbecile to risk the wrath of his betrothed should he botch the circumcision of their only child.

Samuel was whisked into the broadloomed living room overlooking the Sydenham River, and placed into Michael's father's arms, being a position of honor. The *moyle* slowly began his work. First the anesthetic: a drop or two or red wine, then slowly, very slowly, the shearing began.

"My god was he using a straight edge!" Michael's mind neurotically screamed. After what seemed an eternity, but in reality may have been a few minutes, it was over, the deed was done. "*Mazel Tov!*" rang out while the Mogen David poured and flowed with diabolical diabetic sweetness. More drinking and chatter and eating ensued, and all was well for the time being.

Michael was not sure, but since he had no means to inspect the quality of the work, and whether the job was done in a good and workmanlike manner, decided to let bygones be bygones. He was not going to cry about a little foreskin, for even the law did not recognize minimal deficiencies as demonstrated in the maxim "*a little bit does not a big deal make.*" Michael had forgotten his wee concerns until he ran into a friend a few years later that had also contracted the services of *Dr. Name Forgotten* to contract the foreskin of his son. Such friend asked Michael if Sam's wee wee looked funny.

To this question Michael did not have an answer, and like all those really big questions in life the answer must forever remain a mystery. Michael never delved deeply into the private recesses of his son, who grew up to be a very private and force-ful person. In any event, the quality of the services rendered has no relevance whatsoever to this story.

# 4

## BACK TO THE NOW

But now it was a sunny October day, and Michael was in his sixth floor one bedroom condo in Hamilton. It was just a bit after noon. Michael knew that many things had happened to him in the past, and his memories were accurate to a point, but he could not think of them all at once, yet they remained in his mind, at least his evolving take on them, somehow miraculously available for him to play back when he wished (before in video and now digitally). Michael never liked to use the word "miraculous" because he did not believe in miracles. Otherwise, God would have to play favorites and make exceptions to the rules and laws of the universe, and science could not exist.

Michael did not feel like going through a detailed proof in support of his position to try and persuade others. He had done enough of that in the practice of law and study of philosophy. He was tired of fighting. He was tired of trying to move mountains. Suffice it to say that he believed there must be order in the universe or there would be no order, and all would be in disorder and chaos—an unrecognizable fucking mess!

Michael slid open the first glass patio door and then the next glass patio door to step onto his balcony where he viewed the not unpleasing sight of downtown Hamilton framed under a bonnie blue sky—a mélange of houses and buildings varying in height and color—a view not unlike many seen from a sixth floor apartment in a city that was of substantial size but not a mega city or the capital. Trees of red, yellow and orange mixed with some vestige of green were interspersed with tall rectangular buildings of grey, yellow and red brick and off-white concrete.

On this super-sunny day everything seemed to be infused and imbued with an extra vital force, a certain *je ne se quoi*. The birds, perhaps gulls, flew in patterns of an arc, as if to trace taut bows drawn against the sky. Then they suddenly swooped or turned as if they were trying to fool someone or duck something. Perhaps they were just playing. Maybe they had forgotten where they were flying to—was it hither or thither?

Michael thought of asking the birds, but what answer could they give? Surely they would squawk at such a rude, crass and base enquiry, and refuse to dive into and indulge any such dialogue or discussion with a son of man who spoke not the language of unbounded flight. Michael was but at ground level in terms of understanding the magnitude of the birdbrain logic that propelled the unpredictable soaring evident before his eyes.

Michael went back inside. He no longer had the patience to dwell on the esthetically pleasing scene. How long can one stare at anything, let alone beauty, without getting bored—unless it is pornographic or obscene?

Michael began to write an email to his son to inform him of the decision to sell the store, and of the planned party where a short story would stealthily serve as an invitation. Michael carefully and painstakingly crafted and drafted a long and detailed email to Samuel explaining the plotted course in minutiae, trying to balance Samuel's sensitivities with Michael's own interests, both in content and tone. To be clear and not to mislead, such considerations were counterbalanced with the firmness of Churchillian conviction that Michael felt he felt. He would not back down—he would never surrender—no matter what! His mind was made up—he had decided!

The word *"decision"* comes from the word *"cede"* which means "to give up," but is at its root derived from the word meaning "to cut" or "to shear." Like the glass broken at a Jewish wedding—or Humpty Dumpty's great fall—there is no turning back.

The email to Samuel took more than an hour to compose, review and edit. Finally, when Michael was satisfied that it was just right, he sent it off. Soon a response was received, not by email, but rather by way of a message on Facebook. All it said was "hey"—that was all! Billy Bishop did it again. The boy from Wroclaw was shot down by just one word!

What an unexpected let down for Michael who was never short on words! Samuel was just the opposite—what could account for such contrast in verbosity between father and son? Did it have anything to do with the universal law that all things manifest in opposites? Michael had never been given a middle name. Could this have caused his addiction to overuse words, his not being able to resist the urge to talk too much; akin to what is implied in the expression: *Spare the rod, spoil the child*?

Samuel did have a middle name. It was "David." In Judaism "David" is considered one of the big three names, ranking in importance only behind Moses and *"the name that can't be spoken."* David was the warrior king, child hero, lamenting poet. Michael believed that David probably ordered parts of the bible written to suit his political ends. In Michael's view David exhibited the classic signs of being bipolar. The evidence was all the manic massacring and the depressive psalms David scribed. Perhaps David of biblical fame was no hero, but just another crazy and lost soul driven by obsession and compulsion.

There was also a price that had to be paid for what David did: the house of David bore a curse. Coveting the wife of one of his generals, David commanded such general to do battle where all knew he was certain to die. As David was king, he got his way. After the general's death the beautiful recently widowed widow was added to King David's stable of wives. Some people however, did notice and they were not at all pleased...

David did not have to pay for his sins. He was able to lust and conquer and lament as much as he wanted, and yet still be blessed by God. It was his issue who bore the burden—who had to carry the weight—a sort of Judaic karma.

Michael had thought of calling his son, "Samson," believing intuitively that his firstborn would be strong. It was a good thing that he avoided the name—it probably would have had the opposite effect—like naming a boy "Sue"!

Samuel had recently moved out to go to law school in Ottawa allowing Michael to downsize and move into his present condo. Did Samuel choose law as a career to spite his father, to outdo his own flesh and blood? Perhaps Sam had what it took to be a successful lawyer—all the right stuff—a big mouth or what is known as a big "*pisk*" in Yiddish. Samuel might have been slim and short; in fact about 2 inches shorter than Michael, but Samuel would never back down, no matter what. No one dared to challenge him when they saw the fire in his eyes!

Sam was very astute as a child and quickly recognized trademarks and brand names. His capability to ape and imitate poses and stances of athletes or others accurately was uncanny. This led to his being a good actor in high school which naturally evolved into drive and then overdrive, and finally to *warp speed*!

Now Sam, like many children of his generation, was an aficionado of James Bond starting with Pierce Brosnan, but in time he bonded with the best Bond, Sean Connery. He was also raised and reared on the Batman, movies and cartoons, both light and dark like rye bread; but what may have been his favorite fantasy in all its generations was *Star Trek*. Sam was always the Captain while Michael was always relegated to be the subordinate second-in-command known as *"Number One."* Michael's duty was to make it *so*, as Captain Sam commanded.

Perhaps Michael and Sam were much alike although they may have been blind to this. They both always had to be right, and when they disagreed, something always went wrong!

Then again, they were very different. To Samuel confiding was weakness. He pushed and caffeinated himself like a bottomless cup, and would reply in the same sarcastic manner as Michael's mother had to similar assertions when warned "you need to rest, you'll burn out" but in a more of a *mind your own business* tone: "I'll rest in the next world." This always irked Michael because he feared tempting fate.

Sam as an infant carried around a toy hockey stick which although small matched his size. It did not look like a toy as for example would a real pistol in Arnold Schwarzenegger's massive hands. And he developed a wicked slapshot: very impressive in a country called Canada.

Samuel's hands were eerily similar to Michael's. Michael had always admired his father's hands with their long perfectly shaped fleshed-out ivory fingers. They were elegant, spiritual, and artistic—possibly "aristocratic"—even though Mendel labored in a factory his entire working life. When young, Michael thought his stubby fingers and large palms should have belonged to a peasant, being more suitable to working the earth than for professional pursuits, but their attraction grew on him with age. His hands were nimble and strong and possessed a well-forged utilitarian charm.

Michael could not see if Sam had any scars from life's trials and tribulations and seemingly unrepentant onslaught of acts and incidents which are always hurled at those walking down her path when they least expect it. Michael just wanted to hug his son, to tell him that he loved him, but Michael did not know if it was he who didn't know how to do so, or if it was simply a case of Samuel not letting down his force field, his protective shield, to let the words be spoken. Michael had never felt inadequate as a father when Samuel was young, so why was he having problems reaching him now, communicating with him?

Michael was almost never at a loss for words. He never had to deal with such issues with his own father. It always seemed and felt right, the way it was. Michael rarely thought about it, at least not until Samuel was born. In Michael's mind his own father had somehow reached perfection in the last few years of his life, when Mendel would tell other people exactly how he felt about them without hesitancy or ulterior motive—and it was always something positive.

Sure Mendel was human. He would not invest in anything that could cause him to lose sleep. Michael passed on such sage advice, telling others of this litmus test for investments. Michael found it incredible that his father was not frosted or tainted with bitterness after suffering the great and undeserved losses that befell him in his life through no fault of his own.

Should Michael compare himself to his own father? Mendel was a man of routine who woke up early each day and prepared an extravagant breakfast. This was the only cooking and cleaning which Michael's mother would permit anyone other than herself to do. Each day before supper Mendel "made *a schnaps*" having a shot or two of whiskey. But rarely did he get drunk, and only when he planned to. When he went to events like a wedding or *Bar Mitzvah* Mendel would fill up a glass with hard liquor to the desired level of drunkenness he sought—usually from four to eight ounces—and then down it all at once straight! Afterwards, he would sit there with a self-satisfied silly drunken smile plastered on his face for the entire night as Michael's mother derided him for not knowing how to dance!

Still, Mendel loved Michael's mother so deeply it was unfathomable to Michael. She so often heaped scorn and railed against him, especially when he came home late for dinner from the park after playing cards all day. And in spite of his love of playing cards, he gave it up when he was no longer at the top of his game; more than can be said of many professional athletes or performers!

But when Michael's father lost his temper, which was seldom, he was torn asunder, and it was *Paradise Lost*! The pain and hurt once held in, checked and balanced, erupted from the ocean within, rupturing and fissuring the flesh of his soul.

Michael was like this too, for when his rage raged, it was red and all consuming (but to a much lesser extent than his father's). But now, Michael felt no rage. It was an extremely sunny October day in Hamilton. If someone had invented a *"sun-o-meter"* to measure daylight brightness, this fall day would surely register high. And if intensity of light were audible, the dogs would be howling!

# 5

---

# A FEW COMPLICATIONS

The 20th century produced a particular and peculiar type of madness beyond the confines of the law schools and the medical schools. No condescending aspersions or dispersions are meant to be cast on the neurotic theories of Freud or the lunacy of the pill pushers, but when the paint of life gets squirted out at 20 megatons per microsecond, the result might be a bit of a mess, especially if painted in panoramic color by the paranoid mind, not merely in the tainted stain of water colored ink or the pastels of a mad artist's brush, but in the depth and endlessness of a permanent vacation of the body and mind!

After the Second World War the oils of hate were seeping into the rivers of time and draining into the ocean which like a great churning washing machine left the garments of what remained of humanity smelling refreshingly clean. And so the dispossessed returned home to not find their homes. Mendel and Michael's mother met on the planked wooden floor of the garment shop in that particular Bohemian part of the world known as Walbrzych which might have meant "wild thing" or "wild place" in some old Germanic dialect. The name conjures visions of dark dense forests and variations of wild pig roasting on an open spit over a smoking wood fire. The Soviets were gracious and generous enough to gift such vanquished lands to Poland, and this is where Mendel consummated the union with his bride, jabbing his needle into the patterned cloth of life with the repeated expertise of a sewing machine operator.

On what could have been Labour Day, or the fist Monday in September, if that particular piece or tract of land was under the jurisdiction of the government of Ontario (in those days everyday was a pretending to labor day under the eye of the red yoke) dropped the first fruit of the afore sewn union. The eldest son of Mendel and his young energetic bride was named after Mendel's deceased father as it was the custom to honor the deceased of Mendel's heritage by recycling names, which coincided with the name of the father of the race, "Abraham," who also happens to be the father of a somewhat equal and often conflicting race in the lopsided place called the world.

"Abe" or "Abie," as Michael's brother was called, is a name not to be confused with Abel, for that would make Michael Cain, who he was not. But Abe complicated Michael's life in a way which Michael was still trying to understand and unravel.

Does the pot know what forces have shaped it when it is already formed, full and boiling? Does it have the right to call the kettle black? Were they not partners the two brothers, like yin and yang, each a part of the other, sharing the same ancestry and blood, carrying the same genes, wearing the same jeans? Michael did not mind hand-me-downs. But unlike Cain and Abel, they were amicably able to share and divide the bountiful inheritance that their parents had saved and left them, without even one fight. Could not all their other fights, disagreements and spats be construed merely as outpourings of love in accordance with the law of the manifestation of opposites?

And were they not both there with their father, respectful of their duty, when he suddenly took ill and quickly lost his mind shortly after his wife, Abe's and Michael's mother, died? There was then nowhere for Mendel to turn. He did not want to leave the house, go to a nursing home, or have someone come to the home to take care of him. So Mendel returned to the house of his father, to the house of Abraham, to no longer weep in his sleep.

Michael recalled seeing his father in the hospital hours before he passed away. The doctors predicted he had another week to live. His breathing was labored. A mischievous grin played on his face which appeared to lack any sign of age as if he was an imp caught in the lights of a midsummer night's dream. The thought that this life on earth which often spans scores of years is in but an infinitesimal flash of light, that each person exists in some sustained state of unremembered reality other than this existence, edged on Michael's mind.

Michael knew that his father could not recognize him. Only perplexity emanated from the two soft almond-shaped orbs set in Mendel's face which moved to the left and right as they searched for something—something lost and misplaced on the verge of dreaming, never to be found. Mendel's eyes were asking: "who are you?"

Michael calmly and clearly expressed in Yiddish: "I am your son," as he sought a hint of acknowledgement, a glint of recognition, in his father's confused grey eyes. Perhaps a light, a lamp of some sort, lay around the corner in the labyrinth of Mendel's fleeting consciousness. Perhaps it was only Michael's desire that projected such hope.

The primate understands only survival and reproduction. Michael tried not to take it personally. "He is dying and I am alive" was the summation of Michael's thoughts. His feelings seemed foreign, with a sterile numbness to them, as if they were negated, cancelled out. Michael felt the subtle glow of all the love his father had radiated during his life. The prime imperative and overriding meaning of Mendel's life had been to care and provide for Michael and his brother. The job was done. The case was closed. What else could Michael do but put on his hat, coat and gloves and go out into that cold and clear December day with the courage and single-minded conviction bestowed on one who knows with certainty that all living creatures walk in the shadow of the mountain of life: the valley of death? A few hours later a telephone call came from the hospital. Michael's father had died.

Michael had to get ready for work. He picked up the phone and called the store. Jambalaya answered: "Hello, Wild Rice."

"Jambalaya—it's Michael. Do you have a moment? Listen— I've been doing a lot of thinking. I've decided to sell the store." Michael continued: "I got this great idea to have a party to celebrate the selling of the store and to write an invitation in the form of a short story to be delivered by Canada Post to everyone nearby. Once people read the story, they will realize that it is an invitation, but not before, so they will be curious enough to read it and not throw it out. The story would essentially be about me and would explain why I was selling the store. It'll be great promotion. Should I tell Lasiandra or do you want to tell her? I don't want to surprise her. What do you think?"

"Lassie knows. You already told us. There's a customer here. I've got to go."

"Oh—okay. I'll be in late this afternoon. Maybe I'll see you then." With those words Michael hung up the phone. His mind was turning, void of content. After a few minutes Michael returned to the there and then, his little nest on the sixth floor in Hamilton in the early afternoon on a sunny October day. He had to get ready to go to work.

# 6

## SOME QUESTIONS

What is the measure of success? What is a life worth? Someone once said that a life doesn't add up to a hill of beans in this crazy world. That person was better to do and more handsome than Michael, yet he could not make heads or tails of life. What hope did Michael have if a chain smoking actor caught in a triangle of beauty, authority and piano playing in French-speaking North Africa could not make heads or tails of life? Yes, a hill of beans, at least that was something tangible which could be eaten, taken to the bank. And yes, beans, no less a hill of them—the possibilities though not endless were quite audible. *"Hark! The beans trumpet."* A whole army of bean eaters waiting at the gates of heaven and then in unison a giant *"HARK!"* and down go the gates with a huge onslaught of souls trampling over the fallen golden gates disappearing into white peaceful bliss—all because of the earthy little bean. If only it were so easy...

Feelings of self pity and doubt coagulated in Michael's mind like so many bubbles of water ready to boil. The frustrations and angst of all his endings and losses aligned in "woe is me" fashion as he stared into the mirror of advancing age and depleting resources.

All the negative thoughts and feelings so aggregated caught and trapped Michael forming a net around him. Though but sentiments and conceptions he had conjured, they weighed heavily on him. Now, he planned to run away from his current situation as he done previously with the practice of law. Could he *not* be the hero of his own story? He did not need a whole hill of beans. Perhaps a little pile of peas would be enough? But where were the peas? Life, like a hydra-headed monster, was no fucking fairy tale. It was full of hard cold banality and red hot compulsions, all muddled, mixed and tangled. And now Michael simmered in his own emotional stew.

Where did it start? What happened to the young eager boy adventurously advancing down the gangplank in Halifax harbor, secure but free in the firm, gentle grip of his father's right hand? Michael was now almost 60 years old and in the autumn of his life if his earthly existence were but a year. He had no mate and was all alone. His son was far away and distant, and so too was his brother. Michael was alone, running, gyrating in circles, round and round, trying to escape but held captive, chained by illusions and mental constructs, shouting and growling like a trapped, chained dancing bear beseeching all who would listen to hear. He yearned for waves of *"don't take yourself over"* to wash over him like a sea to assuage his anguish. Those who had brought him into life had departed and left.

Heaven too was not there, it was occupied, hidden in the brisk chill wind as it flogged the leaves that remained on trees or lay on the ground, sucking through osmosis and evaporation their life force. In the agony of their death and dying, the foliage, once alive and green, shrieked in crimsons, yellows and rusty golds, waiting for the rake or worm to be recycled. Perhaps it is at this point that the butterfly emerges from the cocoon, or if the tube is squeezed too tightly there is an explosion, and blobs of toothpaste go flying everywhere to mar the mirror's reflection. If one would know the answer to the question: which of the two possibilities will occur—transformation or death—it would be a worthwhile answer indeed, and worthy of scientific investigation, but the color of pain seeped along the curbs and arteries, making navigation dangerous and worth averting.

So where did it all begin, all the confusion and reflecting? Was it when the little 6 year old Polish Jew-boy straight off the boat from Israel was accused of killing Jesus by his Italian immigrant friends? "No, we got you, the Romans, to do it for us" Michael could have replied had he been a smart-assed little jerk, but he was just an intelligent one-dimensional kid who argued against the existence of God. He knew that the Romans crucified and that the Jews stoned—that was a historical and biblical fact. In any event, Michael had nothing personal to do with the crucifixion. Why would the church be teaching such prejudicial *trife* to little boys and girls?

The Jews and the Italians were very much alike there in Little Italy in downtown Toronto. Sure, more Italians lived in one house than Jews, and the Italians had rougher hands, but they were both hard-working family folk, so that is not where Michael's problems began.

Later on as a young teenager Michael's family moved up to North York where he met and became a different type of Jew. A back-talking, cool, rebellious Jew with tucked out shirt and checked or striped shirt and *Beach Boy* haircut, who with friends the product of middle or upper class families rushed to *My Generation*—"Why *don't you all just f-f-f-f-fade away...*"

At the Heights of Bathurst Secondary School, the Jews were smoking pot and hash, and the Italians were shooting up! It was just a natural extension of their forefathers' favorite method of extermination and exemplification; thus accounting for Michael's natural preference for being stoned, rather than having a spike driven right through his veins. *"But it's all right— Jumping Jack Flash is a gas, gas, gas..."*

But that's not where it began. That was just schoolboy fun. Michael chose "against," which later became "for," but he might have been ahead of his time. The first trace of the crack or blistering of that happy, blissful, science-will-explain-it-all rational world of Michael began at a much earlier age; an inkling of which appeared in the following incidents.

# 7

## CAMP STICKROCK

Oh you Muses who amuse with the trying tales of the
contrived conundrums stirred in the caldron of cares of
this earthly existence give form to those idyllic days of almost
forgotten youth and innocence of Michael during his days at
Camp Stickrock on the shores of Albatross Lake full of blood
sucking leeches, in beautiful Muskoka cottage country and
the Province of Ontario, across which shore lay the town of
Gravenhurst, a morbid name hidden to all but the most initiated in delving too deeply into the morass of fecund verbosity.

Murmur of the milk train snaking its chugging way up from
Toronto to third term camp in August as the young and not of
legal age occupants played "spin the bottle," and Michael would
premeditate the spin cast so as to get the girl. Sure, he as a 10
year old had practiced kissing with his Italian friends who were
all boys, but that was merely academic and not a pleasantry
even if lips had been locked for more than a minute with breath

not so sweet. It was done only and in so far as necessary to develop the art and skill to use in a pinch or squeeze. Whisper too how later on in life, Michael was not above a sleight of hand to deal from the bottom of the deck so as to peel the veiling robes from one desired when playing strip poker; but it was all for fun and no one lost an eye!

Sing of the massive cliff of Canadian Shield dotted with cedar and pine carved with scores of granite stairs rising from the shore of Albatross Lake that greeted the campers as they disembarked from canoes laden with suitcases and bags that by strength of paddles and counselors' arms traversed the murky bottomed lake beneath the three quarters moon hanging in the evening sky like a not quite full ball of cheese.

Pray tell how at the summit of the cliff on a cleared plane lay the mess hall, the administration building and the wooden cabins where the campers slept. Shield the senses of all who live from the dreaded hidden outhouse, reeking to high heaven with a smell that would make even a drunken sailor swoon. The thought and sight of which filled Michael with such fear and loathing he might as well have been lost in the rotting under-belly of Las Vegas. The sheer ugliness of the immense well of shit impressed itself on Michael's tender young nostrils as he was coming of age right down to the pit of his stomach. And it is here that Michael first experienced the hardening of the bowel, visiting the dreaded john but once in 18 days.

The doctors of today do not connect the bowel to the heart, but any child who can tie themselves in knots will attest to the fact that a twisted bowel goes right to the brain and makes thoughts of the heart vacant indeed—the foulness of flatulence being proportionate to the time one has not been out-housed. Matters reached a crescendo of dastardliness when someone put clear cellophane wrap on the outhouse seat and covered it with peanut butter. This last aforesaid smear was too much for Michael and his bowels hardened and hardened, and caused the blood that flowed through his veins, arteries and brain to trickle ever so slightly less.

But before the slow turning of the screw and the hardening of the sap, camp was fun with all its outdoor activities: canoeing, swimming and archery. Michael learned what it was like to live in the great Canadian outdoors: feeding frogs to snakes, singing songs about the Titanic and things that sunk and stunk. During the third term camp Stickrock was a music camp and the instrument that Michael studied with mathematical precision (and a mechanical tin ear) was the violin, the most famous of Viennese torture devices. Michael reveled, with little practice, under the tutelage of the thin instruction of the nose picking, pale, baby-faced Transylvanian, Mr. Googoola.

Then it happened—a hint to Michael's future. Competition Day came and the campers were divided into several teams, each having a roughly equal number of campers from the various age groups. Each team was named after a country in Africa which had so many newly named exotic countries emerging from the bridle of colonialism. The names were strange to Michael who had yet to study geography or history. His country and team was Ghana. He knew little of Ghana and never heard the name before, but it was his team and he must do his all for the team, for at such time Michael thought that such thinking was right, and did so without hesitation, to the same extent, no doubt, that her Majesty believes that her subjects serve at her pleasure and leisure.

After such time, Michael did indeed meet people from Ghana. In Prague or Tokyo he met many that steered tourists towards titillating and sizzling clubs and scenes—doing work that the home folk cared for little, and paid for even less. But that was then and this is now, and Ghana was still young and innocent and darkly mysterious and beautiful, at least in Michael's imagination.

The big race involved all the campers and started at noon. It took the form of various legs, wherein each age group would complete in a different activity. The starter pistol's ring broke the silence of anticipation with a big bang. The swimmers swam, the runners ran, the canoeists rounded corners and returned, their paddles frantically splashing and dipping. Michael's leg was to run on all fours, after the eggs were carried up the cliff on a spoon, and he ran over rocks and moss. He ran with manic adrenaline and abandon like a wild animal, perhaps a wolverine, running fast and furious, surprising himself how fast he could run with so much control like a wild animal, but with such soft smooth hands and a racing mind. And he was the fastest of his leg!

The afternoon passed into evening, and the evening waned with the stars crowding together making luminous the dark canopy of night as it swelled up like the inside of a hot air balloon flecked with a million marks from the crackling fire as the campers sat like little Buddhas in a semicircle. Now came the most powerful, magical time: *story time!*

When Michael's turn came to speak he walked slowly and surely to stand before the crowd. All eyes were on him, hushed in anticipation. He was filled with so much joy! The thought of how happy he was brought a smile to his face as he told a story about his beloved Ghana which he made up on the spot, there and then. It just flowed out of him irrepressibly! He was so full of emotion and happiness that when he finished his little rant the smile on his face grew and grew. For the first time, as if some screw within him had been turned but a touch, he saw himself separate, standing there unable to move. The smile on his face grew more and more powerful and unyielding, without regard to the interests of its host.

With the force of gravity and light combined, the monstrous and hideous smile had latched onto him like a blood sucking leech and rode him like he was a rocking horse. He could not stop it! It was his master. He stood there with that alien smile gleaming, beaming from his face like a supernova; and it scared the hell out of him—but not the shit! How could he love himself so much as to lose all control of his facial muscles at Camp Stickrock?

He knew then and there that life was too powerful him. He must hide! The smile was his inner demon let out, and little Michael was deep inside hiding somewhere in a dark recess, lost and holding back for fear of exploding—scattering solid, liquid and gas to the vicinity and infinity—allowing him to forget but for a moment the hard ball of lead that weighed heavy in his gut, his intoxicating constipation. *There were forces not in his control—the teeter-totter could tip at any time!*

With wings of wax Michael had tried to reach the sun. With each flap, farther from the fertile field did he fly, rising higher and higher in the night. His pleasure cord could only reach so far. He fluttered up out of sight of the pleasure gods to his cloud on high, to hide there with his tearless pain covered by an alien smile.

Jesus was asked what the two most important commandments were. He answered: "The lord is one and there is no other; and that people must love each other no matter what." If God was one, that is all there would be, and there could be no more. If everyone loved everybody else, then all would be love—*no more and no less!*

But what is love? Where did all the lust and desire come from? What tree bore such fruit? In what garden does it grow? Michael bit. The smell and taste satisfied at first; but soon that which he ate consumed him. He thrust it to the ground as the worms crawled out to complete the circle of life.

How can God be trusted? Are all the ordeals but tests to measure the mettle or armor one has to manufacture? Inside, hiding and scared, Michael still carried the little child, and the sun would rise again to give morning to his hopes, plans, dreams and schemes.

# 8

## GETTING READY FOR WORK

But now the sky was blue, and natural light filled Michael's condo apartment. He was still in what is called reality, in a time deemed to be now. It was a cool, breezy, sunny day in a city named Hamilton in the province legally known as Ontario, in the Dominion of Canada which was a country. Michael was there with all his books and furniture; with the walls, windows, floors, doors, ceiling and appliances in his one bedroom unit. It was not a prison. It contained the chattels of his life's accumulation. It was his home, secure liberation, his little abode on the sixth floor, for him to come and go as he pleased 24 hours a day. Although he was no angel, at least not yet, Michael had hands that could feel, a mouth that could speak, and a mind which created time and place and thought itself to be in the here and now.

Did Michael hear a needle dropping in the vast void as if his inside was out, *helter skelter*, no louder than the sound of one hand clapping? He saw angels dancing on the eye of finisher's needle as it fell and fell and fell. Their sardonic high pitched shrieks of laughter pricked his ears. Perhaps they were but fairies and dragonflies gyrating in flames of fire, like tattoos on the wall in *Plato's cave*. The devil's harem, angels with ivory-white feet and dragonfly wings, danced to a demon beat on the head of a falling needle—feet bleeding and pierced.

Watching Jesus in his final glory days was surely no picnic. He was full throttled, made exemplary, transported mainline in front of his prostrate fans, and then went biblical. Michael was no Jesus, at least not yet. The echo of the sound of the pin dropping was the shadow of his loneliness: longing lacking words. He had fallen, was cast unto the cold, muddy ground waiting to be saved and resurrected, wallowing in the muck of his own mire.

It has been said that birds have nests, moles have holes and foxes have dens. What better seduction pad? Perhaps there is a tree that a monkey can call its own. What street or scene or stone can a man own? Where in the urban outdoors can a man freely pee? Where can one rest a weary head when the toil of endless thought and slanted sight is the clock that ticks the hours away? Though thoughts are fast, the minutes were slipping away like excited hands under a black evening dress, so Michael began his preparations to leave for work.

Teeth were brushed, hair was combed and lavender was splashed on the face and rubbed into the neck for its healing, relaxing and odiferous properties. Next, Michael broke off a piece of fresh organic ginger that was sitting in his fruit bowl about the size of the tip of a thumb, washed it, and wrapped it in half a piece of paper towel and put it into a little wicker box that looked like a cigarette package which also contained organic ground turmeric. These were for an infusion (not to confused with tea which is a particular specie of plant) that Michael would make at Starbucks when and where he would order a triple espresso and a tall cup of hot water for his ginger and turmeric drink, while on his way to work.

Ginger and turmeric were related species, cousins so to speak, and taste good together. Both grow in India where Michael thought he would like to go to see what they looked like alive—cinnamon as well—there to be enchanted by the vibrant jungle of odor and noise.

Michael would put the turmeric powder in his water with a wooden stir stick. The turmeric was a golden yellow color and smelled earthy and mildly sweet. Michael knew that it was worth more than gold because you could not eat gold. Gold was cold and a watery tinny yellow, good for trinkets and exciting the savage fool, to rush the blood fever high of a crucifying conquistador. And what church or temple would be complete if not replete and gilded with gold and be speckled in jewels to make the gawking eye go agog in supposed celestial serenity?

Turmeric had so many benefits: good for inflammation, brain function and anti-carcinogenic. Michael would take the ginger and masticate it with his teeth to release the juices when he mixed it with hot water and the turmeric. He liked the attention it would attract. He, the fun loving, sad and lonely, happy, laughing, enlightened animal making and drinking his hot, spicy, earthy, healthy drink. But first after chewing the ginger in preparation for the mix, he would drink the espresso, sometimes adding and stirring in some raw sugar. He liked the spicy hot sensation that the ginger left in his mouth that was amplified by the drinking of the espresso. He would wait for the turmeric/ginger infusion to cool before drinking it, sometimes taking it with him for the drive into Toronto, or at other times, for a walk first.

Michael washed the organic fruits that he would take with him except the banana which needs no washing: an apple, a pear and an orange; and placed them into his shoulder bag along with his cheque book and his appointment book. To make sure he took the store keys with him, they were always put in a certain pocket. Each thing had a designated place. Michael was glad of this because at times he forgot where he put things and would be happy to find them where they should be.

Michael then put on his brown corduroy sports jacket which was so old all the buttons had already fallen off. It did not matter as the jacket fit him well and still looked good on him, making him look like an artist or a professor. Samuel had worn this jacket for a while, as he did with some of Michael's other old clothes, but the jacket was a bit too big on Sam and looked more formal than it did on Michael who wore it comfortably.

# 9

## LOTTYLOU

Michael recalled a picture of him wearing the jacket over a brown and grey checked shirt in which he looked handsomely radiant, full cheeked and clean shaven, except for a reddish brown mustache that hung over his broad, beaming smile. His girl at the time, her name was Lottylou, looked enchanting and happy with her red smiling lips, ivory skin and curly sandy blond hair. He met her while articling at the small law firm in Malton some thirty years ago.

He might not have thought about Lottylou if not for putting on the jacket and having looked at some old photos when unpacking from his recent move, but having lived up to the present his life had been full of incidents and many thoughts, many of which he thought about over and over, especially under Justin's smile; but he liked to think about Lottylou because he did not think of her often, and had fond memories of her. As the frequency with which Michael had girlfriends diminished as he got older, he liked to dwell on a time when he did have girlfriends more often. It stroked and soothed his ego.

When Michael met Lottylou he would have been considered a good catch as he was a party and fun loving lawyer-to-be with his certain look and smiling charm. Lottylou worked as a legal clerk for a large law firm doing title and real estate conveyance work. It may have been dry, but it matched her sense of humor. She was a country girl at heart and talked like a country girl: straightforward and down-to-earth, lacking duplicity. Michael liked her no nonsense, uncomplicated, easy-going practical approach to things—it was a foil to his somewhat "out-there-always-thinking" anima.

Michael and Lottylou did not get along like oil and water in spite of their differences, which were essentially minor, marked by energetic mental minutiae. Although she was the country girl concerned with the day to day, and Michael the wild urban pensive dreamer schemer, they both enjoyed imbibing liquids, talking and getting along.

For a while Lottylou lived in the west end of Toronto renting a second floor apartment of a two story house from a hospitable Serbian landlord who occupied the main floor and always insisted that Michael have some shots of Slivovitz whenever they crossed paths. Michael always obliged as he thought it impolite to say "no." He also liked partaking in the customs of other cultures when it came to partying!

There was however a tragic flaw in the relationship between Michael and Lottylou, for otherwise it might have blossomed and born fruits like little brats hanging around. But for this tragic flaw, Michael and Lottylou might have practiced and plied their trades together often and for a long time as they were in complimentary professions, and Lottylou was very accepting and giving.

Michael recalled a certain memorable night spent at Lottylou's apartment and the date, for it was exactly nine months before Michael's birthday. They drank a whole bottle of Dom Perignon champagne in celebration of Michael completion of the Bar Admission Course. Champagne may be in a league of its own when it comes to inciting *amor*, and no less should be expected based on its price tag.

That night the champagne divinely inspired Michael in his love making. He felt compelled to beget; to have a child born on his birthday garnered great significance in his bubbled up mind. Was it not a sign—a clear idiosynchronicity? Brimming headstrong with champagne, and sure in the erection of his logic of coinciding dates, Michael was hard with desire to beget there and then, and plow his seed into Lottylou's fertile ovarian field! But Lottylou, the practical, clear-headed country girl who could hold her champagne better than Michael, put a kybosh to his plan, making Michael put a condom on to corral his milky seeds.

There occurred a strange but true phenomenon that Michael believed made it impossible for him to continue to intercourse with Lottylou, which the so-called men of science might scoff at, but it is no stranger than a flying fish or a talking bird, and that is whenever Michael had sex with Lottylou it fatigued him and would give him a headache. He considered this to be a bad omen for the future of the relationship because he liked sex, and the tiredness lasted for a whole day afterward making him ineffectual, which he didn't like. Because something can't be explained does not mean that it is only psychological and not real, except in the dogma of the pretenders to science, and the practice of the modern doctors who want to control all minds and rule the world with their sick theories which they pass out as truth. Perhaps Lottylou had the type of metabolism that turned copper green and made silver tarnish when she wore such jewelry. Maybe a watch would stop if she strapped one on. Michael could not remember if such was the case as he prepared to leave for work, but he was now tired from just thinking about it.

Was the Lottylou effect chemical or energetic? Nomenclature did not really matter. Was not a rose a rose? He knew that he had not jumped too quickly to his conclusion because he tested his hypothesis repeatedly by continuing to have sex with her. Always the debilitating tiredness and fatigue came after he did. Sure, with other woman Michael might have got tired and fallen asleep but that was different. Michael knew that it was not due to drinking as Michael drank all the time back then and was familiar with the effects alcohol had on him—it prolonged rather than lessened his ardor. But he could stand the *après-climax* no more, so he *acted* like a jerk when he broke up with Lottylou to make it look like it was his fault. Michael liked and respected her, and he did not want to hurt her feelings.

# 10

---

# MELVA

Before sinking nose and mouth first into the idiosyn-chronicities of an affair between Michael and a woman named Dorothy, and the brief time the quarrelling and jealous gods that rule fate and play with mortals' lives allowed them to remain together like the spin of a bottle, the light and dark shades of the inquiry lamp needs to be turned on the relation-ship between Michael and Jeff who were best friends for many years, and through whom Michael met Dorothy. As the details of the "Mutt and Jeff" show are too numerous and multifold for this modest mazurka, they will be waltzed over with salsa so as only to quickly polka at the foibles, fortuity and fastidiousness of friendship.

Michael and Jeff met at Leadbelly Junior High School where Michael attended from grade 7 in North York after Michael's Italian adventures in downtown living. They both took lessons in Viennese torture (the violin) in the class of the neck-less instructor who shall remain nameless.

In grade 8, after watching some breasts sprout in grade 7, and being part of a learned circle of colorful commentators, Michael went out with a certain girl named Melva who lived near Jeff. Although the affair was brief and the kissing and petting lasted but one month, Michael developed that religious devotion with his pants still on from the anticipation and excitement of his first feel of the mystical and exalted source of nourishment, the mama gland, and in that land of milk with his young honey he took the first steps on the factual ladder of life and pure desire, and "hallelujah!" he experienced the gush without sex, still a virgin like Mary, his first being the one that precedes the anticipated second of Jesus. Being overcome with all and one in darkness and light, he hungered and thirsted for more knowledge and triumphs that he could brag to his friends about.

The relationship between Michael and Melva was short and relatively innocent, lasting only a month, being but "puppy love" where kisses and pets abound, but Jeff had a hot and heavy relationship with Melva afterwards, lasting a few years. Only God knew why, for no one else did. It was a hot and sordid affair, full of jealousy, arguments, and passion. Michael learned of the frequent vicious arguments from little clues dropped here and there, such as lips pried open and yammering wide under the influence of tequila, beer or whiskey might provide, but usually it occurred when he was in earshot of the line of fire between the two combatants spitting vituperate cannon balls at each other.

Melva was a healthy girl with a healthy appetite for socializing and food. She came from a close-knit, well-to-do family happy to let her do as she pleased. Finally reaching her senses, she dumped the rocky, long haired Jeff. It is through the connection with Melva that Michael met Jeff and they became best friends for many years including most of high school, where they shared many nights together—but never exchanging fluids—partaking in the exotic whiff of blondes and reds from the intoxicating Middle East, having fun, and partying their brains out. That was high school!

Michael became friends with Melva again later when he was a young lawyer practicing law in Toronto. He and Melva had a good relationship. It was a mutually rewarding easy-going friendship with no commitments or pressure.

One day while she and Michael were at her parents' farm near the town of Windy, Ontario, Melva proposed to Michael that they be more than just friends—she asked him to have sex with her! Michael by this time had a few years under his belt as a lawyer in a general practice, and was starting to know about people. He knew Melva well enough, and told her that she was the type of person that did not maintain friendships with her ex-lovers, so if they became more than friends and broke up, they would no longer remain friends. He thus cautioned her to be very careful about having sex with him, and to think hard and long about whether it was such a good idea.

But Melva had a voracious appetite, and was a head strong Taurus, while Michael was weak-kneed Capricorn who could not say "no," so they did it then and there and quite often afterwards for a while, as the monkeys or minks might do. But there came a time, as there always seemed to in Michael's life, which he in boredom, frustration or possibly in just plain mean spirit let his thoughts slip out, and called her a "glutton." That was it for the relationship: "*Ker plunk, it sunk.*"

Perhaps Michael was ready for the affair, the head to tail, to end. Although the dispersion cast did contain an element of truth, for Melva truly loved eating more than Michael, it was in fact her most favored and flavored pass time, but for Michael to actually tell her so was base, low and mean—especially directly to her face as she stuffed it!

Michael felt guilt and shame, and loathed himself for doing just that. Is not the making of a derogatory remark in reference to someone's most beloved weakness, the lowest and basest thing one can do when it comes to any relationship—like rubbing salt into someone's deepest wound? Yes, loose lips can sink more than ships, and Michael's malicious uttering pulled the plug on their tryst, sinking beneath wisdom like a stone. And so he got kicked off their boat ride together.

Michael however, could not let go of the "sorrowfulness" he felt. Not because of what he thought, but rather over his lack of self-control to let what slipped out of his lips slip out in a moment of anger and frustration. It transpired in the days before he knew that he did not know that one could *not* divine the effects of words spoken on actions, whether thought true or false, or considered good or bad because the twisting fingers of fate were twisted, and things would always end up as they should—the more quickly so by mixing things up—for every nature finds its own level. Everything must find itself in time, or it will be lost; and it will find its rightful place more quickly if knocked out of the hole it is lodged or jammed in!

If some semblance of the truth be told, the real underlying reason Michael might have been as callous as a bunion with Melva was that her social life centered on her family. They were accepting, loving, well-to-do, providing Michael with ample lucrative legal work, but Michael wanted to be the sun, god and king of his own family. He did not want to go to someone else's Versailles, and thus, so to speak, he sent Melva away with her cake and he had none of it. But at least he was still the centre, sun and king of his peasant, if at times not so pleasant, life. Perhaps if he had towed the line and married Melva it would be like sticking his head in a guillotine, a spectacle for those who knitted, and his background was operating on him, sewing and finishing his fate. Knitting was so WASP, or possibly French, and very foreign to him. The bridges he battered loomed over his destiny like burnt-out ships. He would never be able to return to the harbor of her love. His future was being knotted by the naughty fingers of fate tailoring the tapestry of his life that so sealed and sewed it shut.

# 11

## DOROTHY

While working as a young lawyer, before buying the house in the Annex, Michael met a woman named Dorothy. He met her at a party that his friend Jeff had thrown when Jeff was living in London, Ontario. Being a good and longtime friend of Jeff, Michael was of course invited.

Dorothy was a short, well-proportioned, attractive university girl who tied her long black hair in a pony tail, and whose smooth, ivory skin looked all the whiter because of her thick black rimmed glasses. She was Michael's type and size: intelligent, charming and chatty, and a few inches shorter than he. She had recently been accepted into a master's program in Toronto so they were soon to reside in the same city.

Although Michael may have had many types, being open-minded and taking life in lustful leisurely steps, she rated very high on the "being his type" scale due to her good looks, size (compact and firm) and her level of education. In fact Michael thought that she was perfect for him, possibly heaven sent, and the clincher was that she was born on the same day as he, being but a few years younger. That was surely an unmistakable sign that the relationship was "meant to be"!

The fates held her out as if on a silver platter at Jeff's house in London for Michael to delight in her delicious, dainty, delicacy. She and Michael hit it off and started dating immediately. What could be more beautiful than the apparent apparition of harmony and meant-to-be happy, young and lustful cupidity?

But as there is always trouble in paradise, she was to throw a monkey wrench in the gears of Michael's imagination of perpetual marital merriment. She was part of a tight-knit (oh no, not knit!) community of Slovenians whose cloistered Christianity and cultural purity precluded her to marry an outsider, or to have premarital sex, period! Thus in the days before slick Willy, Michael and Dorothy did not have "sexual relations" according to *Clintonian* terminology, but Willy was indeed orated, and Michael's attention was rhetorically erected to provide him with some satisfaction. Thank god for cunning linguistics that allow for the wind of words to blow and speak of the deeds of brave Fellatio.

Michael invited Dorothy up to his law office in downtown Toronto which was on the 14th floor of a building on prestigious University Avenue aptly and idiosynchronistically named "Phoenix House" to show her what "file" lay in his drawers. Michael had risen not once but many times up to this point in his muddled life, but he had yet to experience total freedom and rebirth, as his past risings dealt only with that which leads to birth, rather than that which *creates* rebirth.

Michael's office would actually have been on the 13th floor had there been a thirteenth floor in the building, but the architects of the Phoenix House were less courageous than the architects of Ontario's education system which until recently had a grade called thirteen, possibly the only province in Canada not to fear the unlucky number.

Michael must have forgotten to notify security at the front desk that he was taking a friend up to his office, for when he and Dorothy were on the floor in a compromising position the night watchman entered the office and spied Dorothy discoursing with Michael's Willy. Recognizing Michael, he apologized and left. Michael was not at all upset, but instead proud to be caught in his office at night in a compromising position with such a beautiful and intelligent woman practicing her orations on him.

Michael tried to make the relation work, but Dorothy would not listen to him. Blood was thicker than love—the family must be obeyed! Resistance is futile to the conditioned mind, thus condemning Michael's hopes. He had imagined converting although he had no stomach or appetite for organized religion and was not quite sure what her organization was. But because he thought that she might be *the one*—was a sacrifice *not* in order? What can be greater than love? All the signs were there.

Michael pictured himself dressed in the attire of a Jesuit—a black robe. He saw himself darkly and seriously draped in what may have been a pope's attire, but in black. What a far cry from the chromatic dinner jacket of silk worn by his ancestors as they danced in Hassidic ecstasy! Love, though said to be blind, paints the scene. Michael wanted to "*paint it black.*"

The vision of himself in those fine and constricting vestments, the lightless color of night, made him think of a movie he had seen which may have been called *Black Robe*. The movie took place in Canada several hundred years ago when the Jesuits came to convert the heathen natives who were misnamed Indians. The young, handsome, bearded Jesuit, who looked much like Jeremy Irons, should have been perplexed by all the whiteness of snow and the fury of the wilderness, but did not waver; he was ruled by the steady hand of discipline.

His mind may have been whitewashed, for he continued to wear his formal, elegant black robes, even though totally inappropriate for the savage, unrelenting winter cold of the "Great White North"—and he stood out like a sore thumb!

Michael's recollection of the movie was sketchy. What he thought he remembered was that the Black Robe went on a journey with the chief of a tribe and the chief's beautiful daughter. Along the way the Jesuit and his fellow travelers were attacked and captured by a party from a hostile tribe. The chief was summarily killed and the Jesuit and the beautiful princess were taken prisoner, tied up in a tent where they and their two captors slept.

During the night the beautiful Indian princess was able to convince one of her captors to have sex with her, and to untie her body, but not her hands, so she could lie down and receive the longing of his desire. As he fucked her, he probably thought it was the luckiest night of his life to be so favored by one as attractive and shapely. He probably couldn't wait to tell his friends about the score—she was one hot luscious babe! But once they got hot and heavy—into the convulsions of coitus— she grabbed his knife (having previously surreptitiously freed her hands) and repeatedly plunged its large, sharp blade into the back of its pumping owner who soon lay limp on top of her. Did he even notice he was dying? Was it the best sex he ever had?

Michael wondered whether the sound produced by the cold steel blade going in and out of the heated, heart-a-throbbing body lubricated by warm, gushing blood, might not be the same as the sound of the penis penetrating her warm, wet, love tunnel, but the loud music striking a crescendo might have covered up the sound, in the same manner as redness of emotion blackens the whiteness of sober second thought. Michael could not remember. The princess then pushed her expired partner off like he was nothing more than a sack of potatoes and went on to stealthily stab the other captor, sending him to his eternal rest as he soundly slept.

The Black Robe was freed, but showed no signs of strain from the ordeal. He nonchalantly got out of the tent as if to stretch, like nothing had happened! He just stared at the vast expanse of white snow in the thin grey of early morning. He was ready to continue with his mission.

Michael wondered how anyone witnessing red blood steaming over pristine white snow could still believe, still go on dressed in black robes and think that all was in order—still follow the order! Heaven might know, if only it were not too busy creating nasty weather.

Dorothy soon left Michael. Her dam could not resist family pressure, nor was it ever constructed to do so. She and Michael last met on the banks of the Don River overlooking the Don Jail. She would not listen to Michael's pleas and pleadings. She wore the black robe of a mind set to an end, like a script written in stone, unmoved by his red blood that might as well have been streaming over the dirty snow of late winter. He had opened his heart to her and she *let it bleed*.

Michael thought of how he had visited a client in the Don Jail—his first and only time there. The large metal door swung shut with the heavy sound of closure, locking in what was there. It was then that Michael resolved never to practice criminal law again.

# 12

## THE SNOW

The thought of snow took Michael's mind, like a magic carpet ride, to a much more peaceful and tranquil scene. He was in the broadloomed living room of his parents' bungalow in North York. Samuel, still a young boy, was playing with toys scattered over the coffee table. Michael's father entered the room and slowly lifted the very large shade (also called a blind). It rolled and wound its way up guided by Mendel's sure hand, uncovering the front yard as seen through a large window. It was early evening but already dark outside; the further north, the longer are the nights in winter. The street lights cast their dullness over the dried brown grass and leafless trees in the park across the street. The vista was imbued with a nascent navy blue hue like that seen just before dawn. The evening was still, and the earth was breathing slowly, deeply and regularly. Christmas was coming, but not for the Jews.

Then a few large flakes of snow began floating ever so slowly downward, crescent-shaped, swaying to and fro cradle-like, peacefully descending as if to a gentle lullaby. Then more and more flakes began to fall until the view was obscured by a wall of whiteness on that windless night. Michael's father uttered the word "*shnei*," which in Yiddish means snow, and the "i" sound is pronounced hard and long like in the word "eye." Michael's father emphasized and sustained the hard "i" sound at the end.

Even though it might have been said as a mere statement of fact with only the slightest hint of awe, Samuel repeated the word several times exactly as Michael's father had, who by then had already left the room. Then Michael did the same. It may have sounded like the din that emanates from a temple on the Sabbath, or the drone of a repeated mantra—all done mindlessly without thought—but the sound so spoken sparkled in subtle, shared joy, a thread that banded, bound and bonded three generations of the family Rice in a common, calm contentment, there and then in that warm house on a wet snowy night.

The sacred sight of snow, the congealed side of life-giving water, froze out all worries or cares caused by the cold, hard, undeniable fact of its harsh, beautiful being. Michael and Sam would often thereafter imitate the manner in which Mendel had uttered the word "*shnei*"—it was so laden and loaded with wonder!

Now it is impossible to write the word "*shnei*" correctly in English script because the Yiddish characters are archaic and biblical like the Hebrew letters, and thus totally different than their English or German counterparts. In German one would say "*schnee*"—not the same word as it lacks the long "i" sound at the end.

Coincidently, the fellow Michael's parents hired to replace the large front window in their living room *was* of German heritage. Michael's mother agonized over finding someone to replace the window—and *hallelujah*—she was referred to this German tradesperson who did a great job. He was also a very nice man—a real *mensh*.

Michael's mother always fretted about repairs to be done to the house, or any decision like the choosing of a fruit when she shopped. She did not want people to look down on her. She would not let her husband, the *guppy*, decide, for she thought him incapable. But in this case she had chosen well with the tradesperson she hired to do the work whose name may have been Hans.

He was a real *fachmann*, which in German means expert, but Michael's slant on *"fahman"* was slightly different, for in Yiddish he thought it meant an extraordinary worker that imbues some higher level of energy or caliber to the work done, something special that would be noticed, a near divine or supernatural quality. Michael thought that his father, Mendel, was a *fahman*, for when Mendel ironed for example, which was seldom indeed, the result was always a cut about. Perhaps it was due to those holy hands, sewn by love into flesh.

Michael's father was a *shneider*, or a tailor in Yiddish, which comes from the word "to cut," not to be confused with someone that plays with snow, or is made from snow, being a *"shneiman."* Michael considered himself a *fahman* too. For when he did something like sweep the floor, which was seldom, the result of his labor would shine and glow. Michael thought that if there is a God, then God would definitely be a *Fahman*, for is not the "Nameless One" reputed to have created the world by design? And did not the sun shine so bright and clear, like all things had been washed in *Ultra Cheer*, this October day in Hamilton?

After installing the picture window at the Rice residence in North York, Hans had stopped on the shoulder of Highway 401 to adjust the load on his pick-up truck, and: *"Wham, bamm, thank you mamm!"* he was taken out of play, never to return to North York, or to any earthly abode for that matter, unless burial be considered a form of lodging. God proved once again to be the real *Fahman*, the "*Fachmann uber alles*," hiding behind the next corner with a snowball ready to pelt one and all: the good, the bad and the indifferent. All one can do is rant and rave: "*Fahman; Fachmann; Fuck man!*"

Through the association of carnage, Michael's mind was propelled to Melva's parents' farm near Windy, Ontario. She and Michael had arrived at the red brick farmhouse on a drizzly, grey autumn afternoon to spend a few days alone, which should have been peaceful, but for the fowl about the house: the cocks, hens, ducks and geese that pecked at Michael worse than his mother henpecked Mendel. Upon entry they noticed signs of intrusion. Items were scattered on the floor willy-nilly, strewn about in a disorganized *ad hoc* sort of way. A lamp had also been knocked over!

In the fireplace, ashen logs were askew, some breaching the boundary of the hearth. Michael looked to see if perhaps Santa Claus had got stuck in the chimney while struggling to get into the house, but it was much too early before Christmas—the malls had yet to start playing the torturous Christmas music. In any event, there were no signs of the existence of Old St. Nick. Pieces of foam were strewn and scrambled on the hardwood floor of the main room. Inside a white pillow case they found an emaciated, dead black squirrel with teeth bared, smiling sardonically.

The signs were that it had struggled and fought against the painful pulses of ceasing after entering through the chimney in a carefree and squirrely sort of way. When trapped in an unknown stand of couches, tables and chairs it must have gone berserk—wild, frantic—burying itself deeply into the headrest of sleep, clawing out its final resting place, returning to the dark timeless womb from whence it came.

Michael sensed it was an omen—his skin covered in goose bumps. Soon thereafter, Melva's mother, still in her fifties, passed away. She was an artist, as well as a housewife, signing her works of painted birds and flowers with the name "*Birdie.*" The bright blues, reds and whites, and clean uncluttered lines of her creations reminded Michael of Mozart, if his music were set to paint, and the fine culinary offerings of Austria. And Birdie, who was not happy in spite of the family's wealth and material possessions, flew like a dove from the trappings of this world to beyond its borders and boundaries—all foreboded by a thin, dead, sneering squirrel.

# 13

## THE DONNING OF
## THE PONCHO

After putting on his corduroy jacket, Michael donned his poncho. Now he could be called *Don Miguel* or Mister Michael, such is the look the poncho bestowed on him. It was not a Sears' or store-bought poncho. No—it was no ordinary poncho! Michael had bought it in a craft market in that strangely spelled city in Mexico, Oaxaca, over thirty years ago. He had rediscovered it on his recent move when it appeared in a pile of things; and it came out sparkling clean after laundering with a non-toxic, biodegradable detergent sold at the Wild Rice store. Michael had traveled through Mexico and Guatemala when he took a hiatus from articling after curtailing his position in that downtown Toronto law firm where he was looked upon strangely by his principals, whom he thought of as being Kalfkaesque, high functioning, formalized thought police.

Michael could have bought an ordinary Mexican poncho at any of Oaxaca's busy markets, but he fell in love with the one he now wore. It had worn so well, and now he was sure that he had made a good decision, even though he agonized over the purchase at the time because of its higher price.

The poncho, now donned, might have been made of alpaca, being thick and well woven, but it was unlikely to have come from Peru, being bought in a craft market in the salt of the earth, the big "O," so it probably was just loomed from thick, fine cotton. One could not be sure, for if it had been sold in Canada, it would be mandatory to have a label in both official languages, French and English, but there was no label of any kind. So what could one be sure of? It looked like, smelled liked and served the purpose of a poncho, so must it not be concluded that it might rightly be called and considered a poncho?

When Michael was bedecked by the poncho people noticed it, and thus him, bringing a degree of gladness to the *"corazon"* of señor *Don Miguel*, making him feel regal in a humble sort of way. Michael was transformed and transmuted into an artistic, learned, gentrified Bohemian. When he wore it people would often say to him: "Hey, that's a nice poncho."

"Thanks, it's a real Mexican poncho," would be his modest low keyed response as if the compliment was no big deal. "I got it in Oaxaca, Mexico, over 30 years ago when I was there. I could have bought a cheaper poncho, and lord knows there are many ponchos for sale in Mexico, but instead I got this one which I really liked a lot when I saw it at a craft market. It was much more expensive, but I think worth it. Thank you for noticing."

Michael thought of an incident that occurred a few days ago near the Wild Rice store when he was nonchalantly walking by the Liquor Store on a broad, busy street that might have been an "Avenue" or "Boulevard," but in this case was simply named

"Street." Michael heard: "Is that a Sear's poncho, or a Mexican poncho?" directed at him.

"Thanks. It's a real Mexican poncho, blah, blah, blah..." Michael began and went on with his *spiel*. Although Michael was intelligent, imaginative and able, he tended to repeat himself, especially when he talked about himself.

Suddenly it struck Michael. "Hey, those are the words from a Frank Zappa song. I know the album!" Then Michael and the fellow, let us call him "Doug," for Michael did not know his name but had seen him many times in front of the liquor store—and it might have been his name although it is hard to guess someone's name if you don't know it—started singing in unison the words to some songs from the album including *"Dynamo Hum/ Dynamo Hum/ Where's that dynamo coming from?....I got the spot that gets me hot, and you ain't been to it yet/ Oh no no no..."*

Then Doug let into singing *"She wore an Amarillo Brillo/ I don't mean no Mendocino vino/ She had a snake for a pet and an amulet,"* which Michael happily joined when it came to the chorus.

There they sang together with no care for the busy world buzzing about them, sharing nostalgic unction—two men singing. Michael's singing voice, though very enthusiastic, was out of tune. Then they began to sing the title track: *"Moving to Montana soon/ Gonna be a dental floss tycoon/ Yes I am-m-m... Riding into the sunset with my zircon encrusted tweezers..."*

It was so much fun—it brought joy and peace to Michael's heart—that real Mexican poncho was a magnet of attention and happiness. Michael began speaking to Doug as one man speaks to another once he has stripped and ripped off the cloak of convention and fabrication, and the shackles of servitude which *homo sapiens* may find themselves dressed and enmeshed in, if they only stopped to take the time to look. There they stood face to face, *mano a mano*, looking into each other eyes, so close that when they spoke with words spouting from the primordial well of humanity, the spit was almost blinding. Two men who may have danced barefoot on the point of a needle—one who may have pointed said needle into his arm—each understanding the other as if the air between them had been sucked out dry. There was no need for words, which was very strange and unusual for Michael.

Michael did not judge Doug, because Michael had not stood in or worn Doug's shoes, although they looked quite nice! Michael knew about judgment and other people's shoes all the way from his childhood growing up in Little Italy. During the winters he often went skating at an outdoor ice rink about a mile from his home. There he learned how to skate: to weave in and out of the crowds, expertly and agile to avoid collisions even at high speed, his body gliding like a locomotive, the steamy vapor of his warm breath transfused with the wintry air. Michael felt free as he weaved and waltzed though the hoards and herds of people like a needle and thread pushed and pulled through fine cloth by a practiced hand.

The only problem was that at this particular ice rink run by City of Toronto, Parks and Wrecks Department, and possibly all rinks run by the said department, everyone always skated in the same direction, and although Michael learned how to skate well, he only became adept at turning left. This proved a detriment later on in his life. When things were heading in the wrong direction, he did not know how to make a right turn!

It so happened that one evening when the young skaters returned to the warmth of the dressing room, rosy cheeked and smiling prior to the rink's nightly closing, Michael's shoes were gone and he could find them nowhere! What was he to do? He could not walk home in the cold winter night shoeless! So he did what any right-minded boy of nine or so might do, not yet having a university degree in ethics or the life experience to question an eye for an eye in all its ramifications, he chose a nice pair of comfortable tan suede shoes that fit him; and they were comfortable all the way home.

He wore those shoes, which could be considered god sent, if not for their being stolen, until the souls wore holy. Those shoes were his tit for tat—his Old Testament justice. How the devil works in strange ways! Lord, pity the last boy to leave the skating rink shoeless on that cold winter night! Michael *had* felt guilty for a moment, but what could he have done at such a young innocent age, having to make a real life decision on the spot, there and then, which was here and now to him then, although he did not think about it like that at the time? What would anyone in his shoes have done if they were in his skates and found no shoes? One should not judge too harshly for life can play *musical shoes* with anyone when they least expect it!

Michael concluded with the sage advice not to judge someone by their position in life. Doug's position was always in front of the Liquor Store. Doug was intelligent and well dressed, witty and friendly, and provided the useful service of holding people's dogs while they bought their booze, beer or wine. He sold a sliver of a newspaper called *"Outreach,"* printed specifically so people like him could hand them out for a hand out— the paper not being worth the paper it was printed on—but at least it established a façade of respectability.

When Doug spoke his wisdom showed despite his being a drunk for all his life, now being well over 50. Notwithstanding the know-nothing, upright, uptight, white collared pinheads of Gotham (an allusion to Toronto) scurrying like chickens without heads in their downtown coop bounded by opaque chicken wire of their own imaginary creation, who may have many times looked upon Doug condescendingly, thus spoke Doug:

"I remember when I was a young man watching TV with my friends. There was a group of six of us that hung around. Now there are only two of us still left alive. It's funny that I, the alcoholic, am still *here*, while the other fellow is in jail. I'm not sure on what bum rap he is in for. A third friend became an accountant and now resides in a nice small mansion in Etobicoke, so he can't even be considered to be alive! Ha! Ha! Ha! Who would have thought that when we watched black and white TV back then the world would become so colorful? Life sure is funny. All it takes is a few pills, some pot, and a lot of alcohol to get by. Ha! Ha! I guess I should be happy and not complain. I'm still alive and have a tax free business... and I'm not an accountant! Ha! Ha! Ha!"

Michael looked at Doug, and he looked into Doug's eyes that announced Doug was a man that looked into people's eyes and said what he meant, and meant what he said when he was not inebriated, which was probably next to never. But hey, Michael used to have a few drinks, a few times a day, almost every day, in the good old days that he vaguely, fondly remembered. The natural urge and unquestioned meaning of life back then was to get as fucked up as possible, so it did not, and would not, matter.

Michael felt warm inside, even though it was a cold over-cast day, for he found a bond with humanity and discerned this truth: that humanity can care about humanity if it is humane, and caring for a dog is possibly the most humane of all human acts. Perhaps Michael and Doug were two outcasts there in front of the newly expanded Liquor Store on a wide, busy downtown Toronto street as they sang funny old songs; but they could just as well have been two acquaintances meeting and greeting each other in a busy outdoor market in Athens, an "*agora*," in ancient classical Greek times, but for the perceived reality of this dream dreamt, and its narrative termed "our life." In conclusion of his splendid meeting with and parting from Doug, Michael thought, "Good work if you can get it." But the position in front of the Liquor Store was already taken.

And then Michael, still in his condo apartment in Hamilton with his poncho on and ready to leave for work, had a new idea which he thought was brilliantly funny, reveling over it with brimming glee, congratulating himself on conjuring up such a splendid idea. "I will print the invitation to the Selling Party in the form of a short story in a small booklet, and I will have it distributed by people like Doug in front of liquor stores. I will give the Dougs of this world the booklets/invitations free of charge and they can sell each one for only 99 cents. Then I will write and create more invitations/short stories for them to sell at the very low price of just under a dollar, and these stories of questionable meaning shall be part of what shall be boldly labeled: "*Almost a Loony Series.*"

"Ha! Ha!" Michael wallowed. "Write it and they will come. It will be a smart and good thing that I do, perhaps a smarter and better thing than I have ever done, helping the needy while at the same time needing their help. The dazed, amazed masses of busy downtown Torontonians will be amused, but not abused, by my brilliance, because when they least expect it will get the joke, that 99 cents is almost a loony! Perhaps then I will be rich and famous! Ha! Ha!"

Michael continued to chuckle over what was probably at best a real loony idea. The wringing of his hands could be heard all the way to North York as the scheme churned round and around in his mind. Perhaps after decades of inhaling life's varied fineries a subtle impression of Justin's smile had been permanently etched on Michael's mental mirror.

Then, a fresh vision visited him. It was like a video, with guess who as the star, Michael riding a cool scooter like a *Vespa* along the shore of what appeared to be the Mediterranean Ocean with music from a *Spaghetti Western* playing in the background. Were he in France, Italy, Greece or Spain, it was not important. Past dry cardboard colored hills on the right, and a navy blue sea on the left, he rode like a comfortable expert at a lawyerly pace wearing his real Mexican poncho over his brown corduroy jacket. He had found his niche, poncho fluttering in the breeze like a hometown banner dancing in the wind, proudly leading a parade in some holy crusade. Through the collar of the poncho his head poked, projected and protruded like a piston of a flower.

And *this* was life—his salt blood mingled with the salty taste on his lips. Motion, time and scene were one. The scooter under the sun between sea and hill, the central focal point of the sphere of his longed for life, brought a split second of silence and peace. Some awesome poncho—eh!

# 14

## MOVING TO MONTANA SOON

Now, the journey of Michael's tale must take a rest, a stop to give meaning to the notes so discordantly arranged on his stroll down the garden path, partaking in Adam's carnivorous rib fest always on the eve of tomorrow. Would an apple cleanse the palate? Could a drink quench the thirst?

Knowledge has been likened to a fruit, but what insight can be gleaned in a word or a foreign phrase? Should a judgment be based on the tilt of a hat or the slant of a veil? With all languages so similar, why is it that foreign languages sound so foreign and strange? How can anything be true in a world where the artist's eye makes light through shade, weds the earth, water and sky with color, but can never paint a scent?

As the spaces between the notes makes music potent and powerful, so too was Michael spaced in the days of *Supertramp*,

*Genesis,* and Frank Zappa in the foggy Oktoberfest fields of Kitchener while studying philosophy at the University of Waterloo, during a weekend pried open by a miniscule microscopic dot of low ph factor, aptly named *"Moving to Montana Soon,"* in honor of the prevailing theme music.

The weekend, which was not merely memorable in a minor sort of way, had some odd results. Michael's friend Gary, whom Michael knew from high school, was certain that he would receive a call from God. Whether the call came or not, no one ever heard, but Gary waited patiently beside the phone—the spirit having sprinkled its angel dust on him. He looked exasperatingly elated and profoundly serious in his state of expectation!

Michael's friend Jeff, who had seemed to fare quite well during the weekend festivities, checked himself into the hospital on his return to Toronto for a reality check, returning to a world that had rotated a degree or two—but one can never be too sure of these things to really be sure of them.

Michael basically made it through the weekend OK. Maybe he would have thought better of it if he remembered more, but he *did* determine that AIDS was an anti gay CIA plot ordered by Nixon. Not to worry however, Michael did not lose his moral compass or the passion for the study of philosophy and discoursing. He was now one step further along the walk down the proverbial path, which meant that he was one step further away from where he had started!

Was Michael walking down the path of life with no heed to where he was heading, with no thought of where he had been or from where he came, blind to the steps he had taken, unaware of the missteps he had mistaken, to get to where he was?

Was he looking up at the trees, searching for a bird, a monkey, a snake or a legendary phoenix? Did he not notice that the future was coming while the earth rotated? He was going nowhere because the earth was turning in the opposite direction from which the future came. Michael was stuck going nowhere—his wheels spun as if raised in thin air! He couldn't see what was coming or going to happen on that not so cold but windy autumn night, when the leaves covered and colored the sidewalks and roads of Waterloo like honey oil, making them skittish and sweetly slick.

Waterloo is the sister city of Kitchener with which it forms one municipality. Kitchener used to be called "Berlin," but changed its name at the outbreak of the First World War. As the line of aggression of the Great War was choreographed by a chorus line directed from Berlin, symbolically speaking, the head of the enemy was severed by the sword of diction when the name change was executed. But the smell of a rose or a spicy sausage cannot remain hidden for long, notwithstanding the rebranding attempt to cleanse; so *"lederhosen"* and *"umpapa"* could not be eradicated, and Kitchener nee Berlin, still retained its taste for sour kraut and love of polka.

And on that night when Michael was driving with nothing to do, but searching for something, fate and its shadow waited for him in the form of two hitchhikers to be intertwined with one seedy and shady, but at the time popular, watering hole of a hotel named after a duke: the "Kent."

For those not versed in proper history, namely the type propagated by the British Colonial Office, Waterloo is not an English name although one should not be criticized for thinking so, for it was there in the fields where the finest chocolate and beers are made that Wellington met and tore his Bonaparte apart. Now Wellington definitively sounds English, but with so many dukes and pubs and breweries blotted and micro dotted all over the countryside, finding the next whiskey bar definitely gets confusing, as is remembering what county in southern Ontario one is in when sensing all energy at once without a filter or smoke!

And Sam, who had yet to be born, or even conceived of at the beginning of second year of university for Michael, might have had the ambition and stature of Napoleon, but how can one measure and compare the size of what is when there is no volume to it, when it is just a thought, a feeling , a propensity, a desire, a mere word which has been twisted by abuse and overuse, and powerfully shoved into the recipient, not from behind when they were neither ready or looking, but fed directly mouth to gaping mind—a direct frontal assault—lodged into the dark sponge region of the mind: details, facts and beliefs which otherwise might have been of no use, like history, but bound to be repeated like buried lessons percolating, unless like a good lawyer, the ass is covered, and the past is let go, with the future left to come as it will.

# 15

## ON FINDING MORE LOVE

Waiting at the side of the road on that October night on a route bordering the University of Waterloo campus were two pretty girls, banging at the door of womanhood. Their teenage years had waned, but they were of ripe age for the primordial prerogative of procreation for primates, and probably so primed by their independent and rebellious natures. Michael's desire waxed with imaginings of well formed breasts and soft shaven skin. That night Michael could not believe his luck. It is seldom that the things one hopes for—longs and pines dreamingly for—actually come to pass. Often one hesitates and opines that if something is too good to be true, it probably is—and correctly so usually—but not always! On this night the *"too good to be true"* was really waiting for Michael, believe it or not!

Michael searched for a dark cloud, and there were probably some in the sky that windy night, but it was too dark to see.

Michael was well oiled and quite versed in the power of poetry. Hope and desire were stringing him on along their spider's web, stirring the underground stream in his heart to the point of near boiling eruption. Oh how quickly he, the young man, had forgotten the smelly and sticky lessons that fate had not so stingily taught him to date—and who and when not to date if smelly and stinky—but you who know will know, that "honey oil" is sweet, seductive and powerful! The butterfly could be stung by a bee, as you shall see, and if you have the ears to truly taste the tale, the words of the poet loosely and wantonly foreshadow what is to come:

*POEM OF FORESHADOWING*

*Oh muse, may your drops drip onto our lips*
*Shower us with inspiration that we may succinctly sing*
*To tell the succulent tale how male met female*
*And how the erection of swollen male desire*
*Rising in an edifice of love and fire*
*Ardent in union formed a head to a tail.*
*Pray tell how together they did drink some ale,*
*How as one they did wail and wail*
*Hoping for a sign like a note from heaven by mail.*
*But woe and alas, it did not arrive as they patiently waited*
*Not realizing that the future had come—*
*And all communications had become digital!*
*When the first taste of technology was taken*
*No one thought that it would be bought and sold*
*So often—but now there is only foreboding*
*For the future of hand written mail!*
*So drink more ale and wail baby wail*
*For that which you wait for*
*Must you always and forever*
*Wait for to appear in this tale.*

*And you, you who have a mouth to taste*
*All of life's giving goo garburated*
*Must have the strength, when you come*
*To that hole in the road not to falter*
*Not to lose the load which you harbor*
*Like a martyr!*
*Courage and stamina for one more stroke*
*Must you secure as your motto.*
*That arduous road must you endure full throttle!*
*Until that moment when Ecstasy occurs*
*And all is a blur!*
*On the road that you have taken*
*On the road that takes you.*

Into the car jumped the young women, to Michael's delight, not quite catlike, as if his subconscious was a whip. "Where are you heading to?" he asked.

"Downtown, we're going out for a beer at the Kent," replied the one with darker curlier hair, as she giggled her way into the back seat. Although in truth, they both might be considered blondes with straight hair, the one with blonder straighter hair sat in the front seat beside Michael. She was quiet, thin and attractive with large blue eyes.

Michael had to open the doors manually from the inside because in those days having automatic car doors was a luxury, while rust was standard. Michael did not know that he was a poor student because he had never been a rich student, so he could not compare. He did notice that they hesitated for a second to determine who would sit in the front seat next to him. It was a good sign he thought—they were thinking of pairing. Michael was up to the luck of the draw or the spin of the bottle, so to speak, as he still trusted fate, and had yet to understand its sinister shadowy shady side which kept its marks or victims in the dark and unenlightened—but not untouched.

"Well, I don't know where it is, but I am not doing anything tonight, so I don't mind finding out where it is, and I can take you there" said Michael not quite sure if he was being funny.

Whatever he did worked, for they told him where and how it is, in words and chirping snickers, "a real *dive* on King Street," and he drove them there on their guidance, and they let him attend with them in that most popular past time—especially in those parts of the world where the mind needs and seeks to be pacified—the drinking of beer!

The bug-eyed slim *fräulein* who sat in the front, destined by chance to be picked up by Michael, was named Hilda, and her talkative friend that sat in the back, less slim but no less shapely or attractive, bore the name of Wendy. Michael would have been happy to bore either, not in the sense of making them uninterested, but in the sense whereby and wherefrom children might be born if a condom had been bored. Falling in love was still easy for Michael, like imagining himself a handsome prince in the mirror, although much of his time was filled with self-doubt and anxiety, as is often the case with those recently past teenage years that drink and smoke too much, looking for and believing in answers with an absolute ruler of an adolescent, yet unable to erase the lead penciled in by tradition and convention.

As it turned out, the three newly encountered friends all studied at the university, and they got along famously as if they were old friends; but that is the usual course under the stewardship of *Madam Beer*, who abates silence, loosens tongues and makes socialization simply fabulous in her foamy froth. The same *Mrs. Beer*, who can set tongues wagging and lips smacking, can leave a trace of sickly sea in her wake if one sways and swaggers on board for too long and has to navigate her fermented waters. Then the only remedy is to bite the bitch back, like she bit you—but that was her plan all along. Once you are caught in her passive-aggressive pendulum you are trapped in time before you know it, drinking all the time!

But drinking back then was still fun, and Michael was a naïve young man, who aptly could have been called a "lucky boy" that night, and unaware of the deep pit which the demon alcohol could drown anyone in. Although Michael had on several occasions turned green from drinking too much, he was still green when it came to drinking too much as he was still an innocent who believed in love and drinking. Woe to those who live to be a ripe old age and must choose between making love, or getting drunk—able only to dream of doing both together as they had once done! It is a great mystery why everyone wants to grow old, when no one actually wants to *be* old.

What was the Kent hotel like? Unfortunately, Michael was too drunk whenever he was there to remember. Obviously there was beer and drinking, and it was dark, and the music was loud. It was always referred to as a "dive." Michael did recall that when he suggested going there people would decline saying it was a dive, and so it must have been. The heavy wooden tables, carved with the names and drunken inscriptions of many inebriated patrons, and heavy black wooden chairs stood up to the wear and tear of the endless repetition of beer being drank, and more beer being drunk, and the sweet and sickly smell of more beer—and then vomit—varying from vile to bile depending on what one has or has not eaten.

Perhaps it was called a dive because of what in Ontario is known as a washroom or restroom. No one really rests in or on the toilette, unless they have really drank a lot, in imperial gallons and have blacked out, or unless a headrest is needed after overindulging in more than one's lot. Then they can get a close up of some dark, short and curlies set against the white porcelain of the crapper throne's rim, usually royally stained yellow at the Kent. One must then return to the gods of primordial bliss the clear bubbly ambrosia they have over-guzzled in gallons (i.e. many liters).

As often happens in watering holes like the Kent, the patrons would use their knives for literary purposes to engrave and mark the furniture to prove that they had been there, unlike some country and western bars where the etching was done on someone's face for just looking. The name "dive" came about because the frolicking imbibers got so drunk and wasted they could not hit the urinal or toilette bowl, and the bathroom turned into a room where one could *dive* into a floor full of piss, or slide in it as if they were pretending to skate on ice, joyously making a grand entrance on stage to sing a heartfelt song, and then slog over the soaked carpet on exiting; unless after seeing the pubic hair of god close up, they went catatonic, losing all the joy, that certain *je ne sais quoi,* of beer drinking!

But things must have gone well because Michael started going out with Hilda.

# 16

## OFF TO HIGHER SCHOOL

Back in high school, Michael had started grade 13 taking all maths and sciences which were the subjects he was naturally best at. Back then, one got to choose their courses in magical grade thirteen. Grade 13 *was* necessary to attend university. What else would Michael do? He was not ready for work—his hands were too soft.

The undercurrents of the government and culture clearly promised him a future where he would be taken care of—not in so many words—but in no uncertain whispers. All he had to do was live, party, enjoy and patiently wait. The scientific-medical-legal establishment was in the process of making everything perfect and right, and Michael's generation would not have to worry about anything: it would all be taken care of by logic, which had finally been discovered. The technological advances made ensured that Michael and his buddies could *"keep on rocking in the free world."* There would be no needs and wants that science and modern living could not meet in the future, and everyone would be as happy as they ever wanted to be! Even religion would be tolerated with childlike affection!

Perhaps though only a myth, religion might have been secretly entrenched in the Canadian Constitution. No one wanted to rock the boat, start another crusade, anger the ministry, priesthood or clergy—most of whom were angry enough having to remain celibate! Society as a whole was sold a bill of goods—and most swallowed the hook and sinker after being fed the line that the future looked bright and shiny!

How could they, they then in charge, whoever they may have been, have lied? Was the garden not a garden? Some said that God was dead, but man, could he or she or it rise again? What went wrong? Were all the illusions really just illusions?

But Michael with all his math and sciences became alienated from certainty. His heart longed for poetic justice, and his soul longed for a feeling of oneness which may have been lost or misplaced when Michael was torn from the womb—but that is just an unproven theory! So Michael, when he could not remember the answer to a math question because he could not remember the question, after smoking Export A's and a pipe full of short-term memory loss, decided to call high school quits and take time to find the meaning of his life: to search for his destiny.

So Michael with the excuse of being a rebel, and pretending that he wanted to write, dropped out of Grade 13, got a job as a mail room clerk, read existential authors, and went out into the world and sought time to find himself through a mundane job, only to discover that work was time-consuming and boring, and that it was hard to sail without an engine. Reorienting his course, he enrolled in free school to study English literature and poetry, because that would not interfere with partying, and he *could* pretend that he was doing something deep and meaningful.

Now for those of you which have studied or know something of mathematics, which may be considered an abstract absolute, once off the progressive path, once one ceases the training, they cannot just start from where they are, but have to go back to where they were to get back on the wagon, but the wagon is no longer there. In any event, Michael did not want to repeat grade 13. This may have been for reasons of superstition, or just plain laziness, so upon his return from a European vacation lasting the whole summer he applied to university, and was accepted at the University of Waterloo, famous for mathematics, computer science and engineering, to study arts and humanities.

Although he did not have grade 13, which normally would have been a prerequisite to university admission, he did have good grades before he dropped out. He had also completed two courses in free school, and got a letter from his brother saying he was smart and proficient. On this basis he was accepted, notwithstanding the rigid rules—coincidently the mascot of the Faculty of Engineering at said university was an oversized monkey wrench called the "rigid tool"—because he was alive and breathing, and to that academic institute of higher learning a monetary unit, a commodity, a BIU (an anachronism for Basic Income Unit) the life and blood of any institution created by government that may legally be considered a person but not an individual. And Michael should have gotten the hint as to why the idealism of the 60's and 70's faded and failed, and why the road he was travelling on was littered with lies and twists of truth, but he was young and naïve, and a heavy partier preferring twists of lemon or lime or to dance, and soon to be lost in the Kitchener fog.

And where was Michael now? He was in his condo apartment in Hamilton ready to go to work, with his mind bathing in the revitalizing dream waters of *The Selling Party*. It is funny how the mind can do more than one thing at a time, sometimes, and at other times it will go over and over the same old grooves like a needle in an old 45. Michael was now leaving the apartment to go to work, pulling the heavy veneered door shut behind him, locking it with the key that he had in his hand ready for the task. Michael was glad that he had to lock the door each time with a key so that he would not lock himself out. Then, he walked down the hall to the elevator and pushed the button with the arrow pointing down. It lit up after being pushed.

Things were sure different when Michael attended first year of university at the University of Waterloo in the early 70's. Believe it or not, it was permissible to smoke cigarettes in class back then. Any Buddhist worth their weight in waiting knows that cigarettes are not harmful until they were discovered to be so. Such logic however is smoky, and just a screen hiding the deeper and more meaningful question of whether a cigarette exists at all after being smoked, or is it just an illusion of memory that makes you cough?

In the centre of campus, there was a building called the "Campus Centre" with some shops, a pub, and a big central open space where people could just hang out or space out. Michael fondly remembered how he enjoyed the orange pineapple flavored ice cream. Little did he know then what he knew now, being a health food store man, that commercially sold ice cream could cause brain damage, a tongue licked brain freeze, but it sure did taste good without the knowledge. He thought he knew something about priorities, if not proportions, and that was that smoking, drinking and use of other substances that altered mind and body could possibly cause more duality and depreciate the value of one's conditional and unguaranteed life more than any toxic flavored frozen dairy treat could, but perhaps that was because the ice cream did not totally freeze his brain.

As Michael only found out that he would be attending university after it had started, he needed to find accommodation *post haste* for his first moving away from his parents' house. As downtown rooming houses always have room for one more, being the first stop of last resort, Michael deposited himself in one located in downtown Kitchener to temporarily tenant until the opportunity to step up a rung on the ladder in the pecking order of student housing popped up.

His friend from high school, Gary, who also enrolled tardily due to late acceptance, likewise lacked accommodation. It was only natural that he and Michael should room together, which they did, not as a romantic couple, but to save money, for back then it was not acceptable that one should have sex with anyone, anywhere, and at any time, without being ribbed and bugged about it, as it is now.

Both Michael and Gary were exceedingly excited about their first contact with a more mature and demure *"Lady Learning,"* and to be able to touch her naked truths without losing composure in spite of all the doubters. Gary was also just entering the early stages of higher education—just another *Piper* at the *Gates of Dawn*, his first foray far afield away from the fretful watching eyes of his folks. All he wanted to do was rock and roll and smoke a few!

In the rooming house scene Michael was introduced to a new angle on life, tilted differently than he was used to in the *Gaza Strip* of North York. The denizens of the rooming house seemed to be off-kilter, living in a *helter skelter* sort of way, while seeking *shelter from the storm*. His previous bonnie vista was bludgeoned apart by meeting people who did not have parents that sent care packages or even cared—people who were looking for something, but incapable of remembering what it was they sought. And he encountered his first alcoholic, or one who ails for and from spirits. Michael was not exactly introduced to him, the addict stuck in the endless cycle of suds, sauce and rye, so he never met or knew him, but Michael overheard delirious screams of pain throughout the night while trying to sleep in the small adjacent room on the third floor that served as interim lodging while waiting for Gary to arrive and share a larger room on the second floor.

Michael lay awake the whole night disturbed by the whining wailing of *withdrawal*. In the morning he peeped through the flimsy door banged together from wooden slats pried open slightly ajar, to peek without being seen, to see what was going on. He spied a thin prune of a man whose wrinkles appeared much older than his youthful ginseng colored hair (perhaps drinking hair spray did have its benefits) bending over a bucket in the landing hacking up blood. Michael saw him, the one from which the life force was agonizingly abating, only once but never again.

"The demon alcohol is hauling him away from this earthly plane to a plateau free of pain," Michael thought as if chanting. Michael then imagined hearing the *inaudible*: the sound of one hand grabbing. The *other world* was calling—from the raven darkness spoke the *Cuervo*: "*nevermore!*" The tequila had stopped flowing on that *midnight dreary*. Another soul, *weak and weary*, was taken; to suffer—*nevermore!*

And Michael had a great time during first year studying general arts and taking courses like psychology, sociology, religion and the film, philosophy and English literature, which he found interesting when he went to class—which was not often. Michael tried very hard for the first two weeks of each semester to keep up with the assignments and readings, but smoky and liquid distractions flooded his mind and drowned his will. There were so many people to party with that loved to party too, and loved to party some: people that Michael knew from high school and Toronto, and others whom he had recently met. Why should he let them down when he could be up or down, possibly at the same time? He asked himself a good ethical question: Why should attending class get in the way?

And the Campus Centre Pub at the centre of U. of W. was sure a good place to hang out, and Michael's belief that his attitude and behavior was morally in tune with the prevailing counterculture norms was affirmed by *Supertramp* who sang to him in English, and in no uncertain terms: "*you're right, you're right, you're bloody well right, you know you got the right...*" Mixing liquids and vapors derived from smoking solid chunks put to the flame, allowed Michael to cover all the elements. He had no need to question the morality of what he was doing because when the saxophone solo let loose he knew that he was right, "*bloody well right!*" and it felt great that he was in the right place at the right time, listening to the *Right Song* and the *Logical Song,* then and there in the centre of his universe of higher learning, feeling like a *super tramp* free of the constricting threads of responsibility and conformity. In reality however, he was just grooving to the changing times contoured and conformed to the then, which to Michael was then now.

Michael knew that he had made the right choice going to university because although he attended a minority of the classes, he got good grades in majority of his courses—mostly B+'s in his first year. His brain was tuned to think that he was right and logical, and thus he decided to major in Philosophy. This however, might have merely been a pseudo-reason for his love of the seductive, sleek, slippery and shapely *Lady of Wisdom*: "*Sophia.*" The real reason was closer to the fact that the lovers of thinking need only to think and write a lot after reading just a little, Michael's *juris* being that he loved *diction* of the spouted sort, and not of the read variety, although at this time he had no designs to be a lawyer, still being intoxicated and intrigued by an ocean full of wine, beer, Southern Comfort, Metaxa, or whatever else floated his way. The lure of freshly fired up blonde, red or gold went to his head, and took him out of his head—but not so much as to interfere with the practice of philosophizing, the temptation of which he could not resist.

Perhaps Jesus could have resisted. He hung out with sinners, and might not have been a saint if he had not been crossed by those he ran across. Jesus could have laughed from the high wooden perch to which he was elevated and set—but a double cross is no laughing matter! Instead Jesus asked one simple yet profoundly important question, to which there was no answer: "why?" Then made by his mockers and murderers to return in a fable, fabulous and foreshadowed, his shadow resurrected without the necessity to use the sword, to be taken up by those wearing the righted cross, who would in turn, so to speak, turn off the light of anyone that saw a different hue, and cut the cord of anyone that was foolish enough to shine in any forum.

When someone cannot see, should the log when taken out of their eyes be used to preach and flog what they should see? Should someone, who recently saw not, be forced to hear the national anthem when shown the log, and asked: "*Oh say can you see?*"

Jesus said the log *should* be removed from one's own eyes first so that they can see to be able to remove the speck from the other person's eye. How else could the operation be performed? Jesus knew that a tiny splinter in one's own eyes looks much larger than it does in someone else's *far away eyes*, although the obstructions are in reality the same more or less.

Thus one should not judge harshly, even if the news Jesus brought might be considered good news or bad news, or just plain old news. For what is news? Is it something that papers don't cover to hide, or is it something hidden when covered by newspapers? *There's something going on here, but you don't know what it is, do you Mr. Jones?*

Is it not true that the cross is mightier than the sword? The sword requires physical strength and a skilled hand to wield and strike with it. Some may be able to strike back, while others may shield themselves. The cross however, is sweetly stitched by emblematic blood in the mind to form a net, an ideological web to collect and catch lost souls by those who wear robes so black they cannot be seen. *Do you not believe—you who have been stitched and sewn shut by the hands of those who in faith's name sacrificed you on the cold stone alter of restricting belief and left you abandoned and naked in a world of touch?*

And so Michael's thoughts danced as another log was thrown into the pyre of the fire that burns with desire, consuming itself and all temptation in time. And then *"Bong!"* the sun rises again in cyclical and cynical sameness. "Good day, is there still a log in your eye?"

# 17

## WHAT THE HILDA IS GOING ON?

When two rooms became available, Michael and Gary moved from the rooming house into a house adjacent to Victoria Park in Kitchener, where some of Michael's friends from Toronto lived.

It is an indisputable fact that in every city ruled by Britannia there are typically important streets, not usually named "Avenues," "Boulevards" or "Roads," but rather "King" or "Queen," and they often intersect and produce a "Prince" or "Princess" something or other. Of course streets can't beget other streets— that's a silly thought—they get people and things to places. But once begotten, twice shy, a famous president of the United States who could not get fooled three times once said, for a fool would be a fool to be fooled that often!

Although Britain may have had a parliamentary democratic system for quite some time, one cannot help but notice how many roads and places are named after the monarchy, and that the most important thing, money, carries facsimiles of royal visages, with the face of monarchs included on postage stamps. In contrast, countries or places under the sword of Spanish imposition often bear the burden of being named after a saint, or through some other religious reference.

Many may not be aware of the fact that belief is but a form of psychosis proclaimed by most. Michael did not know this yet in first year university. While studying philosophy he opined there to be grades of beliefs, like marks in school or varieties of hash. The harsh reality is that many lives that once flickered have been flayed and flicked away like an old butt—grilled, char-broiled and staked—for nudity, use of natural forces, herbal remedies, or for following any notion not conforming to the prevailing norm.

But while those that rule may do so with upturned nose because one's own shit never smells that bad, it is usually the farts that are silent and deadly. Feces is natural and like all things perceived as physical is in accord with the most up to date theory of science and exists in the three states: solid, liquid and gas, and is therefore real. The liquid state has yet to be referred to, but everyone knows the run and flow of the inverted volcano when they really have to go.

It is interesting to note how many parks named "Victoria" were mortared by the British cast and are usually found in the seedy part of town. Victoria was a long serving queen when the British Empire was at its swollen peak. Some say that servitude to the administration of the royal figurehead while it plunged into the affairs of foreign lands was not for the common wealth of all the inhabitants. Balderdash! A good fornication and fleecing never really hurt anyone, but you know how prudish some people are—especially those who can stand her majesty's pious imposition.

Two notable things happened to Michael while he was living in the house adjacent to Victoria Park in Kitchener during his first year at Waterloo U. One was that Gary built the most awesome and incredible hockey net in the basement of the house. On completion he discovered it was too big to fit through the basement door, and thus was of no use at all –but it was still awesome! Also, Michael got sick on some vodka and orange juice, and vowed never to drink vodka again!

Something else very serious and close to maddening also happened, teaching Michael much about psychology which Michael was studying at an introductory level at university, the professor not being leery or timid to broach such topic: the expansion of mind and altering the conception of perceived reality, but Michael did not confuse him with the famous professor, Timothy, of whom Michael knew to be Leary. The truth is that time, like a pair of underwear, will never fit again after dilation to the point where a second stretches out to more than a lifetime!

The owner of the Victoria Park house came by one day. He was dressed in black with a cape, not like a religious vestment, but more like a member of crime organized, or some darkly garbed sinister secret service sort of the *"das ist nicht sehr gut"* variety, or so it seemed to Michael. For no apparent reason other than his perceived perceptions had possibly stirred up subconscious sediments and were thus disturbed, Michael's organ of love started pounding uncontrollably, palpitating throughout his entire body, manifesting most in his stomach, mouth and head. He was overcome with an intense feeling of impending doom, although he knew that there was no rational reason to feel the way he did!

Nothing at all happened, and in time, the uncontrollable fear that engulfed him subsided, but it had been very scary.

Now he knew for sure that he was neurotic—*Oy vey!* Michael did not like Halloween very much to begin with—and now he understood why! And Kitchener could be very Halloween-like and spooky, full of fallen orange leaves and frequently foggy, especially in October.

Due to the negative "vibrations" experienced by Michael in the Victoria Park house, and also due to the fact that some of the inhabitants of said house were slovenly pigs—not uncommon for male university students or even some female ones who tend to leave the carcass of a dead, roasted, half eaten fowl on the kitchen table for days without refrigeration, possibly a way to age meat, but a putrid and petrifying assault on the senses for most, Michael, Gary and some other friends moved out, and into another house in downtown Kitchener near the Farmer's Market on Irvin St. for the second year of university.

Michael fondly recalled the crowds that gathered on Saturdays at the Farmer's Market, and the smell and taste of the Oktoberfest sausage with its tangy sour kraut that he so fully and fartastically enjoyed to consume. Michael had a great time living in that house during second and third year at the University of Waterloo while majoring in philosophy. And he did well in his courses too. He was a natural born thinker—he could drink, smoke and talk at the same time without even having to think about it!

And it was at this epic time at that legendary house on Irvin St. where the joyous and ecstatic "Original Thursday Night Madness" occurred—the first of many a great and crazy Thursday nights! And it was to this house that Michael took Hilda, who he had started to date after he had picked her and Wendy up hitch hiking, for a tryst.

Michael's room was on the main floor of the house with a door that locked. His memories of the incidents of Irvin Street are sketchy and scattered, not only because they occurred so long ago, but due to the state he was in, mostly stoned and often drunk at the time. He did recall Hilda being in his room and it being dark, but not so dark that he could not make out the outline and features of her face.

Hilda was of medium height but very slim, with straight thin natural blond hair that reached just below her shoulders. That night she wore blue jeans and a blue jean jacket, and a tight dark colored sweater, which were casual and vogue at the time. Her large bulging eyes were as blue as Lake Ontario on a sunny day—not to mention that she had such big breasts for a thin girl! Even though generally quiet, she was not overly so, to be considered abnormal. The truth is—and one may believe or disbelieve it as they will—the reality is that although things are perceived to occur in time, all one knows of them are the memories, because the incidents have already passed when first realized to occur, and when reflected on are not just memories, but memories of memories, so the truth is that Michael at the present time in his Hamilton condo could remember very little of Hilda, and what transpired with her.

Michael could not remember whether he had sex with Hilda, that is if he had put his broom into her closet or not, nor could he recall how deeply consumed with each other they got. Michael would probably have remembered if he had poked Hilda, for things like taking store and keeping score were important for him to keep stock of.

Hilda was pretty enough, being a true blonde with a narrow face and frame, and her big blue bulging eyes. And Michael and she must have done something together as they were both in his room alone in semidarkness. All cats may look the same in the dark, and one may affectionately call a cat, a "pussy," but the feline facsimile did not apply as Michael could not see in the dark. His only clear recollection, which is actually quite hazy and bizarre, was that Hilda's face kept changing and altering as he gazed upon her visage in that quarter light where they were face to face—and he became fixated with this going on, which might have happened only in his mind. Michael was not at the time under the influence of anything that could account for the morphing sight of her, as real as real could be to him then and there. He saw it with his own eyes and pondered upon it while it was happening, and it freaked him out! He could no longer go out with Hilda, although he was not so cruel as to tell her the real reason for terminating the relationship—she might have thought he was a loony! He was definitely sane enough to know what had occurred could be considered crazy.

But was it crazy? What can one really know of this world, outside of, or other that the conditioning they are subject to, with all the tempering and uninvited mind tampering resulting in the inability to see things as they are, from the outside in or the inside out? Even to look is a limitation that can be broken down to a lens and light, if looked at in a certain light.

Would one's belief change if they knew that Michael jumped from Hilda to Wendy to have a fun filled, rewarding, intense long-term relationship? Wendy and Hilda had grown up as friends in Kitchener. They both went to high school cloistered together at St. Mary's, but they would have none of the nuns' orthodoxy of abstinence preached down their deep throats. Wendy told Michael many years later when by chance talking about Hilda, that Hilda had joined a well-known organization that could be considered a cult. Does this addendum affect or change how the situation ought to be judged? One should not be too quick to decide, for the truth can be elusive and slip one's grasp like a squirming snake. Things are never really true, or perhaps they are true and not true at the same time.

Michael's interpretation and explanation of what happened is this. Hilda did not know who she was, so her perception of herself kept shifting so, so to speak, she was a "changeling," as evidenced by her later joining a cult, which Michael somehow picked up intuitively. Perhaps, and on the other hand (as a lawyer would say) Michael ought to have taken the log out of his eye, and then he might have been able to see so he could take the speck out of Hilda's eye. However, her eyes were very big and stuck out a lot, so it should have been easy for him to see if anything was lodged therein obscuring her vision. Perhaps Michael should have let his love light shine, then and there, so he could see and be seen, but that was then and this is now, and there exists an un-crossable schism between the two.

# 18

## IRVIN STREET AND JAKE

What can be said about second and third year of University at the house near the famous Farmer's Market in Kitchener on Irvin St.? The pliable minds of the youthful occupants were being filled with fluids, formed and shaped, and at times spilled or bent out of shape through the smoky and maze-like ways of a university education. Four post-adolescents free from the watchful eye of their parents lived in one detached house with no curfews—the only rules being to clean up your own mess, and to share your drugs and alcohol.

There was Tinger MacInsky, a tall thin brooding English major working on his master's degree. Michael had met him the previous year on the "Moving to Montana Soon" weekend. Tinger calmly and quietly shared his tin foil knowledge that a Bic pen could be used for more than writing or taking slap shots—the knowledge of which the undergrads inhaled like smoke from a Bic pen pipe as Tinger exhaled the profound and practical wisdom. Looking through the glass of smoke darkly, one could not be blamed for mistaking MacInsky for a young and emaciated Shakespeare, his hair and pale face spoke of that simile—and he had no doubt studied Shakespeare being an English graduate—but Tinger had enough street smarts not to talk too much, and to know that "to be" or "not to be" added up to nothing in terms of getting a job in the real world versus the play world of English academics, except for getting a job as a teacher, which is what in fact Tinger did, getting a teaching job with the force of an institution that turns men into robots: the military.

Although Tinger could appear as a villain, an idea possibly hashed out through the haze of smoke from a Bic pen pipe because his pallid face lacked color, thus hi-lighting both his thin, black mustache set in the middle, and his black as mood, thinning hair which framed it. Tinger was no villain however, although hearsay has it that his temperment could swing wildly like an unlatched gate in a wind storm, or like the multiple mulligans needed to be taken by a cross-eyed drunk to score par in a friendly game of golf.

Then there was Jake, Jake Plum, or plum Jake as his farcical friends who were fond of jesting often joked. Michael and Jake went a long way back. They both attended the same grade school. Jake's mother and Michael's mother also worked in the same factory (called a "shop") where they had the same job, sewing by hand, and they were about the same age, and both their girlhoods were sewn up and finished in the darkness of the shadow cast by the far right!

Back then, Jake's mother went by the name of Leah, and Michael thought it *was* her name for why else would she use it? On the death of her husband, Leah changed her name to Lilly, which might have actually been her name to begin with, but at least it was from then on.

Jake and Michael both studied the bowing on the violin at the University Settlement in an area of downtown Toronto called the Grange, but Jake was actually able to make music come out of his instrument! Why was the violin not an instrument of torture in Jake's hands as it was in Michael's? Perhaps all Transylvanians, which was Jake's background as well as Mr. Googoola's, had a talent or gift for music. Michael did not. For when he stroked his instrument, his nimbleness with numbers translated only into the numbing notes calculated and manufactured in his mind, instead of heard with the ear of his heart.

Jake's nickname while at university was "the bear" because he had a thick black beard and fine white skin, as Transylvanians often do, and was a tad overweight, looking a bit like a bearded Cat Stevens or Paul McCartney. Michael knew little about Transylvania except for tidbits he had picked up here and there, but enough to reach the following conclusions.

The Dracula legend was probably based on the fact that many Transylvanians have pale white skin contrasted with jet black hair, which makes their lack of color, their facial pallor, all the more striking. It is not true however, that Transylvanians are all nocturnal drinkers of blood who wear formal capes and jackets and have died, but yet are undead. In fact many, like Jake, were full of vigor—he could grow a 5 o'clock shadow within an hour of shaving!

Secondly, garlic is popular in Transylvania along with paprika. The "stinking rose" does not just keep vampires at bay, it keeps everyone away. Garlic is not a rose that smells so sweet by any other name.

Thirdly, Transylvania is a region in Romania, where the inhabitants speak Hungarian. Romania was named after the multitude of Romani residents that reside there nomadically, and not after the Romans, as some mistakenly maintain. The Roma are very musical, and thus the Transylvanians acquired the talent for and love of music from their beloved roaming Romani compatriots.

Jake's parents spoke Yiddish as well as Hungarian and thus the Rices could communicate with the Plums with aplomb. Most Hungarian Jews did not speak Yiddish, which set them apart from other Central European Jews who mostly did, and that set apart the Transylvanians, who mostly did speak Yiddish. Hungarian is supposed to be a very difficult language to speak, a sort of "*goulash*" or mishmash of a tongue. This might explain why the dead that live are called "*ghouls*"!

Michael's parents moved to North York from downtown Toronto shortly after Jake's parents did, and bought their bungalow just around the corner from the Plum's, on a crescent shaped street facing a park named after the street on which it fronted except of course the park was named "Park," and the street was a "Drive." In true British tradition, the park and street were named after a certain prince.

Things haven't changed much in the sixty years or so since the street and park were named. Some people claim that Canada is now no longer a colony, but those who cling to power through oppression, no longer having the strength of arms to hold the people pinned down with force, will go to any length to maintain control, like retaining imperial measurement, or using the royal family to distract the masses from what is really going on. And Charles is *still* a *bloody* prince after all these years! When will his mother ever let him grow up?

Back in Hamilton, the elevator call light went out, and the shiny chrome elevator door slid open automatically with a soft pleasing ring of "*ding.*" Michael stepped in and pushed the round button that said "B" which lit up after he pushed it. It stood for basement. Then the door closed. On the passing of each floor, the pleasing bell's sound was reproduced.

Michael thought of how nice it would be if the ring for each floor was the ring of the cash register at his health food store. In his flight of fancy, he would ride the elevator all day, going up and down the seven, or eight floors of the building if the basement were included. Each ring would bring more coin into his coffers—he would be rich and possess big bags bulging with money! Why hadn't the store done well enough so he could show one and all how good and successful a capitalist he was—and not have to work? Then he could hold his head up with pride!

Pride sprang up often in Michael, subtly like a hand stroking the instrument of its self importance before it is noticed, slowly at first. It would burn its way up the spinal cord, and then explode with the haywire force of freed fire when the irresistible urge made contact with the brain, igniting and consuming everything—everything but itself.

Perhaps things had happened subconsciously. Maybe Michael really wanted to fail so that he did not have to carry the burden any more. Maybe he wanted to be free to roam; to possess only the things he knew he could use and carry; to pare down and become a practitioner of practicality. Didn't he wear the clothes he liked to the point of being worn threadbare when they wore well? What more did he need?

Perhaps all his melancholy, sadness, and unfulfilled desires were as a result of an imbalance of hormones or chemicals. As a male he had been taught and conditioned to push, and *not* to yield—not realizing that in the position of open armed yielding he *could* yield everything that life pushed his way or placed on his path. At least he would stand a chance to side step and duck whenever life threw a curve-ball at him. He would not be a sitting duck!

Physics teaches that for every force there is an equal and opposite force. When more is taken of what there is, then more has been given. But the more demanded of what there isn't, then the less of what is expected *is* received. Michael thought this battle or interplay of forces, the joust between the self and the world, was really but two sides of one coin, all being one, and the sport of juggling the forces could aptly be named "*mental judo.*"

The word "judo" brought his mind to ponder on things *Japanese,* a race known to take the position that small things are good, rather than the more proportionate perspective summed up in the adage: *everything in its appropriate measure.* But the quality of a thing should not be based on size—just ask any self conscious male!

It is easy to take issue with the inverse subversion that goes on in Japan, a culture that considers shrunken trees and flower arranging to be the most wonderful and worthwhile of pastimes and pursuits. What *gooblygob* or *gobblygoo*! Can a country that considers fish above and higher than birds be trusted or taken seriously? Any bird brain, even one that has not eaten fish (which is touted as being "brain food") knows that fish swim in bodies of water, and birds fly in the sky, which is made of air. At least on this planet, air, the home of birds, is always above water, the abode of fish, which is always in nature below air, and thus in nature there can be no conclusion other than birds are above and higher than fish.

Should not the Japanese however be forgiven? Is not their notorious conformity a result of their contagious infirmity, banged out by the smithy hammer of harsh and unrelenting despots? Oh, but what fine and delicate pottery they kilned!

Now in the elevator, Michael knew where he was, and he knew where he was going. He was going either up or down. He trusted the elevator in his condo building as he had been on it many times, and it always took him to the floors he wanted to go to without fear or much thought. He just had to push the right buttons and that was easy.

But there was an elevator filled with fear and loathing in midtown Toronto, which Michael had ascended and descended in only once in his pre-university, late adolescent days, in a building on Bloor Street, part of or affiliated with the University of Toronto, named Roachdale College—not referring to the well-known insect on which no opinion is made due to respect for life—but rather in the sense of what is left when a joint is smoked. The joint in this case was a building of some eighteen stories or so, full of drug dealers. One would have to know where to go and where to get off, the things to be beware of, and what to be aware of upon entering the building and taking the elevator to make a score; but after sampling wares, the ability to properly navigate the ups and downs was lost as one got extremely elevated and high—and *paranoia* set in! Then, the elevator seemed to have a diabolic mind of its own, moving up and down with the door opening and closing as it willed!

Michael's heart raced. Had he not had dreams of being both stabbed and shot in an elevator? The door would open, a tall, thin man in a hat and overcoat whose face Michael could not make out would enter and ride all the way to the basement with him. The mystery man would then stab Michael with a large knife in one version, or shoot him with a pistol at close range in the other variation, always in the abdomen. The silent stranger would then get off the elevator and leave Michael there, presumably to die. Michael could not remember if he did die in any of the dreams. The shot or stab did not really feel all that bad, it was just a sensation like indigestion—oh but the fear—that *was* unbearable! And the elevators in Roachdale never functioned properly!

Michael never was a drug dealer. There is no need to argue about the difference between a "dealer" and a "pusher." It is a distinction of pure semantics artificially inseminated into the minds of the drug, sex, and rock and roll crazed youth so some Canadian band named after a Swiss book could make and eat a great deal of cheese. Michael only went to Roachdale because he did not like to pay retail—he wanted to save a few bucks. Roachdale turned out to be the trippy market where instead of having stalls or shops all on the same floor, level or plane, as in a normal market or mall, they were set, located and situated on different levels, floors or planes, where one would travel in the elevator, like a time machine, which went from the more distant past to the less distant past in the reflection of memory.

Then somehow, as if by magic, but most probably due to his fractured and fragmented memory, Michael found himself outside in the light of day behind busy Bloor Street, his stoned heart pounding with purgatorial fear under the intense blinding blaze of the sun, surrounded by the tall buildings and the heavy traffic of midtown Toronto. Surely the cops were educated enough to know what degree the people that went to Roachdale College received and carried out with them, and Michael was worried about being caught carrying to any degree, whether in metric or imperial, and then being interrogated under the blinding light of the truly inspiring third degree which would surely cause him to wax poetic in stream of consciousness *mumbo jumbo ad nauseam.*

The elevator made Michael think of his trip to Japan several years ago. Japan was like one giant urban area with lots of elevators except for the mountainous areas. Even parking lots for cars would use elevators—it was so crowded. Things were built up instead of out. In Tokyo, or possibly in other large cities, commercial establishment and restaurants and bars and clubs would be in high rises. "*Ding,*" the door opens—one could be anywhere. The door might open up to a swanky bar, a bathroom, or perhaps a dream. One had no control, could not see, and could not escape if there was a trap!

In the movie, *Inglorious Bastards*, Brad Pitt's brusque Tennessee Sgt. feared ambushes in basements, so how freaked out would he be to have to meet someone in a high rise where the only means of ingress or egress was the elevator? If the building were a contract, there would be no exculpatory clause!

Michael could not recall if there were stairs in Japan because he had never seen them used. And everything was new, except for religion! The Japanese are known for being technically proficient, with the possible exception of nuclear power. But fusion or fission is nothing to laugh at—the overreaction of a reactor in the land of the rising sun and falling yen is a sad and serious matter especially in light and heat of their having been nuked as punishment for their naughtiness in choosing the wrong side in the last big war. A case of ambition overstepping ability and sensibilities perhaps, but imperialism is such a powerful motivator!

No fun should be poked at fusion. It is OK when dealing with cuisine, where the taste *is* in the taste, but it is not the case that the state should state the taste. Saké may be likeable even when served warm, and the taste for Scotch may need to be acquired, but everyone should be left to their own devices notwithstanding the Japanese attempt to control with their doctrine of small is swell, and fish above all. Such notions of what is esthetically pleasing need empirical proof, not imperial force!

Michael was still descending in the elevator in his condo building in Hamilton, Ontario, when he was struck by a great idea for a TV or internet series. A person is riding on an elevator and it could open up anywhere, to any time, at any time. The show could be a comedy, a drama, a soap opera, or an adventure. Like real life, anything could happen. The renewal of life, every day, every second—every binary electron turning on and off like an elevator opening its door continuously anew. Michael thought: "I should note that idea" and it elevated his mood, even though he was going down.

The door opened on its own accord after a final "*ding*," and Michael exited the elevator. He was now in the basement parking lot where a constitutional right entitled him the right to the exclusive use of one parking space, as set out in the declaration of his Condominium Corporation. His parked car waited.

In honor of the device that has lifted and raised, lowered and brought down mountains of people and products, join in song to pay homage to that great invention which has allowed for the ascension or descending in this world more rapidly than by a ladder or stairs, without Luddite dissention, and of one brave soul dedicating his crazy manic depressive life to its riding, without derision, full time: "*Elevator Man.*"

## *THE ELEVATOR MAN SONG*

*Elevator man, how high or low can you go?*
*What waits for you when the bell rings and the door opens?*
*What level will you be on? What time will you get there?*
*Oh elevator man, will your feet ever touch the ground?*
*And when you get there how will you know*
*That you are not just in another elevator?*
*Oh elevator man, elevator man, does it matter*
*How fast or slow you go? How will you*
*Get there when you know you're there?*

# 19

## A FATHER'S IRE

As friends in high school, Michael and Jake mentally skipped through the Panasonic and panoramic Floydian fields of *Ummagumma* with their heads between the speakers of a Grundig stereo, listening and howling to the solid piece of wood furniture with high fidelity on the broadloomed floor of Jake's parents' living room in their North York bungalow.

Michael recalled that one day back then, and even before, when his head might have been clearer with less strain from trying to hash out life's proclivities and disturbances, Jake related to Michael the detail that Jake's father was not speaking to him, Jake that is, because he was angry with him for some minor matter. The silent treatment was being applied by the elder Plum as a form of discipline and punishment. Michael found this behavior odd and perplexing because he could not understand the logic or emotion behind it.

Michael, who even back then as a teenager had to have an explanation for everything that needed to make sense to him, comprehended that such behavior was incomprehensible, and was probably meted out as a result of Jake's father being so much older than Jake's mother, then Leah, which difference might have been thirty years or more, and thus Michael perceived Jake's father to be out of touch—doing an old man thing resulting from a generation gap. It seemed to Michael that such gulf or divide existed between the generations back then, but no longer, as now there is no gaping hole between the desires and actions of young and old. Whether one now enjoys partying or is entrenched to tow the party line is no longer a function of age!

Michael did not understand why Leah, who had a soft and friendly personality, pleasant appearance and a likeable plumpness, fair complexion, and dark Transylvanian hair, would want or need to marry a man so set and stern in his ways, thirty years or more her senior, that would use the withholding of chatter as a form of child control. Leah was kind and social, and always agreeable to Michael's mother's opinions which were spoken in a tone leaving no doubt they were correct and true opinions fastidiously fastened to factuality—spoken by someone that was full of the spirit and demeanor of "*I know, and aren't you glad that I am letting you know*," and not by a guppy-like wet "*shmateh*" ("rag" in Yiddish).

Michael thought that not speaking to one's own son, the punishment Jake's father not so boisterously belted out and interjected into his relationship with Jake, was not fair and just, well before Michael had any inclination that he would be versed in philosophy and law. Michael saw it on par with cutting off one's nose to spite one's face.

Perhaps many people would not lend credence to Michael's point of view, or weigh in on his side so as to tip the scales of the *blind lady* in his favor. That may explain why so many people do not, or are unable to smell injustice and hypocrisy in this world, perpetrated and populated by many humans seeming unkind and unwise. People scramble about like eggs breaking each other, steamed over something or other, ignoring the fried mess. They do not have a nose anymore to smell that something is rotten and needs castigation due to their own nasal castration! They need to face up to their own cracked, hard-boiled premeditations—and smell the skunkweed!

In contrast, for example, when Michael did something that his father disapproved of, it would be pointed out that it was wrong, and he would be told not to do it anymore, but not in so many words. Michael's father might just ignore it altogether as not important enough to interrupt his watching bowling on TV, while peeling and eating overripe fruit bought at a discount price no doubt from the bargain bin. Michael's mother might snap at him and yell; but that was all, it would soon blow over like an inconsequential tropical storm. In short order, each person would go back to their place in the family: Michael going out all the time to amuse himself—and going to school to fill in the gaps—while his parents went to work to support the family and provide the necessities of life.

Michael's father had a calm temperament, balancing caring with not caring, hardly ever losing his temper except when he did. To reach such stormy state he needed a lot of egging and goading to get irate, all fired up and enraged. (Incidentally *"ire"* means eggs and is also slang for testicles in Yiddish.) Then all the hurts and pains stored up mushroomed nuclear—the harder and longer he tried to restrain his composure from decomposing, the greater the eruptive explosion and fallout! The yolks and whites and cracked shells would be scattered everywhere. Mendel would withdraw after the tempest blew over. He tried so hard to avoid slipping into the world where the *tainted stain* marred everything.

Michael remembered an incident which occurred when he may have been but four years old, where he must have done something to steam his father's eggs, because his father took off his belt as a precursor and in preparation to punish Michael with *the strap*. Michael was not afraid because he sensed no real anger or urgency. His father had always spared the rod, so Michael was already starting to show the signs of early spoilage.

Michael nimbly darted away and chuckled as if he was playing a game of *"catch me if you can"* while hiding from his father. From the vantage of a cranny he watched his father falter, belt in hand and pants falling, searching for Michael. But then, what may have been poetic justice, occurred. Michael in all his fun and excitement had not noticed that when he crouched down, he had sat on broken glass. Now, he could not help but notice as he got up because he was bleeding profusely!

From then on Michael wore and bore a large scar on his right shin, the shape and size of a lip. The kiss of glass was a clear reminder, Michael believed, that one should never laugh at or tempt fate. Had it been more visible, it would have looked like a pretty cool tattoo, in the days before tattoos were cool.

Michael also learned a lesson for life, which was to be careful in choosing where to sit, essentially to be mindful of details, for a little oversight might come back to haunt a person in a manner of malevolence and hurt unimaginable at the time of the oversight. Perhaps similar in meaning and scope to the expression, *the bed you make is the bed you sleep in*, which was one of Michael's favorite aphorisms. Michael's mother had a different take on the expression in Yiddish, the directness and vulgarity of which appealed to Michael. It loosely translated as: *"As you shit, so shall you eat."* Yiddish is such a sensual language!

Although the gash did not hurt, the cutting edge properties of glass being more than just reflection and transparency, and the fervency of Michael's sobbing and wailing were directly proportionate with the flow and gush of his dark red blood, it was his apprehension of being hurt that pained Michael most, although he was not mature enough to realize this at the time.

Although Michael's father temper could be pushed to the point of no return, Michael had never been lashed by the straps unleashed during these tumultuous storms unfurled when Mendel's composure was torn and rend asunder, when the hurt and pain became unbearable to bear, constrain and hold in any longer, and then the scars of sufferings accrued in his lifetime, or perhaps in the lifetime of the Jewish race, or during the entire tenor of the human race, like dark clouds colliding, crashing amidst lightning and thunder was let loose with abandon like a scab ripped from a wound! Not once however, did Michael recall his father's anger being directed at him. It was always posturing by Mendel to make it appear that he was the head of the family and in control.

What Michael did recall, since his father had passed away over ten years ago, was his father's wet kisses. Michael was always surprised how warm they were. They did not come often, the Rices were not a "touchy feely" type family, but when receiving a heartfelt labial missive from his father Michael felt the rarified essence of love transmitted to him.

In later years, when any receptionist of Michael's kisses complained of their being sloppy and wet, Michael just smiled, and his heart filled with fond memories of his father. Recalling his father holding and kissing Samuel as a baby, when Samuel was too young to speak and pretend to object, Michael sensed that Samuel must have felt the same, for the smile on Samuel's face radiated silent contentment.

Then, there came a day of black uncontrolled cyclonic anger, while the family was living in Israel and Michael was but a four year old child. It happened without warning, and with no context available for Michael to make sense of it. At such a young age he was not made privy to what was going on in the adult world. His world consisted only of what he needed, felt or thought about, and no more. He had yet to acquire the desire to accumulate and differentiate.

All of a sudden he noticed his father roiled in a mountainous rage that had erupted like a volcano from the deepest depths of the earth! With savage incendiary force Mendel was trying to pummel Michael's brother with a belt. Each blow, some striking with the force that would make mother earth herself quake, seemed to come directly from the hand of Jehovah! Terror stricken, Abe tried to dodge the blows as nimbly as he could, while Michael's mother franticly tried with all her strength to hold her husband back.

*"Stop, stop! You're going to kill him!"* she yelled hysterically crying at the same time, in what language being unimportant and inconsequential. Unquantifiable fear overtook Michael as if he were the recipient his father's unencumbered Olympian bolts of blind, mad rage. Titanic fear consumed Michael—the apocalypse had arrived—which no doubt dwarfed any pain which could be inflicted by mere physical blows! His parents had always been even-handed, so Michael *knew* his turn was next! He had done nothing wrong—what caused his father ire to blaze like a bonfire out of control! Michael did not know. He loved his father, and the fear that his father no longer loved him, that the love and protection of this kind and gentle man was forever lost, smote him to the core.

The color of Michael's terror was red and black, blotting out all light, soaking and saturating his pulsating insides, as if they had been pounded and pulverized by the iron fists of a boxer on the verge of victory; Michael was ready to be knocked out—to disappear! In fathomless fear Michael waited for his turn, like a dutiful son. His turn however, did not come: anger diffused into curses and tears; and then shame.

The dark sky of day was cleared by the cool breeze of restoring night. Michael bore no physical harm, which his heart told him he would have weathered and could have healed from, but the forecast was now overcast by a shadow of emotional torrents that he did not understand or comprehend, denting his previous "all's-well-in-Michael-land" disposition.

No one took the time to explain to Michael what had happened and why. In the caring Canada of today, no doubt a social worker would attend after the occurrence of such a traumatic incident to make sure everyone was OK, and such state professional would earn her or his keep, but this was Israel in the 50's and life was hard. The focus was on war and survival in a land forged from the desert, reclaimed as a historical and biblical imperative, whether rightly or wrongly so is a matter for the obfuscation of historians, apologists, politicians and fanatics, but is nothing new under the rising and setting sun.

Michael later assimilated this incident by framing it in the context that his brother, Abe, who was more than three years his senior, was hanging around with the wrong kids who exerted a bad influence, and Abe had done something which angered their father, but Michael did not know what could scramble his father's eggs to such point of ire; but things conceived in the abstract are never as good or bad as they are in actual detail, if the conception ever reaches the light of day at all.

Abe was what one might call a little "hood"; and whether one is for him or against him probably boils down to which group, band or gang one belongs to, or is associated with. His actions might have been acceptable and humorous in the *"Happy Days"* of North America; but where should the line be drawn? Who is to judge? Should one play the blame or excuse game, flip the coin, or just take the money and run? If there were an answer to such questions, one could be all knowing and wise, but mortals live in a *shadow-land* where light and truth is kept veiled and hidden by the refraction and reflection of the senses and the mind.

Michael thought that his father was a great and spiritual man that maintained his balance and poise well through the ferocity and turbulence that rained upon him. Michael's brother however, as he recently asserted to Michael in a long and argumentative telephone conversation, viewed Mendel as a trivial and little man, a wimp and a guppy. Now how can two people that lived in the same house, more or less subject to the same conditions perceiving the same phenomena, arrive at such divergent and differing observations and conclusions. It isn't logical, but there is no doubt that it happens all the time. The only logical conclusion is that there exist at least as many realities as people, and perhaps more—or perhaps the "log" in one's eye is the root of all *log*ic. That is what makes the multi-faceted and fascinating world so psycho, crazy and il*log*ical.

In such recent telephone conversation Abe disclosed to Michael what fueled Mendel to go ballistic. What happened was that Abe had stolen money that was set aside for rent, the father having to work two jobs sewing in the day and sewing in the night to stitch enough money together to tailor ends to meet, and Abe the little hood, cut the seams sharply as if done with a razor blade, and in a very unseemly manner. But Abe shifted the blame, he was a master of the game, and to this day believes that the father had over reacted, and that the anger was all about saving face and pride. "Big deal if the Rices didn't make the rent" he stated to Michael, "our father was out of control. He could have killed me! I was only seven years old!"

*"Good thing that Jehovah of the Old Testament was not our father,"* Michael thought after he had calmed down.

What type of man was Mendel in this confused world? Of what cloth was he cut? Was his action an appropriate reaction or just another a knee-jerk response based on preconditioned mores and morals gone emotionally amuck and awry? Should one side with *Robin Hood* or *the Sheriff*? The plastic dial of the virtually indestructible Northern Telecom rotary telephone, that at one time belonged to Michael's parents and was inherited by Michael, bears witness to the extent of Michael's wrath:

he struck it with all his might with the handle that one listens and speaks through, when he, like his father before him, lost his temper during a conversation with his brother, when his brother told him what happened.

Michael regretted losing his temper and damaging the phone, but it still works even though it does not look so good anymore, unlike that great shining light of Canadian financial and technological achievement, Northern Telecom, which was by greed pinned to the mat for the count and taken out. Yes, Michael was ready to take off the belt if not for the fear that his pants would fall and he would be standing there in the court of law ready to plead his case or his father's case in his underwear if need be, like he had done in so many dreams; but this might have been caused by the inheritance of genes, or the by imbibing of the old school values of retributive justice prevalent in the Old Testament which any scholar worth their weight in library dust knows has been succeeded and superseded by the love of the New Testament—notwithstanding the fear mongering that is so fundamental to some sects with their emphasis on burning in the flaming eternity of Hell as punishment for not doing as they say.

Jesus was asked how many times someone must forgive a brother by whom he has been wronged. Jesus said that seven times was not enough, and that the brother should be forgiven at least seventy-seven times! Boy, did Jesus ever have a sense of humor! Michael was no Jesus, at least not yet, although he had nothing against the so-called sinners who may have been strapped by life. Perhaps Michael had a sense of humor too, but how could he compare himself to Jesus?

Finally, who or what is to blame? Is "blame" the right word to use? Do the pants, the belt or even the underwear matter in the eyes of life, and the all, and what is called: *what is, was, and will be,* that needs not to review the various and limited works of not-so-human-kind with its X-rays, ultra-sounds, death ways and other manifestations of energy and vibes? Is the human mind in opposition to the natural, which like a perverse inverse prism refracts and reflects things into their opposite and what they are not? Is it only in the mind that one is well dressed or naked—or somewhere in between? Why should the world care about a species that cares so much about itself that is manifested in freedom and limited by nature, or limited in freedom and manifested by nature? Like the blink of an eye, the disintegration of the solar system, nay the universe as known, is less than a baby fingernail's scratch on the boundless skin of all that is all.

# 20

## STILL ON JAKE

Now you could forgive Michael for thinking Jake's father's mode of punishment as old fashioned, or that this somewhat quiet man who refused to partake in social trivialities, like saying a friendly "hello" to Michael, seemed more of an aloof and serious octogenarian than a contemporary of Michael's parents, but when Michael found out his history as disclosed by Jake and Michael's mother, Michael's mother having great respect for Mr. Plum, the tilt of Michael's predilection towards blame and his predisposition to find fault leveled off.

Jake's humble father was then, when Michael knew him living around the corner in North York, a retired "presser," someone who irons the finished product in a garment factory. Michael considered this a much less esteemed position than the occupation of his own father, who was a sewing machine operator, and had been one all his working life. The sewing machine operator and the "cutter" (one who cuts the cloth into a pattern), were the heart and soul of a shop and both could be called "*shneiders*." The sewing machine operator's job was glamorous and prestigious. He could fly with muscularity and force the sewing machine's pistons to pound in the performance of their duties, joining material to material seemingly seamlessly through skillful operation of a machine, but a lowly presser could only "glide" over the finished product in the heated application of his trade, thus but straightening things out and making then look nicer.

That was not really the old and senior Plum's original calling or profession however, he had in fact been a mayor of a small town in the old country, Romania, if politics can be considered a profession, and if so, possibly the oldest, vying with lawyers, liars and layers. But when number two was made, the all so efficient master race decided to clean up and wiped the said mayor's then wife and children—yes the mayor had a family suitable to his age and position—from the face of this dirty earth and sent Mr. Plum to camp for "re-creation" or "de-creation" depending on how the pastime is viewed. Now it is well known that the master race which saw only black and white, accepted only pure discipline to their commands, and was well-suited in terms of attire, disappeared when the world discovered that color was much more attractive ideally and ideologically—and also because they lost the last big one too!

It was at such a "facing creation camp," where people concentrated on philosophical issues such as the meaning of life, or lack thereof, that Jake's father met Jake's mother. She was all alone, a teenager, trimmed of all kin like him. When the camp's term ended, he took her under his broken wings. The two nested together and started a family, and then took the boat to Canada because hardly anyone could afford to fly in those days.

After several years, Jake's father passed away from old age. It happened sooner than with the other parents of Michael's friends due to his old age. Mr. Plum *had* done things in an old world way, his way, the way he had learned and seen in the old country, from growing fruit trees in the back yard, pickling and making his own liqueurs, to the transferring all the family property into Jake's mother's name before his demise to avoid the necessity and costs of having the lawyers do the devising, demising, and division of the estate.

Can one learn how to love? If love were shoes, most people would not be very well shod. They'd be walking down the jagged, icy path of life in bare feet. Being barren and stripped of love makes the longing for it all the greater: the weight of loneliness all the more unbearable. But if one wore love—dressed in its elegant and practical footwear—they would be seen as worthy of love, and people would notice. One is so often judged by the shoes that adorn their feet!

When Jake's father passed away, his mother who was an attractive and friendly middle-aged woman full of life, suddenly became "Lilly." Perhaps that was her name all along, but no one knew. Lilly was not overbearing like some women are. It would be foolish to think, and even more foolish to make the assertion, that the greasy hand of such trait reaches and touches only the female gender. Of course not: thinking that one is always right and thus entitled to call the shots can point its finger of blame at all genders without discrimination.

And Lilly who was at such time retired, seemed content without a husband, having two fine sons, a nice bungalow in North York, and enjoyed cooking, baking, cleaning and chatting, as did her friend, Michael's mother, who had similar interests—but Michael's mother knew that she, Michael's mother, knew, and let everybody else know that she knew as well.

Michael never thought that Lilly would be interested in another man, even though she was probably still only in her 50's. Perhaps at his young age Michael was naïve enough to believe that people his parent's age did not get lonely; that they were somehow asexual. Michael tended to think a lot, and that is why he even thought about it. But fate was to prove him wrong once again.

Was fate actually conspiring against him, or was he just a little paranoid? Lilly in due course met a man named Johnny. They married, and Johnny moved into her bungalow. For a while everybody got along and was happy. Life disguised herself as being Rosy. Johnny did not ask Lilly to change her name.

Johnny was a nice enough and friendly man, retired and a contemporary in age of Lilly—and he loved to talk! He had the particular habit of talking so much as not to listen, and was in fact a know-it-all, but Michael knew that Johnny did not know everything.

But as all good things must end some day, just like in the song about the necessity of the leaves of autumn to fall, so it passed not after a few years, but not a multitude either, that Johnny for no apparent reason started to get suspicious and act selfishly and meanly, and he made it a habit to make untrue and hurtful accusations and statements that made Lilly suffer, and alienated her then adult sons to the point that they kicked him out of the house. It was simply a case that the way he acted was impossible to deal with, and so the sons, one of whom was Jake, got rid of the impossibility.

Perhaps Johnny had simply gone crazy. There may or may not be a technical diagnosis concocted to categorize the way he behaved, or if his condition was yet discovered or uncovered, but would it really matter? Could something without a name or label really exist? Would it be not be like a smoked cigarette, a tree fallen in the forest when no one was around, or a cigarette yet to be rolled? These questions may be viewed as academic, or a lawyer might say that they are moot points, but the simple prognosis is that the craziness was always there—at first like a small seed so it was tolerable, hardly noticeable. Then it grew so big—like a weed it took over! And then, lo and behold, it was able to be seen by all for what it was: a big nut tree! Johnny passed on shortly afterwards. In fickle ferociousness, fate snapped its uncaring fingers to order the dishonorable discharge of Johnny, and so it was.

And then soon after, it was Lilly's turn. The big "C" came. Her number was up! She was incurably claimed. The big "C," of course, stands for cancer. It, and the industry constructed around it, might be the biggest enterprise in the world, towering monstrous above other undertakings organized for profit, growing malignantly ever larger like a tumor that has come to dominate the medical, pharmaceutical, and so called scientific establishment and its thinking. Most have jumped on its bandwagon as it rolled down Main Street with endless cries of "*crisis*" to cover and obscure the shrieks of pain resulting from the barbaric and callous methods tied to the savage tactics of scorch, slash and poison established for more than a century that it has been able to rule the thought waves.

The flower that was Lilly's friendly and outgoing nature wilted from the chemotherapeutic and X-rayed moment she began to receive the state-sanctioned "treatment." Her life rippled with fear, pain and nausea. She resorted to wearing a wig to hide her shamed bare and naked head. Even though her case was considered incurable, the usual procedures were followed. She died in agony in the wake of the tow of the modern health care tug. Her sail had been trimmed before she could set sail on her final sortie to the setting sun.

The law states that a doctor cannot be held culpable if they follow standard procedures. Although everyone is different, the same procedure must be followed. Resistance is futile! "*We were just following orders.*" There is no problem if the war is won—no one listens to the loser's complaints!

Doctors are now the high priests, and the medical establishment their temple, and the so called scientists their sycophants. Should they not be questioned? Today, instead of burning someone at the stake or excommunicating them, anyone who has a different take on reality can simply be labeled *insane*, and taken out that way. It is an apt categorization no doubt, to the extent that "insane" means being *in sanity*—and not knowing how to hide it! It is as dangerous as a cancerous growth that must be cut, burned or toxically removed.

Doctors now perform all the ritual tasks that were once the purview and domain of their priestly kin. The rationalizing reductionists have been so esoterically successful in the application and mastery of ideology and propaganda that the general population believes the arbitrary labels, classifications, and categorizations to be truth. How can anyone, not so authorized, dare to assault with challenging questions those who stand and guard the bastion of unquestionable *scientific truth*? The doors of membership in the all powerful and all knowing "brotherhood of scientists" are open only to those fully initiated and indoctrinated by a degree as dictated and sanctioned by the ruling and governing societies, associations and colleges!

Doctors stand at the pinnacle of science—they are the cops of reality. They are not only in charge of bringing people into the world—they are also responsible for taking them out! Talk about a monopoly! Few people have a *clue* that they are being played, and that "*Truth*" is but a name game!

# 21

## JAKE, JEAN AND TINGER

Michael was now in the underground parking garage of his condo walking towards his car. Perhaps his plans would work out. He had downsized, sold his house and bought his one bedroom condo not only to pay down the debts of Wild Rice, but also to have to do as little maintenance as possible. *"You don't have to cut the lawn, condo, condo, condo."* A condo was just right, if Michael sold the business and wanted to go away, all he had to do was close the door, turn off the utilities; he could go to his dream land for months without a care in the world—no worries about cutting the grass, repairs, or security—it was all taken care of.

His car too, would be secure, safe and warm in the enclosed, underground parking garage. Having just moved at the beginning of the summer, Michael had yet to experience the benefits of underground parking during the winter, but if he *had* thought of it, it would have melted away frigid thoughts of heavy snow, and ease the burden on his heart and shoulders of shoveling a driveway and cleaning the car of the nasty precipitation so prevalent in the cold Canadian winter.

Michael's car was a Toyota Corolla. In fact his last few cars were Toyota Corollas. They had all the features he wanted and were reliable, practical and economical. Whenever he bought a new car every five or six years or so as a replacement, Toyota had improved the model while keeping the price increase in line with inflation. It was quite a feat to provide more for less, especially now-a-days when many commercial enterprises were charging more for the same, more for less, or the same for less. Michael noticed some suppliers of Wild Rice had performed this magic trick: the price stayed the same—but the package was new and improved to contain less.

But Toyota, a Japanese company, and now the largest auto manufacturer in the world, bigger even than the US companies that used to own the road, seemed to get it right. It now dominated the highways and byways, and was the champion that everyone wanted to challenge: take a jab at and knock down. Toyota had done such a good job with the Corolla that one could hardly feel the road while driving—a feature favored by some in a car—but certainly not in condoms! Due to safety reasons, Michael especially liked the Corolla. No self respecting thief or joy-rider would ever be caught dead stealing a Corolla, and thus Michael felt secure that wherever he went or parked, it was safe.

There was a time however, when Japan was allied with the Nazis. This occurred in the last big one, perhaps because the inhabitants of the land of the rising sun had three things in common with the black shirts: orderliness, obedience, and attention to detail. Though things made in Japan were many years ago considered junk, not so for the centre of the axis that spoke to the wheel of industry much sooner after the war.

That the products manufactured in Japan were of poor quality was a commonly held belief in Canada way back when Michael was in grade school. He remembered a school trip to the ROM (Royal Ontario Museum) in Toronto in grade 5 or 6. In that regal edifice of stately stone, where mummies and dinosaurs are on display (literally speaking and not as a reference to the royal family) there is a large wooden totem pole in the middle of the marble staircase that spans three flights, on which artistic indigenous artifact were inscribed the words, probably etched by some young prankster, "*Made in Japan.*" When someone in the class noticed that the big native phallic symbol was deigned to be fabricated in Japan, the whole class broke into laughter after it was pointed out and someone shouted: "*what junk!*"

With no disrespect to the great people of all races, although indigenous people may refer to a whole bunch of races—one must be very careful in the use of the term "race," as well as "nationality," because they are not clear legal terms of art and consequently confusing. In law, one must always be wary and leery of opening up the floodgates, for like *Pandora's Box*, one never knows what chocolate will be pulled out if the thumb is stuck into the wrong place, do they? The dividing line between races is at best sketchy, and at worst asinine!

Michael learned to take issue with any doctrine or dogma, the more so in direct proportion to the degree of certainty professed by the propagators. People have been conditioned in homogeneity as advertised to "*rather fight than switch.*" It matters not whether one would "*walk a mile for a camel*"—"hey buddy, you're in the wrong continent!" or "*Winston tastes good like a cigarette should*"—homosexuality is now legal in Canada.

There was a famous House of Lords legal decision, the House of Lords in Westminster, England, being until recently the highest court of appeal in Canada, which held "one cannot *approbate* and *reprobate* in the same breath." This just goes to show how elevated the law deities are above the regular *suck* and *blow* vernacular of the street person. But while "fuck," "fornication" or "coitus," but not "colitis," may smell the same, the average Joe Blow or Sheila in Canada understands and uses "fuck" all the frigging time for emphasis, so much so that no one except the dogmatic doctrinal pushers of restricting and disempowering propaganda which is pornographic in its pure perversity really give a shit about such fucking nonsense!

It might not have been too long ago that the makers of totems were in some square circles religiously viewed as taboo. Was it due to envy or jealousy that such natural, large, hard, erect phallic symbols caused burning hostility to erupt without climax? One need only point to history for absolution: it provides ample examples of burning and ardent desire to quash debate. But so as not to approbate and reprobate in the same breath, the lovers of the pagan wooden pole and those who worship the man on the wooden cross must be forgiven, for as Jesus said: "they know not what they do."

Speaking of cars, the first car that the Rice family bought was a used 1960 *Pontiac Parisienne*, initially for Abe, and it was the car in which Michael learned how to drive. As his first car, he loved it like everyone loves their first something or other—like the first beer of the day is always the best. (Perhaps excluded from this generalization would be sex, because Hyman can be a jealous and hurtful deity.)

And the car was a car when cars were still noble mechanical iron beasts, not computerized commodities. It had bench seats, and was so large that it floated along the road like a boat going, lo and behold, miles per hour. Michael would have loved to have sex in it, it was big enough, but his years were still too little. At the time he had no idea that "Parisienne" referred to Paris, which is the city of love, and thus would have made having sex in the car even more romantic. Such ignorance of cultural nuances, punctilios, or what a lawyer might call niceties, is but one example of the handicaps that children of immigrants must contend with—such children not being able to afford the opportunity to even learn the game of golf so as to be on par with the non-immigrant kids when it comes to being culturally conversant.

Michael recalled how he, the little eager, well-liked brainy kid, would be confounded by linguistic conundrums, but back in those days kids were tough, and the use of torture and physical punishment was still legal for teachers, especially for the sadist "discipline freaks." No one had ADD or ADHD back then—they were yet to be invented or made up! Sure some kids were naturally more enthusiastic, while others paid little attention in class—that's how it was! There was no army of social workers, special needs teachers, or psychologists looking for work and mining the fields for more work.

Things in the nostalgic *Good Old Days* were much more normal and sane. For example, goalies in the game that Canada is known for, being hockey and perhaps lacrosse, wore no masks so they could see the puck better. Goalies were real men back then—brave heroes—although they might have looked more like mummies with all the stitches!

One day in class, maybe in grade 5, the teacher asked if anyone had seen what happened in the previous night's hockey game. Hockey is more than just a pastime: it plays an integral part in Canadian life and education teaching the virtues of teamwork, assault and battery.

Michael put up his hand in class eager to answer the question as he always did. He had indeed watched the game and knew that the salient point the teacher was looking for was that a star player for Toronto had been injured, and had to be carried off the ice. Back in those days they had hockey with the occasional fight, as opposed to now-a-days when there is occasional hockey between the fights, and the star players rarely got injured; so it was a big deal if a marquee player did get hurt! Michael knew exactly what happened, but during the game the announcer seemed to use words in a strange manner. Nonetheless, Michael answered as precisely as possible, his vocabulary not yet overblown with itself back then, in a clear and terse answering voice saying that so and so, the actual name of a player now forgotten, "got a *stretcher* and was carried off the ice on a *charley horse*."

The whole class, at least those paying attention, including the teacher, broke into a cacophony of laughter at this *faux pas*. The teacher, an Australian who always talked about things Australian, had for once deviated from his usual discourses on either the assorted, sordid wild beasts of the Outback or his *shtick* on "the banana benders," to actually talk about something Canadian, corrected Michael: "No, the hockey player got a *charley horse* and was carried off on a *stretcher*."

Michael then recalled that those were the words that the announcer had if fact used, but it made less sense than how Michael had strung the words together. Did it not make more sense to call an injury a "stretcher," and a thing that can carry a person a "charley horse"? Maybe it was invented by someone named Charley! Was it a stretch of the imagination for someone to ride a *charley horse*? Kids or nymphomaniacs would love it! Think of all the laughing drug addicts! Language is such a strange creature: arbitrary, true by definition only. Little was Michael aware of the possibility that language might be so high and mighty as to actually define reality too! That is the contention of some modern philosophers, as Michael was yet to learn, as he would, during his time of higher education at the University of Waterloo still to come.

In high school at the Heights of Bathurst Secondary School in North York Jake had a girl friend whose name was Jean. They were compatible sweethearts, or so it appeared, both being friendly and down-to-earth sorts. Jean had blonde hair, but not so blond as to make her dumb. Though well figured in a more matronly sense, she was not overly plump, and she was attractive without being starkly beautiful. Jake had dark black hair and fine fair skin, being considered by many as good looking. The general consensus was that Jake and Jean would end up married to each other as they appeared, for want of a better expression, *the perfect couple.* The fact that they were both enrolled to attend the University of Waterloo upon their graduation from high school, should have clinched and consummated their relationship.

But as impious fate would have it with its groping and meddling hands and fingers, or more correctly, not have it, things did not go according to Hoyle, i.e. plan. When Tinger MacInsky moved into the famous infamous house on Irvin Street while Jake and Michael were living there, Jean left Jake, to everyone's surprise, for the Tinger.

"How could this be?" Michael thought. "Jake and Jean seemed like the perfect pair, but Tinger and Jean are so different!" Jean was earthy, motherly and not moody. Tinger was brooding, intellectual—air and fire—letting off mostly dark smoke. His skinny frame was the odd to her even rack. But yet they, Jean and Tinger, lived together, got married, and had children. Then they stayed together for quite a while until they separated and divorced—and had nervous breakdowns! Michael was not sure if they parted amicably, but that was unlikely. It was probably quite a bitter prying apart, even though the repulsion and animosity they must have felt for each other by such time should have made it easier.

Ominously, they went through what Tinger used to joke of long before as the four "M"s: Marriage, Mortgage, Monsters, and Madness. This humorous word play is cleanly a step above the lewd four "W"s: Whip it in, Whip it out, Wipe it off, and Worry! The four "M"s proved portentous, foreshadowing the wailing and gnashing of teeth by Tinger. Was it poetic justice or just a tragedy?

Does reality always trumps desire? An analysis of the rock-scissors-paper game may hold a clue to the answer of this question. The scissors cut the material of life that is sewn together by desire to make people who they are. The rock, like hard and insensitive reality, then smashes the scissors. The rock however is not bad. It does what it has to do because that is its nature—it has no choice. In reality it is just like water: it always finds its own level. Morality however, the study of desires and how people intercourse, is like language or paper, it can always be worded to suit one's purpose, and can thus wrap around and defeat the reality of the rock. And so it goes round and round—no wonder they had breakdowns!

In today's world it is no longer acceptable or *politically correct* to use the expression: "nervous breakdown." Now it must be said that someone suffers from a *condition, complex* or *syndrome,* the likes of which can only be treated by a medical professional so the profession may profit and the established system suffers no harm. The term "nervous breakdown" is preferable. When things are not put together or assembled in a manner where each component or energy is at or in its natural place or level, there has to be a breakdown so that a new order can rise up; a resurrection so to speak. Nature in its blind ruthlessness knows best, no matter what the experts or father may know or say. Unfortunately, when authority feeds its dogmatic theories to unsuspecting recipients, such *gruel* is often mistaken for nourishment, even if more often than not it is just plain hogwash or bullshit.

The final outcome of the dissolution and divorce of Tinger and Jean was that Jake and Jean, and Jake and Tinger, remained friends, but the relationship between Jean and Tinger could not be reconciled or put back together. The egg of oneness had been forever cracked, shattered and scrambled.

Looking back at it now, Michael was not sure if it was all a matter of fate. Perhaps the science of psychology could explain some things. The initial marital mash-up could be chalked up to Jean's nurturing nature, and to Tinger being someone she saw as a baby. As Jean was well-endowed in the maternal, mammary sense, she was ready to take Tinger on her lap and keep him fed a breast at a time. Even though things may have ended up badly, due to immense irreconcilable differences, Michael considered that things turned out as they had to, for those that have broken down must rebuild and restructure after the fall from the dizzying heights of marriage. At least Tinger, who might have been devastated beyond words by the whole ordeal, will not die a virgin!

And then Jake, during the latter years of university, married a skinny blond that some people classified as a bitch, who Jake subsequently divorced to later find his soul mate. He worked as a teacher, and then retired and headed off to *Lotus Land* (British Columbia). Michael however, thought that she, Jake's first wife, was pretty hot, at least the way he remembered her looking back in university. Michael was ever a gentleman preferring skinny blondes—at least as one of his types.

# 22

## HOPE, GRAMMAR, AND CAPITAL PUNISHMENT

Michael stuck his car key into the key hole and unlocked and opened his car door manually from the driver's side. The remote control was not functioning. Sometimes it worked, and at other times not. Michael wondered if somehow his "vibes" interfered with things functioning, but he only thought the chances of this being the case remote, and only some of the times. But he did think, "what a pain in the ass," because in the past both the passenger side and diver's side of cars had key holes that permitted unlocking the car manually from either side, but now that there were remote controls, one could only open the driver's side manually with the key, it being a cost saving measure to have no key hole on the passenger side. This angered Michael, because he wanted to be a gentleman and open the passenger door for any lucky little lady that might ride with him, but now it was too much work for him to have to open the door on the driver's side, unlock the car and then go around the car to open the passenger door. In effect, the malfunctioning of his remote control effectively interfered with his ability to get laid.

Michael roiled and railed that even in his lifetime, the short period from his arrival to Canada at the age of 6 years old to now, his being almost 60 years old, was like no time at all: zero years. This must be true and is verified by the fact that if one adds "0" to "6" it makes "60," and thus not so strange that the years passed like the blink of an eye in the unreality of time.

When Michael came to Canada life was simple. Things were black and white. There was classic TV with straightforward stereotyped ideal role model families like in *Father Knows Best*, and *Leave it to Beaver*. Michael initially thought that the *Beaver* was a Canadian show because beaver, the animal, is a symbol of Canada, often referred to as the "Canadian Beaver" and is on the five cent coin called a nickel. Canadians take this animal seriously and don't just give it lip service—they put their money where our mouth is. The "good old" days of black and white TV may have been a misnomer however, because there were very few blacks on TV back then—that only came with the technological advent of color. It is funny that black people can be referred to as people of color, and colored people can be referred to as blacks. It makes the whole racial thing chromatically confusing!

In regard to "*Beaver*," what a misapprehension to think that it is a cute little boy's name. The truth about subversive naming and mind control is to have the message sucked in and licked up subliminally without the consumer being aware of it being pre-plotted, planted and potted, and planned. Everyone knows what a beaver is and no apology is needed for any crassness and vulgarity used to describe such hairy critter. All true Canadians are no doubt accustomed to dialectic depravity, and if one is American, they might as well learn how to pretend to be Canadian when travelling; so here it comes.

A beaver is a soft and sometimes friendly, and at other times not so friendly, furry creature that dams the intercourse between two bodies of water when the one above wants to flow into the one below, with damn large teeth that would spread fear into the heart of any pole, if trees had a heart and a mind. Don't even mention "*beaver tails*": they are so flat and awkward. "Beaver" and "tail" have one and the same meaning in the jocular vernacular of the hockey rink. Although rumored to taste good, the tail allows the beaver not only to swim, but to play and frolic in the water. This dexterity is further demonstrated in that the beaver is at home in the water like a fish, or out of the water like a mink, or in its damn den, like a fox. But no matter what its name be, for if it were from the *Land Down Under* such strange and delightful animal might have a weird name like a duckbilled platypus. That old Shakespearean refrain is worthy of repetition: "would not a *beaver, tail, fish,* or *platypus* by any other name smell so sweet"?

From the time of the early sixties to now, from the the two "K"s: Kennedy and Khrushchev, when young boys drilled in school to prepare for the really big one, the big and possibly last one, "number 3," where the specter of combining number 1 and 2 with the number 3 of nauseous projectile vomiting from the giant mushroom while not magical, still hangs over all heads like a cloud of questions. But now is the time of HOPE, that Harper, Obama and Putin won't apply Einstein's atomic theory, for from the time of KK to HOPE the progression has been along the eight fold path of enlightenment through 8 tracks, V8's, crazy 8's and *Eight is Enough*. But annihilation is no joke even if all living things by definition must die. The learned opinion is that dying is better done a little at a time, not all at once! There needs to be a witness to make an event's occurrence a reality by perception and announcing its passing, or else it would be like one hand clapping. It would not be right if there was no one left to mourn, lament and grieve, and say the appropriate prayers. Think of all the goodies, candies and chocolates that would go to waste!

What happened to Wendy? She was left dangling like a participle; but English is a language where one doesn't need to know grammar to speak adequately, not like Spanish where grammar is king, so there is really no point in knowing what a *dangling participle* is. Michael learned Spanish grammar to help him understand the language spoken in Cuba in his multiple trips to such isle over the last ten years or so.

Michael learned that in Spanish the rules are always followed, while in English they are not. The worn out expression that "there is an exception to every rule" when it comes to English will not be used, because it is a trite cliché. The amazing thing is that there are rules at all if there is an exception to every rule, for how without rules can anything make sense and be consistent and predictable? It is only a crazy person that believes everything they perceive, feel and think, so how can one really know if they are right when they think something is an exception or a rule? If one *is* sure, is that a sure sign that they *are* crazy?

A lot of information can be gleaned about a culture or a country by the way it inflicts capital punishment on its own population. "Capital" as used here does not refer to money or assets. The infliction of that type of punishment is called *taxation*, which some "non bleeding-heart non-liberal types" consider a punishment *worse* than death. Nor is "capital" used here to mean a city where the seat of government is situated. Washington DC is proof that this type of capital can depreciate greatly. It is the execution of the word of a duly constituted court of law to terminate someone's contract with life upon a just and thorough judicial determination in consideration of only the most serious and heinous breach of the code of conduct that precipitates such need for extinguishment that is the subject of the present inquiry . The question is: how does a race, culture, society or country legally kill someone for which in a country like Canada the poor plebe who cannot afford a good tax lawyer has to pay?

Some jokingly say that humankind has no right to take the life of one of its own because it would be neither kind or humane—and possibly repulsive—although not to the extent of cannibalism or incest! Is it not the purview and bailiwick of nature to determine and snub out being so naturally, efficiently and without a care? Why do humans race to try and improve and compete with Mother Nature in what she does so perfectly well? The jurisdiction of the state does not apply to Mother Nature, but *law*, which is the judicial arm of the state, does take notice, and tries to imitate, albeit poorly and never perfectly, as history has so often demonstrated.

But lawyers, they who practice law, are hypocrites. They call an occurrence of nature an *"Act of God,"* and thus the insurance company does not have to pay, even though all the while the greedy insurer smilingly collected payments pursuant to a contract that was indecipherable! That's fucking sucking and blowing in the same breath! No one had to prove the existence of God in a court of law! Someone once tried, but they called it a "monkey trial"!

Judges have a trick up their sleeve which is analogous to the sleight of hand used by "creative" accountants, and the judges' "fudge factor" is called taking "judicial notice," in a court of law. One may be shocked at this revelation which seems neither judicious nor biblical, but is more a case of *monkey brain mash* or *The Three Wise Monkeys.* But for god's sake, why did the creationists lose that famous "Monkey Trial"? When the judges pronounced the sentence, it was really premeditated and predicated on the phrase: *"Act of God"*—not a sentence but a clause and not even a *cause célèbre*! All that needs to be said is that accountants and lawyers go well together. While accountants fudge numbers, and lawyers milk files, they are deliciously rewarded together, *"yum, yum... chocolate!"*

But to continue the inquiry into different languages and different grammars, and the pronouncement of sentences, and the ending of life by the statement of the governing state, one may ask which influenced what? Did language and grammar come first, and then influence the state, and thus the manner in which terminating sentences were metered out in their final punctuation—or did the race, state, culture, people, nationality, country or whatever one wants to call it, choose the means of meaning, i.e. language and grammar, and did this then result in the manner in which capital punishment was meted out? One might consider this a trivial point, a matter of splitting hairs, but no one was ever killed by split hairs, but rather by splitting the head or severing it from the body.

A group in power exerts the lawful modes of extermination by fiat, statute, precedent, custom, or whatever means they can manufacture or muster. The more tried and ancient methods of stoning and crucifixion of the Jews and Romans respectively have been spoken of. Now, the dangling participle which was left dangling is a construct of English grammar, and this method or mode, dangling, or commonly called "hanging," was preferred in England, the country where the language, English, originated, and it was sure a crowd pleaser, most enjoying the suspense and marveling at the spectacular cathartic display. Of course, by due course, hanging carried over into Canada, as an English speaking colony.

In the United States where English is also spoken, but a modified, shortened and more sensible version—thank you American know how—called "American English," some states in that great united beneath Canada, elected the electric chair as their current mode of execution, which shocked a few people, but that is how democracy works in its great utility and power. Other states in Uncle Sam's turf went for lethal injection, a nod to the *knowhow* and technical achievements of the *Great United,* demonstrating the prominence and predominance of the drug and chemical companies. Some states retained good old-fashioned dangling on a rope by the neck to death, which might be shocking to some as they are no longer colonies of Great Britain.

Please recall that Americans call the war where their ancestors threw a tea party and moved their greenbacks to Washington the "War of Independence" while the Brits call it the "American Revolution," but is this not all words and semantics? Yes, but some say words are "worth fighting for!" And is not *the pen mightier than the sword?* In the beginning there was the word that did all the creating which then caused the Tower of Babel to fall and everyone to blab and blabber. The word was the root all wars and conflict, and thus one may be led into temptation and conclude that *grammar led to the means of all murder!*

In France where the people took matters into their own hands with a royal beheading befitting any world-class nation, they did not have a "war of independence" but rather a "revolution," because it would be crazy to battle for independence against one's self, and also they did not speak English, but in the turning tides of tyranny, or revolution of heads, the French so cultured and elegant, but some may say lacking in good old know how, went from royal to mundane, from monarchy to mob, and made a clean cut, their *modus operandi, de rigueur,* befitting such fine culinary craftiness, was of course the clean chop and swift silent slice of the guillotine, *voila!*

And the Spanish, whose colonies rivaled hail Britannica, but whose ships were too slow when weighed down with all that plundered and conquested gold, sure had the *drek* kicked out of them by Drake. But in Canada, or more precisely the

Province of Ontario, because education is a provincial matter as dictated by the British Colonial Office when Canada confederated, little is taught about the inquiring catholic kings, and their love of etiquette and ritual, so inquisitive of Jews and Moors and all people indigenous, whether in the old world or the brave new world—why there is a distinction at all between worlds is unknown as both worlds were presumably created at the same time and by the same word—chose with altruistic, selfless sacrifice to send varied races and peoples to a far better world that was neither old or new, but timeless, with the courtly quality of being considerate, chivalrous and caring enough to baptize them first. And it was probably by the end of the sword, or decapitation by the razor sharp blade of the sword that so many met their end. Now, not any hack could do that with one stoke—and castration by the use of Flamenco clackers is probably slow, unproven and uncertain, and assuredly noisy and irritating.

"What has the Spanish method of mortality got to do with language?" one may ask—to which may be replied: "Spanish speakers, no matter what the color of their yoke, are referred to as *Latinos*, or *Latinas*, depending on their gender, which is no doubt based on the fact that the language they speak is a derivation of Latin. Now who spoke Latin? The Romans of course were the speakers of that once catholic language."

"But the Romans crucified, and not the Spanish," one may say in rebuttal.

Yes, but that is a half truth, which in wisdom is more dangerous that an outright lie. All one needs to do is look at the sword, the Spanish sword: does it not form a cross, and was not the cross emblematic of Spain, viz. the sails of their galleons and shields? So, did language lead to the means of extermination, or did the mode of making one "*no more*" precede the lingo? It's a bit more difficult to determine than whether to use a fork or spoon, isn't it?

# 23

## THE ORIGINAL THURSDAY NIGHT MADNESS

Almost all the characters living in the house on Irvin St. in Kitchener while Michael attended second year at the University of Waterloo have now been introduced. There was Michael of course; and Jake, Tinger, Gary, and one other notable person, D'Arcy Deveus. Rest assured that matters pertaining to him will be illuminated. No words will be spared, nor sparsely sprinkled in the quest for truth, the whole truth, and nothing but the truth.

With the care reserved for hand feeding an infant, every grubby detail will be passed on, like a mother bird feeding her hatchlings directly, mouth to mouth, without an intermediary, interpreter or meddler, until every spoonful, every drop and morsel of such transcendental dripping is transmitted, to ensure that every kernel is germinated, that all grain is sprouted, and that each nut is cracked open and unshelled.

Here then is the tale of the young men that drank too much and smoked too much, and thought they were enlightened with the Dionysian joy of oneness by their Apollonian affinity for analyzing. The highlighted night in question was called "The Original Thursday Night Madness" because it first occurred on a Thursday night, and is deserving of being preceded by a definite article.

Along with the human cast of characters hereinbefore detailed, who by querying objective categorization could by behavior be classified as animals: laughing hyenas, manic monkeys, babbling baboons or spiritual squirrels; Cherry Herring was Ouzoing into the Metaxacated minds in slow Southern Comfort style without regard to the winey warnings of the religiously drunk Beaujolais Superior so that even the feel-good Scotch did not fear to share his acquired taste indiscriminately. The self-satisfied mix of mind and spirits led to the nix of any stirrings of reality with *feel no pain* severance.

In hunger of the looming munchies, Gary highly heated a pot full of cooking oil on top of the electric stove to the maximum, as if he had set the controls on the range to the heart of the sun, to fry some fabulous fries for appeasing the appetite of the merry, alcoholated mirthers. But as intoxication dulls the wits, and Gary's needed no whittling, when the basket of fries was submerged into the smoking boiling oil there erupted with a great "whoosh" a blazing bonfire of devilish size in the middle of the kitchen, there and then on Irvin St. in downtown Kitchener! The drunken revelers looked on gawking, goo goo eyed red, mesmerized by the byzantine flames dancing like a scared scarecrow ablaze!

Stunned shit faced stupid youth needs no excuse and knows no danger when it comes stoned faced, face to face, with ferocious flames of fire, and Michael wondered how they were now going to cook the fries, as it might be too dangerous? No matter what Gary did he could not put out the fire, for the oil had ignited and it danced ever higher and higher, like the revelers pranced entranced by the pulsating pyre!

But lo and behold, just like in a movie where the cavalry arrives at the last minute to save the day, the man living next door, who was a normal person with a real job, came in with a fire extinguisher and put out the flames. He did not need to admonish the partiers, for they being in the process of receiving a university education, knew or ought to have known that they were being fucking stupid by getting so wasted and placing themselves in harm's way, but they must be forgiven for they were hungry and did not know the properties of oil when heat is applied, nor could they be expected to understand the laws of physics in their overtly over-intoxicated, happily drunken delirium. Still the neighbor, Lester, who had good manners, was man enough to pretend it was funny, and sat down and had a beer with the boys in his blue-collared way. Michael thought he was OK, but now Michael definitely knew that no fries would be fried.

And so this night of multiple mixing of drinks, and drinking an amazing amount, became known and referred to by the tenants of that house on Irvin Street as "The Original Thursday Night Madness"—and was thoroughly enjoyed by all!

It just goes to show that sometimes one just *had* to be there to fully understand and appreciate the feelings and sentiments shared by those that were *there*, but is it not the mind, and the manner in which it mediates and meditates that provides magnitude to an event? Luster, or in short, lust, is in the eye of the beholder, and whether something shines bright or is dull, or whether it is big or small, is relative to the size of the hole one tries to cram or shove it into.

But Thursday night *is* a great night for partying because no true and righteous follower of Dionysian frivolous drunken festivities can wait until Friday to get wasted and fully fucked up, so the original Thursday night that almost brought the house down in ardent embers of burning brotherhood must be honored and revered with ritual homage seminally (i.e. weekly and religiously) with fervent ardor on each succeeding same named day for such sake and in such name! And that night was ranked mighty high in the minds of the partakers, and possibly made or broke the *Akashic Record*, even if such drastic drinking leaves one limp and unexcited pursuant to this sober reporting of the same. One *just* had to be there!

# 24

---

# THE VILLAIN,
# D'ARCY DEVEUS?

One might believe that there is no such a thing as a villain, for that is a moral or normative determinative found in fiction only where stories have plots. Michael's tortuous mental terrain of unacceptable actions postulated based on D'Arcy's transformation from friend to foe will be delved into in detail. Soon the knowledge of what is not fair in love and law (and the entry and admission thereto) will be revealed, as will the *sine qua non* that fornication with your best friend's *fräulein* is definitively *verboten*, and a rotten thing to do, even outside the state of Denmark!

What "is to be" should not be capriciously bantered about so as to prematurely come to the climax of the pertinent part of the intricate, entangled and enticing tale of Michael, his life, women and woes, with accidental and inadvertent foreplay that got out of hand before the scene was laid, or the bed was made. It is generally not a good idea to put the chicken before the horse, count the eggs before they're fertilized, or let the cat out of the bag. Suffice it to say that the trembling hands of fate shake in laughter at man's and some women's folly at adherence to fickle fidelity whether high or not, and in any season or stage of life.

Michael recalled re-encountering Wendy at a coffee shop at the University of Waterloo where they again talked, but now soberly and clear-headedly, as if they were old friends and joked, and Michael was post and past Hilda. And a funny thing happened: Michael discovered that they were both in the same class, Greek Culture, but because he was yet to attend in over a month, he was ignorant of the fact. As two young, gay and happy heterosexuals habituated to smiling and laughing they laughed about it! Back then, Michael did not mind being behind or having to come from behind to pull up from the rear, for he knew that he could ram and cram the full load of the interesting course into his head, and discharge his duties as a student through an "all nighter." Greek culture had happened so long ago; it would not change before he got around to stimulating his mind with it, to grow and harden his intellect with the ancient classical knowledge springing forth from the strong erected pillars and columns of such arcane and erudite wisdom and architecture.

Michael told Wendy that he found her more attractive than Hilda, which was actually quite a good line. Michael however, was not seduced by Wendy's loveliness, for he knew that Platonic love was the highest love of all—having been high and studying Plato in his first year. He also knew that truth is beauty, and beauty is truth, and that was all he needed to know if he could express it in at least fifty words on an essay or exam. No—it was Wendy's infectious, inquisitive, intelligent, fun, bubbly, party loving personality and her love of hours and hours of discoursing that attracted Michael and turned him on—and it was her good looks and great body that allowed him to want go out and be seen in public with her.

They, Michael and Wendy, began to spend a lot of time together: laughing together, drinking together, getting high on life together, conjugating the happy tenses of life's grammar of young and eager love, engaging in the joys of unlocked and unwed nuptials talking endlessly, earnestly, and eagerly about the unsolvable and insolvable questions in life like: "Does God or god exist?"

They had fun having and making fun, but as it always happens, or had always happened, fate has fun and then fucks one, and all the fealties, fondling, phallic sizing, and fornicating become but faint, fading almost foreign fragments of forgetfulness. Desire raging like a fire always consumes itself. The once flaming and smoldering embers then turn to cold ashes and dust crushable to naught—only to be rekindled again by more desire—going in circles like a wheel on a journey around a round orb. So without end does fate conspire!

Michael met D'Arcy in his first year at Waterloo where they both found themselves in the same philosophy class. D'Arcy was from the nation's capital, son of a military man and a mother. He was of sturdy stature and average height, and carried the demeanor of "*I am a people person*" persona strongly on the square shoulders of his brown tweed sports jacket. Some saw him as acutely handsome with his captivatingly blue, blue eyes, set like two precious gems shining from his rugged but smooth face and sandy brown, Robert Redford hair. Michael did not initially make a judgment on D'Arcy's appearance but was instead drawn in, lulled and lured by the sound of Darcy's inquisitive, assured elocution. But in due course, Michael discerned that D'Arcy had the ability to bait and hook the catch, to open the latch and get into the snatch when he turned on the charm, like in that famous bilious adolescent poem song: *"Barnacle Bill the Sailor."* A few verses follow:

*BARNACLE BILL THE SAILOR (sung to its well-known tune)*

*"Who's that knocking at my door? Who's that knocking at my door?" said the fair and young maiden.*
*"Who's that knocking at my door? Who's that knocking at my door?" said the fair and young maiden.*
*"Open the door and lay on the floor!" said Barnacle Bill the Sailor.*
*"Open the door and lay on the floor!" said Barnacle Bill the Sailor.*

*"What's the thing between your legs? What's that thing between your legs?" said the fair and young maiden.*
*"What's the thing between your legs? What's that thing between your legs?" said the fair and young maiden.*
*"That's my cock to pick your lock!" said Barnacle Bill the Sailor.*
*"That's my cock to pick your lock!" said Barnacle Bill the Sailor.*

*"What if we should have a child? What is we should have a child?" said the fair and young maiden.*
*"What if we should have a child? What is we should have a child?" said the fair and young maiden.*
*"We'll dig a ditch and bury the bitch!" said Barnacle Bill the sailor.*
*"We'll dig a ditch and bury the bitch!" said Barnacle Bill the sailor.*
*And so on...*

Michael and D'Arcy were two young adult heterosexuals in heat, but they had more than that in common. They both liked to philosophize, pontificate and postulate while imbibing intoxicating fermented liquid formulations. D'Arcy's supposed slant being apparently to the Marxist left, while Michael's was more to the abstract roundness of a question mark and the echo-like laugh of knowing mocking mirth—they were both extroverted types!

Michael admired Darcy's ability to score in the beaver tail full contact league where Michael himself, being cute and physically trim, was no slouch or sloth either. Although unsure of D'Arcy's amplitude, Michael knew that he was no match when it came to frequency. D'Arcy had it in his heart to share the spoils of his carnal conquests now and then, for Michael vaguely recalled one such offer, which Michael might have even accepted if it were not politically incorrect to do so—and if the vanquished were not so varnished in spirits so as to be unable to provide informed consent to further shellacking. But such are the forms that young men's fancy takes; and no formal course in, or edict of etiquette, is going to dictate otherwise, whether provincial, federal or municipal, and whether stated imperatively or implied, directly or indirectly.

Michael was happy with the friendship for he was a trusting, happy little tipsy hippie philosopher in blissful and carelessly easy higher education doing what came naturally to him— imbibing and inhaling life and love's immutable inspirations and exhaling—and singing melodic and rhythmic incantations in self-satisfied stokes of hazy, smoky self.

And it so happened that D'Arcy and Michael decided to major in Philosophy in second year at Waterloo, and they co-rented along with the other tenants aforementioned that fabulously famous house on Irvin Street. They both became executives of The Philosophy Undergraduate Association (The PUA) which granted them the rights and privileges to an office with the other executives on campus, where they philosophized about life and all other matters they could do so over, overdoing it, including existence, which when concretely deconstructed was but an abstract, artificial edifice structured by linguistics and lubrication of the tongue that made the words flow.

And then Michael and Wendy became an item, and fornicated with fidelity while Deveus, D'Arcy forayed into the fecund fields of Kitchener and Waterloo to plunder pussy. And one day, Michael, who still naïve—though book-smart but not street-smart—got a taste of things to come, not Primo or hydroponic for that might have been nice, but ominous foreshadowing. Michael realized that when D'Arcy was bad mouthing someone towards who he, D'Arcy, appeared to be a friend, that he, D'Arcy, was acting duplicitously, and Michael thought: "he, D'Arcy, could be doing the same with me and be bad mouthing me behind my back—all the while appearing to be my friend—for even if people are not ruled by principles, they are governed by patterns"—and the erection, elevation and expansion, in Michael's mind, of the possibility that he was being used to a probability, saddened and hurt him, for D'Arcy had come on as a true friend. He even told Michael so several times! Michael would later in hindsight (which is 20/20), be able to see this matter for what it was, analyzed legally. D'Arcy's credibility had been impugned by his inconsistent statements, and thus all his assertions would have to be weighed to determine how much credence should be given to them.

It is quite interesting how the conceptions and beliefs forged in the hearth of the mind, with no metal edge, can inflict pain that is quite real... but philosophy in her beauty of leading one to the revelation of the ugly naked truth can be hard-edged and steely cold, lacking regard for all the wants or cares of anyone in her way of applying the universal principle to the particular instance: by showing utter disregard for an individual's needs and desires!

Now how many times has one thought someone else to be their friend, a true best friend, having drank and gotten drunk from the same cup, having smoked from the same chillum;

even indulging in probing analysis together—but not physi-cally—sharing virtues, values, virility and sometimes viruses, to have it then turn out that they misconceived and misconstrued the manifestation of motions meant to manipulate rather than being Philadelphia-bound to the city of *brotherly love*. Perhaps Philadelphia was the key, for all have no doubt heard about Philadelphia lawyers, meaning exploitation, which is what some lawyers and all gold diggers do. In a city of brotherly love exploitation is all the more difficult to accept because of its jux-taposed incongruence and contrast to what is expected.

And after some time of seeming serenity, it so happened that D'Arcy's desired goal was to get into law school, but not so for Michael who had read Dickens, and thought that the law was an animal begat by cross-species coitus meant to carry people's burdens and loads, namely an ass, or "arse" if you prefer the queen's tongue. Michael was wary and had no appetite for cunning linguistics when it came to probing loopholes or other forms of *a posteriori logic*, nor did he want to overly distend himself and possibly pull a muscle to cover his own behind, which lawyers are noted for. Additionally, the work involved in the schooling of law would likely be prohibitive of procrastina-tion, and Michael preferred the reality and physicality of the *skirt chase* to the flimsy, disposable and exhausting nature of the *paper chase*. Even though Michael lacked the burning itch or fire that could be caused by unprotected sex, he could not resist the sweet seductive singing of bar-hood, barrister-being and all its solicitations, not to mention the ensuing perceived prestige, plus the bonus of bulging, bulbous, billability!

After Michael wrote the LSAT (Law School Admission Test) on the coaxing of D'Arcy—and scored very high—the thought of grandiose barrister-mania enshrined itself into the constitution of Michael's consciousness without dereliction, and his previous predilection and preference for philosophi-cal professor status *"poofed"* into thin air like passing puffs of a panoramic phantasmagoria. And so whether a pipe full of pot was a prerequisite for a deliciously delusional desire of monetary materialization through unmitigated machinations was a moot and academic point as it was no longer hypothetical—but at what cost! Rest assured that law school tuition was tolerable and doable back then. No large brown paper bag full of money with holes cut out for eyes was requisite to embark on the journey through such an eloquent education.

It must be stressed that it was D'Arcy, and not Michael, who always wanted to go to law school. Michael was nonchalant and philosophically flippant about such professional pursuit preferring abstract postulations; but the lure of material titillations proved too tempting and tantalizing for Michael to avoid and evade, and so he enrolled at the University of Western Ontario, which was in fact in London, Ontario, where he attended after receiving a B.A. in Philosophy from the University of Waterloo.

# 25

---

# THE BIG "V" AND
# THE LITTLE "V"

One need not be a genius to notice how furtive fate is in flipping fortunes, choosing to forget the fancy of one's desires to leave the holder thereof unfulfilled, instead cruelly showering the favor on another who had no taste for the former's favorite flavor; and the latter who did not desire, once tasting the treat finds it so sweet, gets drawn to the course, becomes dumb to say "nay," thinks it OK, and deftly disavows any prior position held.

But is not position relative, as is time—dependent on the observer, the frame of reference, direction, velocity, and rate of change? The *I Ching*, or *Book of Changes*, teaches that everything turns into its opposite, meaning in a mathematical and physical sense, in time and space, and in quantity and quality. Two objects travelling at different rates of speed starting from the same place at the same time may reunite at a different point at the same time, leading to the conclusion that all is joined. But when fate does its flip or reversal, it has done nothing at all, for the *Logical Positives*, as they were called, concluded that it does not matter if there is a different explanation for the same things, they are still the same. Shakespeare's expression of this truism however, is more poetic and rosy.

But despite all the philosophical underpinnings and mental gymnastics relating to fate, reversals and opposites, they may be but the bed of a straw man, for D'Arcy was pissed and peeved that Michael who did not want to go to law school got in and was going, and he, D'Arcy, who wanted to, was not, and things changed from that time on, and not for the better!

Jealousy is not a judicious attribute. No one wants to face the wrath of a woman scorned. What happened with the two friends, D'Arcy and Michael, who at one time were like brothers? They were by the flames of fate unfurled torn apart by a jealous mistress, the lady holding the balance in her bared arms. She without sight or seeing, "*Señorita Law*," chose the mocking, curly haired Michael over the dashingly handsome D'Arcy, proving once again that the law is truly blind.

From that simple twist of fate, like the snapping of fingers to a Bob Dylan song, who did tell us "*the times they are a changing*"; but even the great Zimmy was not aware that the times would go so far, so fast, and so often, like a nymphomaniac at a barn dance turning to and on her opposite, and then back to and on herself again in an instant—unbelievable! D'Arcy started to go downhill, without direction. Michael went uphill, having found direction—he cut down on the smokes and consumables, and even trimmed his hair!

D'Arcy began to hit the bottle harder and more often—so frequently that he was no longer hitting but holding—and he took to wearing his pajamas (pants and tops) beneath his brown tweed sports jacket during the day when he ventured and bused to school. Michael and Wendy noticed this, and talked about his new attire which they found to be style-less and selfish, as they were fond of talking.

Perhaps some people might have viewed D'Arcy as an enlightened, indigenous Peruvian with his brightly colored, patterned night pants and *chemise*, but Michael and Wendy knew that D'Arcy was sliding down that slippery Andean slope with his lack of respect for proper attire, and his inflated philosophizing and more fervent frequent fornicating with whoever could be found, finagled and seduced were signs, cries in the dark, of a frustrated, jealous, envious man who was but a child inside, reared in strict military discipline.

Michael became more cautious of D'Arcy and cognizant of his possible insincerity for he now saw that D'Arcy had an insatiable appetite for self-aggrandizement and tearing other people down. Perhaps the increase in caution was due to Michael's being pre-law—he was trying to cover his behind—but D'Arcy, as far as Michael knew, was not of the *Sodom and Gomorrah* type! Michael could see the predator in D'Arcy's blood red lips and mesmerizing blue eyes. He imagined D'Arcy's mouth filled with the red blood of young and innocent prey—and not so young and innocent prey. But maybe the stains were there because D'Arcy drank so much red wine!

Before continuing to render an account of Wendy, Michael, D'Arcy and law school, the outcome of which has already been hinted at, it might be a good time as any to bad-mouth the non-recreational drug industry. Someone came up with the term the "military-industrial-complex" in a steely hour after the Second World War, but be warned of the "medical-pharmaceutical-marketing-axis" which is more insidious, scurrilous and vexatious still. The establishment of such evil axis leads one to believe that all the common conditions of life: old age and dying, moods and personalities, are but diseases and not a normal part of life. The average Jill or Joe is enjoined to believe the spin that the axis is on the side of right: that the drugs they have a monopoly to provide are good medicine so they can spend hard-earned taxpayer money like a goat in a whorehouse on a slew of high priced professionals, equipment and pharmaceuticals to seek and not find a cure, but instead to maintain conditions and compound prescriptions! Like drunken sailors with landlines to the pockets of poor plebes they turn on, they drink from the tap of fear on the public tab, feeling all powerful, loosey-goosey, doctored up, to fuck and fleece the poor patient, John Doe, in jaundiced, self-serving, righteous entitlement! Whether from the front, where they can be seen, or from behind, is not important, for like sailors reared in isolated conditions they just want to put it in while making believe that they are helping out, like *Little Red Riding Hoods.*

One may find this vitriol too vituperate or virulent, but it will be proven not to be jejune by way of example with a word that begins with the letter "v," which word is derived from the name of a sweet-scented, sedating root and honey of a locally grown herb, *valeriana officinalis,* producing the popular drug, probably trademarked, that terrifically tranquilizes, sooths, silences and makes smooth jangled and jagged nerves to satis- fied stillness: "valium." Sounds great, doesn't it?

Michael got his first taste of the little "v," valium, when he was in high school and probably 18 years old like the song that confuses every day says. Maybe that was also the age that Michael got his first plunge and taste of the distinguished big "V" that brings to mind oysters and clams and vulvas, when at the first breach of cross-kneed security, the "V" of virginity is forever lost.

Michael recalled that he was shaking like a leaf the first time his dipstick was oiled (unlike the Michael of later years) when he was deflowered by a pretty, trailer-park type gentile girl named Lorna. Lorna lived near the Pits of Christy on the north tip of Little Italy where Michael and his family had resided.

Like many things Michael had when he was young, she was a hand-me-down from his brother. Michael grew up in a prudish house, notwithstanding that he was not Catholic or Baptist, and his parents never talked about recreation or procreation, not being drawn towards the licentious, or perhaps having a limited vocabulary. Michael would never have thought his parents had done the deed but for the seeds that were planted and had grown into he and his brother.

But Lorna took a real shining to Michael, and he had the desire to perform the act, it having been so frequently discussed and prostrated before in exaltation and worshipped with his adolescent friends who sought to complete copulation in religious fervor, and then to boast even more fanatically about it when found, fondled and finished as if it were a competition.

Even though Michael was scared shitless and trembled scared, she was easy, young and pretty; and he was not scared of sex as much as shit, but that is for another story to be sung and not to be sullied, soiled or spoiled here. But it turned out that Lorna was so submissive and lacked what Michael's mother had called "personality" in spite of her attractive appearance and great body! Isn't it ironic that her submissiveness allowed Michael to do what he wanted, but was also the cause of his curtailing continuing to come and see her? He thus stopped having sex with her quite quickly, rather than repeatedly having sex with her and coming quickly. He had thought that sex was all he wanted and cared for, but fate had once again tempted him, bringing and building him up just to let him down and fall flat on the face of his own misapprehension.

What a strange concept that personality has anything to do with sex; but the empirical evidence just presented to fortify this position notwithstanding the mythical drive and wanton lust of horny youth cannot be overlooked. A few years after he ceased copulating with Lorna, Michael forgot how boring she was and decided to look her up. He now had experience and a few notches under his belt. Michael knew that Lorna was drawn to his appearance and attracted to him, so why should he not do a good deed, a *mitzvah*, and give her what she wanted? She was easy and pretty, making her pretty easy, and as the saying goes: "if you don't use it, you lose it."

What a surprise! When Michael got to her house she was no longer a skinny little thing, but had transformed into a beautiful woman in the prime of her life, her sexual apex, perhaps 19 or 20 years old. She had filled in proportionately perfect, or so her body appeared from the outside, with shiny, straight, flaxen blond hair flowing over her shapely shoulders. Michael was really turned on! He thought *"to hell with personality, and big deal if she was as submissive as a wet noodle—how could that have really mattered?"* while sitting beside her on the cloth covered couch in her living room in that working class neighborhood of midtown Toronto, erecting the scene of what was to come in his mind. She was ready to receive him *all the way* home!

But as fate decided to have some fun, her husband who was a big and jealous man returned home unexpectedly, and Michael skedaddled expeditiously, before even having begun disrobing, so it might have appeared they were just friends talking. Michael was glad to leave and get away unmarked and untouched. Although perhaps a tad frustrated, he could still find humor in the situation. Perhaps however, there was justice after all: he did not love the girl, and probably never would; but he would have loved to fuck her, so what could he do? Access was denied by the forces that be—the gate was closed—locked shut! The discussion was over, zipped up.

On further reflection, sadness and grayness colored Michael's world, as he intuited that she would be severely beaten, for somewhere in the bible it is written that the thought of an act is worse than the act itself. The thought that their tryst would result in her thrashing, nagged at Michael. It stuck in his gizzard, drizzling down on him obsessively like a filthy guilty shower which he was unable to cleanse or wash from his dirty mind. What could he do? Should he crucify himself? He was but a novice, essentially an innocent, in the fucking world!

Back to valiums: Michael was proof of the worn out warning at the time that smoking pot would lead to harder drugs—although all users or people with habits live in denial and will deny even this—and the fact of their denial. Although it seemed like a joke at the time that the use of certain drugs would cause people to jump out of windows believing they could fly, this was in fact proven by some scientists at the CIA, and later reaffirmed by a U.S. senate sub-committee probe.

But on second thought perhaps the scientists did not really believe they could fly, that would be counter intuitive, and really silly without wings or a jet pack—a very unscientific belief indeed! The more plausible explanation is that the scientists, being scientific, knew they would die from the fall as they were no doubt aware of the elementary law of gravity which even a dense schoolboy without a massive brain knows, but seeing the truth of all the conspiracies going on around them they became so paranoid and freaked out that they killed themselves. That wasn't said, was it? Was it?

Valium was such a perfect money maker that sales were guaranteed to skyrocket. People would be so calm that they would not get paranoid, and there would be no worries. No one would even want to sue. A user might jokingly state: "*Sue, shmoo, who me, ha, ha, ha!*"

Some might think that the effect of valium on memory would be a drawback, but it was so effective that people forgot that they could not remember, and if it feels so good, who cares? Memory was probably the root of all evil anyways: the strychnine laced apple in the garden. *Tastes good but makes you feel like shit.* And what was the effect of Valium on sex?

*"Who cares when you feel so good?"* It was probably endorsed by the Catholic Church!

Michael was experimenting with drugs in high school, and that is probably why he may have dropped out of school and not become a doctor or an engineer, but instead became a lawyer where talk, words, pleadings and motions are of prime importance. But he did have a doctor at such time, and figured out the best way to get his valium was to tell the doctor that he suffered from the symptoms listed on the bottle. He would thus be assured to get the product because doctors are so well trained—better than seals!

Michael ended up getting a prescription for 12, but he was not satisfied with so few, so he changed the number on the prescription from 12 to 42. All it took was two strokes of a pen! The "1" was turned into a "4" all so carefully in the same colored ink with the same weight of stroke. But when he returned to the pharmacist to pick up his pills, they were not prepared for him—the pharmacist was still waiting to hear back from the doctor to verify the prescription. Michael, like a little jerk took off, never to return to the same pharmacist or doctor.

What lesson did Michael learn from this? He really blew it. If he was not greedy, he could have continued to get the pills prescribed, with the amount and strength increasing as his resistance gradually rose. But now nothing—he would have to buy his pills illegally: no doctor prescribes in lots of 42! Although it is an even number it is quite odd, and would no doubt be subject to suspicion by any prudent pharmacist. What lesson did he learn? It was this. If you commit an act which might be construed as illegal make sure to do it in such a way so that no one will know. In fact, the best way to something illegal and get away with it is when each step of the process is by itself legal and there is paperwork to prove it. Michael would need a legal education to fully understand this, but he never was tempted to apply the unprincipled principle once law became his principal profession.

Is this a shocking revelation? Look at the drug and pharmaceutical companies, and organized religions. What are the two greatest causes of death and bodily harm in the world? They are of course pharmaceuticals and religion—terrorism, genocide and wars can all be subsumed under the heading of religion. Death by pharmaceuticals is in pseudo-scientific terminology statistically significant. No shit, Big Pharma knows how to manufacture some kick-ass pills!

Big Pharma has gotten more seductive and subversive in its ability to farm the hoard of humanity like cattle, never to cure but to maintain "conditions" so as to sell more and more of their products. Today a patient just doesn't take one pill, but a whole *cocktail* or cornucopia. How much does that cost and who is profiting? And "cocktail"—that could be right out of Madison Avenue! How sexy putting "cock" and "tail" together! So sleek and seductive! How profitable! No assertions or accusations are being made, but in *loving kindness,* and for fuck's sake, open your eyes, perk up your ears, and taste what's going down!

What lesson did Michael really learn from the "altered" prescription mishap? The answer previously given was in fact facetious. Michael may have done a few unethical things when he was young; and perhaps some as an adult—even though his mother admonished him for being holier than the pope—but should he not be forgiven? Is it not written that all the saints were once sinners?

Michael had a few more adventures with the little "v." One day when he had planned to go a friend's party in the north end of Toronto, while still in high school, he decided to purchase some valiums midtown. Michael knew that the pills would take about half an hour to kick in, so he popped about five times the therapeutic dose to make sure that he would feel really good. He was not into prescription drugs except for recreational use which required exceeding the recommended dose to amplify the desired effect. He was only 20 minutes drive from the party, so there was ample time to drive and arrive safely before *mother's little helpers* performed their magic and impaired his motor skills to down him out in non-caring contentment.

But just as he was leaving the house where he scored the pills, he was asked if he would drop some people off at a downtown bar. Although it was in the opposite direction he was going, and would add 15 to 20 minutes to the drive, Michael was a nice fellow, so of course he said "of course."

Everyone piled into Michael's car, and off they went southbound, and in about ten minutes the passengers were dropped off without a hitch. Michael U-turned immediately, and headed straight north towards the party knowing it would be a race to get there before the valiums kicked in. When Michael got north of midtown, but still south of where the party was, he began to notice his reaction time had slowed down: he was responding so slowly that the car kept stopping in the middle of intersections for red lights, clearly a contravention of *The Highway Traffic Act*, and possibly sufficient to merit a conviction of *dangerous driving* under the *Criminal Code of Canada*!

Although Michael was mainly focused on partying and his own pleasure, his intelligence being in the form of book smart, he decided to compensate and counter the contraindications of the sedatives he had ingested, which were the effects he sought, by driving very, very slowly and planning to stop well in advance of when required. It was clear from the thick haze that invisibly clouded his judgment that he was really downed out! When he was almost there, only a few kilometers from the party, as if in slow motion he lifted his head to see the traffic light way ahead turning red, so he put his foot to the brake as quickly as he could, which was quite slow, to slow down and stop well ahead of time as he was trying to be super-safe and cautious. Instead of coming to a full stop, he glided and smashed right into the car stopped ahead at the red light, with a big "*Bang!*"

He was so downed out he could not worry, but the instinct for self-preservation runs deep. What could he do? He was too out of it to even write! Amazingly however, Michael came up with a very bright idea. He just stayed in front seat and feigned shock!

"I'm in shock" he repeated, repeatedly, as if he was stunned and unable to do anything, which really was not far from the truth—except for the "shock" part. It probably worked; he got no ticket, nor was he charged with any offence. But back in the days before *zero tolerance* and political correctness, people were much more reasonable.

Michael was fortunate. The car he hit was a big old car full of black people. Looking back at it now, Michael seemed to recall that the occupants of the car that he ran into appeared to be a lot more scared than he was. Perhaps they did not have the pleasure to be downed out like him. He was the middle classed white boy—circumcision aside—but no one could see that! The police might have thought: "What right did those black people have stopping in front of the cute, young, white boy with the innocent baby face sporting a sports jacket? Surely they had stopped abruptly creating a situation of *force majeure*."

Michael did not have the where-with-all to inquire about the well-being of the people he hit in his super-sedated state, nor would such a course of inquiry be in accord with his feigned shock. Why should he look a gift horse in the mouth? Perhaps the occupants of the car he hit were in the country illegally. He did not know.

All the paperwork was taken care of in fairly short order. The whole process from smash to finish seemed to Michael to take less than an hour. There was still a party to attend to. The car was drivable, even though the front end looked like an accordion, so he asked the tow truck driver to tow his car and him to the party. Michael knew he was in no condition to operate any equipment at all!

Michael arrived at the party house in the north end of the city, North York, where his good buddy, Bob, resided with his parents who were out of town for the weekend. The tow truck pulled up in front of the house with Michael's car dragging behind, front end off the ground like a fish being hauled in. Michael was excited to finally arrive at the party so he could have a few drinks, or whatever was around, but mostly to tell everyone about the accident and how smart he was to plead shock and get off scot-free. But why were there no cars parked around the house? Had everyone planned to get so totally shit-faced and not drive?

Michael sauntered to the side door of the bungalow, and knocked on the door. No lights were on and there was no music playing. The valium allowed Michael to notice these things, but not to care too much about the answer.

A light soon came on. Bob slowly opened the door. "What happened?" Michael asked. "Didn't anyone show up for the party?"

"What?" Bob said in a deep voice while rubbing an eye. "What—Oh, the party's over. Everybody's gone home."

"So early—not much of a party was it, eh?" was Michael's chipper retort. Bob did not respond. Michael continued: "What time is it?"

"It's around 3 o'clock," said Bob.

"I can't believe it! I thought it was around midnight—go figure!" Michael exclaimed as he shook his head, obviously pleased that time had demonstrated its relativity. Even as events dilated, it had rocketed by! "Are you still up to party?" he asked his friend.

"Twist my arm." Bob replied while lifting and moving his clenched right hand slowly in the arc of a hook until the clenched fist touched Michael's left shoulder. Michael grabbed

Bob's closed hand from his shoulder, and rotated it 90 degrees. Both friends laughed.

Michael spoke to the tow truck driver who then unhitched Michael's car and left it parked in front of the house. As Michael walked back towards the house he reflected on how cool it was to arrive at the party in a tow truck, and how lucky he was to be feeling so good. Those were sure the good ole *"happy days."*

So Michael and his buddy Bob partied through the not so wee hours of the morning anymore. They made it to "first light" as the sun kissed the green grass of the fair city "good morning" with a soft red hue, followed by gentle rays of warm gold. Michael slept like a baby on the couch in the basement, his mind empty of thoughts and filled only with the contented feeling of a purring sleeping cat, stretched out cozy under a sleeping bag. The little "v" had tucked Michael in nicely!

Michael had another memorable experience with the little "v" in his early days at the University of Waterloo. He had gone to see the famously absurd play, *Waiting for Godot*, by Samuel Beckett, about nothing, waiting around, and discussing what was worse: thinking or doing. The play doesn't make any sense—that it is why it is called *absurd*! Michael had decided to take some valium to enjoy the evening more. It must have been boring, because he fell asleep right away, sleeping through the whole performance, only to be woken up by the applause at the end, when he like everyone else got up and left.

One might think that Michael felt angry or cheated because he had paid good money to see a play that he saw none of; but on the contrary he was very happy and artistically satisfied. His going to the theatre and sleeping through the entire production, only to awake once it was over, seemed to Michael a much greater work of art than the play itself could ever be. It was real life art, more absurd and meaninglessness than the play he went to see. As it passed by unseen and unheard, he was present. How absurd!

How was Michael able to break the spell of the perfectly engineered little "v," and avoid passing his whole life under its influence, happy and carefree, if not particularly productive? Some might think that religion is the answer (particularly those suffering from psychosis); but that was not how.

Others may say that Michael was lucky; but luck is much like miracles: impossible in a universe governed by law and order; and like religion and dreams, simply semantics or an exhibition of wish fulfillment. The answer, which one might find funny or cute, a sort of "Michael answer," is ironic and points to how matters work in reverse in this simple but complex world.

It was Michael's propensity to anxiety and neurosis that saved him from becoming addicted to a drug that was meant to treat the condition that saved him from its sheep in wolves' clothing ravages. Michael was neurotic about knowing the time, just like Freud, whose theories though popular should have been specific to Vienna, the big city centre of empire stress. Michael kept forgetting what time it was under the downing influence of valium, and would have to ask every minute what time it was. He did however remember that he could not remember, and that he had to keep asking what the time was. The memory of this so irked and riled him, although not when under the influence of the little "v," that he resolved to be able to remember what time it was all the time, and not have to keep asking—so he stopped valium.

But because he believed in balance, at least on a lip service level, he upped his intake of alcohol and partook more frequently in other mind-numbing or stimulating substances; but no more pharmaceuticals for the reformed young man! He was now one step further down the circular road of life, and had moved up a rung on the ladder of learning that life's higher lessons are available to all that stray from the long and winding road.

Though appearing incredible, this story is awesome and true. Often, the most incredible things are true, while the most seemingly credible things are not, even if generally believed to be true. That is more incredible still—and a very awesome fact!

# 26

---

## WILL THERE BE BLOOD?

The study of philosophy ended uneventfully for Michael, which is not to say unenjoyably, for he was still in a seriously fun and fulfilling relationship with Wendy. He tried to be serious about studying philosophy, partying seriously with D'Arcy and philosophizing. So he graduated after three years, although having completed many of the prerequisite courses for a four year Honor's B.A. There is no need to list the courses Michael took to earn his bachelor's degree. Suffice it to say that he was well-steeped in *Queen Sophia's* teapot of conjecture from conjunction to conclusion having sipped from the wonderland of her *Mad Hatter* chalice amply and eagerly.

The summer before law school Michael stationed himself at his parents' house in North York while Wendy stayed in Kitchener in an apartment that she shared with another girl. Wendy planned to work during the summer to earn enough money to continue her undergrad studies at Waterloo. It was a good arrangement; they were but an hour away from each other by bus, train or automobile, and Michael did not have to pay rent at his parents' place.

Slowly, Michael and Wendy started to slip apart. Not really an unraveling, but more like a neglected shoelace left untied. The relationship which had once flamed with ardor and splendor now flickered ordinary and mundane, dulled and diluted, doused by the drizzle of time. So separated by space and time, Michael and Wendy drifted, each caught on their own ice floe. The fierce winter winds of passion had abated and shifted. The gentle spring thawed with warm breezes and currents. Michael and Wendy, lulled by the buzz of blooming buds and the chirping of green young twigs, let the memory of the passion which once heated the cold winter nights slip into forgetfulness— their relationship was dozing off.

Perhaps the gradual dispersion was due to the subversive subterfuge of centrifugal force as fate spun its victims like tops. The force radiated outward, spiraling, turning and diluting as it pushed from the centre, drawing and pulling to infinity—the victims falling face-down dizzy, like drunken whirling dervishes.

Wendy rented an apartment near downtown Kitchener on the second floor of a two story old red brick house accessible by a side door stairway. Michael recalled the apartment because of an incident that involved Wendy's roommate, Anne, a tall, athletic girl with short dark hair. One day when Michael was staying over he noticed a huge well-formed turd sitting trapped in the toilette which no amount of flushing could dislodge or dissuade. Although its sight disgusted Michael, he mentioned it to Wendy. They had a good laugh—it was incredible that Anne could have produced such a humongous one-piece outpouring! Would she not be embarrassed enough to do whatever was necessary to destroy the evidence proving her inside did not smell as sweet as her outside appeared?

As Michael was looking for a job in Toronto for the summer, he decided to try his hand at taxi driving, and took a two day course offered by the City. Of the about thirty or so students registered in the class, Michael spied a girl about his age that reminded him of Lorna. She was pretty enough in a trailer park sort of way: slim, well-built with straight, slightly greasy, dirty blond hair and a minor case of acne. Michael, confident by slotting her in the same pigeonhole as Lorna, thought she would be easy pickings, and he was right.

Michael and the Lorna look-a-like got together after the second class, graduation day, and went over to her place where they smoked some pot, drank some wine, and had sex. Although Michael felt good about coming to his desired end of getting into her pants, for it stroked his ego, it was all too easy— anti climactic in fact! It was the first time he fooled around on Wendy; now he realized that he loved her! He was afraid of losing her.

Although it is not strange to have sex with a stranger, and *a change can be as good as a rest*, or so goes the old adage, when one is in love all sort of excuses are made to depreciate and not appreciate sex with anyone but the loved one.

The good thing that came out of Michael's philandering and infidelity was that he now knew that he and Wendy had had a wonderful and happy relationship worth working on, that should not be taken for granted and let just fade away. When one gets what they think they really want, initially they fall into an elated manic state where they rave ecstatically and incessantly of the thing encountered. Then over time as they become used to that which has been found, they come to believe that they were always entitled to it, possessing a legal interest as if it was their province and purview. Then having had the thing for a while more, one no longer cares about caring—only to be proven wrong when they lose that which they thought they had tired of. Then the fire rekindles, burning more painfully bright than before! In such a manner, bad can be good, just as beauty can turn to ugliness, or love to hate.

Michael agonized about whether he was going to tell Wendy; and if so, what. They had not made any compacts or contracts about the rules and regulations governing their relationship. It had flowed sweetly and organically like liquid honey with no provisos, restrictions and conditions needed to be negotiated or put in place. Perhaps however, coming clean might just be the rag that could remove the rust and tarnish accumulated over time, and buff up their relationship with some new luster and shine.

Michael weaseled for words, and talked hesitatingly and tentatively to Wendy on their next meeting, as if something in him came out on its own propensity and was not planned. He downplayed the significance of the actual act, it being done because he sensed a "drifting apart." He "now knew" that they "had something worth working on, something worth saving." Framing the situation thus allowed him to evade culpability.

Wendy became emotional, no longer acting in her usual giggly manner of happy insignificance. Her face turned bright red, as if somewhere something solid inside had turned to liquid and then to gas, and had expanded and strained to escape: Wendy confessed to Michael that she had recently had sex with D'Arcy!

Michael had hoped that he had not heard correctly: "confessed" was not the best chosen verb to describe what she had done, with its religious connotations. Michael in his mind connected the dots and filled in the blanks: D'Arcy had seduced her. They were drinking and having fun as friends, and then when she was liquored up, he turned on the charm and she became helplessly captivated by his mesmerizing Paul Newman blue eyes and drawn to his magnetic blood red lips. Caught in his spell, he struck—the rest is history.

Michael said he forgave her. He realized she had no choice: no chance. She was the prey that strayed too close to D'Arcy's charismatic hook to resist. Then Wendy said that she forgave Michael for his wandering, wavering and transgression. Through *"fessing up"* and some tears they recommitted themselves to a relationship that was worth saving, that was worth having—that is how they felt!

But now, insidious fate was nipping at their heels, trying to bite at and tear off their pants. The forces of entropy, chaos, disorder and disintegration were eroding and wearing out their mutual attraction to each other, like a crowbar prying to lever them apart; but they, there and then, through what may be considered mutual wrongdoing, had righted the relationship and reset it straight, to sail on a smooth and steady course.

Perhaps there was an element of psychic or intuitive ability involved that made them dance to the same dissonant, discordant aria. Anyone can make up theories and believe them, their conjectured veracity open to vexatious debate. What can be seen, tasted and touched, that is something one can get a hold of and try to never let go of or lose—like the sweet smell of a flower.

Michael did forgive Wendy, for he knew in his mind that she was blameless, but a lamb; and that the wolf, nay more heinous than an animal that is compelled and impelled by nature, was D'Arcy, who Michael knew had with afore sight, malice and premeditation seduced Wendy, Michael's girlfriend, to "one up" Michael, who got into law school, when D'Arcy could not. He, that villain Deveus, struck secretly, covertly and under the covers, without love or thought for Wendy and what it might do to her, in lust and the sinister stabbing of "I'll get you"— something only people, not animals, could do.

Michael considered Wendy's transgression greater than his, in a purely abstract theoretical sense, for Michael had sex with but a stranger that he had just met—a meaningless momentary thing of a fling—but she did it with someone that she and Michael had at times put down and criticized, and socialized with: possibly Michael's best friend! Although Michael thought it best to just let it go, he could not let it go, because he was a man first and foremost, romantically conditioned by Hollywood movies and mores deep inside, and believed to the girth of the pith of his being that fucking your friend's girlfriend was a breach to the core, as well as not a very nice thing to do, and in the old days would have resulted in a duel to the death. Though the resentment tortured him like a painful stabbing ache, he tried to philosophize it away repeating to himself: "Well there you have it. He tried to hurt me because I got into law school and he couldn't. He was jealous, but I'm not going to let it get to me"—and Michael's nose grew...

Many cities in Southern Ontario are laid out on a grid pattern, the streets being at right angles to each other and form squares or rectangles, geometrical figures that are easy on the mind, and navigating such good streets does not lead to perdition. But then again, each city has a street that goes off on an angle, awry and askew, not heeding the orderliness of its straight-laced surveyed kin. Perhaps such routes, roads or ways had existed before the learned man came along with pencil, transit and telescope to measure, demarcate and scribe the best laid plans. They exist in all their curiosity going somewhere and make things confusing—but no doubt more interesting!

Michael had noticed that he could not grasp how Kitchener Waterloo was laid out. The same main street that went through both Kitchener and Waterloo, called King St., not Main Street as it might have been called had the corset of British colonialism not been so tight, went in a different direction in each of the said cities: north/south in one, east/west in the other; said street curving somewhere along the way and leading to confusion and loss of direction for those who did not know where they were heading, and for those who did not know where they were. But after a certain amount of time and familiarity, like when moisture reaches a saturation point precipitating rain trumpeted by thunderous clouds and flashes of lightning, so an unseen flash in the mind forms a template to understand the layout of the city all at once—one has stepped up to a new threshold!

No amount of work or effort or study will disclose or make evident when one can cross into the next level: it happens automatically, a sort of "act of nature." Lawyers would perhaps then call it an "act of god" and take judicial notice. Other people might call it a miracle. It happens if one is immersed long enough in something like learning a new language, how to play an instrument or ride a bicycle. One day it just happens!

And on such street that went on an angle in Kitchener, and confused Michael until he reached higher consciousness of the layout of streets in Kitchener Waterloo, there was a town called Breslau, which by now had been subsumed in the aforesaid metropolis of Kitchener Waterloo, and a bar named the "Loo," short for Waterloo, also meaning the "john" or washroom. The Loo might have been a dive, but not as determinatively, definitively or definitely as the Kent was.

# 27

## A LESSON IN HISTORY

Many German speaking people settled in the Kitchener region of Southern Ontario and that it is why Kitchener was called Berlin until the First World War when the name was changed to punish the enemy and metaphorically rub sour kraut into their wounds, which no doubt not only hurt feelings, but also stung and stunk! Breslau was also named after what used to be a major German city, the beautiful city of Breslau which peacefully lay on the banks of the Odra River in what was the eastern part of Germany before the end of the Second World War. After the said war the majestic and historical city appeared, as if by a miracle, in the western part of Poland. By a sleight of hand, a cheap trick, the name of the devastated city was changed from Breslau to Wroclaw. The Soviets, who not only were adept at imperialism but also cunning linguists, had by fiat proved that they could approbate and reprobate in the same breath. For those who may have forgotten, this means to suck and blow at the same time, which any moron knows is impossible in physical reality, but not impossible in political expediency, as history has repeatedly demonstrated. One cannot be sure if the city smelled the same after the corpses rotted, but the looting and pillaging helped to clean things up in a material sense. So, Breslau or Wroclaw became an old new city, or a new old city.

It's funny that even though the city had not moved in space, it changed locations to a different place: a different country. That goes to prove the very special theory of relativity as well as the string theory, which simply stated is that space (the traditional first three dimensions) will change in time (thought by some to be the fourth dimension) depending on the change of the observer: the one that controls the experiment in the laboratory of life, or the political master that pulls the strings to control daily life.

Any lawyer or philosopher knows that *"juris,"* as in jurisdiction, is a formal legal matter, and not a matter of substance, just like words and any form of thought, classification and categorization is a matter of form and not substantive reality; forms being but rules and regulations. But when by formal edict, the name Breslau was transformed from Teutonic to Slavic, to Wroclaw, this did in fact change the substantive nature of the city—it was not a mere formality!

Now Michael had for much of his life grown up under a misapprehension, which in essence is an illusion that the mind creates by conjoining or stringing together what one considers to be facts to create a theory, but in fact, such facts are usually but opinions and beliefs that are not well-founded, but which one picks and makes up to support one's conclusion which has already been reached by an emotional attachment thereto, thus making illusion something like the shade of a large tree grown from fictitious facts.

Michael's "tree of falsity" was the belief that he held until recently that Polish people were prejudiced against Jews, i.e. that they were anti-Semitic. This belief, which seemed to be founded on certain occurrences that were construed by him as facts, *was* in fact erroneous. Generalizing from the particular to the universal is fraught with difficulties: the road to hell being paved with the best intentions.

It might be an idiosynchronicity that Michael who was born in Wroclaw, formerly Breslau, was in the Town of Breslau, now part of the City of Kitchener Waterloo, where a bar named the Loo is situated, where something traumatic was to happen, but will not be divulged until after the misbegotten reasons that Michael had taken an eye for an eye approach with his misplaced prejudice of the Poles due to his misperception that the Poles possessed and practiced prejudice against his people and person, the Jews in general, and the central European Jew in particular, is analyzed.

At the onset of the Second World War Poland teemed with Jews, it being estimated that one tenth of the population of Poland at such time was Jewish, and about one third of the capital, Warsaw, saw themselves as such. Few Jews remain in what is now Poland. Most and almost all who had returned after the war have left, just like Michael's family. Poland became virtually Jew-less and Jew-free evolving into a near totally homogeneous country of Catholics, as the fact that until recently even the Pope being Polish will attest to. There has never been a Jewish Pope nor is it likely there ever will be one, notwithstanding a web site on the internet claiming the contrary.

Michael's parents worked in Silesia, which is what the area around Wroclaw had been called when it was still known as Breslau. It was an industrialized region, and Michael's parents were there because work was there, they being the workers that worked in the shops and factories of the garment industry. Back then people had to work to make a living, which is not the case in Canada today where many people believe that the government should be working for them. What a strange notion!

Michael's mother would never let Michael's father talk about Poland, and although unaware of the reason or reasons for such restriction which perhaps stemmed from resentment, it led in part to Michael's aforesaid misapprehension about the Polish people. Michael's mother should be forgiven for her sentiments. She was probably a girl of only nine when the shit, so to speak, hit the fan in Poland, and she fled the country with her family to Russia to survive. Michael did not know what happened to her during the war and in those days, because not only would *she* not, she would also not allow Michael's father to talk about Poland, period; nor did she ever even let a word about her time in Russia to be mentioned or dropped.

Was she too young to remember those years? Probably not. The mind in its efforts to protect one from bad memories, like isolating the *unwanted* in a cyst, cuts off access to such memories, buries and hides them, knotting up the bearer of the negated repressions. Michael did find out something, and that was from his uncle, his mother's oldest brother, who until recently had lived and been lucid in fact to the great age of 99 years in spite of his being a chain smoker for a time, lighting one cigarette from another, but it does help if your son is a doctor. Michael had in recent years become more interested in the history of the family.

The words Michael's uncle had used to describe Michael's mother's experience in the war were: "she did not lick honey." These words stuck in Michael's mind like a post-it ° note, and he ruminated on them like cud in one of a cow's stomachs, and not because they were spoken in Yiddish. Israel is often referred to as "the land of milk and honey," but Michael's uncle spoke in the negative, juxtaposing what did not happen to what might have in reality occurred, which was not disclosed.

Of course no one would expect war, with all its wreckage and displacement and dislocation of multitudinous contingencies to be a piece of cake, or a sweet treat, but in that statement, Michael opined, understatement was mastered. It made one wonder of all the terrors and horrors and difficulties that a girl of tender age would experience by using words that were opposite to what was most likely the case. Now, no one but a sadist wants to ponder on atrocities in detail and graphically, especially when they involve one's own mother where the bonds of love are natural and animalistic.

Michael recalled a situation disclosing the mind's natural propensity to contextualize events and occurrences from when he was practicing law and representing a client. There were allegations of sexual abuse of his client's very young son brought against his client's estranged spouse's partner that she was living with at the time after separation, in a divorce case. Such allegations when spoken of in general and abstract terms were easy to compartmentalize, and it was a piece of cake to shield oneself from their deleterious emotional effects when sheared of details. But on reading the Children's Aid Society report profuse and replete with graphic details, Michael could barely force himself to keep turning the pages in his stunned, saddened shock. Though now a seasoned professional, he could barely keep the sobs from surfacing and cracking his composure as the infinity within him connected to all life, quaked, for with such full pornographic punctuation comes the visualization of the image which was previously only abstractly perceived, but is now elevated by the creation of mental pictures into a reality that affects the responsive mechanism in the human organism and psyche.

Michael feared to tread such territory of imagination in respect of his mother and the war, for in such primordial well of darkness only the painful abyss could be reflected, and Michael preferred instead to savor the delicacy of the turn of the tongue "lick honey," which lack thereof was simply understood and not emotionally threatening; and this was a case where he did want to leave every stone unturned.

Michael's mother had been denied the chance to be a hair-dresser, her lifelong dream according to her, but not having pursued the same in later years perhaps it was just a cop out, fixing her desires on something simple and not attained, instead to become a factory worker unable to read or write, whose life had no meaning but to work, to cook, to clean, to care for the family and to tell everyone how it is or should be.

People who knew Michael's mother when she was young said she was like fire, that she had personality. And she was friendly, kind and accepting, even if strongly opinionated, and perhaps overly sensitive about being independent, and refusing to take gifts from anyone, saying "why, I'm not good enough?," questioning why anyone would even think that she was in need of anything. She didn't need anything from anyone!

Perhaps that was the voice of the young girl buried deep inside of her, inverted in adulthood and maturity, in essence being the reflection of a child's unfathomable wishing well devoid of coinage. Life's magnifying glass may burn a hole in the dark recesses deep inside where the inquiring eye cannot or does not want to see, in the opprobrious light of day with the oppressive rays of the sun.

When Michael was born in then communist Poland he was to be named after his mother's father, "Moishe," who was by then deceased, and it was an honor to be so named. Michael's brother, Abraham, was named after his father's father, or pater-nal grandfather.

The white coated doctors in the Polish hospital where Michael was born, or perhaps the bureaucrats in whatever coats they wore (no doubt bought on the black market and pos-sibly tailored by Michael's father who labored at a second job at night to earn enough money to keep an apartment which could at any time be taken over by a bureaucrat or a friend of a government official since no one worked in the day because communism did not pay, choosing instead to play poker and drink vodka at the shop, pretending to work when the commissar came to town, *oh ho,*) would not accept and register the name, Moishe, that was intended to be Michael's lifelong calling card, as it was a Jewish name, not a Christian name— Jewish names being forbidden in Communist Poland. Instead the officials and powers that be suggested the name "Michal," which thus became Michael's name, being the Polish version of Michael, easily morphing into "Mike" and "Michael."

Michael knew this story for as long as he could remember. It bothered him because he was an undisciplined believer in "freedom." Not being able to call your child an honorable name, in an honored tradition, was definitely an unreasonable limitation of freedom. It turned out that Michael liked the name Michal or Michael better than Moishe. It only goes to show that bad intentions can often lead to good results, complementing the old saying that the best intentions pave the road to you know where. Michael was embarrassed by his Jewish heritage finding it foreign, nonsensical and outdated, believing religion to be mind candy based on myths and dogma: a cause of wars, oppression and intolerance.

But Michael was still called Moishe by many people that spoke Yiddish and affectionately called "Moishela" which is a diminutive, and would be similar to Mikey in English. The truth of the matter is that Michael did not know what his parents called him. Did they call him Moishe or Michal? He had thought about this often after his parents had passed away. Funny he thought, "I know that they called me by a name and often, but I cannot remember what that name was. I cannot remember the sound of my parents calling me by my name." Funny isn't it, Michael had listened, but he did not hear. He did not hear the stone dropping into the pond, but saw only the ripples. *And ripples never come back.*

Just as Michael was denied having the name that he was intended to be given, there may be significance in the fate of names—the belief that words are written in a book that governs life—people placing, imputing and impugning meaning to the stories they impose on the world. At such time in Poland *moyles* were trimmed from the list of approved occupations and were not permitted to ply, apply or display their trade to circumcise. The powers that be cut and snipped with one proclamation and edict, with one stroke of the pointy pen, thousands of years of skill and practice developed together with an accompanying song and dance, and a doctor had to be used, a white coat instead of a learned and specialized black cap, to surgically and not ritually remove the foreskin of baby Michael. Fortunately he was not deboned!

Michael's father was in the Polish army at the outbreak of war, he being over thirteen years older than Michael's mother who he did not meet until after the war. Conscription was mandatory in Poland at the time, and Michael's father told Michael that many Jewish men would injure and maim themselves so they did not have to serve in the Polish army, because the Jews and the Poles were like distinct nations, and if not, then different cultures, like the English and French in Canada.

There was a special word for this self maiming to avoid military service in Yiddish, and it was something like a *"navleh,"* but would it not hurt as much by any name. Michael's father did not injure himself and went to serve in the Polish army, to defend and fight for Poland, for that was his country. Being Jewish was a culture based on a long tradition within such nation. Michael thought that his father should be recognized as doing his part for Poland. The honor to the father could then cast light on the son. Michael felt that he was excluded from Poland: he was born in Poland, but was not Polish!

When Michael's father was serving in the Polish military at the start of the war, his unit was captured by the Germans, and the prisoners, Mendel included, were taken by train to Germany as prisoners of war. Perhaps war had not yet officially been declared. What a crazy thought to think that carnage, killing and destruction needs a legal decree to make them formal. Things must have been in confusion: Michael's father did not look Jewish so he might have been treated like an ordinary soldier. Perhaps the name Mendel could have been a clue, but matters were surely in disarray—Michael was not privy to the details.

Michael's father was not anti-German notwithstanding what happened during the war. Mendel fondly remembered and talked about how during the First World War when he was but a young child, a German soldier passing through town picked little Mendel up in a fatherly way and affectionately told Mendel that he reminded him of his own young son, or so the story goes. There is no doubt that the soldier was a father at heart lost in the game of war, an expendable pawn missing his son.

For some unknown reason, whenever Michael told this story, he would break into tears that could not be dammed or halted, no matter how hard he tried. Michael did not comprehend why it made him so teary rather than just deeply sadden him. How could emptiness produce such a flood? Perhaps the tears swelled up from the deep well of the collective sufferings of humanity, being turbulently shaken and stirred when one ponders the ordeals endured and wrongs incurred by the ones that one loves. Michael was not prone to hysterics or crying, except when really shit-faced drunk, or from watching a very sad movie. The sorrowfulness impressed itself more on Michael when it came to the suffering of his parents, rather than his own self pity—he was quite used to feeling sorry for himself!

It is difficult to argue for or against fate, or conversely free will or lack thereof, because each life is only lived once, or so the theory goes, so there can be no experiment devised to test the hypothesis of whether fate in fact exists. If Michael's father had not survived the war, then Michael would not exist, and then there would no story to write—but Michael's father did survive.

The story of Mendel's survival goes like this and Michael knew it because his father repeated it as often as Michael's mother would let him, and unlike Michael's mother, Mendel liked to talk about some of what went on during the war. It was Michael that was usually the obstructive party, not listening as he had heard the story before, and thus never really hearing it. It now became a situation which Michael regretted as he was very interested in what happened and the details; but it was too late, there was no encore performance.

Although born in Mlawa, which is in north eastern Poland, Mendel had spent much of his time as a boy growing up with his maternal grandparents who lived in the south western part of Poland, as his mother had died when he was a young child, and Mendel's father remarried.

Michael's paternal grandfather whose name was of course Abraham, which means father in some far long ago forgotten language, kept true to his name by *beeing* busying multiplying with a new wife, pumping out progeny, and the four children from the first wife, Mendel's deceased mother, were sent to her parents' home to be cared for. There they were amply provided for, materially and emotionally, because Mendel's maternal grandparents owned a small leather factory, and two milk cows and a goat. A young unwed aunt also lived at home and helped in the raising and upbringing of Mendel and his siblings.

Mendel grew up as a studious, good natured boy with a determined look in his almond-shaped eyes, learned in the

Torah and the operation of a sewing machine, gently touched by a sense of humor that mostly he found funny.

It so happened that the train crammed with the prisoners of war including Mendel stopped in the exact town where Mendel had grown up with his grandparents near the then German border, and through the window of the train Mendel recognized a distant relative and called to him requesting that he throw some civilian clothes to Mendel, which was done. Mendel got changed, walked off the train, and was not noticed. Could it be that simple? Why not?

Of course matters are not as simple as they appear on the surface, but neither are they as complicated as one often complains about. Escaping from the train was just the first step. Mendel had no papers, documents or ID. How was he going to roll his cigarettes? He was a *persona non gratis* unable to say that he was an escaped Polish prisoner—that would be dangerous. Or a Jew: even worse!

Michael's father always stressed the point he considered to be the "*to be or not to be*" moment of his life. He had to cross a bridge or something guarded by a German sentry, and knew that if he was stopped and questioned it would surely and certainly spell his death in capital letters. With that in mind, aware of the grave risk involved, Mendel resolved to cross, and placed his life in the hands of a possible taker. He looked straight ahead and walked with determination, crossing the bridge unhindered. And he lived.

Recently, Michael often thought about what it would have been like if it were he who had to decide: a bit more of a pressure cooker than having to take and make that *big money putt* in front of a gallery in a game of golf. Michael could not bear to continue with the thought! Were he in his father's boots, would he have the strength and courage to make it across the bridge, let alone take the first step? His heart would have beat loud enough to disturb anyone in a stone's throw, possibly to wake even the dead if they were within earshot. It is a moot or hypothetical point however, which lawyers like to avoid as much as getting caught with their pants down, bare-assed and embarrassed, because it was not Michael's choice to make. It was not a philosophical choice, but an existential one, and therein lies the paradox—existentialism is a philosophy!

Michael's father, though learned in the Jewish prayers, was not what could be called a religious man, perhaps practical would be more apt. He believed that one had to work to support his family, with his own peculiar or funny sense of humor. He did not believe in God because how could God allow what happened to happen. Was she busy filing her nails? Mendel did however believe in right and wrong. He was Jewish, and spoke Yiddish partaking in the customary customs of the culture.

Like many of his factory worker contemporaries he leaned towards socialism, even so far as to know and sing many socialist songs, whether in Russian, Polish or Yiddish. He swore in Russian so that Michael and his brother would not be subject to the corrupting influence of highly emotional sexual slurs. In Canada he was a member of the Workmen's Circle Association, or *"Arbetering"* in Yiddish, which promoted Jewish tradition without its theological bullshit aspic, faithfully paying his dues to secure a burial plot for himself and Michael's mother. Their bodies now lie side by side in the Workmen's Circle section of a Jewish cemetery in Toronto marked by two engraved grey slabs of smooth stone.

Michael knew that only his parents' bodies, or what remained of them, were buried there; so *"what would be the point of visiting the cemetery?"* He knew that his father had written in the book of life in strokes of loving kindness, leaving his mark on the wall-less corridor bounding what is called or conceived of as one's life. Mendel's wondrous works could be seen by Michael at any time he chose to look.

To finish the story of Mendel's role in the war, Michael pieced together the following without being able to vouchsafe as to its accuracy. Mendel's two older brothers and baby sister who grew up with him at his maternal grandparents perished during the war. The curtain came down on their acts prematurely. His half brothers and sisters who lived in Mlawa with his father and stepmother all survived, some say thanks to Mendel.

During the war Mendel went to Russia where he was initially jailed as a displaced person, and then shipped off by freight train to labor at a logging camp in Siberia called a *"lager."* It was very cold in Siberia, but healthy for a young man to work hard and be outdoors in the fresh air. No doubt healthier than being crowded in a concentrated camp and having to breath the toxic air in the busy showers that clean one of body and sets them free.

The Jews and the Poles did get along and coexisted for about a thousand years before the Second Great War as they needed each other. Poland was caught between the Teutonic knights on one hand and the Russian empire on the other. Not *shabby* in the long burning lamplight of history: surviving the tight squeeze between the clutches and hugs of the bear and the boar!

Was it somehow analogous to the situation of the Jews and Moors in Spain who also co-existed first by necessity, then garnering mutual respect by sleeping in the same bed and not hogging all the blankets—or coming on too strong when the other party wants to sleep! That is until the red cross of the catholic kings triumphed, and severed the familial conviviality.

With the occupation of Poland, Pole and Jew were forbidden from getting along and being simpatico. The imperial Bolsheviks were but the left hand reflection of the right-handed imperial Reich who like two brothers would kiss and then fight.

# 28

## BACK TO THE PRESENT AGAIN

Back in the underground parking garage of Michael's condo building in Hamilton it was mid-afternoon as Michael was ascending the ramp to exit. The big garage door rose and opened. The bright light of day momentarily blinded Michael so he put on his sun glasses and waited at the top of the ramp for the garage door to close before turning right on the side street. He then took another quick right onto a busy one way street driving past the *Art Deco* GO Station as he headed towards his favorite Starbucks.

It was an exceptionally bright sunny October day. Perhaps Michael was just in one of those moods of greater receptivity to the brightness of light. Michael was the type of person that needed to get out every day. He would not feel right or well if he didn't. Michael was someone who had "ants in his pants." His

mother would accuse him of having "pins in his ass" a translation of course, and "fantasies in his head." At least he used his
body and mind. He didn't mind being a dreamer, or *"gapa,"* but
there was no way anyone was going to call him a "guppy"!

Michael had a theory that over time people developed
certain traits or characteristics that were needed for their
survival and thriving, dependent on their environment and circumstances in a tribal or cultural setting. These characteristics
or traits could overlap with one another or could shade into
each other to varying degrees.

Michael considered himself a prototype hunter. He had to go
out and find the prey. He could be so intensely focused on one
thing that he would not notice anything else, and he believed
this was a trait developed when his ancestors hunted: they
had to make the kill to bring home the bacon, or the brisket
for observant Jews or Moslems to whom succulence is not the
supreme factor in supping.

And this theory explained why, other than at those elevated
times which required extra exerted extreme effort, Michael just
like to putt around, doddle, chat and socialize, and let time slip
tranquilly by. Some people may be archetypically homebodies
and like to keep the hearth fires aglow, enjoying the domestic
duties like cleaning and cooking, but Michael was never one of
those. He considered such duties a chore, and a bore. Getting
out of the house or apartment, driving around seeking, seeing
and doing, was his lifeblood.

Michael believed in some version of the theory of evolution,
although he was not an orthodox Darwinian. (Who has in fact
read one of the most influential books of our epoch: *The Origin
of the Species*?) Michael believed that the wider and greater the
gene pool, the greater the chances of survival of the species,
subspecies or race. Even crazy traits like mania and lunacy
might in some circumstances prove more useful than traits
usually considered as strengths such as strength, size, good

looks, coordination, gifted oratory and rhetoric skills, speed, fertility, etc., for the circumstances a creature finds itself in might be endless—what might be needed to get by and survive in every circumstance was unimaginable! Take for example the myriad and multifold instances and examples of people that survived the said Second World War. One would no doubt concede and concur with the point of view that madness in all its unlimited and incomprehensible manifestations might just be the most important means of maintaining and ensuring mankind's continued survival, without jest.

Michael was not totally satisfied with the static state of survival of the most adapted as it relates to the different genes or traits being randomly strewn by the rules of inheritance, and even thought the notion that traits or genes acquired, altered, or added to in the lifetime of a living entity could be passed on to offspring appealed to Michael, science, had supposedly discredited such Lamarckian belief. Michael's hermetically sealed truth was that the lips of truth always sought out the ears of understanding to whisper sweet nothings to—and the case was not closed as long as truth is as elusive as a slippery snake continually slithering away from one's groping grasp!

Michael also "knew" that the human race was a species related to apes and monkeys for he could see it everywhere: in the hands, the eyes and faces of all people. He knew that *Homo sapiens* were just another type of ape. Take for example any attribute considered important and unique to people: the ability to laugh, lie, joke, cry, cheat, talk, sing, eat with utensils, and write, and also being foolish enough to ritualize marriage as monogamous, and it is evident that people are no smarter than monkeys!

Only an insensitive prejudicial lout would say that all people of a certain race look the same, for example the Chinese, and they might think the same of others, the Jews or Caucasians, but once one gets into and is part of a group, things never do look the same as what one thought they would look like from the outside. Similarity and identity are just a shorthand habituated by the mind to recognize the same person on different hair days, whether good or bad, and permits people to lump people into piles of friend or foe, which is no doubt necessary for continued survival of any distinct group that wishes to remain a distinct group that wishes to remain the same.

Michael saw that all people, all members of team *human race*, looked the same; and that cars were just tin cans on wheels with hidden engines. This insight came to him as clear as day one sunny morning when returning home to his parents' bungalow in North York after an "all nighter" while high in high school. Perhaps the peyote or mescaline ingested had something to do with blowing open the drawers of his perception. He observed this "truth" with his own eyes, and likely an astonished look on his face! Everyone, whether black or white, yellow or brown, looks the same in the *big picture*! Each person, though they act with unmitigated unimaginable cruelty, or with super-caring kindness, is really no different than the average ape—except for all the body hair, and the cult like worship of technology and celebrity.

# 29

## IS THE LAW AN ASS?

For the first year of law school, Michael rented a room in a house with other students in a newer subdivision near the University of Western Ontario in the northwest part of London town on a street surprisingly named White Acres, which is a coincidence because in Michael's real property class in first year law school, parcels of land were named "White Acres" and "Black Acres," so no doubt a lawyer was involved with the subdivision, but that would only make sense because where there is property and money why wouldn't there be a lawyer?

Michael's studies at law school will not be detailed. Suffice it to say that Michael's "illustrious" legal career ended with a whimper and not a bang: he had ceased and desisted from practicing for several years before he was disbarred by the Upper Society of Law in Ontario for failure to file his annual returns. The answer to the question if calling the law an ass is asinine, or a matter worthy of consideration, will be evident when all is revealed and explained.

Lawyers engage in an adversarial system, not a system of love. Love is allegedly and ultimately supposed to be exemplified and incorporated in the institution of marriage. Both wedlock and a court case may formally, or on the surface, seem the same or similar, but they differ substantially and substantively, for though they both start out with pleadings, then go into a discovery stage followed by a trial, which is sometimes long and arduous but always costly, and finally there is a determination or judgment for which sometimes both parties have to pay, the real difference is that in marriage one stops getting fondled and fornicated frequently in time, but in a court case the litigants always get shafted by swollen legal fees, like lambs fleeced and shorn of their shekels.

If lawyers wanted to be outright mean and lowdown nasty they could disrobe any wayward lawyer who strays from the flock. The clergy does this to their "bad boys" by defrocking them. But disrobing lawyers would be cruel and unusual punishment as *"embarazar"* means to get pregnant in Spanish, which would be embarrassing to happen during a trial with the lawyer *in barrister mode* in open court, but not so for marriage where the usual course is that intercourse takes place (although, as aforesaid, diminishing in frequency and amplitude like the ripples of a wave over time). Without an obstacle to sperm or semen (a condom or some other fandangle that clogs up the course of the life force) embarrassment will result if done with someone other than a spouse, if it is discovered of course once the baby is born as determined by a DNA test no less, beyond a reasonable doubt of course!

Michael took many courses in his first year of law school and studied studiously and judiciously, and that strange phenomenon occurred that psychologists call "reticular cognition" which may more easily be understood as something *akin* to "stereotyping" or putting everything into pigeon holes. It relates to similarity and identity, and has been used for mind control and brainwashing. In a nutshell, or for a nutcase, it can be explained as: one sees what one is focused on, or asserted undeniably: one *notices* what *one* notices.

Here are some examples. If a person is pregnant, or their partner is pregnant, then it will seem as if everyone they run across is pregnant. The situation is the same if someone buys a car of a certain type like a Toyota, they will notice that almost every car they notice is a Toyota. But when a cold and callous unbiased count is taken, no variance is noted in the distribution of the phenomena before and after the precipitating event which brought attention to it. The thing focused on does not occur more frequently, but paradoxically is seen and sensed more. Consequently all perceived and conceived *truths* are only psycho*logic*ally true; thus leading to the conclusion that things can be the same and different at the same time, as well as being different and the same at different times, because everyone sees things differently. Now that this has been explained, the paradox no longer seems so paradoxically perplexing.

Everyone has experienced the reticular phenomenon for it is how the human mind is structured, functions and works. Once Michael attended law school, *everything* he experienced seemed to relate to legal or illegal matters. Law suits filled the newspapers—he never realized just how common they were. Torts reared their ugly intentions or neglect everywhere and in everything. Even alphabet soup was subject to interpretation. He began to understand life as a contract, and all actions stood as precedents.

Details of Michael's studies in law will not be divulged in any specificity and particularity which might be misconstrued as the giving of legal advice or practicing law without being properly licensed, for in order to practice law in Ontario not only is the educational requirement of a law degree necessary, but the masters who are called "benchers" must be paid; or one is not permitted to pipe up and belt out legal principles. Year after year, the dues must be paid without fault or else one cannot practice law in the province of Ontario, nor do anything which appears or might be construed as similar.

It is a well-known principle that the law is concerned with appearances as much as it is with actualities and truth. There is an adage, an old refrain, that *not* only must the law be done; it must *appear* to be done. Talk about peer pressure!

The law as a jealous mistress carefully guards its jurisdiction as if she had an unspoiled cherry under that silky, sexy, seductive black satin skirt, always on guard and vigilant to swat anyone who tries to lift and reveal or unveil her formidable fruits without a degree and a formal decree from the Upper Society of Law in Ontario.

Michael's disbarment after ceasing to practice law for the second time was administrative; not at all as glamorous or exciting or as scurrilous as playing with oneself in court— which could be very interesting if anyone had the singularity or testicularity to do it—but such behavior would likely result in contempt of court charges being laid rather than the judgment that such acts lay somewhere between gratifying self-fulfillment and promiscuous self-indulgence!

When Michael knew for sure that he no longer wanted to practice law after keeping his status in good standing after not practicing for a few years, he sent his annual fees and filing form back to the Upper Society without fees, noting thereon that he would not be renewing his membership.

The reply he received stated that he could not resign or discontinue being a member of the Upper Society simply by ceasing to practice as a lawyer and giving notification of his doing so because the Society's rules did not allow for it. The proper and requisite protocol and procedure proscribed by the pompous port-swigging benchers was that Michael had to fill out a special form to be able to resign.

Michael in his easy going manner called the Society and said: "Fine, send me the form so I can sign it and get it over and done with," thinking that it would be no problem, but instead he was told that there was no such form, and that he would have to figure out how to draft the "please let me resign" begging letter, which had to be signed, witnessed and submitted to the omnipotent Society for their review and approval.

Wow, if Michael wasn't already mad, it would have driven him crazy! Most of his life he had been a patient procrastinator, at least ever since he had started smoking pot, but this was the last straw his back could bear. Why should the Upper Society be able to rule his fate? Was there not a rule in law against restraint of trade? What hypocrites? Michael had done absolutely nothing wrong, why should his fate be subject to the discretion of the haughty Upper Society? Why did he have to do all the extra work not to be able to work? Michael could not believe that in this day and age such duplicitous standards still existed, under the auspices of the overseers of the practice of justice in the province of Ontario.

"How ludicrous, lunatic and schizoid can it get? I should have never sworn that oath to the Queen when I was admitted to the bar" Michael fumed as the self-feeding but not self-serving negative feedback cut his composure with the force of a locomotive, and his anger skyrocketed out of control. The toxins accrued in a lifetime—the wrongs suffered, the slings and arrows of outrageous fortune, the junk food, alcohol and dope ingested, imbibed or smoked had been stirred, released to fire his ire!

The people that wanted to control Michael's fate like he was a puppet on a string, that wanted to turn him into a miming, mimicking, marionette dancing to their mindless tune, would never win he vowed, for now his guiding principle was named

"*Defiance*." He would never surrender or subjugate himself to what was essentially *slavery* at the hands of the masters that arbitrarily and capriciously ruled and governed the front line fighters in the battle for rights and justice—lawyers like him! Michael had dared unlink the shackles and divorce himself from the jealous mistress in his quest for liberty and freedom. Would he be humbled and humiliated at the hands of the benchers who by statutes and regulations acted like a gang of little Caesars and Sheiks to keep him in their harem, standing in the way of his wants like a prophylactic?

Michael pictured himself bloodied like Jesus walking down University Avenue with a staff in hand crudely carved from a fallen maple branch. He looked savagely strong, unshaven and disheveled. He was filled with the spirit of *Disobedience*, as he waved his rod and staff in the air wailing and warning loudly and repeatedly: "You hypocrites, I thought that slavery was abolished a long time ago in the province of Ontario!" The diamond clarity in his eyes spoke of the mania which enmeshed and immersed him as if he were an angel befallen, or son of God now cast out and lost. Michael had in fact lived such scene in Cuba many years after his disbarment. He had escaped from a hospital in the City of Cienfuegos. Blood spurted from the insides of his forearms after he stood up from the gurney on his own volition and pulled out the intravenous tubes feeding his veins. It must have come as a complete surprise to the doctors as he rose and just walked out of the hospital into the midday sun bleeding like a modern day Jesus. Perhaps he went psycho or was drugged. He never knew for sure what caused him to wander through the streets in circles as if lost in a labyrinth, singing and shouting repeatedly and rhythmically: "*Yo soy loco, pero poco!*" ("I am crazy, but only a little!")

When it came to formally terminating his standing as a lawyer, Michael was in no uncertain terms angry, but the deep-seated resentment he experienced relating to his desire to cut the cord binding him umbilically to law was completely dwarfed by the venomous hostility he harbored the day he was actually called to the bar—admitted into the fold of *lawyer-dom*—to become both a barrister and solicitor. At the time he wisely kept his mouth shut, but his mountainous rage spat out in silent hate within himself; he was still unsure and insecure as to why he felt the way he did.

What caused his distemper to spike so high? Was it that he had to give, swear and vow an oath of allegiance to the Queen of England in the ceremony that granted him barrister and solicitor status so as to be able to practice law in the Province of Ontario? She, the ruler by bloodline, owner of all property in Ontario, exempt and immune from the application of and prosecution under all laws, the One who wore the crown—how could she cloak herself in democracy? Was it not at best, an insult to someone whose family was fractured and minimized by the war of ultimate solutions to swear allegiance to a monarch who ruled by the right of kings even if she was a queen?

Some argue that the queen is just a figurehead—that swearing allegiance to her is just a formality. But what is hypocrisy? What is Justice? What is Truth? Is it OK to lie if it is conventional and convenient to do so, for example: to get ahead, receive head or get laid?

*"You are free as long as you obey the laws. Don't worry it's just for appearances. Don't rock the boat. It's not a big deal. It's just a formality! It doesn't really mean anything. She's just a figurehead. It's just the way it appears, it's not the reality."* And so on the naysayers' and apologists' words spew forth in expedient diuretic fashion.

But appearance is the concern of the law. It is all anyone can see—unless they are crazy! How many steps does it take to go from swearing a "pretend" oath to complete denial: *"I see nothing; nothing; nothing!"*? If it is a meaningless ritual done only for spectacle, then why the fuck is it done at all? Would not dancing and singing *Kumbayah* be more edifying and entertaining?

When Michael was called to the bar he should have been excited to be starting out on a potentially profitable professional career, but a metaphysical thing (and it can't be disproven) happened. It was attested to by a photograph, evidence beyond a reasonable doubt that is clearly visible and open for all to see. All know that the color of rage is red.

Michael was standing with his co-graduate and former roommate, Steven Davis, in a photo. Each wore suits draped by a black solicitor's graduating gown. Michael wore a light blue suit as it was a warm, late spring day. Davis sported a dark brown suit as he tended to dress conservatively. The color of the graduation gowns was black, at least that is the color they appeared to be in the light of day or by room light, but in the photo of Davis and Rice shaking hands, Davis' robe was black, as it should have been, but lo and behold, the graduation gown adorning Michael, although in reality the same color, appeared blood red!

How could it be explained? "Science" as now preached is at a loss to account for such and other readily observable phenomena because in practice science has been converted into a "black" esoteric art strictly maintained under the authority of "scientists" who permit only other "scientists" already indoctrinated and initiated in a shared dogma to enter the exclusive and exclusionary enclave they have established.

Once upon a time science was based on the search for verifiable and repeatable results rooted in experimentation so that "truth" would not be ordered, ordained or imposed by any authority whether religious, regal or otherwise. Science used to be open to all, discoverable by even a commoner or layperson. Truth depended on what a thing did and how it acted rather than on whom it knew and how it was connected. But an authority or any group that is separate must by the very nature of being what it is, always act to perpetuate itself—otherwise it would not exist and continue to be in the first place—exerting control either by force, which requires the expenditure of great energy, or through the belief of adherents, i.e. brainwashing or mind control. Zealots then become the force that enforce. Having someone do the dirty work voluntarily and fanatically without charge reinforces the authority's belief in its own infallibility.

What could have caused Michael's gown to glow fiery red in his graduation photo? Did the red hot anger sequestered within seethe out of him transmigrating from an internal feeling to an external energy caught on film? Was the force so strong that its emission could not be constricted nor restricted by a black robe, but converged with the black lack of light color in cardinal reflection?

The false science of today and the medical-pharmaceutical complex to which it is bedded and wedded, unofficially and commonly, would say otherwise in its omnipotence and omnipresence. All are forbidden to challenge or question—it would be treason or heresy to do so! If anyone is foolhardy enough to try and assail the steep walls of such fortress they will be branded a nutcase, marginalized as a nut cake, locked up in bin full of loonies and fruit cakes, or drugged up with pharmaceuticals for which they or some poor taxpayer must pay—adding insult to injury! Would being doused with boiling oil or jumping from the frying pan into a fire be any worse?

But all who show the same angry red hue as Michael displayed when he took his lying oath to pledge his feigned oneness with her most exalted and worshipped Regina, the Second, must learn to forgive and love, for the game in not played out till the one end is reached where and when all trivialities and perceived wrongs can be laughed at, shaken off as if they were but water on a duck's back. For in truth—truth is unknowable!

Ultimately, it is not important whether one tell lies or not, as long as they act in *loving kindness*. Nobody knows what the future will hold. Although actions form the chain that link the past, present and future, what the result will be, whether good, bad or indifferent, are but judgments to and by which the believer is tied—as surely as beauty is in the eye of the beholder!

# 30

## BROTHER VS. BROTHER

Although Michael tried during his first year of law school, he could not forget what D'Arcy had done. One may believe that they have deeply interned and buried resentment, and then it is forever gone. But guess what: like a stinking, foul mouth or the forked tongue of a hissing snake, it can rear its sneering condescending hole and strike unexpectedly! Although some may cast blame on frolicking fate, it all has to do with the nature of repression, resentments and interment. One day the negative energies must and will escape to sprout and shoot forth like a furious fountain, a gushing geyser, or just plain diarrhea!

D'Arcy came to a party at White Acres. Wendy and many other people were there. One of the occupants of the house had a dog, and D'Arcy being drunk as usual, did the most disgusting thing in Michael's eyes, although there is no corroboration that it was done to get Michael's goat even if he was a Capricorn.

Michael however, felt like D'Arcy did it intentionally and was trying to rub salt into Michael's wound.

D'Arcy had the audacity to chew pizza, and then feed the pulverized mush to the dog. The dog being a man-loving and simple beast ate the regurgitated mess oblivious to the degradation entailed therein. Michael watched in downright disapproval as D'Arcy teased him with such boorishness, and yet Michael, in spite of all the whiskey and wine, beer and buds, maintained his composure, notwithstanding such egging.

But as every dam must bust or burst, especially when beaver is involved, it so happened that one day when Wendy, D'Arcy and Michael were drinking and partying at the Loo, in Breslau, Ontario, located on an angular street which so perplexes and confuses, Michael had done a little "v" recreationally, and thus his inhibitions were lowered. Then and there he saw D'Arcy before his eyes, his blood red lips in full throttle snidely snarling in such pompous, self-serving philosophizing that Michael thought: "how could you have fucked my girlfriend?" and "how could you have fed chewed up crap to the dog?" Unprovoked and without warning Michael lunged at and attached D'Arcy, wrestling him to the ground.

Michael was downed out and drunk, and D'Arcy was very drunk as well. Neither was in top fighting form. D'Arcy was probably the stronger, being in fact the bigger. Immediately after the initial attack Michael's wrath abated. He noticed D'Arcy had freed himself somewhat, and might soon get the upper hand, so Michael let D'Arcy go, got up, and stepped back a few paces and said: "I just had to do that because I took some valium tonight and I guess I was still feeling ill will over what happened with Wendy. I think that the anger is gone now. Hey, sometimes shit just happens!" Then the three laughed it off, and kept on pretending to have fun and drinking.

At times, strange things happen on streets that are not straight. Michael, not yet having learned not to fear the truth, had lied, but being on valium it did not bother him, and he soon forgot about it.

# 31

## MICHAEL AND WENDY

For a while everything flowed fine and freely like verse unleashed from the core of consciousness which has no meter, rhyme or reason; like tiny smooth particles of sand slipping through the reflecting glass of time meandering as does a river, well-tempered at times and raging with roiled torrents at others, the sediment sands stirred and disturbed to murky clouds long lost beyond the fringe of forgetfulness, which will pass in hindsight if permitted to do so in peace and patience. So was the pace when present became the past in the guise of donning the disguise of the future.

Michael finished his first year of law school, and Wendy completed her third year of humanities at the University of Waterloo, and they decided to live together for the summer, which for those attending university in the province of Ontario begins in the second month of spring: April. Michael had done fairly well in first year law although it took him some time to catch on and be hitched to the constricted and concise nature of legal thinking. The bait was adequate, and with his inherent leaning being tilted to the abstract mathematical incline, such knowledge was able to roll to him without the exertion of much effort, and Michael was able to find balance through continued and prolonged stimulation and simulation in the ratio of cases legally determined by staring decisively at the black and white fine print that renders a living crucial and critical situation into a paper judgment.

Michael knew that in order to do well, that is to get good marks, all he had to do was chew the information provided by the professor during the lecture, who spoon-fed the student as a most prized possession, and then regurgitate the well-masticated slop back to such teacher, which the professor would consume with relish and delight in its originality, and wisely grade highly.

Michael also learned another trick, and that was not to do any of the readings or work till the end of the course when he was in a position to understand how the contents and materials related and fit together, so he didn't have to waste time studying what he did not yet understand or know and still needed to learn.

Michael and Wendy rented an apartment together in a high rise building in London, Ontario and starting living together as man and woman, boyfriend and girlfriend (but not as man and wife) for the extended summer, not ready to navigate the lock of wed. Michael hadn't completed his courses in family law to have a thorough grounding on what could go wrong in the animal-like practice of husbandry, but for all intents and purposes they did what a married couple would do: eat together, sleep together, talk together and copulate—but they drank from separate cups!

Wendy was able to secure a job with Bell Telephone as a telephone operator in London, a part time position which she had held in her home town, Kitchener, while attending the University of Waterloo. Those who know anything about history and telephones, or Ontario and Canada, will know that Bell or Bell Inc. or Bell Telephone, or whatever the hell they're called, had a monopoly on telephones when only landlines were extant. Bell was the only game in town back then: no competition was allowed. Such corporate monopoly was named after Alexander Graham Bell, who came from Brantford, Ontario, which by the way is where the great one, #99, Wayne Gretzky, hails from, a city/town in rural Ontario about 50 km west of Hamilton (about 30 miles) where at one time there was much farm related industry including a huge Massey Ferguson plant, that was shut down when it became much cheaper to manufacture offshore in China and Korea.

Michael was worried about Wendy working as a telephone operator at Bell, even in the days before Bell became unbelievably belligerent, as it is today, hiring MBAs to maximize profit and minimize return for the customer with practices such as unilaterally imposing contracts with long fixed terms that can only be terminated during short intervals on specified dates not specified. Anything that has to do with cancellation or termination of a contract by an irritated and irate customer is routed to a specific operator, a specially trained operative who is a kind and considerate conversationalist trained to thwart the complainant by never losing composure nor budging from the unfair business practices dictated by the master, Bell. Although such practices may be actionable at law and reprehensible morally, they allowed Bell to accumulate every nickel and dime, quarter, loony and toony that could be squeezed out of the hapless customer. Omnipotent and omnipresent *Ma Bell* believes it to be her God given right and prerogative in a democratic and capitalistic country to do so, given that anyone has the right to sue and spend thousands of dollars to potentially recover hundreds! Thank God there are lawyers to do the

dirty, irritating and annoying work of retribution and revenge—
asking only for pay without delay—not one's soul.

No, Michael was not worried about that. Such frustrations
percolated and did boil over once after the consumption of
a copious quantity of coffee, but that is beside the point. As
Wendy had a great figure, Michael was worried about her being
disfigured in a physical and not a monetary sense by working at
a sedentary job all day (i.e. where one sits) and thus develop a
very large and unsightly ass.

You may think that Michael exaggerated, or was taking his
worries too far, but the anatomically incomprehensible sized
rumps that can inhabit the female gender of the human species
in North America, both Canada and the US, speak for themselves in their grotesque grandeur. To avoid a graphic descrip-
tion, a refrain from a well known children's ditty sets out the
magnitude of the matter in plain English: *"not too big, not too
small, just the size of Montreal."*

For you Americans who may not understand, Montreal used
to be the largest city in Canada and is situated in the province of
Quebec, but when the rumblings and rasping of separation and
distinct nationhood were emanating from the said province,
Montreal like a pair of wool underwear washed in hot water,
shrunk, to no longer have the honor of being the largest city
in Canada. The kudos devolved to Toronto, but notwithstanding the shrinking of Montreal like testicles on a cold Quebec
winter day, Montreal is still a big city. It would in fact be the
biggest city in the country—if Quebec separated!

The reason Michael was worried about Wendy developing a
very big and ugly posterior was that as a budding lawyer he was
concerned with appearance as much as substance. Wendy not
only had to be substantially beautiful, she *had* to appear beautiful in Michael's eyes, and those of his peering peers!

Michael decided not to work for the summer to try his
hand at writing for the few month hiatus from his studies. He

still had the passion and desire to be a writer, but being post-philosophy and inter-law, he had come down somewhat from his high horse of lofty ideas to a more practical level of pragmatism. In respect of earning money he thought: "Why should I work hard at a low paying, menial job for the summer, when I can instead borrow money to live on, and then it will be a piece of cake as a fully fledged barrister and solicitor to pay the principal and accrued interest back when I finish law school?"

Although Michael's logic was close to impeccable, it failed to be perfect and thus was still subject to be pecked apart mercilessly. Fate and the future, which is the outcome of the past and present, demonstrated the fatal flaw of the financial formulations that fluttered in and fornicated Michael's mind. When he did practice law, although successful in that he practiced with ethics, not prosaically but of a caliber beyond a reasonable standard, he fell far short of reaping the rich rewards he had envisioned and forecast financially. His strategy though beautiful and elegant—esthetically, artistically and abstractly—failed to be the boon foreseen.

To write, yes, that had been his life. He wrote as a teenager the words: "I am a writer" over and over like a mantra of positive reinforcement, wishing it to be so. But like so many scattered and slightly seeded plans, it had not come to fruition—at least not yet! Now, with some more years under his belt and a year of law school, he had gained some educational weight, and could focus once again on writing, to re-view if he might now have the metal to make and manufacture memorable meter, to write lucidity enough to be lyrically likable. To this end he decided to read many classics including works by Steinbeck, Mann, Dostoyevsky, and Camus hoping that their skillful styles and creative abilities would subliminally and subconsciously seep scientifically into him through osmosis. But alas, he was able to compose only a few "so-so" poems, and complete less than 10 pages of a sucking novel he worked on until he realized that he just blew his time. His output was so dismal in terms of quality and quantity that well before the summer ended he put a kibosh on his writing literally. His aspirations were now limited to just becoming a happy successful lawyer—and partying in the interim!

Although at the time Michael and Wendy both smoked heavily, about a pack a day, the fire that once burned bonding and consuming them had subsided somewhat causing it to smoke less. People say that time has the habit of doing that, and there is the old adage that *"familiarity breeds contempt."* Although too strong of a statement to apply in this case, all such adages, maxims, axioms, proverbs and pithy platitudes are fun for entertainment and amusement purposes like the horoscope, *feng shui*, superstitions, religious myths, and theological stories, doctrines or dogma, but they are only half truths. The other half of the time they are insidious and dangerous, and should never to be taken as gospel. The law of balance applies: *one gets out of something what they put in*, or as stated in physics: *to every force there is an equal and balancing force*. There is no doubt that one needs to work at something to get it done, but in the real world which is not cleanly or clearly cut or shaded into black and white, *shit sometimes happens*.

Michael and Wendy did have sex regularly. Michael recalled one particular occasion which occurred during that summer because the condom that he was using broke! It was no joke! The next month, Wendy missed her period. Michael started to think *"marriage, mortgage, monsters and madness; to abort or not to abort; marriage or no marriage; rest of my life with Wendy—why or why not Wendy?"* All he needed to do was pull the petals off a flower! There was so much to consider. They got along well. Perhaps she *was* the one—the first *one*?

As Michael was studying law, not being a right-wing nut case, he knew that no matter what his feelings were, it was up to the mother. He could not get his head around the whole right to life debate however, did not the lord give and the lord take? "*Whisper words of wisdom, let it be*": the way she wants it!

For three months, Wendy did not get her menstrual period. Michael got hot under the collar; although he usually just wore T shirts, he was not for or against—he could now argue either side—it's just that men get so jittery when they expect their sexual partner to have a period. It was so long of a period-less time period that Wendy made an appointment to see her doctor in Kitchener. Michael stayed home trying to pretend he was not nervous, but was too distracted to read or write, so he just went to and fro in his mind hopping and bopping between "*yea*" and "*nay*."

When Wendy came home she had some big news. Her stepmother, much younger than her father, was pregnant, but Wendy was not! Michael thought it strange and *immaculate* that the condom had broken when he and Wendy made love, and then her stepmother ended up pregnant. It could be construed as a miracle by those foolhardy enough to believe in such disorder, but it seemed synchronistic—converted and elevated in Michael's mind to an idiosynchronicity—a junction of supreme unction!

Throughout that summer until he stopped, Michael wrote on a small desk, a wooden table with but one small central drawer where he kept pens and pencils and a few important notes. As previously stated, this was the desk table that he and his brother had used when they shared a room in that second floor flat in Little Italy, the front room of which doubled as his parents' bedroom and the living room.

Michael did not think his family was poor back then. He had everything he could want: a roof over his head, a house that was heated in winter, lots of fruits, homemade cakes and buns, and other good food to eat. He was well-cared-for, free to come and go as he pleased. The flat was not two dimensional—it was full of love! Though Michael was young and a budding free thinker, soon to become deflected by self-reflection to a point beyond self-absorption, he was almost always happy, for that was his nature and disposition, to be extroverted and smiling. He was not bad or good, in an ethical sense, for he had yet to fully taste the "fruit of knowledge" cultivated by the categorizing and classifying axis.

And on such desk, which now sits as a small display table at the Wild Rice health food store, Michael engraved on the right hand side closest to him, the courses he took in law school together with the years in which they were taken. During this summer he even incorporated the table into a poem. That table, if it was not a thing or a physical object, could be considered a bridge in time, for it spanned the past: Michael in Little Italy living with his parents; law school: the summer in London trying to write; and the future: the health food store. The table served not only a useful utilitarian purpose but also as a symbol of the unity of time. Its four-legged, rectangular, right-angled materialness stands as a testament and monument to the illusion and appearance of time—transcending time.

Is the table then not worthy of reverence or homage? Without idolizing it or turning it into an icon like a golden calf, which like the worship of all gods is not kosher, a few words might suffice as long as they do not cross the line from acknowledgment to fanatic obsession or deification. The last two lines of a poem about the table which Michael wrote that summer with Wendy in London are herein quoted:

*Table Poem (Ending Only)*
*I wonder what non union worker nailed in its legs*
*Now I sit at it unable to move.*

# 32

## HOW IT ENDED

The relationship between Michael and Wendy which at times had been as sweet as licking honey had its determination and climax—not in a dramatic or traumatic scene or sense—but in an anti-climatic long and slow withdrawal. Whereas long and slow and withholding normally heightens an organism, in the drawn-out pulling out of what was once a smoldering affair, the mighty logs that had flamed ardently were now but grey, dusty and charred, too dried even to be considered limp. But Wendy and Michael did hobble and wobble together for almost another year, well into Michael's second year of law school.

After living together that summer in the London high-rise apartment, on the recommencement of school in the Virgo month of September, Wendy went back to her fourth year at Waterloo to complete her Honor's B.A., returning to her home town of Kitchener which was in fact a city, and Michael found accommodations to share with his friend and fellow co-student at law school, Steven Davis: a second floor, two bedroom apartment of a two storey detached brick house in South London. While the University of Western Ontario was in the north side of London, living in the south of the city afforded Michael a chance to experience the real London (Ontario that is)—*Rock and Roll!*

While London was known for its insurance companies and its conservatism, notwithstanding that former Premier of Ontario, David Peterson, was a Liberal from London, London like many towns and cities in South Western Ontario were at their heart "Rock and Roll" towns. They had the drugs and alcohol to go along with such milieu, and the seediness too. Unlike the potent pot hydroponically bio-engineered now-a-days, back then the weed was often imported and still contained seeds, giving it *snap, crackle and pop!*

In truth Michael had cut down on his use of hard drugs. Once he had a bad trip he avoided the same micro-vacation spot, but he still enjoyed the occasional smoke with frequency. For a boy with a Jewish background and not a large stature he could drink spiritedly—binging on spiritually when stirred with smoke. Some people wondered what brought Davis and Rice together as neither of them sang and danced very well—or did standup comedy.

Steven was of average height and bore an understated athletic build that was neither stocky nor slim. His brownish blond hair was cut conservatively but not too short, and made him look a bit like a "goody two shoes." He spoke clearly and concisely, if not passionately. His personality and character may be summed up as sedate, confident and serious. His WASP heritage appeared apparent, but inside there was a bit of a rebel who liked rock and roll and punk music, as well as academics and sports. He enjoyed partaking at parties—proportionately and well measured—but not overly so.

Michael, on the other hand, to use a lawyer's expression, could be passionate and manic, a sort of Levantine Viking, a mixture of fire and earth, water and air; and all over the place. While Davis guided his ship on a steady course and keel, Michael basically ran amok, swayed and tempted by every storm and tempest. Michael kept burning his bridges, which in the island state of Cuba would be a prohibition against burning one's ships, but Michael always found a way—he was well rehearsed in the art and craft of thought where matters could always be divided into opposites—either side could be considered right or left if one turned around.

Perhaps it was their intellects that drew Davis and Rice to each other. They were both good students. Or perhaps Steven was drawn to Michael's wackiness, spontaneity and irreverence, the things he, Davis, lacked and secretly longed for. As for Michael, he might have seen in Davis the steady hand of following through on well-thought-out, reasoned, well laid plans; something Michael lacked the desire to pursue. The truth might have paradoxically been closer to the fact that no one else wanted to share an apartment with Michael in South London, and Michael being a contrarian wanted to demonstrate that not *all* Jews hung around together.

Michael did well in his second year of law school taking courses that were more mathematical, technical and precise in nature such as Income Tax, Taxation of Wealth Transactions, and Corporate and Commercial law. Perhaps some of Davis' good study habits were rubbing off on him.

When Wendy moved back to Kitchener she rented an apartment in the seedy and sketchy part of town near the old bus station. Why is it that the bus station in Southern Ontario is always in the bad part of town? And if some places can be said to have bad vibes, her apartment *oozed-a-plenty*, but Michael was less sensitive to his weird machinations back then and paid no heed to the tingling of his spider sense!

Almost singlehandedly, he helped Wendy move into such apartment, never once bragging about it, or thinking that his *mitzvah* or good deed might someday be rewarded. Isn't that what love is, the doing of something for someone that one *does not* want to do, but does it anyways just to help the other person? How different from sex which some confuse with love! Sex cannot show love because everyone wants to do it, especially with an attractive, fun and friendly, well-endowed woman which Wendy was.

As is so often the case with expectations, they let one down when the unexpected occurs. Expectations will always let one down, not gently generally, because for things to happen as envisaged, and end up as one desires would be sheer fortuitous and gratuitous luck, logically, and nothing more. When the future is a fully dimensional reality with a myriad of multiple possibilities, how could one expect to pinpoint the exact infinitesimally thin slice of what is to be? Would it not be like finding a needle in a haystack? As stated in Zeno's paradox, one can never actually reach something, which would be somewhere, but can only approach it by getting closer and nearer. This may explain why, when someone tries to do something good, the results often turn out very bad.

After Michael helped Wendy move and set up her apartment, he thought they could have some fun and relax, smoke, and screw—but party pooper fate had a different plan plotted. Michael quickly fell ill. People may laugh at the fu, which is short for influenza, but it is much more serious than a mere cold: more people died from the flu during the Great War than from the man made carnage! This is a true fact, even though it is not glamorous or exciting. Many facts are not well-known because they are boring and mundane and thus not considered *newsworthy*. The axis controls the mainstream media and wants to titillate and shock with sensational news items to further its secret public agenda. The stealing of a snow plough and running over a police officer, or just the shooting of a police officer, may be depraved and unacceptable acts, but are really not very common, as are deaths by pharmaceuticals, or by cancers from the toxins spewed into the environment by axis agriculture, and its food and drug preparation practices.

The Texas flu kicked its spurs into Michael hard and relentlessly, and felled him like he was a hog-tied steer at a rodeo. In that apartment of bad karma, he lay in bed limp, lacking the strength to move, suffering fever pitch hallucinations devoid of vivid and lucid images normally encountered in dreams or while high, gazing hazily on mathematical and thought abstractions and formulas, trying to decode the meaning of what was just beyond the fringe of consciousness to decipher and understand, tantalizing his burning, thirsty, aching body.

So Michael, who was not prone to fever, lay there for two days straight on a futon on the floor in the middle of that malicious and menacing apartment, unable to think straight, being too weak to get up out of bed, developing painful bed sores. He thought that he was going to die because he was prone to hypochondria.

"So this is the reward I get for helping Wendy without regard for myself," he ruminated when he gathered enough strength to put a sensible thought together. Looking back on it now in his more mature years in Hamilton after the U.S. was *"Bushwhacked"* by father and son presidents, he related the Texas flu to George Bush Jr., who took on the mantle of Texas so he could be "one of the good ole boys" and become president, and prove to his father that he could do it, i.e. become president.

No one however, is a real Texan because it is just a label, a state of mind, rather than a real state! By claims of manifest destiny, so *A La Mode,* the Americans pried Texas from the Mexicans, most of whom were previously Spanish, who in turn decreed their claim to such territory by sword and heavenly claims of legal "right-of-way," taking such real property from the native inhabitants, who usurped and disturbed the animals and wild life existing there previously. And so on and on and on it goes! The only thing that makes real property real is the claim it exists in *fee simple*! Notwithstanding history and rights claimed, Michael considered both the Texas flu and George W. Bush to be malignant.

But Michael did not die, and on the third day was able to get out of bed and enjoy the regular flu symptoms of sore throat, congestion and a cough for the next two weeks. Wendy soon moved out of the apartment of bad vibes, which Michael did not complain about even though he had to help her move again.

There are basically two routes to get from Kitchener to London by car, or vice versa. One could be called the "high road," and the other the "low road." Michael traversed both such routes in his car to see his bonnie Wendy, while she would take the bus or train. Back then all roads could be considered high because drinking and driving and a little puff, although not condoned was not condemned like it is today. Michael would often go for a drive on Sundays alone with some wine and weed. It was not out of the ordinary—a picnic on wheels so to speak! Back then discretion and measure were exercised, not like the harsh unyielding intolerance of right and wrong pontificated today. It was no big deal to let things slip under the radar. Mores, the determination of what is good and bad, has shifted with time, like the style of cars, haircuts and the cut of one's dress or lack thereof.

One of the two routes between Kitchener and London which by-passed everything, but required the traversing of a greater distance, was to zoom on Highway 401, while the other more direct route was Highway 7 that went through Stratford, and other towns and villages on the way. Highway 401 was the second of the super 400 series of highways, coming after Highway 400. Such highways were divided and access was limited by on and off ramps. One could get to where they were going without impediment of lights, cross streets or stops, travelling quickly in time. Flying down one of these marvelously smooth highways was like sitting on a couch until exiting at the appropriate off-ramp, passing time like a couch potato. However, the lofty expectations of sustained super-speed travel collided with the reality of constant rush hours, construction and accidents, and anyone taking this *super route* could be trapped in stop and go aggravation at any time without notice and an exit.

Highway 401 is the backbone of Ontario spanning over a 1,000 km from border to border, from Quebec to Michigan. Through Toronto it hits upward of eight lanes in either direction—amazingly though, *eight is not enough*!

Highway 7 is an older highway, and like all highways in Ontario, belongs to the Queen. Is that control or what? The Royal family, which changed its name to the House of Windsor during the First World War to hide its German connection because of a family spat, owns all the roads, easements and rights-of-ways as well as all property in Ontario except for native land which it either contracted away or omitted to grant and devise onto itself.

She, the queen even owns the language which all her subjects must speak. Not only is such language spoken in the United Kingdom, which is not so united, it is spoken in almost all of the colonies whether former or not. The syllabic tentacles of English even reach all the way into cyberspace to dominate the internet!

Highway 7 is just an old-fashioned two lane highway that provides a more direct route from Kitchener to London and back, but it often takes a longer time to traverse a shorter distance because of all the stops and starts involved in going through cities, towns, villages and other urban areas on the way. But wasn't that why the route was constructed in the first place, to take people from one place to another? It often

MICHAEL GRANAT

happened that the speed of taking the longer route equated to
the slowness of the shorter one—proof again of the theory of
relativity that two objects, or vehicles, leaving from the same
place and taking different trajectories or vectors through space,
could arrive at the same different place at the same time. It is
analogous to life where each person takes a different journey
or path, but ends up in the same place: the present at different times!

The one big town or small city Highway 7 winds its way
through is Stratford, Ontario. Why is Stratford famous?
One might in a knee-jerk fashion respond: the Stratford
Shakespearean Festival, but that is just an artsy excuse to sell
hamburger at *filet mignon* prices. Stratford is just another
industrial rock and roll, Southern Ontario town, dying an indig-
nant death of a receding hairline of manufacturing. Culture is
the thin veneer staged to hide the rusty steel and sooty bricks
of the aged, derelict fabrication plants; a toupee to cover the
industrial bareness.

The most important thing that happened in Stratford, which
occurred in the mid-nineties, almost twenty years after Michael
drove through it to see his woman, Wendy, is nearly on par or
of equal score to the Great One (all hail Gretzky!) coming from
Brantford, even though it is hard to surpass or come close to
Wayne's meteoric performance. The singing and dancing icon,
Justin Bieber, was born in Stratford! He tried to match the
Great One's record by having as many hits on Twitter as Wayne
had assists. It surely proves that Stratford really has no culture!

But is he, Justin of Stratford, a false prophet trumpeting
Messiah? Say it ain't so—who could Handel that? Is he a rock
star? No, real stars are composed of hydrogen exploding, like
the sun. If he were made of rock, Bieber would fall from the sky
at night, instead of racing his Italian sports car.

Michael was weaned and weeded on the finest classical rock
of the sixties and seventies, with many Lennon and McCartney

songs beatled into his buzzing brain like they were *earworms*. Justin's Bieberic talent would at best land more than a *rolling stone's* throw away from the monumentally real-martyred rock idols and icons like Jim, Jimmy, Janice, and sometimes Zimmy.

Michael considered that there was no need to get into a *deep purple* haze of the *pink Floyds* or *strawberry fields forever*, or *meddle* on the *dark side of the moon* when it came to young Bieber. He was not a punk, although at one time he was as cute as that little TV Beaver, but then he left and grew up Stateside to become more of a menace than *Dennis*.

"Who are you, Justin?" Michael wondered. "Tell me, *who, the fuck, are you?* You're just a hip hop *wannabe*, slim counterfeit clone of the most celebrated celebrity "clown" in Canada who hails from the real city, the megacity, and shuns pride." Michael was referring to none other than that crack-raving, pot-bellowing, rye-guzzling, pot-hole filling, largely-larded, T.O.'s leading elected man, the right honorable Mr. Mayor, the one who had to be called "Your Worship," so cool with his gang, the emperor of celebrity, at least for now.

Too bad Justin boy, not even pretending to be a *bare naked lady* could help you reach the megalomaniacal success you strive for *across the universe*, unless you find love, for love, oh love *will not fade away* even on a *ruby Tuesday*. Justin, when you are a man, you will know this and be able to say goodbye to all the *Beliebers* of false idols, as well as your youth. And then, you will be like a god, for *all you need is love. Love is all you need.*

And Wendy would come and visit Michael often in the second floor apartment in South London which Michael shared with Steven Davis during second year of law school. Michael recalled that the apartment had two bedrooms, each with sloped ceilings being mirror reflections of each other situated at the back. Michael liked sloped ceilings in a room although the volume was less because the floor footprint was the same, and such quaint pads were angularly not square. Money was saved in matters related to and affected by volume, such as heating bills and taxes.

When Wendy came, Michael would usher her into his cozy and comfortable bedroom as he had missed her, and longed for her presence, company and touch. They would listen to Steven Davis in the adjoining sister bedroom practicing classical guitar. That way, Davis would not have to listen to Michael and Wendy grinding their organs as they made rhythmic passionate love.

Michael recalled that Steven would trim each fingernail, one at a time, carefully and thoughtfully in an understated almost nonchalant manner before he would begin to practice, which he did often. Watching Davis trim his nails reminded Michael of his father's hands: the loving, giving and gifted fingers and hands of the sewing machine operator used to feed and push materials to be joined and united by the rapidly bobbing and jabbing needle of the humming sewing machine with thread. There was enough light in the bedroom, as it was still day, for Michael to make out the curves and contours of Wendy's naked body. He looked at her bountiful breasts trying to pretend he was not staring. One was slightly bigger than the other—was that normal? Michael had never ever been so close and intimate with anyone before to notice such a difference!

But soon the light of day faded into the twilight of the evening. The fingers of fate set the hands of the clock to night. In darkness the two once laughing and bemused lovers languished in the limbo of apathy, taking the relationship for granted. That is how it ended—with a whimper and not a bang—unlike the so-called birth of the universe.

The notion that the time of the birth of the universe can be fixed, or that the universe was even born at all, is more infantile than childish, for how could anyone talk a tick or lick of time before the invention of clocks or tongues, or the advent of day or night, which surely did not exist before the first moment that creation was struck. It makes one want to shout the berserker's cry: *"there can be no time before time!"* And just as there can be no time before time, neither can there be time after time. All time must be joined and self-contained like a circle inside of which another circle is found, and outside of which there is everything but a circle. Time appears to occur in the apparent world or realm of phenomena, as time or some time is all time in the dimension of time if time is analogous to space, and could be considered to all happen at the same time if it is stretched out all at once like space.

The conventional view that depth, breadth and height are three dimensions is misconstrued. They should together be considered as one dimension called "space" or volume. If this newly defined "space" is the first dimension, then time would of course move into second place. What then would become the third dimension? Is there such a thing—if a thing it is—and could it be known? The answer is certainly beyond the scope of words. If the mind focuses on the relation that links time and space, and then applies the same relation or function to time/space unified as one, one may from such springboard glimpse a hint, scent a whiff, of the answer to this mystery. For want of better terms, the third dimension can simply be referred to as the "perplexing non-apparent paradox," where space is the first dimension and time is the second.

After Wendy completed her four year degree at Waterloo, coinciding with Michael completing second year of law school, she moved to Toronto to find work. By this time the relationship had shrunk to the point it could be represented by the most foolish number that exists and adds up to nothing, that is fraught with not, that is all being and non being balanced, the unspeakable number which some opine represents a hole: "O," "O?," "Oh!"

When Michael noticed that Wendy was gone and the relationship was over, Michael realized at last what was lost. Isn't it often the case that one does not know what they've got till it's gone? *And on and on it seems to go...* Michael initially thought it would be easy not having Wendy around or available, but the older he got the more difficult it became to find someone that he could screw who turned him on (and would not turn off his friends). When the relationship ended, he moved about stunned as if in shock, being only able to shake his head and ask in disbelief: "What happened?" The numb despondency, the dejection and pain, the intense hurt of subtle lack of fulfillment was probably equal in degree, if not in kind, to the profound loss, frustration and displeasure he experienced when his mother had to hide from him for over a week to wean him from the breast, the source of the early elixir of life, when he was three years old!

But one need not feel sorry for Michael, for it is well known that what doesn't kill a person makes them stronger, unless it maims, wounds or scars, or unnoticeably interferes with the proper functioning of the immune system, or noticeably affects arousal of the sexual appetite and apparatus, for Michael saw many moons and mammary glands after mamma and Wendy. Some might have been minute or miniscule, and others mammoth and monstrous, but all had the same function, generation after generation, needed for the prolonged propagation of the erect species of which Michael was a member, the end result of people begetting since time not recorded, until recently, when the artful axis substituted formula for mother's miraculous milky meal to enhance its profits, already utterly swollen like a huge udder.

Michael and Wendy remained friends. Their lives had followed similar paths as they wandered on different roads which converged for a while. Subsequently, they each had one brief marriage with each begetting one issue that they construed as adding meaning to their otherwise hedonistic, questionable lives. Both tied the knot with people whom they probably would not have, had they known better or got to know their partner better beforehand. But for Michael's it was a case of *beshert* and thus predestined, but not so for Wendy. She was never persuaded to convert to Judaism, so the doctrine did not apply to her. It may have been written in the book of her life which could only be verified if one were able to read that most sublime text, but would not *all that happened* and *was to happen*, come to pass by any other name?

Michael did try to convince Wendy to continue being his one and only after Michael realized how much he panged to be with her after being without her for but a short time. Although his pleadings did not fall on deaf ears—her hearing was still audibly good considering all the loud rock music that passed through them—Michael lacked the persuasiveness of an experienced advocate at the time. Michael did not want to push it too hard or too far. He did not want Wendy to stay with him solely because of his slick oratory skills, for her do something she did not want to do to and would possibly regret later. He let her know how he felt. That was it. He must have loved her to let her go so easily. But then again, he may have thought that she would come back to him. So ends another love story.

What happened to D'Arcy? Michael picked up through the grapevine by way of hearsay that D'Arcy stayed for a while in Kitchener attending university, but never really got anywhere; his spirit was likely trapped in a bottle until released. Michael heard that D'Arcy had passed away a few years ago. "He must be in Valhalla now," Michael mused, "his lips and teeth blood red from the fruit of the vine, free of bodily chains and pains, floating outside time and space, his blue eyes shining through the absolute zero that separates this world and dimension from the reality that is all, and still a part of it. *Shine on you crazy diamonds.*"

Michael reflected on this as he was arriving at his favorite Starbucks in the now trendy part of Hamilton that he so liked.

Perhaps he should not have used an "eye for an eye" and "tooth for a tooth" with D'Arcy. If Michael knew then what he was in the course of learning now, in the course of randomly reviewing the idiosynchronistic happenings and occurrences of his life, there might have been something that Michael could have done that would have made a difference. D'Arcy might have still lived! They might have still been friends! The issue was not about going to law school, but *love* and *forgiveness*. D'Arcy may have been the weak one, his back stabbing and frequent fornicating but a cry for help, a shot in the dark—but Michael was too concerned with proving his own theorems to turn on the light.

Michael for a moment felt a tingle of guilt zip up his spine like low voltage *kundalini* rising, ascending, transcending and passing, leaving him void of down to earth thoughts with corkscrew force igniting his desire to be able to make it right, to do right, like a fuse. But he could not, so he resigned himself to the thought: "I was just a young sapling then. I could only grow in the manner which I grew, competing for space and light, bending and bowing to the blow of the wind. Now I am a mature tree. Even though my branches may not all be well-formed or beautiful, I am still alive and growing. I *can* give shade to the vulnerable creatures unable to stand the revealing, healing and life stealing rays of the midday sun, and the mysteriously maddening beams of the midnight moon."

Michael now saw himself as the centre of the universe—not an uncommon perspective—so prevalent in the "me generation" or any generation from Narcissus to the iconic Jesus sold by the church. Michael was moving towards the fool's paradox of all and nothing, i.e. that one is all and part of the all. The fool's paradox was not a place like Montana, although that is a state, because places exist only in the first dimension. Rather, the fool's paradox is a state of mind, a zone where one's lamp light shines truly in all dimensions—acting and being acted upon at the same time in no time and in no place—full volume in emptiness!

Michael thought that in his heart he loved D'Arcy. Now there was no need for forgiveness. In the soundless echo chamber of the mind, Michael whispered "*shalom*," which in Hebrew, a language that Michael once spoken but since forgotten, means four things. Michael could only remember three: *hello, goodbye and peace.* The forth lay on the tip of his tongue not ready to be revealed or unveiled, but he knew that it was not the orgasmic *love* he had sought throughout his life—love which could be overtly tasted and felt. He was so tantalized and seduced senseless with its shifting, changing persona, that he forgot to let it go.

Michael was looking forward to the triple espresso soon to be enjoyed at Starbucks as he parked the car on a nearby side street. The dream he had recalled that morning with the two large waves breaking happened to etch upon his mind. The dream he now interpreted as representing the two loves of his life, Wendy, and his *beshert* ex wife. Then—holy multiverse—it struck him that the dream could mean whatever he wanted! The mind connects everything together any which way it pleases with binding wires twisted by logic which it labels as "*truth.*" Perhaps he could ride the crest of the waves like a surfer and laugh in the face of fate, the water foaming and spraying about him, the salt stinging his eyes, causing a teardrop of joy to drip down his cheek. Growing up in this world and being of this world he gazed in awe at the long, perfect, unbroken ancestral chain linking all, creationist or evolutionist, to a common ancestor: "Adam" or "Ape," differing only in name. Michael then fondly recalled the overcooked food and bitter herbs eaten by the salt of the earth that should not be thrown into a dung heap or fed to dogs.

# 33

## WAY BACK WHEN

Way back when Michael was young, life was simple and uncomplicated. Why did it have to get so damn confused, confounded and convoluted? He knew that whatever he thought was right back then, and he did not have to question it. What he needed to know he heard or saw, and the conclusions he reached he thought were his own. The explanations came as if they were already within him; all that was needed was to ask the question.

Sure there were things that he needed to learn, like history, English and French, and about indigenous people called "Indians." And there were things he wondered about the answers to which might be classified as being in the realm of physics or science, but he would find the answers to these in books, like the world being composed of atoms, and that sight is based on the reflection of light. When he was possibly 9 or 10 years old, he believed that one day he might do something good, really great, like discover the cure for cancer, yet unaware that his ambition would be the force to propel his ship of dreams and aspirations to crash into the rocks of ice that served as a rye whiskey reminder that one in light seeks the safety and solace of shade, and one in darkness seeks the exhilarating charge of blinding light.

Little did he imagine that his dreams to make a difference would lead him down the path of skirt chasing, bowing to the greenback, and trying to suck in pleasure without blowing out pain, to be cut by the hot knives of desire, hashed out in wanting, groping his way in the dark in the murky and mazy belief that one can get closer by sheer desire.

Michael recalled that when he was young he had it all figured out, and even knew at what age he would be married. He could see himself a young cute little 9 year old Michael, with his little violin and case waiting for his lesson at the University Settlement sitting on a worn brown couch beside a glass top coffee table in the main floor of a two story brick building that was situate at the south end of a small urban park in an area close to downtown called the Grange. He remembered the chestnut leaves, fallen from a chestnut tree no doubt, as he walked to his lesson after taking the streetcar, all on his own, and how each leaf had five petal-like leaflets.

Who decided what to consider a leaf or a leaflet? And the awe so smooth brown oval shaped chestnuts that always had a little off-white color spot on them. Was that their Achilles' heel? The chestnuts themselves would often still be encased in a spiky light green casing, which if much bigger and made of metal could be attached to a chain and handle to create a deadly weapon. When Michael cracked opened the fresh green husk, usually by stepping on it with just the right amount of force, but not too much that would damage the chestnut inside, the nut was still moist but would dry quickly. An older Michael reflected on this, and it made him sad and happy at the same time to think of the cycle of life, the nut being the embryonic seed that would be the tree, and the tree bearing the nut—the perfect circle of imperfect manifestation. If the circles of life were spread out over time and joined they would appear like a *slinky*!

This bittersweet recollection like a bowl of hot and sour soup (one of Michael's favorite dishes) balanced the contradictory flavors like a bow pulled taut, letting him know that he existed in contrast and in balance to not existing. His life was no more than a visible vapor of breath. He thought of what Jesus had said, the kernels of the teachings that survived through parables like a shoot cutting through the earth to reach for the sun, or a needle with its threaded tail stitching through fabric effortlessly, slipping through the censor's blood stained bludgeon.

Jesus admonished the authorities of his time. Some he said saw only the fruits that hung on the trees, while others saw only the trees that bore the fruit. Jesus pointed out that life was comprised of not only of the tree and the fruit, but the growth and decay, the process which united them. Life was the changing changeless, or the changeless changing, a safe strongbox where all is stored secure—a web or cradle that no one can fall out of—the manifestation of laws where one is free except from their own oppressive thoughts, or the reaper's scythe.

On the glass coffee table sat magazines. As Michael waited he picked one up. It might have been a *Time Magazine* or *Newsweek*, the name is not important, but it was a news magazine in any event, and on the cover was a black and white picture of an athletic, handsome, young black man.

Michael was intrigued by the magazine because there were no magazines at the Rice residence. Not only did Michael's parents not read English at the time, magazines were considered a luxury. Michael did not know how to judge his family's economical state or class, or what his family lacked. The providence and state of his environment and upbringing was all he knew and never once considered that he might be seen as lower class by others. He was happy having all he needed. The rest he believed, being whatever he might want, would come to him in time.

He read an article in the magazine which was several pages long, filled with black and white photos about an up and coming young boxer named Cassius Clay who had just changed his name to Mohammed Ali. Perhaps he was from Alabama, but Michael could not remember for sure; he thought there was some reference to Alabama. Michael was a bit bewildered at the time, and wondered why someone with such a classy, classic, alliterated and strong name such as Cassius Clay, which had been given to him by his parents with full blessings no doubt, and probably borne and worn by his forbearers with pride for centuries, would ever want to change it to a foreign sounding name which had no punch, pizzazz or jazz to it.

As well, "Mohammed" and "Ali" both sounded very Arabic and Muslim. Michael's family had recently arrived from Israel, still harboring animosity and mistrust of Arabs, many of whom did not want Israel or Jews to be in Israel, desiring that every single Jew that lived and breathed—at least in Israel—be annihilated. All this was beyond the understanding of Michael. His interests lay in trying to figure out how the world worked. He thought science had an answer to everything, just waiting to be discovered. He was now confused: how could the world be in such a state of hate? He and his family were not filled with hate. Fear perhaps, but not hate.

Michael was not prejudiced *per se*. He was still young, innocent and naïve, and had met few, if any, black people up to then. The closest thing was probably a swarthy Sicilian, but the sins of the forefathers seem to slip into the unconscious of their sons subliminally, as if in the genes, contrary to the theory of evolution.

When Michael read about the transformation of Clay to Ali, from caterpillar and larva to butterfly or bee, Michael did not understand the deep torrents and undercurrents coiled therein, for he had yet to slip into, and then try to escape and run away from the clutches of the Upper Society of Law in Ontario that subsequently refused to un-enslave him.

Reading the magazine, Michael noticed that Clay Ali was of marrying age, and Michael thought that the ideal age to marry would be at 28 years old. Not too young and not too old—but just right—and that became his goal.

But Michael was wrong again. He did not get married at 28, but was in fact almost 35 years old when he plunged into the deed. It could be argued from here to eternity what the best age to marry might be, or whether one should get married at all. Today, matters are further complicated by questions relating to sex. Will there be enough, and if so, with whom? It is a moot point however, which for some reason lawyers don't mind—as opposed to hypothetical which they always stay away from. Michael had no choice: his union, bond and covenant covered him like an artistic mosaic of Mosaic Law linking him to his *beshert*, pre-scripted and preordained by what could injudiciously be called an act of god unless spoken in court. *Amen.*

Now Steven Davis, there was a man who knew what he wanted. He wasted little words, used and spoke only those necessary without artifice, embellishment or consternation. Michael secretly envied this, but not overly or overtly so, as he never put it into practice or displayed such predilection, inclination or propensity.

Where was Davis now? After law school Davis had gone overseas to study law for a year at some medieval university notorious for learning and teaching in the queen's own bailiwick named perhaps Cambridge or Oxford. The exact name is unimportant as both names are equally impressive. No doubt Davis is a legend there as he played on the ice hockey team, shining head and shoulders above the other players across the big pond. It ain't cricket, is it?

Davis was never one to take short cuts or shirk his duty; quite the contrast to Michael who threw out the baby with the bath water when it came to getting from point A to B. Davis went on to become a professor of law. He went through all the steps including articling and bar admission course although he could have skipped both because he had a graduate degree. He chose to take the *long way home*, not the short cut that was available to him, because he had the stiff upper lip displayed when one possesses the bulldog quality.

When Davis decided he was going to get married, his wife appeared out of nowhere as if placed by fate on his path. She was exactly what Davis wanted her to be, an independent, strong bodied, capable big-boned blond with the capacity and verve to carry the five children Davis divined and desired. They came after he came without much ado. Did he know the secret of how to grease the wheel of life or what goose was good for the gander?

Some may gawk at the way they see the world work. Some say that the lord works in mysterious ways. Any reference to the divine or to a god-like something is made strictly on a without prejudice basis not to be construed as a metaphysical admission of the truth thereof. It is a mystery why someone, something, or the whole thing, reputed for holiness, purity and cleanliness, would make desirous that which is most prohibited and considered dirty and taboo. Not only desired but *really* wanted. The human race is in reality totally dependent on such shunned singularity that is needed for its very being, existence and rebirth: its propagation! Begetting and sex can and ought to be considered on par with the life force itself in terms of importance and necessity; they may even be one and the same. Although some characterize disbelief in the divine as "ungodly," one can fight such cynical *worldview* by being like a boxer that is quick on their feet and able to punch and jab powerfully at lightning speed with both hands, and clap hands and sing, and really sting, while still being literate! Such someone does not need to change the name of the boundless to divine, which by any name would smell as sweet, stinky or sublime.

The "act of god," reproduction or sex, can be seen as a bright, joyous and sunny wonder. Why do so many abide in a seedy den cultivating rotten fruits bruised by the dark and lustful shades generated and germinated in the artificial light emitted and radiated by the medical-religious-monarchical axis to alarm and beguile, antagonistic to the free and plentiful inter-course of *Homo erectus* among each other? The faltering light obscures one's natural light. In the shadow the world becomes a valley of fear, war, oppression, frustration and guilt; begetting becomes a sin of nightmarish lust. Why is it so difficult to com-prehend that the day and night together make up the days of life, before all time, after all time, and in all time?

# 34

## ON INFINITY AND LOSING

Michael got out of the car after parking on the side street in the last available space before such street intersected with the now trendy Locke Street where the Starbucks Michael liked was located. As there were now trendy shops, cafes and stores on Locke Street and the rents had gone up, even street parking had to be paid for. When Michael first came to Hamilton he was drawn to the area with its tree-lined streets and brick houses, bushes and flowers. The houses were not too big and not too small. The owners and occupants thereof were not too poor or too affluent—sort of middle class right. Locke Street was calm and not heavily trafficked—it was not on the way to somewhere. It was a good area to walk, bike or drive, and near enough downtown to walk there.

When Michael arrived a dozen or so years ago, most of the shops and storefronts sold antiques or were occupied by beauty salons, hairdressers and barber shops (the beauty industry never being short of needy customers), but now there were fewer antique shops as the rents had escalated with the gentrification of the area. When the yuppie denizens from Oakville and Burlington started talking about moving to this part of blue-collar, steel town Hamilton, the "Hammer," Michael knew that it was time for him to get out, so he sold his two story brick house in the area to buy the one bedroom Condo where he currently resided. Not only did he make money on the downsizing, he also captured non-taxable capital gains, which in layman's terms means that he paid no taxes on the profits. Michael's logic was: "Why not live in a less desirable area which is much cheaper, when I can still hang around in an upscale café in a good area for free?" His condo, Starbucks and Locke Street filled the bill and shrunk it too!

Michael looked both ways to make sure no cars were coming as he walked across Locke Street. Looking down he noticed the thick white lines marking the cross walk, painted just a few days ago. The white of the lines was very clear and bright; easy for those driving to notice so they could proceed with caution.

"So this is where our tax money goes" Michael mused as he continued to cross the trendy street, "to paint lines on intersections, and for fancier traffic lights that count down the seconds before the light changes. But is it really necessary?" He recalled a simpler time when hockey goalies wore no masks while the other players of that fast moving game sported no helmets. Kids even walked to and from grade school unaccompanied. But that was then and this is now. The evil axis had filled the hearts and minds of North Americans with fear!

Back before the axis materialized, individual freedom abounded. People were able to do as they pleased, free from so many rules and regulations, watchful cameras, listening microphones, and most recently, the drones of "big brother" watching over them, just like Michael's brother tried to watch over him when he was young. Abe was still trying to tell Michael what to do! But the "watchers" and "monitors" were so secret: they had been sewn within, among all. Most people are blind to the axis as its rays spin invisibly outward from a non-existent point to roll and control their minds!

But what could any one person do? It was a democracy, wasn't it, so any one interest, one vote, was of infinitesimal value—hardly worth crossing an "X." Who could match the power and castigating strength of the established system—it had grown insidiously out of its own members and constituents—the whole was now more monstrous and greater than its parts. Initially it started out benign, but in the soft and sweet bowl of culture it grew and grew, feeding on poor citizens' and taxpayers' hard earned dough with such an insatiable hunger and appetite that there was never enough, creating crisis after crisis, causing shortage after shortage; falsity and failure were said to be lack and need to justify devouring more and more. And the bigger it got, the more it grew. And the bigger it grew, the more it needed to eat and feed itself to sustain and grow more!

"They are sly, cunning and clever, and make us believe they are acting in our best interests" were Michael's thoughts of the powers which uphold themselves to maintain the status quo. "The grey matter of our minds is but putty in their hands, to mold us as they will and bid, to do as we are told. We are expendable and unknowing pawns in the game they play with our lives."

Michael was in Starbucks now and he was going to order his triple espresso and hot water as usual. It was his habit to always make a funny quip, unless he was in a real foul mood, and say something while ordering, such as calling the triple espresso, "triple X."

Starbucks was the epitome of success for a corporation. They had a formula to replicate and clone success it being strictly executed and enforced at all the stores, unlike his store,

Wild Rice, to which Michael had to constantly shovel in more capital to keep the furnace of his operation fired up and boiling. If his business was a patient, it would be in critical condition and on life support.

It could be argued that he must have liked it that way, for that is what he did, if not by his own choosing, then by not choosing not to, by letting it happen over an extended time without exerting an effort to make it otherwise. Perhaps that was what the "Wild" in Wild Rice signified, the untamed natural force occurring when things happen according to their nature without interference of order and control. Maybe it was sheer laziness, but just letting the business survive and continue marginally was like walking the razor's edge, but what could that mean? No one can walk on a razor's edge without the proper footwear due to the law of gravity pulling their feet down and slicing them apart!

But wait, to walk the razor's edge one must be balanced so as not to fall over, and so light as not to exert more downward pressure than a sole could withstand. Or does the razor's edge somehow relate to Zeno's paradox: one can never arrive at, but can only get closer to? The razor's edge could get shaved so thin as to disappear, to be cut or divided by nothing and everything, so just like the present it would not exist because the past and future leave no time or room between them, like a boundary where two contiguous or adjoining things or states touch each other: there is no room between them except an invisible boundary line to mark the perceived difference. *Loki's head can never be had—without touching his neck!*

How is Starbuck's code of conduct so well reproduced and mentored into the being of each of its managers and employees, drilled fervently and furiously into the very being of all who work there as if by a lance sergeant, and begotten into a barista's consciousness as if planted by genetic inheritance? Michael imagined overseer enforcers from head office officiously wearing immaculately pressed black uniforms each with a small round green and white mermaid logo. Each member of such elite group of behavior police would cast a shadow of doubt in the mind of any barista caught acting friendly for more than the allotted thirty seconds in fear of the third degree and being scolded: "*You vill not tell za truth—*" in the blinding light of the confusing rigmarole.

Going up to the counter Michael imagined that one day all of Starbucks' procedure would be automated and digitalized and there would be no chance of human error. The Starbucks' experience would be perfect: profits would rise exponentially by having to pay no wages. At the counter a holograph to suit the customer's mood as indicated by their body language would ask what they would like, and then take the money directly out of their account as they would automatically be recognized. Everything would be made by machines, as it is now, except more so. The order would end up deposited perfectly at the end of the counter without human involvement. It could even be refined to the point where each patron would be recognized on entering—the technology already exists. Each customer would hear different music particular to their liking, projected directly to them for only them to hear. There would be as many different symphonies or songs going on at once as there would be people to hear them, without interference from each other. "*Oh children, it's just a step away, it's just a slip away.*"

Perhaps the sky high costs of the high tech gadgets could be skipped or leapfrogged. Each customer could be given a little pill or a whiff of something as they entered to make them imagine the experience which they desired, to let out the inner soul in full expression. Surely it would be allowed as long as it were prescribed by a doctor, or endorsed by the Health Canada, the F.D.A., or the C.I.A. It would be the zenith and apex of contentment—the cat's meow—possibly the most popular thing around next to masturbation which no one likes to brag about, because almost anyone can do it, and it costs nothing! And why could not stimulating an experience be nearly as good as the real thing—Coca Cola notwithstanding? Should it not be possible with the plethora of digitalized marvels available for one's disposal, in light of and considering the unbounded and uncharted nature of reality that the mind is lost and found in, not to mention the highways, byways, laneways and dark alleys?

Michael discovered infinity while very young in a place that may be considered crappy—although for Michael it was just in the ordinary course of doing business. Michael did not know if he was remembering an occurrence directly, or if his recollection was a memory of a memory. With no evidence to the contrary available, the latter is more likely than the former because over such a long period of time he would have probably forgotten the actual initial incident that instigated its remembrance.

Michael was sitting on the potty making number two, and it was on a pot filled with water the size in which potatoes are often boiled. Fortunately *"poo"* or *"poo-poo"* does not need to be peeled like potatoes, but that is just a silly and gross idea. Michael was about three years old, and while sitting there and making *"caca,"* he realized that he could count to infinity with just the simple knowledge he possessed, having recently learned how to count. He deduced that the pattern in counting was based on repetition, and there were only 10 digits. The same pattern was repeated no matter how high or big the number got, punctuating and permeating the sequence forever, or to infinity, as endlessness is often called. Even though the names of the numbers changed as they grew, Michael saw the big picture. And would not the number have the same value or be worth the same no matter what word or language was used to count? It was a good thing that Michael was on a pot, and not on pot, for then he wouldn't be able to remember how to count so high! In essence Math, or arithmetic, is just another language, where words are true by definition in the coinage, capital and currency of symbols rather than words.

Life would have been much simpler and more enjoyable had "number" just remained another word for a method of smoking pot, instead of something which has no beginning or end, and thus impossible to light when one was on the pot taking a shit!

Speaking of higher thought, Michael's father taught him how to play chess when he, Michael, was in grade school, and by the time Michael was in grade 4 he was on the school's chess team. When Michael was in grade 5 his school placed third in the Toronto chess championship for grades 4, 5 and 6. The City of Toronto back then was not the same as the City of Toronto now, for the City of Toronto now would have been called the Municipality of Metropolitan Toronto back then. The City of Toronto back then did not include what were first called boroughs (a holdover from the crown that pricks through the English language like a thorn) and later matured, growing into cities, such as North York, the other Yorks, Scarborough (it would be fairly easy to guess it is was a borough) and Etobicoke. Such details are provided to point out that the boroughs and other cities had their own school boards back then and did not partake in the Toronto chess championship.

By grade 6 Michael had a lot of experience playing chess, which has been called the game of masters putting in on par with the haggis eater game of golf, but for golf being an outdoor game one plays against oneself, and when angry or frustrated a player cries out in anguish: "*what for!*" and then throws the club (if it did not go flying with the swing) as far as possible. What a stress release!

Chess is an ancient binary game where two sides oppose each other and play on a checkered board called a chessboard which has an unknown past. Each piece is limited to its own particular moves due the nature of what piece it is. Pieces can be captured, players move alternatively or take alternate moves, and when the king of the opposing player is taken or captured the game is won or lost depending on who does the capturing, or gets taken—just like real life!

There are many other similarities between the game of chess and life, or "analogies" or "similes" if one likes to use "like" as well as "as." Life has been referred to by the name "game" as has love. As in life, so it is in chess: white always gets to go first, the queen is a more powerful than the king, and when the king is in danger of being taken or captured the word "*check*" is called—which means someone has to pay! Back when Michael was in grade school there were no credit cards.

Finally, "*checkmate*" is called when the king is in danger of being taken by the opposing side, and has no escape from mating with a piece not of its own color which would certainly lead to banishment and shunning—at least a long time ago—banishment being considered by some a fate worse than death!

Again finally, just like life, the king and queen of the same colors do not mate each other because they have been together for a long time—as long as anyone can or cares to remember since the rules of the game are so ancient!

And Michael played and practiced chess hard and frequently, for he had the time, not yet being distracted by sex, drugs, alcohol and rock and roll. He studied openings and endings endured by the masters, who even at their elevated level of enlightenment could not avoid or escape the fact that each game had a beginning and an end. When a player would not play out the game to the end, they would be forced to resign so all games ended in either the agony of defeat or the ecstasy of victory, unless it was a boring draw. What a cruel and heartless game chess is, but if one wanted to play the game they had suck it up, because being checkmated is part of the game that has to swallowed, and better "to always lose than never to have played."

Michael was the captain of the chess team in grade 6 and also the first board. Being ranked top seed he could be as mouthy as he liked, sprouting and spouting off, as he pleased and pleased him, at any time!

Finally the exiting days of the annual tournament arrived, and the chess team enthusiastically piled into a car operated by the teacher who went along for the ride to drive the competitors to the school hosting the event. The first day was the elimination round. Anyone that lost a game that day was eliminated from further competition. If a player won all of the games played on the first day, they would come back for the second day, or the round-robin round, where everyone played a game against everyone else that survived, and there was no more elimination. The champion or winner would be the person who had the best record for each grade after all the games were played!

Chess is a lot like boxing, but much more brutal because boxing has strict rules and etiquette, being quite often referred to as a "gentlemen's sport." No boxer takes the gloves off and goes for the jugular or a kill without mercy and pounds the hell out of the opponent when they are down and out, as is so common in chess. It would be *"unmanly,"* and sure as hell no referee would allow it!

Can anyone imagine yelling *"check"* in a boxing match like the white side often does to the black side in chess? It would be unimaginably degrading and impermissible in this day and age to strip search a black boxer in a ring during a match in front of all the spectators—even in Alabama! Well perhaps not so when Michael was growing up.

Finally, the crescendo or peak of the difference in the two sports or games relates to the calling of *"checkmate,"* or *"mate,"* as it is often called by serious opponents or proponents, or sex-starved do-it-themselfers, which many chess playing geek/nerds are—only in chess and not in pugilism—signifying the final victory, the complete and utter decimation of the adversary.

Not only for the reasons cited does chess paint a nasty picture compared to boxing, but what would happen if a boxer yelled *"checkmate"* during a match when delivering the final knock out? Would he not be jabbing at his opposite, hurling insult after injury after knocking the other man out senselessly, or at minimum after beating his opponent, even if only on technically grounds, hinting in sort of boxer's code all so smugly while dancing and prancing around like a bragging clown at a one ring circus, something which could be taken to mean: "your wife has been unfaithful," under the rubric of exclaiming *"checkmate,"* to someone who has just had the crap knocked out of them. It's like kicking someone who is down and out!

Michael's team had a full roster of three players for each grade. Out of such nine players, six made it through the eye of the elimination round to return for round-robin round the following day: all three *boards* (as chess players in their own jocular are called) from grade 6, of which Michael was one; two from grade 5; and one from grade 4.

The round-robin matches began. Michael played and beat the player who was touted as the best player in grade 6, an Indian from the land of curry. Michael, like a hurricane, was on his way to blowing out the competition and being the chess champion in grade 6 for Toronto, which to him was like being the champion of the world. It would provide the recognition he craved because he thought he deserved it—to be crowned the best player in elementary school of Canada's largest city!

But, woe to Michael, he may have counted his chickens before they hatched. Fate conspired against him by putting a hole in his mind whereby he overlooked a clear and present danger or threat that even a player nowhere near his caliber would not have overlooked, in a game where he had gained the upper hand and was overpowering the other weaker player. Such elementary oversight, which is not something he missed, but instead forgot that he had considered it before he forgot about it, caused him to lose, and the game. Perhaps it was cockiness, or sheer fatigue, but shit happens. So it was, it happened, notwithstanding Michael being prepared and having practiced to avoid such slip ups that he was prone to now and then. But what can be done once the move has been played and the die cast? Michael still had a chance to win the tournament. Every player had lost at least one game so far, and Michael had beaten the player perceived as the one to beat to win.

Finally, the time came for the last and final game of the tournament to determine who would be the champion, and who would be the loser. Michael faced the third board from his own school, a Ukrainian named Paul Fartic, for the *make it or break it* match. The tension was taut and covered the room as tightly as designer jeans worn by a skinny teenage girl. An intense crowd swirled intently around Rice and Fartic watching in silent interest, time suspended as if all existence was caught motionless in the eye of a hurricane, the hard fought out and close match, move by move, boring to all but hard-boiled chess aficionados. But when the time allotted for the determinative game ran out, no one had been mated. It was a surprise that the clock was able to run out at all, after moving so slowly throughout the entire match!

Michael hoped the judges would call it a draw, for although he would not concede that he was in the weaker position, it would be an uphill battle to persuade the judges that he was in a position to win. Soon the judges made a decision, one that was whispered covertly into the right ear of the referee. Then the referee, wearing a jailbird style black and white striped shirt thrust his right hand forcefully and dramatically forward three times ending with a snap of the wrist each time in a counting motion, as if he were casting a fishing rod, and then looked straight into the querying eyes of the exhausted combatants, Rice and Fartic, one at a time.

The room was so quiet that even a needle could be heard dropping. The referee turned his head slightly to the right, and with a forward lunging motion grabbed Fartic's wrist and raised his left arm high in the air. Fartic was jumping up and down in exhilarated exuberance, pounding his fists excitedly above his head in victory, before, during and after the referee had raised and let go of his hand!

Fartic had won. Michael had lost! The crowd, as if conducted by a celestial wand, uttered in unison a mixture of "*ooos*" and "*aahhs*," sounding like a religious mourning knell—all were in shock and surprised that Michael had fallen! But there was no appeal from the decision of the judges because a minor, as Michael then was, does not have legal standing to appeal a decision, or to ask for leave to have a decision judicially reviewed.

Michael felt badly. Not only had he lost the prize that was rightfully his, he had been beaten and humiliated by the third board of his own school! Michael tried to console himself by claiming that he was the runner-up, but that meant diddly-squat. No one cares about an "also-ran." He had taken a terrific tumble and lost his first major trial. There was no consolation prize. Winning meant everything to him as he had worked so hard for its attainment. He had bathed in the hope of expectancy. However, it was not to be. For some time after his defeat he felt like he was worth nothing, even though paradoxically, it could not be said that losing meant *nothing* to him. Chess was the ultimate blood sport, fought face-to-face, *mano a mano*, without any protection or padding to soften the unrelenting blows that are inflicted in its hardscrabble world.

Although it turned out that Michael's school and his team had won the tournament and the overall trophy, having garnered the most points, and had also won the award as most improved team moving from third place the previous year to first place the current year—no mean feat standing on its own, and not shabby by any measure it is cut or undressed!

Additionally, his team could boast the individual champions for both grades 4 and 6, failing to win such title only for grade 5. Michael could have had bragging rights as the captain and the guiding and driving force and leader of the team, but such was not the case. Michael instead felt dejected, forlorn and became seriously sad and despondent. Perhaps he was not a true team player after all!

He thought that he should have won and deserved to win the championship, and thus justifiably concluded that there was no justice in the world. He went around for days on end sulking, sobbing and crying, at times uncontrollably when he thought of his loss. He came so close, within a few small pieces, only to fall to a sub-earthly low. It was as if he had arrived at the gates of heaven, but felicity had by the fate of a slight oversight been foreclosed to him—he was banished from bliss and the benedictions and salutary congratulations of his school mates among whom he was much more popular than that stinking third board, Fartic, the fucker! Michael had been brought to his knees, an almost unbearable fate because Michael's father taught him that Jews don't kneel—to taste life's bitter fruits and herbs and he found them not to his liking. From then on Michael decided not to try so hard anymore at anything— never to dedicate himself to anything with full fanatical, utter and complete devotion! Failure had felled him ferociously, and possibly forever: there was no justice in the world for little boys.

No one, except Michael alone, understood and felt the depth of his anguish for they could not see his misshapen aura, or hear the echo of his longing locked within, no longer to be found, now that he had lost.

# 35

---

# REVISITING THE PAST

After grade 6 Michael's family moved from the immigrant area in downtown Toronto called Little Italy, north to what were then the suburbs, essentially taking the bus straight up Bathurst Street to cross the sentry-less and unguarded border with North York to what was euphemistically called the "Gaza Strip," as it was an area that that was occupied by many Israelite offspring. Michael's family in one thirty minute trip moved from an area populated by working class people like them, to an area proportionally more prosperous permeated with professionals and proprietors of businesses and capital, speakers of good English with plenty of possessions and property who had a propensity and disposition to promote and propagate the derogatory and disrespectful in the spoiled fruits of their progeny. Michael didn't mind. He enjoyed the raving rapture of such rhapsody, and the rhythmic rant of sarcasm and mockery.

But Michael was no longer at the top of the heap in the pile of his peers. He was now just a small fish in a big new pond. He now realized the relative reality that his parents were uneducated working class folk, often referred to as "lower class," as he pondered the perplexing world from a transposed and transplanted perspective. The gasoline of class consciousness he had siphoned from his new surroundings fueled his consternation, and fed the flames of his shame. What he probably most wanted, but was unable to see or admit, sense or feel, was to be accepted and appreciated—in essence to be loved and cared for and treated with respect—but his analytic determination had delineated expectations and distinctions which could never be met. Things never turn out as envisioned even with the best laid plans of any creature whether a mighty mouse, or a ratty man. Michael was unknowingly the author of his own tome, making it like a bed in which he would have to sleep in, even if he could not sleep.

Michael became ashamed of all things Jewish: the dress, the ceremonies, the rituals, and the prayers. They were so obscure, out of place and out of date—no one dressed like that anymore with long unruly beards and prayer shawls—wrapped up in red or black tape. The arcane practices, holdovers from millenniums past, did not resonate with the modern western sound of the Canadian new world clanging in the culture of scientific and mechanical machismo—the shiny sound of the brave new world. He became a secular sort, abstaining from even being *bar mitzvahed.* There was one thing Jewish that he did not mind, or at least liked for the most part, and that was Jewish food—his mother was a good cook and baker!

The cultural stock that stirred and flavored Michael's emotional make up was inherited. The Jews in Poland were an unruly, out of control lot, searching for messiahs, prying to spy peeks of the divine, dancing and jumping ecstatically to their own beat and chime. Michael's family was a modern offshoot:

the modern working class, socialist leaning Jew, emphasizing culture, tradition, education and tolerance with just an acerbic dash of theology. Michael was not versed in his tradition's history at the time. He learned on becoming a lawyer that all traditions, cultures, and races are open and subject to interpretation and revision as they evolve and change.

What of his root stock, the Hassidic Polish Jew, who valued the experience of being and celebration of life more than theology? They were plentiful and multifold and numbered in the millions in Poland before the war. Were they dangerous? Were they a threat, always different, joyously dancing and singing and complaining? Jesus certainly was. No empire that spanned across thousands of kilometers over a thousand years could allow the stone to drop and ripple, but it did. His words were turned inside out, upside down, theologized, dogmatized and doctored so that the waters no longer flowed down towards the sea for all to bathe and be baptized in the cleansing, liquid freedom. Instead the waters were dammed, corralled and pumped into aqueducts and reservoirs, dispensed at the pleasure of the high priests, Caesars and Czars. All had to pay the minimum tithe or tax: lip service and subservience!

Of the Jews in Poland of which there was a multitude before the Second World War only about ten percent survived the smoking and curing of the meaty "final solution." No need to ask: "*What am I, chopped liver?*" Science teaches that nothing is final or absolute. A solution only dissolves, solves and resolves to the point of saturation.

What is the meaning of *decimation*? If a group of ten gets decimated, they can no longer meet, for one is the loneliest number. It is not a group even though it may have been sung. What could it be called? Devastating? Drastically diminished? Deeply discounted? "*Oy, you took a bit too much off the top!*"

The breakthrough novel of Joseph Opatoshu, *In Polish Woods*, written in Yiddish by the author in New York and published prior to the Second World War, sold over 30,000 copies in Poland alone, double the purported number of the sales in all of North America. How many bright reading lights were turned off? Millions of lives expunged—an exit without much ado and no *adieu*, the blackboard wiped ninety percent clean by a black sponge! A once flourishing forest cut down and thinned with only one out of ten trees left standing. A tragedy lacking poetic justice!

Did someone forget that all people are brothers and sisters? Will the memory of the clothes that once housed flesh die after being hung out to dry in the Aryan breeze? What is the shape of mortality: the trumpet tapping or the ram's horn blowing *"nevermore"*?

In grade 7 Michael attended Junior High School in North York where all the people that thought they *could* be cool were trying to *act* cool, and part of being cool was dating. Michael had a crush on a classmate in his grade and she was an identical twin, about Michael's size if Michael were a woman, which is petite for a she, with his type of build, neither fat nor thin, but leaning towards the stocky side. She was a pleasant looking girl with short black curly hair.

The good thing about a twin, Michael thought, was that if one does not like you, perhaps her sister might, and there would be little difference. *"Who could tell them apart?"* Identity bracelets were popular at the time, so Michael bought one and scratched his name on it. He gave it to the girl he had an eye on. Perhaps her name was Suzie. Michael thought that she would really appreciate his token of affection and its embellishment, given the personal touch he added, but Suzie was not at all impressed with the cheap, silver-colored crap Michael gave her with his name amateurishly etched thereon, not being professionally or aesthetically engraved—she would not accept it!

Michael made short order of his foray for the twin's affection and quickly and silently slipped away extricating himself from the scene and situation which he kept quiet about. He was more embarrassed by his naivety and what a loser lout he looked like, rather than being hurt by the rejection. He wanted to be cool and suave, but his actions derided the classiness he cared for and sought to achieve. Then and there he decided that it was time to take up smoking weed for he was too young, and looked way too young, to drink! That would be cool and fun and then who the fuck would care!

Was Michael rash in his decision to smoke hash? Back then there was little of the bud around that was green. The black, brown, red or blond resin was everywhere to be seen, smoked and toked. But if the truth be told, smoke is just a screen for something that is lacking and remains unseen. No one needs an excuse to dance and sing, laugh or cry, or even to get high, but alas, no one spoke the truth for they were too busy being right.

# 36

## THE MIRTH STATION NO. 9

Michael was back in the car after consuming his triple espresso. He brought the infusion of turmeric and ginger with him to slowly sip as he raced and navigated his way on the limited-access super highways of the queen, which linked Hamilton to Toronto like a 60 km long hole on a golf course. Forty-five minutes was par to get to from Hamilton to the Wild Rice store if the day and the way was fair, free of the traps and hazards of rain or snow. But if too many players decided to partake in the driving game at the same time, then the course became congested with traffic, and the time of traversal would be handicapped, which was usually the case, causing one to arrive several strokes of the clock later than anticipated!

The course from Hamilton to Toronto was also often retarded and delayed by manmade obstacles: road repairs and construction like the erection of poles and the laying of asphalt and filling in of holes, all of which had to be paid for by taxes wedged from taxpayers to line the pockets of the politicos in power who had to ensure their pockets had sufficient integrity to hold so much coin in rapture without rupturing!

Although Toronto is east of Hamilton, because Hamilton lies under Lake Ontario, initially one must go west to get around the lake to go east. Michael ramped onto Highway 403. He then dog-legged north between Hamilton Harbour and a scenic body of water called Princess Point (Oh no, not the offspring of royalty again!) He then went east, once north of the lake, until merging with the Queen Elizabeth Way, which was equal to a super highway of the 400 series in every aspect, manner or respect, except as to being named after a number: so was the QEW or QE for short, royally robed without numeric guise!

Michael drove at speeds of between 110 and 120 km per hour as the traffic moved well on that bright, sunny October afternoon. The posted speed limit was 100 km per hour, quite fast one may think, but it was merely a convention—no one went that slowly! Rules, like bones, were made to be broken—not by sticks and stones—but by disobedience to the words of acts and statutes, due to peer pressure.

Thinking as he drove now to work about work, or more precisely how he was going to get out of having to work, that is to say, how he was going to put the ball into the hole and putt out, hit the bull's eye, sew the button on the coat, call a spade a shovel: the question of how was he going to extricate himself from the situation he was in by selling the store, Michael began to dwell on the endgame of his marriage. If one were to spend the same effort in the doing something as one expends in trying to get out it, it, the thing could and would have been done and completed—signed, sealed and delivered, lock, stock and barrel—more easily and with less effort than running away and hiding from it. Done and gone once and for all (which is forever and always)—but humans enjoy to torture and torment themselves with ties to the *mast of must* on the *deck of most,* never knowing when to bluff, if anyone else is bluffing, what the stakes of the game are, or if it is in fact a game they are playing, or just a practice round.

Though the ball which flies and rolls along the course of life appears but small, it needs to be smacked with full concentration and force without reflection or thought as to where it will land, whether on the green or rough, or out of bounds. No matter how the stroke turns out, the ball *has* to be played from where it lands, without giving in to second guesses that can only arouse anger and frustration. That is the lie of the land, and those are the rules of the game. If one cheats, they not only cheat themselves, but everyone else that might find out.

But does it really make a difference unless one is playing for money or keeps? Who really knows the rules of the game? Who will be the first to accuse and chastise another for bending or breaking the rules when they themselves may be bent out of shape? Where does one draw the line in the sand trap of life between bending and breaking in the subjective and subjunctive language of imperatives? Who, without knowledge of the word that created, would know the difference between life after death or death after life, or the separation of thought and action?

These questions have plagued the greatest minds like a bubonic melody sung in an ill key, locking away the greatest sublime treasure there be—*the ability to love, give and forgive*—to just let it be!

What happened to Michael's marriage? Did he really duff it? Was he daft to let it end? Why did he take no *mulligan*? Everything seemed to have been faring fairly well: the practice of law, a dog named Jenny, a young son named Samuel, a house on Millionaire's Drive in Owen Sound, and a young and lovely bride—these were all his! Well, as well as one could expect. Even if Michael was denied to socialize, comport, contort and snort with his friends, it could be overlooked, marginalized and minimized. Could not being sheltered in the sealed vessel of wedlock be construed as adequate compensation to weather such trivial turbulences, the usual ups and downs on the sea of married life? So while Michael had his druthers and doubts as he dithered in nuptials, he was content and complacent to float along the convenient conjugal course which provided some steady consolation of intercourse. But being a real man, he could not let things go by without the occasional bitchy bark and bite!

Like a titanic iceberg where only ten percent (10%) is visible and ninety percent (90%) is submerged in the murky, menacing, marine medium, hideously hiding in ambush, waiting to hinder, halt, decimate and destroy that which merrily skips and bobs along the surface not suspecting that in its pre-plotted path propelled and pulled by the friendly facade of fate serenity will soon be shattered and sunk by what was in store. It happened this way.

Although the law practice in Owen Sound was for a while essentially lucrative, there never seemed to be enough money to go merrily around. Then the real estate market like a living roller coaster, or the tide of a bay, went down: dipped, dropped, and receded into low tide. Much of the work Michael was doing dried up, diminished, disappeared into thin air, due to what the economical pundits or talking heads call a *"recession."* There will always be valleys in any mountainous landscape—it goes with the territory—even in capital markets.

Michael was getting tired of law, always practicing and practicing, carrying the weight of his clients' cases on his shoulders, always fighting but unable to throw a real punch! Although headaches have no mass, Michael did not consider himself an ass, but he felt like a mule. He could not see himself juggling, weight lifting and dancing at the same time at the behest and retainer of his clients, as was his professional duty. He did not want to remain trapped in his suffering in the ring and rink of manmade justice's circus in the Province of Ontario for the rest of his life. Rather, he longed for adventure and risk, something creative to get his adrenaline and juices flowing, and make him lots of money, a pecuniary puddle the size of a pond! He would concoct a brilliant plan to escape his hopeless situation. Michael, who had always done well in the buying and selling of property, hatched a scheme that seemed like a good idea at the time. But as it turned out, which is that it didn't, nothing emerged or was born of it but the cracked shell of his marriage—his life scrambled, and he burnt out!

Michael was soon to be unfortunate enough to learn a little lesson in linguistics: what is meant by the expression *"going over like a lead balloon."* Perhaps it was a case of bad timing, that's all. The project that so electrified Michael's excitement—enthusing and infusing him with the manic energy of a Led Zeppelin song—led him not to ascend and climb to heaven, but instead to fall and descend into separation and divorce, to the shattering of dreams and dinnerware—sad to all except lawyers! The cause of the catastrophe that castrated his conjugal cohabitation and gaiety, the fatal foreclosure to the now forgotten vows of *"forever"* and *"always,"* was sardonically misrepresented by being named the *Mirth Station No. 9*, as is so often the case with names: they end up signifying the opposite of what they mean. Take for example the name, "Little John," or the word "bad" to a black man, and the case is made.

There were two reasons why Michael ventured on with the plan that ended up being worthless, mirthless and meager of merriment. The first was *reticular*, and the second *necessity*. Firstly, as Michael had a son three years of age, everything Michael saw was through the eyes of a father of a three year old son. Secondly, Michael needed to produce enough beans or knead ample dough to maintain and keep the Rice family simmering in the staples of the lifestyle they had been steeped in.

The *Mirth Station* fitted the bill because it was a cooked up scheme to swell and expand his fiscal fortune by converting an old abandoned industrial building at the foot of the mouth of Owen Sound harbor which had suffered the disease and indignity of neglect—a dormant and idle fabrication plant with high ceilings and large open space—into an indoor playground where would lie a mini putt golf course, a snack bar, and stalls or kiosks strung together to appear as cars of a train, to amuse the young and infant patrons who would plead to peel and pry the shekels from their helpless obliging parents.

Taking into account and incorporating the legal advice not to do anything directly which can be done indirectly, and to add beauty and art to the enterprise so as to showcase his craftiness and nimble legal prowess, a pearl in the oyster was hidden in his scheme, which like a a rabbit or dove he would pull out from a bag or hat and shout: *voila!*—Michael would sell a part of the property, a parcel legally described as: a *whole lot pursuant to a registered plan of subdivision*, not essential to the operation of the planned business, which as a whole lot could be sold without the approval the planning department of the local municipality. It was money for nothing, which like chicks for free, was possibly too good to be true.

In accordance with the furtherance of such plan Michael negotiated and secured an agreement of purchase and sale of the freehold interest for a worthy price, payable by way of a deposit on acceptance of the agreement, and only a further small amount on closing, due to a large vender take back mortgage agreed to for the balance of the purchase price. Michael's corporation was the party of the first part to the agreement, so if anything went wrong he could just walk away—depart with no personal liability on his part—and not have to pay for the party of any part!

Engineers inspected the site to make sure it was visibly clear of contaminants to alleviate the concern some parents might have that their children's pliable minds would be warped by the waves of heavy metals. All are cognizant of the psychological and physiological dangers such a toxic stew can spew. Radioactive rock can turn a young, innocent girl into an *Iron Maiden* on hearing the soaring and roaring grinding gears of an *Iron Butterfly*. The invisible rays, worse than X-rated, could darken any holy day into a *Black Sabbath* when one is sequestered in the satanic, sardonic, demonic, ultrasonic sound considered by some holy rollers, but not by rockers, to be worse than sacrilege.

Michael pieced together a prospectus to entice investors so he could borrow money to proceed with the improvements plotted to put into practice the nescience of his joy and imagined money making toy, the station of mirth mingled and mixed with the lucky and charming number, nine, for girls' and boys' leisure and pleasure. Although nine is the number of completion in numerology—it was not to be! Unlike a cat, the project did not even experience one lick at life.

Michael was complimented by a lending officer at a financial institution that his prospectus, which painstakingly set out the steps planned for his proposed project, was impressive; but the bank was opposed to lending a monetary hand because there was a recession going on: banks will only lend money if a borrower doesn't need funds. Notwithstanding that Michael's plans did not unfold in such a way as to make them fly, not even like a paper airplane, he still had plan B planned, which was to put a second mortgage on his house on Millionaire's Drive to borrow enough money to complete the purchase and buy time to find a way to fulfill his plans.

Although the house where he and his wife resided had been bought entirely with money Michael brought into the marriage, in the Province of Ontario the "other spouse" (exactly half of all married couples) has a *matrimonial interest* in the *matrimonial home* as it was called, and thus perhaps wisely, Michael's

wife had an interest in the house, and was required to sign
and consent to the mortgage that was going to be arranged to
help bring merriment to many munchkins. She had previously
agreed to sign such mortgage, without any hint of doubt, hesitancy or duplicity.

In spite of all the difficulties that Michael encountered, he
was poised to complete and get the deal done for he was like
a gnat: once he set his mind to something he would not let
go and would gnaw to the core to enjoy the juicy fruits of his
labor. He so wanted, and thus thought he needed, to get out of
practicing law and get into the "making kids happy" business to
make himself happy; but the more he tried, the more he feared
being trapped forever!

Little did he expect that party pooper fate would be a *nixer*,
to the *nth* degree, to stop him from being the fixer to hobble,
hinge and stitch together the deal which was about to unravel.
But more than this, callous and uncaring fate like a sociopathic,
not a sycophant, street fighter would kick Michael when he
was down, to add insult to injury. It would do so in the most
mean, mocking and mundane manner without glamour, but
with understated acute avarice—and not by the advocacy of
a worthy opponent! If it were a comedy, it would surely be
classified as deadpan! The way the relentless urge or force was
fended off from flowering into fruition was to place an immov-
able object in the way: a dormant, dim dolt that did not know
it was obtrusive and obstructive. That was to be the loose link
to break the chain and derail the train of hoped for runaway
success to condom and condemn Michael's well-laid plan to
non-completion and failure before it even got a chance to get
off the ground to be begotten, born and fly.

Michael's neighbor to the east, on Millionaire's drive, was an
elderly lawyer of Scottish decent, tall and thin and somewhat
stooped from peering too often at copious amounts of periodi-
cals and Playboys, whose wispy white hair hinted and regaled

with barely audible streaks the faded red of haggis and bagpipe shrieks. His name was Mason McClung. He had two sons, twins, but not identical, who were graced by the matching names of Morton and Martin. They all lived together, including the mother, Margaret.

Morton was an animated advocate: tall, thin and stooped like his father, crowned with fiery thinning red hair combed back exposing a somewhat receding hairline. He spoke forcefully, passionately and rapidly with jerky motions of his hands and head so that his anima and aspect was ardent and burning. If he were a cock, no one loath to engage him in a fight could be accused of being chicken if they fled rather than fought, once they saw Morton's demeanor.

Michael had dealt professionally with Morton, and despite his aggressive appearance he was OK one-on-one, never making much of a big deal out of things; but Martin was the apparent opposite of Morton: shorter, dark haired and balding, docile, dormant and dull, chubby and potbellied. When he spoke he did so slowly in a single tone. One had to wonder how he had landed his lawyer's license. With all due respect, he seemed to play the part of a simpleton perfectly. Although looks can be deceiving, in Martin's case the book could be judged by the cover! In spite of his practicing law for several years in Owen Sound, at no time had Michael ever had any adversarial or transactional intercourse with Martin McClung, of the firm *McClung and McClung*, and sometimes *and McClung*, so it caught Michael's attention when Martin was listed as lawyer for the vendor in the sale of the property that would envelop the future *Mirth Station*.

Michael thought that everything would be straight forward. "He is pleasant and polite enough when he says hello, even if he seems a bit slow" was the summation of Michael's thoughts when it came to Martin. "How could he screw up the deal?"

Michael should have stilled and quieted his trepidations for they must have tempted fate. It is funny and arguably unfair, that fate can and does tempt people, but they in turn, are not allowed to reciprocate and return the favor. It would be wise to recognize that there is no tit for tat when it comes to the future, for the good can die young, good things happen to bad people, and fate fucks everybody indiscriminately—whether they like it or not!

The purchase of the property for the planned mirth station, the terminal of gaiety, was set for completion the latter part of May. Michael was working fervently and feverishly to get everything set in place, sewn up, tied up and anchored, including the financing, but at every turn it seemed that fate was conspiring against him. Michael felt like singing that old Yiddish refrain: *"How does one have a bit of luck, where does one find a little happiness?"* But fate, or what is sometimes referred to as the divine, cannot be influenced or petitioned with a song, a prayer, or even a dance—even though many have tried with *rain* and *sun dance*s. If things did turn out as desired or prayed for, would they actually end up agreeable and wanted when they occur? There is a big argument which system better accounts for what transpires in life: cash or accrual. This is an academic question like a hot potato or a *red herring*, a hypothetical or moot point, superficially appearing appetizing to the intellect, but not ripe, ready or worthy of an answer. (Further, it has been quipped that *what one takes in will not defile them, but what comes out will*—no matter what it is called; however it won't smell like a rose!)

Since Michael had studied income tax in law school and was always trying to get rich, he prepared the annual tax returns for both he and his wife, and asked her to mail them on the last day they were due without penalty or interest, as she was going out and by the post office.

Michael waited for her short return, but she did not. Michael was confounded and not amused, until a so called friend of his wife called to warn him that his wife was OK and would be getting in touch with him soon and not to worry, and to continue to take care of Sam; so Michael was even more dazed and confused hoping it wasn't true, and he worried and fretted and wondered what the hell was going on!

It was a good thing that Michael knew how to use a can opener and how to boil water, and also how to use a credit card to dine out. The marriage had been a conventional one. His wife did all the cooking, cleaning and shopping, and Michael did the earning—trying to learn how not to be cleaned out from too much shopping.

After several days it came, not in the mail, but personally served, the papers from the wife's lawyer, the Petition for Divorce, essentially asking for more than everything. In the parlance of the lawyer: "If you don't ask, you don't get."

Legal lexicon has its humoristic, if not humanistic, aspects. The remedies a lawyer asks for in court are called a *"Prayer for Relief,"* and the divorce papers are called a *"Petition for Divorce."* Everyone knows that you *cannot petition the lord with prayer.* This does not apply to the judges of the high and mighty courts, the law lords, who are to be addressed as *"my lord"* or *"me lord"* if one is English, to the judge sitting on his high chair misleadingly called a "bench."

Although some have claimed that their only friend is *the end,* to Michael the end of his marriage was not a friend! It struck him when he wasn't looking—like a left hook out of nowhere! His wife had fluttered and smelled like a butterfly, now she stung like a bee. Although Michael still stood, he was knocked senseless and so taken for a loop that he did not know what he stood for anymore. No amount of loopholes, no matter how clever, ingenuous, money saving, *airy-fairy* or *artsy-fartsy* could put his "humpty dumpty" mood back together again.

He was stunned and shocked and his neck and shoulders ached. Had he not been a faithful providing husband, and a kindly, caring, concerned father? His wife was no mind reader— why did she leave him? Like so many of the unanswerable and irresolvable questions in life, he did not have an answer, but suspected that, like so many things fallaciously and salaciously perceived as real, it had to do with money.

Michael felt abandoned and unwanted until he saw Jenny's happy button eyes staring at him, panting a smile with her tongue hanging out between her discolored fangs. He *knew* that *she* loved him. He now fully understood the significance of the old saying *that a dog is man's best friend*. Michael did not know what he would have done without the unconditional and unquestioning love of the dog, or on the other hand, what he would do with it.

And there was still Samuel to take care of. One can only guess at how bewildered Samuel felt at the tender age of three, considering that Michael, a professional with two university degrees who could argue anything, could not figure out what was going on.

Details of the course of the divorce, all the intricacies of the long and winded battles and curves, court appearances, interim and interlocutory motions, piles of papers, reams of motion records, orders, judgments and other temporary determinations, affidavits and further affidavits that could fill a filing cabinet full, and some more, will not be enumerated even if words written and alleged are the barrister's and solicitor's stock and trade: a veritable vat of fun and a barrel full of monkeys.

The divorce proceedings were finally concluded after 18 years, which is a lucky number in Jewish mysticism and stands for life. "Why," one may ask. God only knows but is remaining silent so that the words can't be used to prove inconsistent prior statements in a court of law, or in any monkey trial. It is an open question whether God would ever be granted standing by a court—definitely not being an "individual"—but at least it is arguable that like a corporation, union or other creature of statute, God is perhaps a "person." Notwithstanding whether standing would or would not be granted, God would have to have to be given some status based on the argument through acknowledgement (sometimes referred to as *estoppel*) because acts of god are judicially noticed, and it would set a dangerous precedent not to follow precedent. And if a judgment against God were rendered, would appealing to God make sense?

Finally the divorce was totally determined and completed with a provisional decree for divorce then called a *"Decree Nisi,"* which soon became absolute. By that time the parties forgot what they were fighting over and about—the stated limitations of memory have been codified and carved into stone in the *Statue of Limitations.*

As the major concern in any court case involving a minor is the best interest of the child, intimate and intrinsic details of the case will not be recanted or revealed. Who would want to read or hear all the scandalous, scurrilous and sensational accusations of irreconcilable differences in the breakdown of the marriage contained in most divorce proceedings anyways? Sounds like reality TV, doesn't it? Thank god for lawyers who drag, draw, and guide overwhelmed clients through the contours of a court case and its perplexing legal passages to safely part with them at the end of the ordeal, if adequately retained and rewarded.

Michael did not think he fared badly for although he had to give up and pay half of his net value, which value decreased and diminished during the course of the marriage, he at least got to stay in the house on Millionaire's Drive, and Jenny and Sam stayed with him. But as surely as the wife was adept at playing the game *"Red Rover,"* she first asked for the son and support, then the dog, singing "Red Rover, Red Rover, let Jenny come over," and finally Michael had to sell the house to have enough money to pay the settlement. When she asked for more he said "*go fish*" (not "*go fuck yourself*"), because that would be a very childish thing for an adult to say and would amount to acting out.

Things slowly got better. First Michael realized that he could see and party with his old friends any time he liked. Nor did he have to worry about cleaning: he could let things be and settle while the dust and mess piled up—and then move out—applying the principle that he would move, instead of trying to move the mountain of dirt.

Michael and his wife both loved Samuel. Because Michael loved him enough to let him go, Samuel came back to live with Michael when he became a teenager, like in the movie or story, *Love Story*. But here it was more a case of Sam being asked to leave the residence of his mother and her new partner, because Sam did not like to listen, obey or share; but Michael was happy to let Sam do whatever he wanted, for Michael too grew up cared for and loved, carefree and free except for his own thoughts and feelings. Perhaps Sam was the same, except that Michael was a mouthpiece who wore his heart on his sleeve and was never short or shy of a complaint. Samuel was the stoic, strong and silent type.

Love makes the world go round and round, and Michael would have lasted a few more rounds in the marriage if his wife had let him and not left him. Love is not at all painful if one when waking up from its fragrant, rose-colored trance can forget about possessions, forgive debts, and let bygones be bygones.

While Michael was severely shaken and stirred, disturbed and distraught by his wife's sudden and unanticipated absconding, departure, vacation and evacuation, he still had to deal with the completion of the hapless venture of the mirth station which his corporation was bound by words and paper and other good and valuable consideration to complete or otherwise be subject and liable to pay damages for failure to perform and live up to its agreement. Michael was still trying to do his part and raise the small amount of money needed to close the deal. It was not a lot, considering the vendor had agreed to provide most of the financing by way of a mortgage back.

While Michael acted as the lawyer for his corporation who was the purchaser, he did not have a fool for a client, because according to the *Land of Oz* and *Alice in Wonderland* fantasy that is Ontario law, a corporation is a person but not an individual, and as such cannot act for itself not having flesh and blood, guts and a heart; and Michael could and did. It might be argued that he was a split hair removed from having a fool for a client, or a part in the middle away from being a fool himself, but split hairs only matter in the beauty industry, and close only counts in sex and horseshoes.

As lawyer for the purchaser corporation, Michael requisitioned among other things a Statement of Adjustments (a legal accounting document) and a draft mortgage back. A lawyer's requisition letter outlines the documents that a lawyer requests. It may expose issues or problems that need to be *rectified* or *bonefied* to close the deal so no hole is left open for the lawyer's preoccupation. A measure of a lawyer's *panache* is to be wary, leery and weary of pitfalls, and not to fall into gaping holes, overlooking, or underestimating the pith of a problem, biting into an oversight, and hitting a nerve, thus necessitating painful and costly repair work which the court at its leisure or pleasure may impose and dispense as it sees fit.

To the requisitions of M. Rice, lawyer, the curt though not discourteous reply from Martin McClung, B.A., LL.B., Barrister and Solicitor, contained no cover letter, only a Statement of Adjustments not showing the mortgage to be given back, thus indicating that all the funds less the deposit were due on closing. Michael, realizing that Martin might not be the brightest light bulb, called him up on the phone.

"Hello Martin—Michael Rice here. You omitted to include a credit for the mortgage back on the Statement of Adjustments, and you did not send me a draft of the mortgage back with your draft documents."

"What mortgage back?" Martin replied.

"The agreement of purchase and sale clearly calls for, provides and stipulates that *"the vendor shall give a mortgage back in the sum of..."*" retorted Michael quoting and reading from the agreement of purchase and sale, quite sure that Martin's preposterous position was just at worst poor posturing or at best, a simple-minded oversight.

"There should be no mortgage back in this transaction," said Martin.

"But the agreement of purchase and sale calls for it in black and white, as clear as day," Michael continued exasperated: "The parties turned their minds to this matter and addressed the issue, unequivocally incorporating the giving of the mortgage back as a term of the transaction, and the agreement of purchase and sale is the document that governs. It is written into the agreement in plain words, in black and white!"

"I told the client not to give a mortgage back," said Martin.

"Without prejudice, that would be well and fine if you wanted to advise your client otherwise beforehand, but the details of the deal have been determined and agreed to, set down, signed and sealed. The parties have made their agreement, and what they agreed to was for the vendor to provide financing by giving a mortgage back on closing. I don't know how it could be any clearer! We have a firm and binding agreement! Your client is opening itself up to a law suit if they do not abide by the terms agreed to!" Michael exclaimed and continued not knowing whether he should be angry or frustrated, laugh or cry. His emotions had been drained dry, stultified by his wife's willful and total disregard for his happiness and well being. He was not comfortably numb—he could barely move his neck!

If what was happening in respect of the purchase transaction was compared to a baseball game, Martin would be coming out of no field at all. Michael did not have the energy to draw the smiting sword of justice from its scabbard to eviscerate and emasculate his unworthy adversary as he had learned to wield in the multi *lawyered* trenches in the high rate office towers of downtown Toronto with the "big boys" of the "big firms." Michael did not have it in him to give Martin a good dressing down or tongue lashing and tell him: "*You fucking idiot, you don't know what the fuck you're doing! My wife just left me, and now I have to deal with this fucking bullshit!*" But what would be the good in saying these things, except to make Michael feel better by letting him air his ire to fuel and fan his fire, to bellow and fume and snort, and let it all out. He was just so tired and confused.

"I have instructed the client not to give a mortgage back. All money must be paid on closing." Martin asserted.

"You cannot instruct the client!" Michael lectured. "It is the client that gives the instructions!"

No reply came from Martin, so Michael then added in conclusion: "I will write you a letter confirming this conversation and my client's position. Beware and govern yourself accordingly!" On that not so veiled threat Michael hung up the Northern Telecom phone.

Now one man might have been angry, and another man might have been hurt, Michael just wanted to save his shirt, so on cold and sober reflection after internalizing enough chilled wobbly pops to drink himself silly and give this matter sober second thought, Michael reigned in his rashness determining that his head and heart weren't into the deal anymore. He being recently de-wifed, it was not in his physical, emotional, mental and spiritual best interests to push and hammer the deal shut, or take on the costs, burden, weight and waits of a law suit. The wind of will had been knocked out of him. His desire was dead and done. He could no longer pose in the puffery needed to threaten the wrath of litigation.

Thus the following day, Michael wrote a terse and short letter to Martin McClung stating verbatim: *"My client has instructed me not to complete this transaction,"* signed *"Yours very truly, Michael Rice."* That was all he wrote. Perhaps his wife had done him a favor by leaving. Michael was not yet forty years old and possibly could have a few good years of cavorting, consorting and contorting left in him. Perhaps the Mirth Station was a bad idea as an investment after all, to begin with. Was it not but a desperate stab at the financial pot of gold at the end of a rainbow? And "hope" in Spanish also means *to wait*—implying that the object of hope never arrives and thus all hope is in vain! There is no rich vein of gold to be struck in the selfish prospecting for hope. All achievement and success requires doing: action cures anxiety!

Michael's wife had pricked his ego to the point that he bristled with indignation. Usually the word "prick" is used in disrespect for the male of the species, perhaps based on the male sex organ being like a needle or something used for pricking. It is funny how "prick" and "bitch" are complementary gender based reflections of each other, but they have totally different meanings and connotations.

Michael did not backtrack or second-guess his decision to walk away from the purchase: he knew it was right for it *felt* right, even though it would take Michael several years to emerge from the darkness of a delayed and protracted divorce to the light of forgetfulness of the pain of not having and being denied. It is a natural law that any buoyant object pushed down to the depths of despair will rise to the surface to bathe in the light of indiscriminating life to emerge from the shadow, because the spirit, though not irrepressible, is compensated for by the temporal memory of mind which forgets in time when it adjusts—as it always does and will, to the status quo—unless it breaks!

What choice did Michael have? He would not have married his wife in the first place if he got to know her in the second place, but double-dealing fate gives and takes, approbating and reprobating in the same breath because it is not subject or subservient to the laws of mice or men, and Michael's *beshert*, his chosen one, was lying in wait on Michael's path so that they could go forth and multiply and beget. Michael was content that he was in a universe and it was working, no matter what state his mind was in. Whether fate was for him or against him however, he was not a hundred percent sure. If he was a betting man he would vote for against—for that is how it seemed *prima facie,* or on the surface, to him.

Would it be an abuse to wallow with Michael in his woe? Those who have been there will know that misfortunes are created by casting *what is* in the shadow of expectancy. A happy marriage and a stable and secure family life was what Michael envisioned for himself, but it seemed no more than a deluded illusion on the dissolution of his marriage.

Two days after mailing the letter indicating that he would be walking away from the purchase of the property to be the future home of intended mirth, Michael received a phone call from the addressee of the said letter, the sparse user of words, Martin McClung, that went something like this.

"I got your letter. Your client has to close the deal. It's in the agreement," a somewhat animated McClung droned in his monotone if one can be generous enough to elevate his miniscule hint of emotion to animation.

"Well, go ahead and sue," Michael gleefully quipped as he proudly and precisely hung up the phone. He was taking the first step, moving on to the next chapter of his life. *En guard* and *touché*! You can take the man out of the practice, but you cannot take the practice out of the man.

And so the saga of the Mirth Station No. 9 that had no existence except in the mind of the creator ends: hapless and meager of mirth or merriment. Was it folly, or a grand idea the fruition of which lay dormant not to unfold in this world, like a seed sprouted not, or a road too narrow and too treacherous to traverse and travel? With such a happy name and lucky number it is curious that it did not see the light of day or the darkness of night to live even one tick of time!

# 37

## IN LIMBO

Michael continued living in Owen Sound as a single lawyer and placed Samuel in a daycare during the work week, thus fulfilling his legal and familial duties in a competent, reasoned and judicious manner, but his interest in the practice of law was subordinate to the care of his son. Although Michael established a reputation as the "go to guy" for complex civil cases that other lawyers were not tempted to undertake, they being too predisposed to produce profit without a penchant, proclivity or partiality to exert a peck or pile of pensive attentiveness, Michael's prime imperative was to get home for his son. The law practice became a golden chain leashed around his neck, yanked by a jealous mistress. Even as the cases Michael undertook became more complicated and multifaceted and often involved multiple malfeasants, Michael was able to astutely manage, maneuver and articulate them. He deconstructed old law to fabricate new arguments that sounded persuasive when bonded, embroidered, embellished and meshed with a little equity.

More than once had he received a compliment from an adversary at a "big boy" law firm who was staggered by the height and extent Michael would stand up and distend himself for his "little guy" client. Michael was quite creative and innovative. He at times advised his client to strike first by seeking a declaration, rather than waiting to be sued, thus framing and formatting the issues to the benefit of his client rather than to defend an action. The natural inclination is to consider any defense an excuse, a defiant denial; but going on the attack is chivalrous and more credible in the courtroom battle—the judge might even listen to the arguments!

Michael recalled a complex case that arose from a commercial contract. There must have been eight or nine "big gun" lawyers in the examination room digging deep into the details as if each fact discovered was a gem of buried treasure uncovered; including lawyers for the parties, lawyers for the lawyers being sued, and lawyers for insurance companies—all plundering blunders so they could party hardy. The gross billability complacent in the room was incredible and undeniably great, and it went on for days and days. In the quest for every drop of data, every dot of detail, the quantity of copious questionings was grotesquely exaggerated to ensure that every grain of ground was upturned and overturned, every iota inspected in minutiae so as not to leave a pebble unturned along the line of fire, the path of inquiry: a pedantic and plodding procession propelled and permeated by the fear of potentially and possibly overlooking a peripheral point, rather than to get to the heart of the matter: the salient issue that would alone make or break the case.

Although such convoluted congregations could be ludicrously lucrative and the file could be farmed and bred to bring and beget financial grain and gain, all Michael could think of was getting out of that chamber of inquisition to go pick up his son from daycare. His heart, mind and soul were not stirred by such legal servitude. The "big boys" had to bill "big hours" to pay the "big bills" of their masters, the partners in the tall steel and glass towers, the grandeur of whose position they coveted and sought to attain. He did not. He was the *alpha* and *omega* of his one man firm, the head and tail, the master and fool of his life.

So Michael decided to call it quits and went into selling real estate which he thought would result in solid returns on flexible time and be much easier. As a lawyer during his previous prior practice, he had procured more than enough technical knowhow and ken needed. Michael came up with the magnificent marketing scheme of offering to pay the clients that used his services as their agent for the purchase of property, rather than they paying him. If it sounds too good to be true it wasn't. This particular ploy was perfectly permissible and developed by Michael pursuant to his awareness of agency obligations. While at first there were the doubters and skeptics, it is now a common place practice because the vendor pays all the commission, even that of the agent working for the buyer, some of which can be refunded to the buyer. Michael grimaced: "It's not a gimmick" when he tried to sell the gimmick.

Although Michael tried, there were at least three reasons why he did not continue with real estate sales as his occupation and preoccupation. Firstly, Michael could not drive and talk at the same time. When he ferried clients around to look at properties he scared the shit out of them every time he took his eyes off the road to open his mouth.

Secondly, real estate was a *sales job*, and Michael was not enamored with beating the bushes to find prospects—he would rather beat his own meat into a frenzy of delight. Michael was also sensitive to rejection which in extreme cases would cause him to extricate himself from the situation if enough negative emotion was aroused. He found that fishing for and baiting buyers was hard work and not a fun pastime.

Finally, most people expected the real estate agent to work at night when they didn't. That was precisely the time Michael wanted to spend with his son. Most people treated the real estate agent as their own personal attendant to jump on call and come running on demand. Michael was sensitive to anything that smelled of servitude.

Thus after giving it a go, hacking at it for about a year, he became discombobulated and wobbled back to Toronto, North York that is, to abide with his parents in the basement of their bungalow taking his son, Samuel with him. There he could seek out brave new business opportunities with the added benefit of built-in babysitters, more properly called "boy watchers," his mama and papa, both then retired.

As to Michael's social life while still in Owen Sound, post-law and pre-return to North York, he longed lustily to discharge the load of his yearnings, seeking and searching for complimentary female companions to seduce with his often spoken opinions to insert into social intercourse and assert his sexuality.

Owen Sound was the largest city and capital of Grey County with only twenty thousand inhabitants; the county seat where county council sat, the outhouse and throne from which it shat, governing in the manner and manure of imposing levies, taxes, tariffs, charges and fees. In such a small population that could easily fit into a football stadium, a large concert hall or a big revival meeting tent it was hard for Michael to meet a complementary sexual partner that was liberal, democratic and open to the various positions—whether on top, below or behind— suitable to his station and status, who had the appearance and personality Michael felt comfortable parading in public, and who was not already locked up in a relationship. This was a tall order for such a short city—if population were height!

There was one woman who seemed a possibility. She was friendly enough with pretty features, at least from far away, and within the age range that Michael preferred at the time: five to ten years younger—but not so young that he might get five to ten in the pen! She was available and a partier too; but on closer inspection she did not look so good after Michael did a "here's looking at you kid" inspection. Once he got near enough to touch her, he lost the inclination to crank her, even if no lubrication was necessary because her complexion was too oily for his liking. As well, he felt that if he got entangled in an intimate relationship with her, she would never let him go without a fight or flight of hysterics! He felt her neediness in her being alone and acting friendly and sociable.

Towns or cities in Ontario the size of Owen Sound, or smaller, seem friendly enough on the surface, but it is very difficult to be accepted as being from there or as "one of them" or "one of us," unless one is born or dies there. Michael had an aversion to being the butt end of missionary conversion as a non-practicing, non-believing, good Jewish boy—what would his parents and relatives say if he were reborn and came back falling and fondling over Jesus? Surely they would complain "*Oy vey!*" and "*never in a million years!*" and possibly more lamentations interjected between "*eat, eat!*"

Michael did meet a woman in a bar who he had not previously encountered, which is unusual for a place the size and sizzle of Owen Sound where one always runs into people they know. He began seeing and being intimate with her quickly and regularly. It would not be inapplicable or inadmissible to label the relationship that almost stretched out for a year or so as one of boyfriend and girlfriend, even though they were both adults.

Bitsy, as she was called, was a slight and petite woman with short red hair, a pleasant face that viewed in a certain way would be called pretty, with smooth, silky, freckled, fair skin. In fact, Michael thought she would be beautiful if her mouth did not have that scrunched, puckered appearance as if she had been weaned on a very sour dill pickle, or perhaps her round little mouth was a bit too small for her pale face which was itself a tad too small for her slight frame, but she was attractive enough from close with tender green eyes, and she felt good to the touch, being well-proportioned for her size. Her tininess made Michael feel big and strong, like a real he-man.

Although Bitsy was tight with her money, as she needed to be having no gainful employment and being a single mother with two pre-teenage boys, she was also shy and indecisive, deferring and demurring to Michael for all decisions, although amply intelligent, caring and a good communicator. However, she was not too tight or prudish when it came to intimacy. They fit well together—his tab into her slot!

Bitsy had one tragic flaw, and it was not a calloused heel or a rough look. She was the type of girl that when she planned to have dinner ready for seven in the evening, starting to cook at 6 pm, the food would not be on the table ready to eat until at least ten at night. Michael did not mind as he had learned that one has to be kind, considerate and understanding to make a relationship work and not blow up in their face, not having fared well in the shipwreck of his marriage. He made waiting worthwhile and passable, marinating his punctual worries in whiskey and wine and curing them with smoke. Those who have locked lips with the strongly spirited *Lady Alcohol know* she smacks harder on an empty stomach—but the smoke does help buzz the blur!

The relationship with Bitsy had hope. Although Michael was not a hundred percent committed because of her wispy, wishy-washy nature, harboring some hidden hesitation, perhaps intuitively, for the subconscious knows much more than it lets on not having a big ego. But Michael was lonely, longing for a steady squeeze to idle and bide the while away—his own echo often rang in tones of anguished angst—but before he could get to know her long enough that she could fall short of meeting his growing expectations (as time together often brings contempt), she broke off the relationship. She felt compelled to focus on her sons, rather than on Michael's swollen desire.

Michael was bruised, but nothing that some *Arnica Montana* could not have healed had he known of it then. She did the deed, pre-empting the potential possibility that Michael would pull the plug to sever their seeing each other sometime soon. The lovers were left bone dry—at least Michael was! That was it. It was over and done. He was left alone in the desert after being deserted, no longer able to fondle and feed on the dessert of her soft, sweet, salty skin and tardy tendencies and tenderness.

At the end Michael perceived part of her character that had been covert and kept under wraps. One may even go so far as to say *repressed*. Bitsy had such strong feelings and beliefs as to what she wanted and thought should be that she manifested the opposite! Her inclinations were so overwhelming that she abated and transmuted them to dust and naught. Go figure! It all makes sense in this *BiZZaro* world, if one has the nose for discerning crap from nourishment, delusion from *drek* (Yiddish for "shit"), or if one read the old time Superman comics. Perhaps however, it was all in Michael's mind that there was a Superman series depicting the man of steel as morally challenged and fallen, with lines cracking his face.

Michael soon moved back to the basement of his parents' North York bungalow, fallen like a forgotten angel into that damp and cold subterranean setting with clipped wings and a shaken sense of self like a dog with its tail between its legs. It was time to rest and heal before he could reappear refreshed and restored and ready for another round on the merry-go-round. For a while, *he just had to let it go!*

# 38

## A COFFEE BREAK

The thought of moving back into the basement made Michael think about his mother. While even the most hardened male criminal loves his mother, the same singular sentiment is often not shared by the fallen female, whether incarcerated or not, from the most embittered convict to one just slightly flea-bitten, such affections towards papa are not always embraced or held.

Michael, though not a convicted criminal, loved his mother deeply in spite of all her blemishes, birth marks and shortcomings, for she had many noble and admirable qualities. She was tolerant and friendly, hard-working and giving, a good provider, and always on Michael's side. Those who have, or have had mothers, will know that love of one's female forbearer is not quantified on the qualities possessed or exhibited by such matron sire as if she were an object or subject to be assessed and graded and stratified like a heartless rock or a prize sow, but is instead based on the current that connects the conduit of caring unconditionally coagulating in the heart and arteries of the cared for one. That *is* love: set like a sponge cake, infracting and impacting the entire being and soul so soaked, steeped and reared.

Was Michael his mother's favorite? To answer this question would be taking sides, pitting brother against brother, which is very bad for household harmony and familial unity. When Michael was born his mother was hoping for a girl, already having a son and being denied toys or dolls by the evil swastika appareled perpetrators of havoc, destruction and depravity, who cared little for little girls or their pastimes even before wartime or bedtime if they were not airy and blond, except to make it a past and last time for many. A frank look at a lost diary will corroborate and dispose, and there is no use hiding it, that young girls are indeed sensitive and some are artistic, but such childishness can be knocked out of them, like the stuffing out of a teddy bear, and who the hell will cast a stone to deny the hollow cost gassed with lying and hating, lip serving eyes! A childhood is not just another thorn on a desert brush to be wrenched out by wretched hateful hands.

Because Michael's mother wanted a girl, she did not cut Michael's hair and let it grow long. She doted on her baby with the fat legs and serious visage (which might have been trying to say something like *"feed me"*), and put his hair into a bun. She thought baby Michael was so beautiful that she worried someone might cast an evil eye on him, or try to steal him. Such were the old wives' tales prevalent at the time, as they were in times before and will be in times to come. The appellation of the perpetrator scapegoat kaleidoscopically shifts in mind altering hate, alternating with fear, a labyrinthine mass hallucination. Michael's clothes were adorned with loose red threads to ward off evil, but Jews, Gypsies, *Jabbas*, *Hutts*, and you name it, have all had bloated biases and prejudicial aspersions spread against them.

Everyone has heard the story of Samson and how long hair gave him strength, but this was not an issue with Michael because the first person to give him a haircut, which didn't occur until he was three years old, was not out to screw him like a Delilah for god sakes, but was his very own mother, who loved him. It was time he started to look like the other little boys his age.

Jewish mothers have a reputation for emasculating or eviscerating their sons, but surely that was not her intention in having Michael's hair grow long for three years before cutting it. Long or short hair does not make one more or less masculine! The truth is that length of hair is just a social convention that can be taken to mean whatever is permanently conditioned into the mind of the observer. It is relative—subject to use or abuse depending on how it's colored—no matter *how* it's cut!

Michael's mind turned to another moment in time when he was with his mother and she was close to *knocking on "heaven's door."* He had driven her to Mount Sinai hospital in downtown Toronto on broad University Avenue where many of the big hospitals are located, because that is what the doctors like, a big street so fancy that it is called an Avenue. Such grand avenue leads north directly to the provincial legislative buildings, the seat of the so-called democratically elected rulers of Ontario sworn to serve the monarch, at whose prerogative and royal fiat the buildings are named "*Queen's Park*" so no one will be confused about who really wears the pants and makes the rules! The surrounding street, no longer belonging to the university or the people, becomes a drive to honor the aged, overly ripe ex-princess, and is called "*Queen's Park Drive.*" Even the adjoining park, around which *Queen's Park Drive* goes around, proclaims her name. This trinity of nomenclature: street, park and building is meant to remind one and all who rules through the manifestation of destiny.

Michael had driven his mother to the hospital for her regular blood transfusion scheduled every few weeks, rather than have her take the bus and then the subway in her weak condition. She did not know how to take a cab, let alone understand why anyone would pay such a hefty fare. The transfusions slowed the seepage of her life force, delaying her *slip sliding away*, helped ease the pain, and likely lengthened the hours she had left to spend on this beautiful and hideous planet until her soul would slip nakedly between the portals of matter from the "*I am*" to "*that's all folks!*"

Michael waited for his mother in the waiting room as she got recharged until her next bloody fix. In the lobby of the high rise medical monolith which stood like Mount Sinai itself, there was a Second Cup Coffee cafe, the Canadian version of Starbucks except that each outlet is franchised and not corporate owned. Upon completion of her filling up with red regular, she and Michael sat down for a coffee and muffin which they both consumed quietly and pensively.

Michael looked at his mother as she sipped the coffee and chewed on the muffin. Her whole being was engrossed in the state of eating and drinking: she chewed slowly and her face winced. Perhaps her teeth hurt. Did her whole life boil down to the fact that she, always a proudly independent woman, now had to live off other people's blood? She was so close to the end zone, ready to score the final touchdown, what else mattered but that she was with her son, and he was with his mother, silently sharing the sacred sacrament of sustenance, both savoring the bitter earthiness of the quality coffee (it wasn't Tim's) and the sweetness of the muffins, knowing that even though they appeared as two separate physical and energetic entities, they were in fact one once. And soon, there would be only one.

There was an unspoken bond like an invisible golden thread that engulfed and united them: uncolored, unpretentious, and unembellished comfort which each other, love of the necessity of eating, and love of each other, striking a still cord that transcended pleasure and pain. They had accepted the moment. Nothing else was important or required thought or analysis.

Neither Michael nor his mother was much into bells and whistles. Michael often thought in the future, which is after his mother died, and before now driving on the QEW heading to work at the Wild Rice store in Toronto, of and about the peace and quietude and perfectness of those moments with his mother, which reminded him of the still surface of a lake in the evening. It would not be a cliché to say such reflections brought a sad and quiet joy to the mixed menagerie of his gyrating emotions with their bittersweet aftertaste.

He was grateful to have such a mother. He knew that he could have no other, and that was it. She loved him unconditionally. Perhaps in some system other than the white coat, evil death paradigm that creates conflict within itself and between brother and brother, father and son, *mano a mano*, man against himself, she was *still* with him and he with her, when time is stretched out all at once like space, separated only by the illusion and seeming separation of opposites in the term of life, determined to have a beginning and an end.

# 39

## A WORD ABOUT APPRECIATION

Michael was roaring eastbound doing 120 km per hour at about four o'clock that sunny autumn afternoon on the queen's wide showpiece highway which incredibly was fairly derelict of cars and traffic for such time of day. The rarified byzantine blue sky, so colored by the seeking eye longing for belonging, found itself covered by infinite translucent temporariness stretched like a sheath over the work of days and thoughts, of time hiding the stars, pulling Michael along like an ideal.

Michael sensed his parents residing in the air and ether. Not their interned casements which lay discarded in the dark, cold, dense ground like cards spread and played out in the mortal game of life, but something which may be but nothing: sensed and imagined. Their span no longer in time, for that was written, but in infinite space. The sky was their home, a place free of torment and pain. They had returned to from whence they came. Perhaps "heaven" had conceived the concept of itself to fall and filter into the cognition of the sapient erect ones, commanding disorder of life's cycles in their disobedience.

The leaves on the trees cried with colors, as they did the falling dance of death and rebirth, laying the groundwork for young and growing sprigs. Their jig and fugue, round and round, spinning and recycling to the timeless tempo of the colorless blowing wind, beat to the meter of the sun's bright unbroken rays.

Michael's mother had manifested the template and blueprint of the perfect relation with a female. In her temple there was never and anxiety or fear related to performance or pretense. She labored in love: cleaned, cooked and cared for him without asking for anything in return. Although she always let her opinion be known, there was no penalty or punishment when such projection of propriety was ignored with impunity. Michael was always immune from consequences.

Often when he was down in the dumps, and declared such dejected state to his mother, she would say: *"Don't let it consume you, or take you over,"* in Yiddish of course. The direct translation is more appropriate and erudite in its simple profundity: *"Don't take yourself over."* Michael could reset content and calm knowing it was not such a big deal after all. He had all the love his heart craved, the answer to his cry.

Yet all the women he loved had left. He was now alone with his thoughts and senses. He still did not know who he was, why he was, often how he was and sometimes where he was, because he did not want to hear the answer to a query that might jar his presupposed notion that would fissure his earthen urn and cause his marbles to plummet precipitously into the depths of purgatorial despair, not matching in color to the picture he had painted.

Although he *had* loved and now had naught, he did not view
life as a game to win or lose. He still sought love as the answer,
whether to his abstract questions or his driving desire, he was
not sure. There was no need to burn a hole, burrow a furrow,
in the hindsight of his logic, the concentrated magnification of
bright ideas. The giving of love without want of reward might
be enough. Love, multiplied in giving, is reproduced when
taken, so the more that is given the more can be received.

And Eureka! He struck the chord in the vein of understanding spelled out in the various meanings and connotations of
the word "appreciation." Appreciation means to rise and grow,
just like the life force that drives human beings to create and
produce, recreate and reproduce. Was it not written and man-
dated in the Torah: "*Go forth and multiply*"? Had the good book
originally been written in English, this could have been more
tersely stated by simply instructing and directing humankind
to "*appreciate*." Wall Street and the Wailing Wall might thus
be idiosynchronistically and mystically linked by the cabalistic
cadence of such sacred word of affirmation, but neither the
Torah, nor the bible was originally scribed in English.

"Appreciation" also means to be grateful and thankful for, or
just plain happy with. It is the taking of giving, one half of love,
which keeps occult the complementary remainder, the giving
of taking, the approbation of reprobation, without which love
cannot exist. Those who live are witness to the spectacle: the
needle and thread uniting and rendering opposites and the
rending of the same at the same time, the simultaneous suck
and blow, the one hand clapping. It is no coincidence that oral
sex is referred to by both these seemingly contradictory appel-
lations, these apparently irreconcilable movements, sucking
and blowing, performed to reach one end, by whatever devi-
ance, means or variation the seed grown in the mind can
muster, master or mustard.

Would Jesus have agreed that appreciation is the key? It is a wonder why Jesus was asked what the two most important commandments were. On the surface it seems a simple and straightforward question, but no one asks what the two most important things are? The question usually asked which is foremost on everyone's mind is "*What is the most important thing?*" No one cares about the runner-up, loser or also-ran, except for one's mother who no doubt is blinded by the prejudice of love, or perhaps Jesus. There can only be one conclusion then: the question was framed to slip through the cracks, to fool the censors (the mind control arbitrators of the time) by not really meaning what it says on the surface, but as a light pointing to something else.

Jesus cared for everyone, advising his disciples to venture forth to heal and help one and all, without denomination or compensation, with no heed of what they took in, but rather for what was put out. How did Jesus answer the question? He said that the two most important commandments are *to love all, and that the lord is one.* But what if these two seemingly different commandments were in fact one? If so, then the only commandment would be to love all, and thus God could and would be nothing other than love—no more and no less would be needed to transform a seeming hell into a wondrous kingdom, bringing heaven to earth by turning earth into heaven!

# 40

## "FINK IS HE WHO READS THIS"

Michael's mind turned to the time when he lived in downtown Toronto and was in grade school. He loved to go to school, to play all sorts of sports and games with his friends, whether on the street, in a school yard or the nearby park. His life was illuminated by the light of love but he did not and could not see this, for he had yet to be lost in the shadows of the specter of the imperatives and demands of conformity: the must and should that leads to differentiation and distinguishing, masked in prejudicial pomposity of pontificated piety postulated and positioned by greed, fear and control, with no appreciation to love indiscriminately, but only to commoditize, subjugate, categorize, apprehend and appreciate the value of one's own cache of assets. To hoard and accumulate things that are Caesar's—indefensible and nonsensical to a contented happy life free from failure, woes and foes.

Michael loved to explore his environs in that then good city, Toronto, walking everywhere from Casa Loma: the fairy tale Scottish castle built by a hydroelectric mogul for his sweetheart he imagined a princess—it being so priceless that it bankrupt him—such feigned fortress stately situated on the now dried-up shore of ice age Lake Iroquois overlooking downtown Toronto with all its quackery and commotion; to High Park at the west end of the city where he fished for minnows in the streams, existentially examining the water spiders, once so fortunate as to land a sunfish on a string and hook. Comic books cost ten cents back then until the price was raised to twelve cents. One could ride the bus or street car for only a nickel or get a small bag of chips for the same metal coin mined in Sudbury which looks more like the surface of the moon than fair Luna does, so the conspiracy theorists say.

In his ideal grade school life, his parents went to work during the week, (the work week being five and a half days back then including Saturday morning), his parents getting tickets to evidence the pieces they sewed and tailored to completion so that they could stitch together the necessities of food and shelter and clothing necessary and save up for a home in North York, while Michael would go to school on his own and come home for lunch during the day.

It was on one day just like any other that Michael learned his first lesson about mind altering addiction, which by fate or some further far-fetched framing of fact, he would have figured out had he had the frame of reference and experience at the time. Michael loved water melons. His parents being frugal of course bought the largest ones they could find. After eating his strawberry sandwich for lunch, for in a Jewish household the mixing of milk and meat is not *kosher*, he started into the largest and most succulently sweet and juicy water melon he had ever tasted. He sliced off and ate one piece, and then another, and then another, and another and another. He could not stop! He kept eating and eating and eating till his stomach was distended and bloated and he had to leave because he was running late for school from not being able to stop eating the water melon. Then a funny thing happened. He had to be pee so very badly, which time it would take to do so ensured greater lateness and tardiness of his return to school, but what could he do? Nature called. An act of god beseeched and beckoned him. He was helpless to disobey, caught mercilessly in an irresistible urge.

He *did* relieve and discharge his urine, or *pee* as it is nontechnically termed, but instead of doing so in the toilette as he was trained, he peed in the kitchen garbage can—and not on purpose! The fault lay with his bladder being filled to the point of bursting with the copious amount of the fruit consumed and its inherent juice. There is good reason why it is called a *water* melon! He had crossed the line of reasonable consumption, impregnated by his consummation with the melon. He might as well have done some lines! It acted like a drug, frazzling his mind and crossing his wires. It was a silly and shameful thing that he had done, pissing in a place impermissible to pee! But so it starts with the insidious and barely perceptible slight oversights that in time lead to full blown substance abuse, mania, phobia and neurosis bloomed and blossomed from the little seed sown in a moment of weak will, waiting to take hold, to overgrow and overthrow the consumer, like an Olympian god destined to rule the world!

On another day while in grade school when walking with a friend he noticed that someone had printed in black marker on a concrete hydro pole the following in heavy capital letters: "FINK IS HE WHO READS THIS."

The word "Fink" was in common usage back then. Today the word "jerk" or "asshole" is likely or more apt to be used in its place and stead to signify similar connotations, so what Michael saw written was emotively charged with strong negative sentiment. "Fink" is probably derived from the compound word "ratfink," meaning a rat, a squealer, a stool pigeon (stoolie) or informer in the unwashed bare knuckled street vernacular of the sixties, representing the basest of creatures, the lowest rung on the totem pole of malicious animal slurs! Not a cute, furry, stuffed blue animal the wimpy wee ones of today might imagine when they hear the word "fink."

At first Michael was taken aback and insulted that he had been called a fink. What choice did he have? He did not know what was written until he read it: a paradox that could be generalized to apply to life in general if one was so inclined to exert the mental effort, for in life one never knows where they are until they are lost—when they see the unseen and are severed— tossed out of the garden in the garden, banished but unable to leave, tied in knots, tempered, formed and blueprinted, locked in a paradigm, energy field set, subconsciously precipitated and saturated, helpless and hapless, caught in the pincer vise grips and clutches of what initially appeared as a fun and seemingly insignificant paradox. More than getting dizzy and losing sight is at stake when one is caught trapped, whirling and twirling in the vortex of a pun in the eye of a paradox!

But Michael did not yet grasp what the word "paradox" with all its incongruity and juxtaposition meant back then, and he started liking the paradox when his focus changed and he started to see it as a funny joke. So impressed was he with his discovery, that he started writing variations of the little vociferous perplexity voraciously, like: *"you're an idiot if you read this,"* or *"don't look at this you jerk"* etc. In time however, the spreading of the joke wore thin. Little did Michael know that in the future he would watch Captain James T. Kirk in the original *Star Trek* series destroy a super powerful computer built and programmed by a superior alien species by simply paradoxically

instructing it with words to the effect of: *"don't listen to me."*
How naïve! That ain't advanced programming. A parent would
never say that to a child, let alone think a child would overload
and explode contemplating such a contradiction, unless they
were using reverse psychology, in which case the child would
listen by not listening. How advanced and superior indeed!

Anyways, everyone growing up on this planet is accustomed
to this type of paradox, or conundrum, which with slight
reconfiguration or modification can be turned into a hypocriti-
cal quip or double speak so to speak, so to speak. The *"do as I
say and not as I do,"* and the mythologized madness of culture,
nationality and religion has poisoned the ability to differentiate bullshit from words, fact from fiction, and is consumed
constantly as *soup de jour* on a daily basis, so much so that the
illogical phrase so uttered phases people less than a *"phaser"*
set on stun.

Michael believed that Jesus had many phrases set on stun.
Yes Jesus, he was a man who in the future was shunned and
ostracized by the Jews, his own brothers and sisters. Perhaps
it was due to the ungodly, incredible and unbelievable manner
he was elevated to a god, breaking all the rules of nature and
resurrected like a fractious child might implore. Surely no one
believes a hard, fervent, ardent adherent when they proclaim in
the heat of passion, *"I won't come in your mouth,"* so why would
anyone believe all the nonsense espoused as the gospel truth.
It's just *gobbly goop* spouted in blinding ecstasy!

No, the Jews at the time of Jesus would not have been in the
least worried if Jesus had preached orthodox catholic doctrine,
including a virgin mother and resurrection from the grave, for
as the man from Missouri would demand: "Show me." The
Jews would have called him *"mishigge,"* if Yiddish rather than
Hebrew or Aramaic was spoken back then, which it wasn't. A
Spanish speaker might in pity exclaim: *"pobrecito loco!"* But to

punish craziness with crucifixion *is* pure madness beyond ordinary madness. Only a sadist could and would do so.

The fear therefore lay in what Jesus must have most likely espoused: *that there is no truth.* The ability to take action lay in one's own hands, a gift granted to all. All could affirm or deny— free to do so aloud or in the silence of their own heart.

Jesus likened people to lamps. A lamp makes what it shines on visible, illuminating the thing noticed, giving life to that which it lights, causing that which is sensed to be, while at the same time not being the cause of its being—just as postulated in the theory of relativity: that the observer affects the reality of the perception. What is perceived or conceived is equal to the ability of that which perceives and conceives to do so! The postulated infinite oneness of all is sensed in fragments, reflections and refractions to the level that the observer is capable of doing so. The observed and the observer cannot and do not exist without the other in the reciprocal energetic dance of life: they are one—the apparently separated sides: subjective/objective, warped and wrapped together like a *Möbius* strip! *The inside is out and the outside is in.*

The nature of life, the use or abuse of consciousness has been likened in parables to a tiny seed growing into a great big bush, to the leaven in bread, or to a sack of flour with a small hole carried by an old woman foolish enough to not see it slip away. At the journey's end upon arriving home, she notices she has naught, her basket is empty.

All people are subject to the same rules or laws which are open to one and all to discover and believe. This is called nature, and the study of the same, science. No one can rule or command except by force, unless the one who obeys subjects, avoiding and negating the gift bestowed equally to all, the gift of life, the gift of freedom to live in one's nature in accordance with the laws of the universe, and to make and take what is available without denial and negation. Rulers cannot survive without their subjects. Such ordination supports the perverse power of autocratic authority to corrupt and make crooked the straight path. Subjects cannot live without rulers.

It has been stated more than once in more than one way that whether one nonchalantly notes only the surface of a thing, or probes passionately to the core, both are essentially one and the same, just as the growth and life cycle of the tree is the tree and its fruit: the two are one, spread out in time, the seeming difference dependent on where the focus lies. All is created by the scalpel of distinction, cutting the staff of life in countless ways to the exponent of infinity: possible and impossible to conceive.

Such was Michael's moment of pretend simple clarity on the "oh so bright and sunny day" as he drove into work. The sale of the store did not matter. Nothing mattered except that he was where he was, who he was, and that he was and would be, for they were all one. He did not know if everything existed at once or if the whole experience of life was but a mental process where all that is sensed and perceived is an interpretation of energy unfolded into a story, a belief in mortality. There can in fact be no time if there is no change and no consciousness. All life is forever and endlessly bounded in its infinite ability to be, laden with the burden of its own denial.

Still, the selling of the store and the loss of loves throughout his life gnawed at Michael's gizzards like tomorrow's storm today. Some say that all pain can be escaped from by living in the *now*. Does the present actually exist? Is it not however thinner than a razor's edge, being but an imaginary line, a border that is not, created by being *between* that which *was* or has past, the past, and what *will be* or is to come, the future. How can a being's organs and instruments of sense and thought dictate the nature of reality except in the sense of making up or acting out a commanding or commanded performance? Words don't lie—only people do! And sex is only a heinous act in the mouth of hypocrites who love to be heard, but not seen!

Have people forgotten how to live life by fooling themselves into believing that categorical classifications and names and labels make substance and truth? No man, woman or child can overcome the laws of nature, the laws of the universe of all that is and is not! Those who understand this are well *multiversed* in the language of life and *know* that what is sown shall be reaped, but what is sewn shall be rendered and torn asunder.

Michael was wading so deep in thought that his head was beginning to spin off his shoulders, for he breathed and *had* inhaled of Justin's smile. Some claim that Justin is not a deep and profound a thinker. Who knows for sure?

The air, which had been pristine and pure, became heavy with humidity and haze. The sun, about 4:10 pm to Michael's back, became a golden gong muffled in silver. The queen's highway, Toronto bound, was now heavily trafficked, packed with cars and trucks, after the merger with Highway 403. The highway, although saturated with vehicles, flowed at super legal speed, like so many drops of water rolling over the black asphalt propelled by the wind of gasoline ignited internal combustion. The mass density of the air evaporating into the time of day insidiously caused Michael's mind to idle with the imperceptible lightness of impending sleep. He pushed the dial on the dash to turn on the radio to *WARP 98, eclectic radio, resonating at the speed of mind.* The music sounded like Mozart, but it was not *"Eine kleine Nachtmusik"*—that he knew.

Michael wondered whether a composer constructed the music from the inside, hanging each note on a hook like so many carcasses moving along a conveyor belt in a slaughterhouse. Could the composer hear how the notes would sound in someone else's ear? Each instrument spoke as if it had a voice. Michael imagined each instrument a different piece of furniture in a French parlor chatting away, as he began to drift.

He slapped himself lightly on the face to try and stay awake. To this end, he began singing, not a song, but by pushing out whole notes in a slow steady exhale attempting to have them resonate in harmony with what he imagined was his being, its hollowness and fullness, trying to unite his wordless longing in sound, to vibrate away the separation between desire and thought. The notes escaped in ladlefuls, streaming upward. Michael varied the pitch of the long sustained tones as a cantor might: his body was the shower stall, his Toyota a mobile sanctuary hurling down the highway on the well-known route travelling at the deadly speed of 110 km per hour.

Was there a God hanging around listening to his chant? Could such God bear to hear a baby cry, or a grown man wail "*save me*"? The pitch and pith of Michael's substance radiated out in audible ripples, waves in the invisible air. His thoughts poured out in a stream flowing to the one great ocean.

There is no fear when sleep lulls: everything is inverted. The more a person worries about falling asleep, the more elusive it is. But once in its breeze, there is no remembering, thoughts are brushed aside. Michael wasn't thinking logically anymore. He was the ape with wild wavy hair flying along the smooth surface of the highway, his tin can with rubber wheels a space ship hovering on automatic pilot.

What was his life? What did it all mean? He had spent the last ten years travelling to Cuba often, searching for love, trying to get his last licks in before he was no longer able to rise to the occasion and meet his desired end erectly head on. Was that a bad thing? Many people thought it was. He had slowly peeled the layers of understanding only to reveal new layers of misunderstanding. He feared that in the end life would prove to be like an onion—after all the layers were peeled, nothing would be left! Absolute zero: zilch, *nada*—the fool's number balancing all there is with all that is not! Would he be further ahead or behind, or was he going in circles fooling himself that all his drives, desires and driving had meaning? What a perilous burning! *Sapiens* should never have been given or found the flame, for now it burned out of control, soon to be put out by creeping imperceptible sleep. Could he instead cut through the onion? That would surely only bring tears.

A vague idea floated in the back of Michael's mind. It had something to do with a book about his life—his family, his labors, his loves and many travels and trials. He could not see it clearly. Was it really there? How big was it? In what color and language was it written? Had the book of his life already been authored waiting for him to read it, or was it up to him to put pen to paper, to scrape the skin of reality and make up the story of his life?

# 41

---

# THE DREAM OF THE HUNGRY MAN

When the past slumbers down the cracked fault of now, the moment becomes all time that is and is not, stumbled across unsought. Motion and stillness churn peacefully in the port of peace. Smiling and sailing hands from the future and past slap and clap simultaneously as they wave "*Goodbye! Goodbye!*" Michael was snuggling in his warm burgundy sheets, stretching in lazy comfort, his wool blanket a sheath under the watchful eyes of the seraphim. He was on his way to completion, the closing of his chosen covenant, not in the least fearful in his dreamlike state. The angel's broad and lithe wings were spreading ready to flutter and depart from the earthly plane theorized in relatively, to a domain of no time and no place of perpetual oneness—the car that Michael was driving was driving him at super-human speed! The heavy hand of fate held Michael's eyelids down and his head started dropping towards his chest. Soon, the universe would be born anew, or forever lost!

Now is the time to commence the lament in the ancient tongue. Repent, and calculate the score! What time comprises the distance between here and gone? The shadow of Judgment mirthfully reclines pliant in mercy to repose, ready to repossess and reposition a life in amusement and familiarity of the end.

Had Michael muddled and faked his way through life, driven by the desire to be the centre of his own opera: a drama queen whose singing wasn't worth a dime when it came to *closing time*? Had he lived? Had he loved? Should he be forgiven? He was an organism very much alive: when his wound was touched, the pain was unbearable, but when the divine pole poked his pleasure spot—oh, how he danced!

Now, all the chained bears were dancing, fading away, chains and all. Further and farther they floated into the haze which obscured and hid the sun. Michael's head and body were now but a balloon, a zeppelin rising ever so slowly, higher and higher, above and away from the battlefield of pleasure and pain, to dream into a dream...

*Michael was in the kitchen of his parents' bungalow in North York. The sheer white curtains that covered the window above the sink were drawn shut, letting in only enough light to make the darkness unnoticeable. Michael sat in his usual place at the oval kitchen table, the laminated brown and white patterns of which could barely be made out through the faded yellow of the plastic table cover.*

*Each member of the Rice family had a place around the table: Michael's mother across from him near the sink and appliances so she could conveniently get up and prepare meals and clean up. His father's place was at one end of the elongated table immediately to Michael's right, close to the centre of the room. It could be considered the head of the table. Michael's father would joke that the "shvantz" ("tail" or "fool" in Yiddish) sat at the head. To the left of Michael was his brother Abe's seat, with the wall directly behind it. Older son sat facing the father, and younger son facing the mother, all in harmony in accordance with lineal namesakes.*

*Michael knew it was early morning. The table was covered with food Mendel was preparing to eat. Breakfast was the only meal Michael's mother allowed anyone to make. Michael's father was an early riser and this morning he had prepared quite the feast. Since his retirement from working, he would fill up with a large meal in the morning and wander the streets during the day to come home in the evening to watch TV and eat supper. This morning Mendel's breakfast consisted of two hard boiled eggs which sat in a small bowl waiting to be shelled. Sardines were piled high on a small plate. Half of an already-been-squeezed at least once lemon shared a saucer with a used tea bag that had seen better days (no doubt to be used again). A small slab of butter was in its clear rectangular glass butter-dish to the right of Michael. Still further to the right, a half full jar of Billy Bee honey was stationed, waiting to have its sweetness spread. Michael noticed the dried drippings caked above the golden-brown liquid "honey line." A small plastic tub of sour cream in front of Michael waited to be opened and consumed.*

*Two pieces of toast popped up out of the toaster with a pleasant ring that would surely have made a dog salivate. Michael could smell the earthy sweetness of the burnt bread. Just then, Michael's father entered the room, placing the hot toast on a large plate one slice after the other quickly, and then Mendel sat down in Michael's mother seat directly across the table from Michael. It must have been early, and Michael's mother had already left for work. Why else would his father sit in her place?*

*But wait—something didn't seem right. Michael strained to determine what it was, but his mind was not sharp, he was having trouble focusing. What was wrong? He wasn't sure, but maybe he should not be sitting there at the table in his parents'*

*kitchen. At the back of his mind he felt like he was forget-*
*ting something, but what was it? It suddenly struck him: his*
*parents were dead—they had died several years ago—he must*
*be dreaming!*

*Normally such a realization would freak Michael out! His*
*natural reaction would be to think or say: "You can't be here,*
*you're dead" and try to find his way to out of the nightmare to*
*wake up. But this did not seem like a nightmare; the images*
*were clear and he was not afraid. A nagging thought gnawed*
*at him, trying to communicate the urgent need to wake up,*
*but he missed his parents so much that he kept the thought at*
*bay. Whether his parents still existed in some form or Michael*
*was just dealing with fragments of his own memory was not*
*important. This was his opportunity to make contact with the*
*"other world" or at least connect with his own subconscious. He*
*would not let the opportunity slip away. He knew that he had*
*the clarity of mind to formulate only one question—but what*
*should it be? With all the strength of will he could muster to*
*avoid the automatic swerves of his somatic state he tried to*
*determine what to ask. What question could solve and resolve*
*the riddle of his life? The words that came out of his mouth were:*
*"Father, what should I do?"*

*Now if he asked his mother this question she would have*
*no doubt replied: "don't take yourself over," but what would his*
*father say? Michael waited for the secret to be revealed!*

*Michael's father lifted his head slowly and looked at Michael—*
*point blank. Were those tears in Mendel's eyes? He then spoke*
*with a steady and clear voice in Yiddish and said: "My child,*
*pass me the butter please." Michael immediately turned his*
*head to the right toward the honey. The room began to spin and*
*swirl in the darkness before Michael's eyes, round and around...*

BANG! The dream was all over. Michael's head bobbed up
with a jolt as his car hit the rough shoulder of the superhigh-
way! His adrenaline-filled eyes popped open catching the light

reflected as commanded and conducted by the wand of physics, striking the digital dashboard clock at exactly 4:20 pm on the button nose noiselessly. Quickly, as if time had almost stopped, Michael turned the steering wheel to the left and pulled back onto the road. His life salivated over its own savior.

Just as the tale began with Justin's smile, Michael's life was resurrected at "light-up time." Was it an idiosynchronicity? He was rewound and restored to his previous perspective: his stomach may have been in his mouth, but he was no longer sleepy. Now he was wide awake, fully alive and able to continue the journey to meet his dilemmas and encounter his enigmas!

Michael had, he knew not for how long, nodded off and slipped into a dream. He almost died! Perhaps he had died in one life, and was continuing with another—memories could be tricky. It did not matter because the pounding of his heart brought his attention to the "here and now." What music was playing on *WARP Radio* when he woke up to find himself still in the land of the living? Was it Beethoven smashing over the gates of the past with the trumpeting in of a new order? Was it the eerie theme from the *Twilight Zone* sending shivers down people's spine? The truth of the matter is that Michael could not remember what music was playing on the radio when he woke up because he was not paying attention.

And what was the meaning of "*pass me the butter*"? Was it nothing more than a joke; fate making a *funny*? And what of reality—were there as many realities as people to dream them up, or possibly more, all fitting together idiosynchronistically so that life could be interpreted in an infinite number of ways based on the same perceptions? Ultimately, are people destined *to be and not to be*?

Michael's skin was covered in *goose bumps.* His blood rushed through his arteries skipping over the ocean of his riled up emotions like he was stoned. In spite of all the ups and downs he had experienced in his life, Michael was now certain that he wanted to go on living. He was grateful to be alive! When he awoke, his first and foremost thought after that of himself, was of his son, Samuel. Michael knew that he had to continue to be there for Sam, to guide him, to continue loving him, to show him right from wrong. Could Michael connect with Sam without losing his way in anger and frustration which so often happens when two beings want to connect but don't know how, leaving love unplugged with its cord dangling in the air?

In any event Michael had learned a monumentally important lesson: *there is nothing like a big scare to act as a wake-up call!* For the moment Michael was simply happy to be where he was: in his car on the Royal Road going from Hamilton to Toronto in the mysterious kingdom of sight and sound, smell, taste and touch—and sometimes thought. The past was behind him and the future lay ahead. He felt alive, and for the moment, that was enough.

CPSIA information can be obtained at www.ICGtesting.com
Printed in the USA
LVOW07s2009250215

428358LV00004B/43/P